THE FORGOTTEN CHILD

Melissa Erin Jackson

ISBN: 978-1-7324134-2-9 (paperback)
ISBN: 978-1-7324134-0-5 (ebook)
ISBN: 978-1-7324134-1-2 (audiobook)

Front cover design by Maggie Hall.
Interior design by Michelle Raymond.
Interior layout by Amanda Webster.

First published in 2018 by Ringtail Press.

www.melissajacksonbooks.com

For Mom, Corey, and Sam—
the only family I need

Contents

1973 1

Chapter 1 3

Chapter 2 10

Chapter 3 26

Chapter 4 36

Chapter 5 45

Chapter 6 62

1960 78

Chapter 7 80

Chapter 8 94

Chapter 9 109

Chapter 10 130

Chapter 11 149

Chapter 12 157

Chapter 13 176

Chapter 14 194

1980-1983 216

Chapter 15 220

Chapter 16 234

Chapter 17 261

Chapter 18 277

Chapter 19 288

Chapter 20 300

Chapter 21 318

Chapter 22 329

Chapter 23 349

1983 361

Chapter 24 367

Chapter 25 379

Chapter 26 410

About the Author 417

Acknowledgments 418

1973

Orin Jacobs was fascinated by the mechanics of things.
"He's going to be an inventor someday," his mother would tell her friends every time she found him in the living room, clock pieces spread out before him on the rug—tiny screws and bolts and wires and springs.

He took things apart so he could see how they worked.

His mother didn't know that beyond the clocks and watches and microwave oven, he also took apart living things. Frogs were the easiest to catch, but he set traps for rabbits and birds, too. Birds were his favorite.

He snapped delicate wing bones to see how they'd heal on their own. He was amazed that just a few cracks here and there robbed them of their ability to fly.

It was when he was eleven, with his little sister tied to a tree, that Orin saw a change in his mother. He knew she no longer thought he'd be an inventor. Now she worried he would become—that he *was*—something else entirely. Sunlight glinted off the small knife in his hand.

His mother ran to him, knocked him aside, and snatched the blade from his fist. Then she boxed him on the ear—slapped and shoved and screamed at him. "What's wrong with you! She's just a baby!"

Was her age the only problem? Did Orin only need to wait until she was older?

His mother used the blade to saw through the ropes binding the six-year-old girl in place.

Orin had never seen his mother so angry. She'd never hit him before.

"I wasn't going to hurt her!" he'd said, sprawled on the ground, hand cupping his hot-to-the-touch ear. Then, softer, he said, "I just wanted to see what's inside."

Clutching the crying girl to her side, his mother's lip curled. "She's not a *clock*, Orin. If you take her apart, you can't put her back together."

So Orin studied human anatomy with only the aid of textbooks. Perhaps he could be a doctor. Doctors were *allowed* to cut people open.

But pictures and diagrams weren't the same as feeling the warmth of flesh as it slowly turned cold. Wasn't the same as getting sticky with blood while rooting around in body cavities, searching for organs and muscles and bones. Wasn't the same as putting a finger on something as small as a nerve, and watching as paws, claws, and feathers twitched of their own accord. Oh, how he yearned to make fingers and toes twitch like that.

He couldn't feel like a puppet master if his mother didn't allow him to pull the strings.

Though as he got older, others denied him access, too. Medical schools wouldn't allow him into their institutions after interviewing him. He couldn't even get hired as a mortician's assistant.

So he waited.

And once his mother died peacefully in her bed on a cool autumn night in 1973, thirty years after she hit him, Orin went looking for his first patient.

CHAPTER 1

A pack of werewolves raced across the television screen. Riley, with bowl of popcorn clutched to her chest, stared wide-eyed, heart thundering in her chest even though she'd seen the movie eight times already. When a knock sounded on her front door, she screamed, sending popcorn everywhere and leaving tiny splotches of white cheddar dust all over her brown couch.

Jade rushed in, hands balled into fists and raised above her head, ready to punch an unknown assailant. "What's wrong? What happen—*oh*." She dropped her arms and propped a hand on her hip. "Good god, girl. You can't seriously be watching this again."

Riley regretted giving her best friend a key to her apartment.

Untangling herself from her blanket, Riley lurched forward to snatch the remote off her coffee table. She hit pause. "What are you doing here?"

"Hello to you, too," Jade said, plopping down next to her and grabbing a handful of the remaining popcorn. "You didn't answer my text this morning. You also didn't reply to a very similar one last month. I know a strategic ignore when I see one."

"I've been busy."

"You're full of lies."

They glared at each other.

Jade looked her usual flawless self, green eyes rimmed with black liner. Riley had worn the same sweatpants every night this week and was almost positive there was popcorn in her bra. Jade's light brown skin—several shades lighter than Riley's—was dusted with the faintest layer of makeup, and her head of gorgeous, wild brown curls was currently pulled up in a messy bun. Several curls had escaped, creating a fuzzy halo around her head.

Riley gave her own head a scratch, wondering when she'd last washed her hair.

She had, in fact, ignored Jade's text. Her initial reaction to the message—We're IN for this weekend, Ry! Jordanville Ranch, here we come!—had been to silence her phone, drop it in her purse, and put on *Battle at Fishrock* for the ninth time.

"*C'mon*, Ry. This kinda thing is right up your super weird alley." Jade waved a hand in the direction of the werewolf frozen on the TV screen and the true crime novels on Riley's bookshelf.

Riley side-eyed her laptop sitting on her coffee table, where dozens of murder-related websites were bookmarked for easy access. "Werewolves aren't real. Ghosts are."

Rolling her eyes, Jade said, "You were obsessed with the ranch ages before the *Paranormal Playground* episode was even announced. You get weirdly fixated on local cases—and you practically go apoplectic about the serial killer ones."

"Apoplectic is a little dramatic," she said, though Jade wasn't wrong. "I like the stuff about catching bad guys and the pursuit of justice and all that. I do *not* like the haunted house stuff."

"Tell you what," Jade said. "If you fess up about why you're so against ghosts, I won't make you go this weekend."

Riley pursed her lips.

"Just as I thought!"

"Why do I need a reason? Ghosts are scary. If I told you I was scared of clowns, would you ask why?"

Jade huffed, sending an errant curl flapping, which meant she'd let it go. For now. "Rochelle and Pamela won't be able to afford that room without you there. Brie's parents promised to stay at the house with her husband and the kids for the *whole* weekend. Brie never gets a vacation. Don't take that from her."

Oh, so now she's resorting to out-and-out guilt?

From the handful of emails Riley had received, and also ignored, five of them were on the guest list: herself, Jade, Rochelle, Pamela, and Brie.

"Look," Jade said, turning to sit cross-legged on the couch so she could stare more fully at the side of Riley's head. "It's not just about affording the room. Or the fact that I've been on the waiting list for a year and this is my dream and don't you dare destroy it …" Riley rolled her eyes at that. "I'm seriously worried about you."

Brow furrowed, Riley turned toward her—back against the armrest of the sofa, knees pulled into her chest. A piece of popcorn crunched underfoot. "Why? I'm fine."

Jade cocked her head to the side, mouth bunched up in the corner.

"What! Don't look at me like that," Riley said.

"Ever since you broke up with Casey, you've been … an anti-social homebody."

That hardly seemed fair.

"You broke up with *him*, remember? You should be partying it up every night and making terrible decisions! You know damn well he hasn't been moping at home for the past six months. That asshole likely didn't wait six *minutes*."

Riley frowned, not sure how Jade thought any of this would help. "I'm not moping …"

Ticking off Riley's offenses finger by finger, Jade said, "You always have an excuse not to do stuff with me and the girls. You only want to hang out with me if we're sitting on a couch watching a movie. You work a ridiculous number of hours, watch an even more ridiculous amount of TV, and you avoid interacting with other human beings at all costs."

Riley's cheeks flamed. "What is this, an intervention? I interact with people all day long, thank you very much."

"I'm talking about interacting with people on a level deeper than, 'Can I get you a refill?'"

Riley gasped in mock-horror.

"*Please?*" Jade's green eyes doubled in size, and she clutched her hands below her chin, looking for all the world like a lost puppy. They'd only been friends since freshman year in college—some seven years ago—but they'd been like sisters ever since. And just like a real sibling, Jade had figured out long ago how to push Riley's buttons.

Ignoring her gut screaming at her to say no, Riley groaned. She'd requested the time off work weeks ago, but she'd also hoped to find a way out of it. She should have known Jade wouldn't have been deterred by mere avoidance tactics. "Ugh! Fine!"

With a whoop, Jade thrust a fist in the air. "I have to get home to Jonah," she said, standing up. "I swear to god that boy would starve to death if it weren't for me."

Riley felt an extra flare of annoyance. Jade had known Riley would be powerless to say no in person. "When do we leave?"

"We'll all meet at my house on Thursday afternoon around four. You still take Thursdays off work to watch your shows, right?"

My shows? Had she really turned into an eighty-year-old woman? "Yeah."

"Okay, good. Then we can take one car—Brie offered to drive.

Shouldn't take more than four hours to get there," Jade said.

"Jonah is going to survive a whole weekend without you?"

"I prepped and froze meals for, like, six nights. All he has to do is warm them up in the microwave." Jade headed for the door. "He's forbidden from using any other appliance. Remember that time he tried to make toast? Damn near burned down the kitchen."

Riley laughed, following Jade to the door.

She hugged Jade goodbye, but her friend held on a second longer than necessary. "Thank you for coming. Really." Pulling away, she held Riley by the arms and flashed an award-winning smile. "We'll have a great time, I promise. Mini road trip, slumber party with the girls—"

"Two nights of paranormal investigations to possibly experience a visitation from a serial killer …" Riley sing-songed.

"Tomato, toe-mah-toe."

Riley shook her head. "Go save Jonah from starvation."

Closing the door behind her friend, she sighed at how epically stupid it was to go to a haunted ranch. She preferred to live in denial about her "sensitivity," as her mother called it, but it was hard to do that when she willingly walked into a place teeming with ghosts.

Between the Great Ouija Board Fiasco when she was thirteen, the old pipe-smoking sea captain who'd followed her around during her first—and only—tour of a cemetery on Halloween in high school, and the haunted apartment she'd moved out of lickety-split just before she'd found her current one, Riley couldn't deny that her mother was probably right. But if Riley didn't go to cemeteries or haunted houses or any place that generally gave her the willies, she didn't have run-ins with the dead. Easy peasy.

And the more she ignored and denied, the easier it was to keep it all at bay. Nothing could come waltzing through the proverbial door if the door was closed, locked, and barricaded.

Because of her aversion, shows like *Paranormal Playground* sent off warning bells in her head. Though, she had to admit, she found the show's co-stars—a boyfriend and girlfriend who'd become husband and wife between seasons three and four—more legit than others she'd seen. Then again, it was a low bar.

Riley stuck to *Cold Case Files*, *The First 48*, *Forensic Files*, and *Dateline*. Shows about justice. Shows about closure.

Not stories of lingering, trapped spirits. Of souls bound to the physical world.

Riley blew out a deep breath. She had to stop thinking about this.

The more she thought about these things, the more she opened herself up. The more the spirits could sense her vulnerability and come knocking at the door.

So, this weekend, she vowed to remain detached during the investigations. She would be the same wet blanket from middle and high school, sitting in the corner and refusing to cooperate. Jade might get upset over it, but she'd deal. Rochelle, Brie, and Pamela would be there to share in the excitement.

A buzz sounded across the room, making Riley jump, but it was only her phone.

She pulled it out of her purse and sighed at the group text that had just come through from Jade.

Ry is in, ladies! We leave in TWO DAYS! Get ready to catch some ghosts!!

She'd added the goofy ghost emoji for good measure.

The women replied rapid-fire, but Riley couldn't even muster up false excitement. She deposited her phone on the coffee table. All desire lost to continue watching the wolf-boys of Fishrock, she turned the TV off, instead opting for a glass of wine, a hot shower, and an early bedtime. Ruining her friends' fun with her pessimism before they'd even left probably wasn't good form.

Standing on the cold tile floor of the kitchen, she uncorked the half-empty wine bottle and poured herself a glass. Her hand shook so badly, a bit of red wine splattered on the counter.

Get a grip.

The *Paranormal Playground* crew hadn't uncovered anything but very ambiguous "evidence." The place probably wasn't even haunted. Denial and avoidance would get her through it. And wine. Could she just fill her suitcase with bottles of Merlot?

Downing the wine in seconds, she headed for the bathroom.

Her phone, still being blasted by her excited friends, vibrated itself right off the table and onto the carpet below with a muted thud.

CHAPTER 2

At 3:50 on Thursday afternoon, Riley sat in her car a block away from Jade's house. Pamela's familiar forest green Jeep rounded the corner and Riley slouched in her seat, face shielded, as her friend zipped past. Heat flooded her cheeks.

"It's just a weekend," she told herself. "Just three days and it'll be over."

The bird's-eye shots of the ranch she'd glanced at—nay, obsessed over—on Google Earth had calmed her a bit, at least. Tightly packed pines rose up around the house, providing an additional wall of protection. Or hiding places, depending on one's perspective.

A robust, active creek wove through the area, closer to the dude ranch on the other end of the property. A hearty hike through the forest would do her some good. While Jade and the girls discussed ghosts and Electronic Voice Phenomena with the investigation team and the other guests, Riley would stroll along the creek and down weaving trails. She'd much rather commune with nature than the tortured spirits of dead girls.

The time on her car's dash ticked over to 3:55. With a sigh, she pulled her car back onto the road and then turned onto picturesque Hyacinth Avenue.

The house was a two-storied, red-brick beauty that sat at the end of a long driveway. The front of the property was surrounded by a low brick wall, and on the left of the driveway, a garden of colorful flowers thrived. A fountain burbled in the middle of it all. Two bathing sparrows flew off as Riley pulled her car in behind Pamela's. Rochelle's clunker with two mismatched front doors was there; Brie's SUV was absent.

Pulling her duffel out of the backseat and heaving the bag over her shoulder along with her purse, Riley strolled to the front door. Thick, green ivy crawled up the walls. Her best friend lived in a freaking fairytale house.

Though Jonah made enough for Jade to not have to work, she didn't want to give up her job. Riley loved that Jade never rubbed her financial success in anyone's face. Hell, Jade was the queen at finding treasures on clearance racks.

Instead of insulting the girls by paying for this little ghost hunting expedition herself, or offering a loan, Jade had made sure to get all five on the list so everyone could manage the fee, despite the fact that the ranch's master suite usually had a "no more than four guests" policy. Jade mentioned in a text last night how "seriously fucking annoying" she'd had to be to pull it off.

Though the ranch house was nestled in the Gila National Forest, you could only actively explore the grounds and stay in the house if you had a reservation and could afford upwards of $800 a night, depending on the size of the room. Even with Riley and the four other girls splitting the cost for the master suite, $160 a night was steep.

Riley shot a glance over her shoulder at Rochelle's old car; it was apparently always a small miracle when the thing started on the first try. Riley would tough it out for her sake.

Jade's front door swung open and Riley jumped.

"Were you ever planning to come in?" Jade asked, one hand on the open door's knob, the other on her hip.

"I was admiring your fancy-pants landscaping."

"Shut up. You saw my fancy-pants landscaping last week. And the week before that. You were planning an escape."

"I'm here, aren't I?"

Jade grinned. "Get your butt inside. We're making road-trip margaritas."

Following Jade in, Riley dropped her duffel in the front hall with the other luggage. Laughter erupted from the kitchen and the urge to hightail it in the other direction hit Riley full force. She already felt like an intruder. *One foot in front of the other*, she told herself as she trailed after Jade. *It's only a weekend.*

"*Ladies!*" sing-songed Jade. "Riley Thomas has finally decided to grace us with her presence."

Pamela Chang fought to dislodge the ice bin from the fridge. Rochelle Humphries sat on one of the stools positioned around the kitchen's center island. Riley knew Pamela from their days as college roommates with Jade. Rochelle—and the yet-to-arrive Brie—had been at an awkward Christmas shindig at Jade's three months ago. Ugly sweaters and too strong eggnog and a White Elephant gift exchange where she'd ended up with a jar full of off-flavor jelly beans like cat vomit and grass and sardine. Riley had slipped out after a hastily sent text message to Jade a few hours in, unable to handle the small talk.

Small talk was hard to manage at the best of times, but with total strangers from Jade's yoga studio and Jonah's tech buddies? It was a miracle Riley had lasted as long as she had. The rest of the night had been spent alone in her apartment, a tiny, unlit, and undecorated Christmas tree sitting on the edge of her coffee table while she binged half of season three of *Tiana's Circle*.

An ominous scrape sounded from the refrigerator while Pamela continued her battle with the ice bin. Shooting a quick grin over her shoulder, Pamela said, "Hey, girl. Long time no see!"

"Work is a time-suck," said Riley.

Jade flashed her a pointed look.

"I'm also a crap friend because I choose Netflix over other humans."

"God, me too," said Rochelle.

If a gust of wind swept through to gently tousle Rochelle's hair without explanation, Riley wouldn't have been surprised. The other woman was a curvaceous 5'4" and had dark brown hair that hung to her mid-back in shiny, expertly styled waves. Without a doubt, she'd missed her calling as a model for shampoo commercials.

Riley did that "I have nothing interesting to say so I'm just going to awkwardly nod a lot for no discernible reason" thing she was so good at. Really, she couldn't come up with a follow-up comment about Netflix? Her one true love?

Her palms grew clammy.

Why was she so damned nervous? It was like the Christmas party all over again. Had she really been sequestering herself for so long that she'd developed some kind of social anxiety?

"Have you seen *Tiana's Circle*?" Rochelle asked.

Riley's focus snapped to the other woman. "Oh my god. You've actually seen it?"

Now fully turned on her stool toward Riley, Rochelle's eyes widened. "Have I *seen* it?"

"Oh hell," muttered Jade, rummaging around in her liquor cabinet on the opposite side of the kitchen. "Are they about to nerd out?"

The question seemed to be directed at Pamela, who'd just freed the ice bin. "Sounds like it."

"I've seen all the available seasons twice," said Rochelle.

Riley grinned. "I'm a little over halfway through viewing number three."

"Oh, sweet heavens, so you're in the middle of season three? Has Cooper—"

"Confessed his undying love for Kendra? Yep. But my next episode is 'Fear Me Not,' so I'm stalling."

"Ugh!" said Rochelle. "I cried for a solid half hour the first time I watched that one."

"The second time I watched it, the moment I saw Howie pull that picture out of his wallet—"

"Stop!" Rochelle fanned her face.

Out of the corner of her eye, she caught Pamela and Jade staring at them like they were aliens who had just crash-landed in her kitchen.

To Riley's surprise, she and Rochelle got so lost in their theories for season five, it wasn't until Jade clapped twice right by her ear that Riley noticed Brie had arrived and a round of frozen strawberry margaritas sat on the counter.

"I didn't even hear the blender turn on," Rochelle said, blinking slowly.

"That was … disturbing," said Jade, looking from Riley to Rochelle and back again.

"Oh, like you aren't just as bad—*worse*—about *Paranormal Playground*," said Riley.

"That's research for my future as a paranormal investigator!" Jade said.

Riley laughed. "The second you see an apparition, you'll be out of there with the quickness."

"How dare you," said Jade. "I'll have you know that I am very brave."

Riley jumped to the side, dancing from foot to foot. "Shit! Spider!"

Jade shrieked, leaping onto a stool with the agility of an antelope. "Where where where!"

Smirking, Riley rested her hip against the counter and crossed her arms.

Jade glared at her, but, perched on the stool like Catwoman, it was hard for Riley to take her seriously. Riley finger-waved at her.

Grabbing a margarita, Pamela said, "Oh, how I missed you girls."

Riley, Rochelle, and Jade—once she climbed off her stool—snatched up the remaining drinks. Brie was handed a virgin one; she was both designated driver *and* trying to conceive baby number three.

"I propose a toast!" Jade hoisted her glass.

The girls followed suit.

"To a weekend of old friendships and new—some of them disturbingly nerdy." She smiled sweetly at Riley and Rochelle. "May we grow closer, enjoy our time away from our everyday lives, and may we see some *motherfucking ghosts*!"

The other three whooped.

Riley let out a mental "*Nope!*" just before they all clinked glasses.

Thanks to the margarita, Riley's nerves were more of a low hum than an all-out scream fest while she helped load up Brie's tricked-out SUV. She could handle this weekend. These ladies were fun and excited and Riley could get through this. She could. Plus, Rochelle was her TV show soulmate. Well, aside from *Paranormal Playground*—but no one was perfect.

Questions and answers about boyfriends and jobs and school and kids were tossed about the car like a beach ball, bouncing from topic to topic in an attempt to catch up on five lives at once. During the second hour, song after song from high school blasted through the speakers.

"This is my *jam!*" Brie and Rochelle called out in unison more than once.

By the time Riley's mild buzz had worn off, they had moved on to talking about a set of people Riley didn't know. People she'd never even heard Jade *mention*. Riley listened, not sure if there was an appropriate time to throw out a "Who are we talking about?"

When Rochelle made a joke about someone named Albert, the four of them erupted in a bout of laughter so intense, Jade was near tears.

The air in the car felt a little thin, too hot. Alone while surrounded by people. She ran clammy palms down her thighs. She was an intruder here. But unlike the Christmas party, she couldn't slip out a door and scurry back to the safety of her apartment.

Hinging forward, she rummaged around in her purse at her feet. She swiped on her phone.

No emails. No text messages. No calls. Not that she expected to hear from anyone.

Another raucous bout of laughter filled the car. Before she'd realized she made the decision, she'd typed "Jordanville Ranch" into her search engine. Somehow, getting sucked into internet wormholes had become her go-to method for calming her anxiety. Yet, despite her penchant for borderline obsessive search habits, she hadn't been to the ranch's website in a couple years. Active avoidance and all that.

"Home of serial killer Orin Jacobs," the headline of the site read. "The site where Orin's Girls lost their lives."

Lost their lives. As if they'd merely misplaced them, not that Orin Jacobs had *taken* them. Stolen them.

Riley still couldn't believe Jade had convinced her to stay in this monster's house. Between the late 1970s and mid-1980s, Jacobs had kidnapped girls, taken them to his cellar to do who-knew-what to them, then brutally cut them open, removed vital organs—some of which were never found; one girl had yet to be identified due to being decapitated—and buried them on his massive property in a neat row of unmarked graves.

He'd been caught when one of the girls, Mindy Cho, managed to escape in the middle of the night and ran for the road. Luckily, she was spotted by a couple out on that back road who had gotten turned around in the dark looking for a nearby dude ranch.

Orin Jacobs' trial made national news, as these things often did. Though the ranch had become a popular tourist stop for people visiting the Gila National Forest—especially after Orin died on death row in the late 1990s—its popularity skyrocketed after the *Paranormal Playground* episode.

Despite the wealth of paranormal shows available, *Paranormal Playground* found an original niche that hadn't been saturated yet: creepy ghost children. The show blew up almost immediately, the show's hosts, Daniel and Heidi, becoming international stars. They traveled all over the world to investigate claims of hauntings. They went from small, obscure places in the beginning—mainly playgrounds, hence the name—to the more obvious ones in later seasons: Alcatraz, Lizzie Borden House, Whaley House, Stanley Hotel.

Mindy, in her late forties now, had come out of her media hiatus to denounce the show for using her tragedy as fodder for better ratings. Given the haunted look in her eye during her plea to the public two years ago, Riley was positive the woman hadn't recovered from her ordeal with Orin. At all.

Riley clicked over to the ranch's chat forum, which was surprisingly active. There were dozens of past guests who claimed to have heard a crying girl at or around three in the morning. Fewer had actually seen the apparition.

On the ranch's episode of *Paranormal Playground*, it was Heidi—offscreen—who'd glimpsed a glowing child just as it rounded a pillar. Riley had watched the episode mainly out of curiosity, and a little out of pride for her home state of New Mexico.

The camera had been focused on Daniel at the time, as he and another crew member attempted to get an EVP. Heidi called out "Oh! I see her!" That was followed by pounding footsteps as Daniel and his crewmate—Mark? Matt?—ran off in the direction of Heidi's voice, the cameraman struggling to keep up. At the end of a short chase, the shot bouncing violently, they caught up with a heaving Heidi, hands on her knees.

Heidi had shaken her head. "She got away. Disappeared right through the wall."

Maybe Heidi had actually seen something. Or maybe Heidi and the crew concocted the scenario to make a mostly boring episode seem more exciting.

From what Riley read on the forum, no one had reported anything like poltergeist activity; things hadn't been tossed across the room by an unseen hand. The only "verified" phenomena were the occasional flickering of lights—which could easily be explained as an electrical glitch—and cold spots, which were usually easily debunked too.

The only consolation Riley had was that the *Paranormal Play-*

ground crew hadn't gone into the cellar, the site of Orin's torture chamber. Daniel and Heidi said the areas below the house had been blocked off from the public at the homeowner's request.

The SUV wove around the curving roads that snaked through the forest. Reading in the car started to give Riley a headache. When her reception bars dropped down to two—Jade had warned her that they'd lose reception entirely once they reached the ranch—and pages took longer and longer to load, Riley gave up and dropped her phone back into her purse.

During her reading binge, the atmosphere in the car had filled with a nervous energy. And night had fallen. Riley hoped Brie's headlights didn't reveal the eyeshine of some forest creature. This was elk country, after all.

"Oh my sweet lord," said Jade. "We're so close. I can *feel* it."

"I'm dying to see an apparition," Brie said, though her usual deadpan tone implied the opposite. "I love the idea of seeing a glowing figure in period dress. A snapshot from the past, you know?"

"What about you?" Rochelle asked, elbowing Riley lightly in the side. "You've been super quiet."

"What about me?" Riley asked, trying to keep her tone casual.

"What are you looking forward to this weekend?"

"Hiking?"

Jade groaned dramatically. "Okay, that's it. You know what, y'all? I have a theory. I've been working on said theory for quite some time." Turning to face the back of the SUV, she said, "I think Riley's a chicken shit."

Riley gasped; the other three girls let out an "*Oooh!*"

"I've known you for, what, seven years now? You only watch scary movies if they've got vampires or werewolves or whatever in them. Haunting, possessions, demons—you always opt out. Now that I think about it, you always seemed to work on Halloween, too! No haunted houses, no costumes …"

"I've had a lot of shitty jobs that don't let me have *holidays* like Halloween off."

"Bullshit." Jade narrowed her eyes at Riley. "Some people just can't handle this stuff. I was thinking you'd get excited about it once we were on our way, since you're so into true crime. Like, I just thought you needed an intervention to get your butt out of the house. But you look … pale, girl. Are you really *this* scared?"

Riley didn't exactly love being called out in front of everyone—Rochelle and Pamela were on either side of her, boring holes into the sides of her head; Brie kept shooting glances in the rearview mirror—but maybe this was the out she needed. Plus, she *was* scared.

"Terrified," said Riley.

"Oh, sweetie." Only Jade could call her that without it sounding patronizing. Reaching an arm over the center console and into the back seat, she clutched Riley's hand. "I feel like an ass now. I really thought you'd like this. Just do whatever makes you comfortable, okay? If something freaks you out, and you need to bolt, just do it."

Riley nodded. "Thanks. I just don't want to ruin the trip because I'm a wimp."

They assured her they thought nothing of the sort. "No, not at all!" and "I totally get it. This stuff freaks me out too" and "We're just happy you're here."

Guilt for lying to them sent her leg bouncing uncontrollably for a while, until Rochelle placed a gentle hand on her knee to still it. Telling them the truth about her sensitivity would be harder. If *she* was uncomfortable with her own skills, why wouldn't they be too?

The Great Ouija Board Fiasco had proven that keeping her ability locked away was the only way to keep others—and herself—safe.

When Brie slowed to make a turn off one two-lane highway onto another, Riley caught sight of a sign illuminated by Brie's headlights: **Jordanville Ranch, 23mi.**

The forest was even denser here; rows and rows of dark sentry trees. Were these the same trees Orin's Girls had seen? Had they peered out of the dark windows of his car, wishing they could fling themselves onto the road to get lost in this massive forest of Douglas-fir and Engelmann spruce?

Brie switched on her high beams; they hadn't passed another car in ages.

Had the captured girls felt a growing dread knowing that even if they escaped, there wasn't anywhere to go?

The couple who found Mindy Cho had been heading to a dude ranch for the weekend to scope the place out for their wedding. They'd gotten desperately lost and while they were idling on a thought-to-be deserted road consulting their map, the frightened, filthy form of a young girl had appeared in the beams of their car's headlights. Riley couldn't imagine how scared the couple had been to see her appear out of the dark, and how scared Mindy must have been that they might not help her. That they might be privy to Orin's depravity and take her back.

Riley's leg started bouncing again. She folded her arms. Unfolded them. Her stomach performed acrobatics.

She really needed another drink.

Checking her phone, she saw "No Service" in the upper left corner.

The steady hum of tires over smooth asphalt gave way to the slow thumping of the SUV rolling onto a semi-uneven road. The blinding glow of her phone's screen bounced erratically, and Riley placed a hand on the back of Jade's chair in front of her. They passed through an open gate set into a stone wall that stretched out in either direction into the tree-laden darkness. The iron gate was one swinging piece, a JR enclosed in a circle taking up a large chunk of the middle. Riley's stomach flipped over again.

Please don't be haunted, please don't be haunted.

A large metal sign rose up just past the gate. "Welcome to Jordanville Ranch!" it said. And in smaller letters beneath: "As seen on *Paranormal Playground*."

Riley's companions clapped as if the sign just performed a magic trick.

Up ahead sat the unmoving red glow of another car's taillights. Jade began rooting around in her bag. "Can you all pass me your IDs? I'm guessing that's the check-in up there."

Brie pulled up behind the SUV stopped next to a guard booth. It reminded Riley of the kiosks that rangers manned outside parks. Riley, Pamela, and Rochelle passed up their IDs, then Jade handed all the pertinent information to Brie. It was a ridiculous amount of paper. It was only a most-likely-not-haunted house, not a government building requiring security clearance.

But, even though this place was in the middle of nowhere, after the popularity of the show's episode, Riley figured there were all kinds of weirdos trying to get onto the property without permission. Skulking about in the woods at night searching for … what? The ghost of a little girl? Of Orin still roaming the premises?

When the other SUV pulled away from the kiosk, Brie inched forward and rolled down the window.

"Hi, folks!" said the man in the booth. He was in his sixties, Riley guessed, and had a full head of white hair. "What's the name on the reservation?"

"Higgins," said Brie. "Jade Higgins."

The man took the paperwork and dipped back into the kiosk. Now it was Jade's leg's turn to bounce violently. The car swayed slightly with the force of it.

"Chill, girl," Riley said.

"Can't!" she hissed, chewing on a thumbnail for a moment. "What if there was some mix-up or I made the reservation wrong and they don't let us in? I'll *die* if I have to wait another year."

The friendly white-haired man reappeared, handing a slightly smaller stack of papers back to Brie. "Always a pleasure to have guests in the master suite. That's where the most activity happens!"

Ugh. Of course it is.

Jade grinned and leaned toward the driver's seat, craning her neck so she could see the old man better. "Thank you! We're very excited."

After a few more particulars, Brie was handed both a parking pass and a map. The man waved them forward to the house. "Have a fabulous stay!"

"We will!" chirped Jade.

The two-story ranch house was made mostly of dark wood. It wasn't nearly as large as Riley had pictured. On the show, the building seemed massive, but the real thing was modest at best. The peaked awning over the front door was supported by a pair of columns with large stone bases. Huge bay windows sat on either side of the front door, and several Adirondack chairs lined the open patio.

Brie pulled into the small parking lot to the left of the house. Three other cars sat in the lot. Riley wondered if any of them belonged to the local paranormal team which helped guests conduct investigations most weekends of the year. The website said the team stayed in one of the detached guesthouses.

The women grabbed their things and made their way toward the front door. They walked together in pairs, chatting quietly in a tight pack. Riley hung back. The spring evening was cool, bordering on chilly. She huddled a little deeper into her thin jacket.

It's just a weekend, it's just a weekend.

The sweep of headlights from a newly arrived car bounced across the front of the house, causing long, jerky shadows to scatter along the façade like startled birds. The car idled at the check-in kiosk.

Something tickled the back of Riley's neck and she shivered. She rubbed the spot against her shoulder as goosebumps sprang up on her arms.

When the same sensation danced like fingertips across her neck again and down her arm, she ran a hand over the thin fabric of her jacket.

It was a breeze, she told herself. She was just cold.

All at once, a looming presence materialized behind her. It was the feeling of being watched, of eyes tracking your every movement. She hunched into her shoulders, turning sharply. Only the quiet, dark forms of the cars and trees stared back. She shook her head. Already psyching herself out. The house wasn't haunted. Her room wasn't haunted. She would have a nice, relaxing weekend. All she needed was to get some sleep and she'd be fine.

An icy breeze swept past her then and her teeth chattered. It felt like a gust off the surface of a glacier. Yet with another two steps, she'd moved out of it.

Heart hammering in her chest, Riley stopped abruptly and

reached a hand out behind her. Cold, biting air stung her palm. She yanked it to her chest.

Just breathe, Ry. It's nothing.

She stood frozen. Waited for an apparition to form, a dark figure to peel away from the shadows. But nothing happened. Her heart rate started to slow to a normal pace.

The end of her jacket tugged down. Not hard. More like a child trying to get her attention. It was the side where she held her duffel and purse. It was the worst case of déjà vu she'd ever had.

Swallowing, she flicked her gaze down, just enough to see if there was someone standing beside her. She half expected to see a small, upturned face peering around the bulk of her belongings on her shoulder. But no one was there.

Shit.

"Ry!"

Her gaze snapped up.

Jade stood on the other end of the patio, a hand on her hip. "You can't run now, girl!"

Shit.

"Coming!"

CHAPTER 3

The first floor was more reminiscent of a hotel lobby than a house. Since Riley had read up on the house's history well before she even knew *Paranormal Playground* was going to feature it, she wasn't surprised to see how different it looked now in comparison to the pictures she'd found from Orin Jacobs' time.

After the property had switched hands, the owner gutted the lower level. From the accounts she'd read, after Mindy Cho made it to safety, the police had raided the house and found it a cluttered mess. Orin Jacobs had been a hoarder of more than young girls—the first floor a maze of boxes filled with books, old magazines, and newspapers. And, oddly enough, bird cages of all sizes. They'd been found empty, but it was clear birds had lived in them once. The man had frequented bookstores and thrift shops on a semi-regular basis.

Mindy, clearly traumatized, had clammed up shortly after she'd escaped. Most speculated she worried Orin would get to her somehow if she talked. So, while she'd told police where to find the ranch, she hadn't told authorities about the other girls. It was the anonymous tip that came in days after her escape that finally sealed Orin's fate.

Riley suspected the call had come in from someone who'd seen him in town. Someone who spotted him with another girl, perhaps. Someone who doubted Orin would have stopped at one victim.

The current owner, Porter Fredricks, wanted to turn the house into a bed and breakfast. He remodeled most of the main house, modernized the kitchen, and added an additional guesthouse; his failing health prevented him from completing the project. Now his family ran the business for him.

A series of cabins and horse stables sat on the other side of the large property. The ranch house itself was only open on weekends and for special occasions.

The wood floor beneath Riley's feet was pristine, gleaming as if freshly waxed. A faint whiff of citrus lay over the more dominant scent of pine wafting in from the open door behind her. The reception desk sat unmanned in the middle of the room, and a few clusters of plush chairs and sofas filled the space to the left of the front door. Most of the chairs and sofas faced the large bay windows overlooking the now-dark grounds. Beyond the seating area was a large, rectangular group dining table. The door opposite likely led to the kitchen.

On the other side of the reception desk, a flight of stairs hugged the wall. Flickering candle flames danced in sconces spaced diagonally, mirroring the rise of the stairs.

The clip of heels on wood drew Riley's attention to a pretty, middle-aged woman in gray slacks and a black cardigan sashaying into view.

"Hello, ladies!" she said, her stick-straight blonde hair swaying as she hurried over. "Come, come, let's get the last of your reservation taken care of."

Jade dropped the smaller stack of paperwork on the polished wood surface of the reception desk.

The woman clacked away on a keyboard Riley couldn't see over the lip of the desk's counter. "Oh, excellent! You have the master suite. That's the Hyssop Room. Go up the stairs, then make a left and head all the way down, then make a right. The room is at the end of the short hall. It's a lovely room." She looked up from her computer screen for a moment to lean forward and say, "And our most active!"

Riley's stomach churned.

"There are two queen-sized beds in the suite and a couch. If you need more sleeping accommodations, we're happy to oblige. It'll be extra, of course. And there will be an extra daily meal charge on your credit card because—"

"Not a problem, not a problem," said Jade. "We're just grateful you could make room for a group this size."

"You were quite persuasive in your emails, Mrs. Higgins."

Rochelle and Riley shared a knowing glance.

After a few more minutes, an unseen printer hummed to life and spit out a few pieces of paper for Jade to sign. Riley tried to look over her shoulder to see what the grand total was, but Jade shielded it from view.

"If you ever need anything during your stay, just call. Either Wilbur, our jack-of-all-trades, or I will be there in a jiff. I'm Angela."

"Thank you so much, Angela," said Jade, handing IDs back to Riley and the others. "Do introductions start this evening?"

Angela nodded. "Yep! The folks from the investigation team arrived about an hour ago and will be here shortly to meet everyone. We'll have late snacks and hot cocoa. In the morning, we'll have a full continental breakfast served between eight and eleven."

"Perfect!" Jade said. "We'll just toss our stuff upstairs real quick."

"They'll meet you at the dining table."

As Riley followed the girls up the stairs, she blew out slow, calming breaths. *Please don't be haunted, please don't be haunted …*

The Hyssop Room was spacious; two queen-sized beds sat to the left and a living-room-like area to the right. In the middle of the back wall were a pair of doors leading to a small balcony. One of the doors stood open, letting in the cool night air. Its white, gauzy curtains fluttered in the breeze.

"Man, this place is nicer than I expected," Pamela said. "I guess on the show we only really saw it with that weird night vision glow."

Riley held her breath, waiting for something creepy to happen now that she stood in the "active" room. But everything stayed still, save for the curtains.

"I volunteer to take the couch," said Rochelle, breaking the tension Riley was sure only she felt. "I'm small enough to fit on it comfortably."

"You sure?" asked Brie. Riley guessed she was merely being polite, given that she was pushing six feet. "Maybe we can trade off."

"Nope! I call couch," said Rochelle. "During my gap year, I did a *lot* of couch surfing. Brings back memories. But it also means I can sleep like a log practically anywhere."

"A bathtub?" Riley asked.

"Oh, I've done that," said Brie.

Riley cocked a brow at her.

"I was totally shitfaced. I have no idea how I ended up there; I woke up in a panic, worried someone had harvested my kidneys."

Riley decided she liked Brie.

When they made their way back downstairs, a new group of people stood in the lobby—two couples, as far as she could tell. They all wore skinny jeans and dark tops. The guys both had short, scraggly hair that likely fell in their eyes a lot. Riley guessed they were in their mid-twenties, too.

In the cluster of chairs and sofas in front of the bay windows, a group of two women and a man sat talking. The guy sported a sensible outfit of jeans and a button-down shirt. The women both wore slacks and blouses, like maybe they'd all driven here straight from work. Thirties, maybe.

Riley employed deep breathing exercises while pretending to listen to her friends as they speculated about the investigation team. Ten minutes later, a group of three men and one woman strolled through the front door. They all wore dark jeans and shirts, like a clan of cat burglars. One of the men carried a bulky duffel.

"Hey, everyone," said a Hispanic guy with graying hair at his temples, a bit of a gut held in place by the black shirt tucked into his pants. "Let's gather at the table over here and have a seat."

The three groups wandered over and squeezed onto the benches on either side. The investigation team stood at the head of the table, their backs to the kitchen. The guy with the duffel placed his bag on the table.

Riley sat squished between Pamela on one side, and one of the thirty-year-old women on the other. Her male and female companions sat across from Riley. She was at the opposite end of the table from the team, so she leaned forward slightly to get a better look.

"We're from Southwest Ghost Investigators. The dude sporting the sweet goatee is Mario, Nina is beside him, Derrick is sporting the not-so-sweet mustache, and I'm Xavier."

"Your mustache is luxuriant," Mario assured Derrick.

Derrick ran a finger and thumb down the length of it twice. "Thanks. But we both know Xavier is just jealous that we can still grow hair while all his is falling out."

Nina laughed.

"Yeah, yeah," Xavier said smiling, waving the other guys off. "You're stuck with us for the weekend, folks. For now, we're going to go over some basics and make some introductions; we'll go into more depth tomorrow."

On cue, Derrick opened the duffel bag and pulled out various investigation tools. Jade squealed. Or maybe it was Pamela. Out came handheld video cameras, electromagnetic field meters, audio recorders for EVPs, thermometers, and dowsing rods.

Riley mostly tuned out the instructional lecture and evaluated the group sitting at the table. The two women who came with the guy took the last spots on either side of the table's end and hung on every word. The guy sat almost directly across from Riley. Up close, he was far more attractive than she'd registered at first. He looked vaguely bored. Likely a friend or partner who'd gotten suckered into coming. A skeptic.

The Skinny Jean Quartet—who sat near the team—looked far more into it. The couple sitting closest seemed even more enthralled than Jade and the rest of their group. The guy tossed his scraggly hair out of his face with a jerk of his head and then reached out to touch a dowsing rod lying nearby; his leather-jacket-wearing girl-friend swatted his hand away playfully. The second pair switched from gazing at the team to eyeing the tools on the table, as if they could master their uses if they just stared at them hard enough. All believers.

Obviously, Riley's four companions were believers too.

And what was Riley? A skeptical believer? A *reluctant* believer?

A poke to her side made her yelp. Pamela's brows were pulled together.

"What?" Riley mouthed, then glanced around the table. The

whole group stared at her, including the team. Lord, had she zoned out and started muttering?

"They're going around the table doing introductions," whispered Pamela. "Say your name and why you're here."

Riley wiped her suddenly sweaty palms down her pant legs before saying, "I'm Riley Thomas and I'm here because my best friend Jade forced me here under threat of death."

Jade leaned forward to glare at her from Pamela's other side, but most of the group chuckled or smiled politely.

"So you're the group skeptic?" asked the female team member. Nina was short and pale with a dyed-black pixie cut. A small gold hoop glittered in her right nostril. "Every group has one; I like figuring out who it is before we get into the nitty gritty of the investigation," she said with a not-unfriendly smile.

"I like to keep an open mind."

Nina and Xavier exchanged knowing smiles. Riley wanted to knock their heads together. She couldn't pinpoint why turning the hunt for the paranormal into a business irked her so badly, but it did.

"An open mind is all we ask," said Nina, addressing the group as a whole. "Just know that most skeptics become believers after a weekend here."

It almost sounded like a threat.

The introductions continued, moving on to Pamela. When they reached the attractive guy, Riley tuned in again. If there was a full-on skeptic, Riley guessed, it was him.

"Hey. I'm Michael Roberts. I'm here with my sister and her wife because … well, honestly? I lost a bet. I never back down from a bet. But I promise to keep an open mind, regardless." He shot a quick glance at Riley then, the corner of his mouth tipping up a fraction.

She bit the inside of her cheek to keep from smiling.

"So we've got *two* skeptics," said Nina. "We'll see which one of you cracks first."

"This place is truly haunted then?" the girl in the leather jacket asked.

"You bet!" said Xavier. "This is one of my favorite locations for investigations. We've recorded scores of EVPs here."

"What did they say?" she asked, voice soft.

"More … weeping than actual words," Xavier said.

"Like the little girl who cries downstairs at three in the morning?" Jade asked.

"I keep trying to convince them it's actually a little *boy*," said Nina.

Xavier smiled at her, then addressed the group. "Nina is our sensitive slash medium."

"I don't quite talk to dead people," Nina said, laughing. "But I do sense spirits. I don't always see them, but I can feel them. The spirit I keep sensing—the one I keep trying to convince the guys is a boy, not a girl—often likes to tease me. He's quite fond of tugging on shirts and jackets."

In the process of stifling a gasp, a coughing fit seized Riley. Her eyes watered; Pamela patted her back. As Riley's cheeks flamed, she was thankful for both the dim lighting and her dark skin.

Trudging on unfazed, Xavier said, "Nina hosts monthly séances and has had some truly remarkable experiences." His chest puffed up like a proud parent. "She was able to make contact with my mother who had passed away long before I'd met Nina. She brought up things only my family would know. It was that experience that made me recruit Nina for my team."

Nina smiled at him. "He didn't have to twist my arm that hard to get me to agree."

The team then launched into an overview of what the weekend would look like—when to meet tomorrow for their first equipment tutorial and when the first investigation would start.

All Riley could think about was the … experience she had out on the patio less than an hour before. Had a little male spirit been trying to get her attention?

This weekend really *was* a terrible idea. It was reminding her too much of Rebecca and being thirteen and that damned Ouija board.

"Well, that should about cover it for tonight," said Xavier, clapping his hands once and startling Riley out of her thoughts. Michael smiled at her like they shared a private joke.

Why hadn't she packed a duffel bag of Merlot again?

"If any of you have any further questions about how the investigations will go, we're happy to answer them. Otherwise, we'll see you back here tomorrow around noon," Xavier said.

The Skinny Jean Quartet disentangled themselves from the table first and wandered back toward the main part of the lobby. The girls were both chatting a mile a minute in hushed tones, hands gesticulating wildly. The boys nodded along, hair flopping as they did.

Michael, his sister, and her wife had wandered to an area behind the receptionist desk and huddled around a large, framed picture. Michael's hands were shoved into the pockets of his jeans; he didn't seem to be paying attention to whatever the two women were discussing.

Riley got up too, intending to hightail it to the Hyssop Room—which, admittedly, didn't sound that inviting, given the "most active" label—wriggle under the bed, and not emerge until it was time to go home. The four others were too caught up in their excitement to notice she'd slipped away. Halfway to the stairs, someone grabbed her arm.

Whirling around, she feared she'd see the ghost boy staring at her. But it was Nina.

"Didn't mean to frighten you!" she said, hands held up in apology.

Riley pressed a hand to her chest. "Sorry. I'm … jumpy tonight."

"I just wanted to let you know that if you need to talk to anyone about … anything you experience here … I'm happy to be that person."

Good gravy, did she know somehow? Was she drawn to Riley because she was a sensitive too? Like two magnets pulled together by a force they couldn't control?

A flash of Rebecca went through Riley's head, her eyes wide and hands shaking. The way her room had looked like a tornado had ripped through it. The Ouija board discarded on the floor. The horrified look on her parents' faces.

"Thanks," was all Riley could manage before she bolted the rest of the way across the lobby, up the stairs, and into the Hyssop Room.

It was going to be a long weekend.

CHAPTER 4

R ebecca Green had been Riley's best friend growing up. From ages eight to thirteen, they were nearly inseparable. She lived across the street and had moved in just days after Riley's family. They went to the same school, were in the same class, and liked all the same things—including the same boy during one particularly harrowing summer. Turned out the boy liked Brenda Fairchild, a girl he'd met through an after-school tennis program. Becca and Riley abhorred her and their friendship was rekindled over both broken hearts and an unparalleled hatred of a girl they'd only met once at Jeffrey's pool party.

The girls spent the night at each other's houses so often, both sets of parents set up their daughters' rooms to accommodate a second child—with an extra desk for homework and a second bed. Their parents got along well and took several vacations together. It was like Riley finally had the sister she always wanted. Riley's mother had a rough pregnancy, and even though Riley's parents wanted more children, her doctor told her she was high-risk. So it had always just been Riley until Becca came along.

Riley had any number of imaginary friends, but they weren't the same as flesh-and-blood people who watched your favorite movies with you, who ate so much candy on Halloween night that you both got *this* close to puking, who laughed so hard with you that you shot grape soda out of your nose and then laughed even harder.

So when weird things started to happen at Becca's house, Riley was torn between being too scared to tell her friend about it in fear of scaring her away, and wanting to tell Becca everything so she could help her fix it.

One night while Riley was sleeping over, she woke with a start to the sound of a baby crying. She gave herself a minute to wake up, thinking it'd been the last remnants of a dream. Then it came again. A series of sharp, short cries that could only be a baby. But Becca was an only child, just like her.

Becca didn't stir. Couldn't she hear it? Couldn't her parents?

Riley tiptoed into the hall. The crying quieted. As Riley crept toward the bathroom, a motion-activated nightlight flicked on. An eerie blue light filled the hall, like the glow of a miniature TV screen. Riley halted halfway between Becca's room and the bathroom, feeling foolish now. She wasn't sure where the cry had come from now that it stopped. Assuming she'd heard it at all.

Then it rang out again, causing goosebumps to break out across her arms and legs. It was coming from behind her. The only other rooms upstairs were Becca's parents' room and a small office. The door to the office stood ajar.

Riley crept toward the crying baby, thankful the floorboards in Becca's house didn't creak the way they did in hers. She stood outside the open door, her back to the wall. She felt like a cop or a spy in a movie, ready to burst into a room with guns blazing. But she wasn't a cop *or* a spy. She was ten and shaking so badly she was surprised Becca's parents couldn't hear her bones knocking together.

Just do it, she told herself. *Don't be a wimp.*

She darted to the doorway, hands out as if that would keep the—what? Monster pretending to be a baby?—*thing* from attacking her. But there was nothing there. No monster. No baby. No monster *pretending* to be a baby. Just a desk, a computer with a dark screen, an office chair, and a small couch.

The cry came again. Loud and piercing and from out of nowhere. The room was empty.

Riley ran back to Becca's room with speed that would have made her dad proud. She slammed Becca's door closed so hard, she startled her friend awake with a shriek. Riley dove onto her bed and threw the blanket over her head.

When Becca's parents ran into the room at the sound of the sudden commotion, Riley did the only thing she could think to do: burst into tears and ask to go home.

It took Riley a month before she stayed the night at the Greens' again. The baby didn't cry—and she knew because she stayed up most of the night listening for it.

Nothing weird happened at the house again until the girls were thirteen. Riley sat at the dining room table while Becca's parents busied themselves with making dinner. Becca had just run to the bathroom, so Riley was alone at the table. Some itchy sixth sense pulled her attention away from the laughing adults and toward the other end of the table. A young girl sat there. She had dark hair like Becca. Riley wasn't sure what color eyes the girl had since the tiny thing could barely see over the table. The tips of her little, pudgy fingers rested on either side of her face, as if she was trying to pull herself up to look over the edge of it. Then she lifted a hand and waved.

Riley's heart pounded painfully in her chest. Maybe one of the neighborhood kids had wandered in and helped herself up to the table. But she knew that was ridiculous. She also knew that the feeling in her gut meant this wasn't a normal little girl.

"Um … Mrs. Green …" said Riley, trying to address Becca's mom without looking away from the little girl. She waved again, a tiny hand above the height of the table. Becca's mom didn't reply. "Mrs. Green?"

"Yes, hon?"

Riley looked at her, then right back at the girl. She was gone. Letting out a startled whimper, she tipped to the side and looked underneath, sure the girl would be making a hasty getaway on hands and knees. But she wasn't there.

Hopping out of her chair, Riley ran to the living room. There was no way the girl could have gotten out of the house. Not that fast. How would she have reached the doorknob?

It was like the crying baby all over again.

When a pair of hands landed on Riley's shoulders from behind, Riley yelped and whirled around. It was Becca's mom, Ashley. Riley's hands shook so badly, she buried them in her armpits.

Ashley bent at the waist and peered at Riley's face, but Riley kept her eyes focused squarely on the tips of her toes. She couldn't tell Ashley that she'd seen a little girl sitting at her table. She'd say she was lying.

Becca came back into the room. "What's going on?"

"I don't know, honey," her mom said over her shoulder. Then she looked back at Riley. "You can tell us anything, you know that, right?"

Something tugged on the side of Riley's shirt and she looked down to see the little girl standing there, a fistful of Riley's shirt in her hand. The thumb of her other hand was shoved into her mouth. She had huge, brown eyes like Becca.

Riley's breath came in short bursts, chest heaving. *They can't see her.*

"Riley," Ashley said, hands still on her shoulders. "Riley!"

She looked up at Ashley's face. Her eyes were huge and brown too. They darted back and forth, searching Riley's face for something.

"What's the matter with you?" asked Becca.

The little girl tugged on Riley's shirt again. Steeling herself, Riley flicked her gaze down and to the right. The girl smiled at her around the thumb in her mouth.

"What do you keep looking at?" asked Becca. "You okay?"

How could they not see her?

Mariah.

Riley's full attention snapped back to the little girl. She was gone again. Poof! Into thin air.

Riley swayed on her feet.

"What's wrong with her, Mom?"

It was the sound of Becca's choked-off sob on the last word that made Riley say it. She wasn't thinking straight. She should have kept her mouth shut. "Who … uh … who's M-Mariah?"

Ashley released her and stumbled back so suddenly, she knocked over a chair, hand to her throat. "What?" It came out like a whisper.

"Mariah," Riley said, breathing even more irregularly now. "Who … um … do you know a Mariah?"

Ashley looked at the spot Riley had been staring at earlier, when the little girl—Mariah—had been holding onto Riley's shirt. "Oh my god." She breathed it more than spoke it. "Did you *see* her?"

A low series of curses sounded from the kitchen, where Becca's dad, Tony, had been standing in the kitchen, watching. Riley had never heard him curse before. Well, other than that time he was trying to fix something in the garage and slammed a hammer on his thumb. He'd said all kinds of things Riley had never heard before.

"Don't do this, Ashley," he said, tossing a dish towel onto the counter before joining them in the dining area. "Don't get yourself worked up. It never helps."

Riley stood frozen by the table, afraid to even twitch a finger given the way Ashley stared at her. Becca's gaze flitted between them all, brow creased.

"How else would she know her *name*, Tony?" Ashley said, spitting the words out as if all this was *his* fault. "How would she know?"

Swallowing, she looked at Becca. Her friend just shrugged.

"Riley, baby," said Ashley, swiping under her eyes before composing herself and squatting before her, taking Riley's small dark hands into her fair, slender ones. "Where did you hear that name?"

How could she tell her she heard the name in her head? That she just knew it was the name of the little girl who was here and then not? That it was the same girl she heard crying three years before?

Ashley shook Riley's hands, hard. Riley winced. "*Riley*. Tell me where you heard that name."

Tears pricked the backs of Riley's eyes. Why was Ashley mad at her? She didn't want her to be mad. Ashley was like her second mom.

"In my head," she whispered.

Tony scoffed. "She's just a kid, Ash. She probably heard one of us say her name and she doesn't remember."

"*No*," Ashley snapped, a tear rolling down her cheek. "We don't talk about her. *You* don't talk about her. You act like she never existed."

Riley wanted Ashley to let her hands go. She'd never feared Ashley before, but she did now. One of her manicured fingernails dug into Riley's skin.

"That's not fair," said Tony. "I haven't forgotten Mariah, but—"

"Mom! Dad. *What's* going on?" Becca asked from her spot just outside the dining room. She wrung her hands. "Who's Mariah?"

"You hear that, Ashley? That's your daughter. *She's* who matters."

That was the wrong thing to say, because Ashley let go of Riley and rounded on him. Tony already had his hands up, showing his innocence.

"You're saying Mariah didn't *matter*?"

"I'm saying she'll always matter, but Rebecca should be our priority. She *is* our priority."

"Stop talking about me like I'm not here!" Becca was crying. More out of confusion than anything else. Riley had never seen them fight before. Not like this.

The room fell silent. Riley didn't want to be there. She wanted to creep out the door and run across the street to her house. Or disappear like the little girl. Like Mariah.

Ashley's arms were folded tight over her chest, shoulders hunched. Tony wrapped his arms around her and she sank against him. He kissed the top of her head.

"We always knew we had to tell her one day," said Tony, his lips still on her hair. "Why not today?"

"I'm not ready," Ashley said, tears rolling down her face.

"You're never going to be ready, baby. Maybe this is the push you needed."

A hand slipped into Riley's and she jumped. But it was just Becca. She stared at her parents. "Tell me."

Tony let Ashley go and she wiped at her eyes.

"It might be time for you to go home, Ry," Ashley said.

"No," said Becca, clapping her other hand onto the back of Riley's, sandwiching it between both of hers. "I want her to stay."

Riley *really* wanted to leave now, but Becca held fast to her hand.

Tony righted the fallen chair, then they all sat down. Parents on one side of the table, the girls on the other. Becca never let Riley go. A united front.

"So, Rebecca …" Ashley began, hands clasped together on the table in front of her. "About a year before you were born, we had a daughter."

Becca tensed, her fingers squeezing Riley's. "I have a sister?"

"Had," Tony said, voice soft.

"She … her name was Mariah," Ashley said. "She died of SIDS when she was two months old." Ashley's eyes welled up and she worked her jaw.

"What's SIDS?" Becca asked.

"Sudden Infant Death Syndrome," Ashley said. "Even when you take all the precautions to keep your baby safe, sometimes SIDS takes them anyway."

"Why didn't you want me to know I had a sister?"

"Oh, honey," said Tony. "It wasn't that we didn't want you to know. We just … losing a child was the hardest thing that's ever happened to either one of us. We still have a tough time with it even though it happened fourteen years ago."

Ashley nodded.

Suddenly turning to Riley, Becca said, "How did *you* know her name when I didn't?"

Riley pursed her lips. "I …" Ashley's clasped hands reached out across the table toward Riley, eyes wide. "I … I saw her. She told me her name. Well, she didn't talk. I just … the name popped in my head."

Ashley burst into tears.

"I'm sorry. I didn't … I didn't mean to—"

"Is she still here?" Ashley choked out, looking around as if she could see her if she just tried hard enough.

"No. She … disappeared."

Ashley slid her clasped hands back toward her, head bowed.

"I'm sorry. I—"

Standing abruptly, Ashley hurried down the hallway.

"I didn't mean to make her sad," Riley said to Tony.

"It's all right, hon," he said. "But maybe you should run on home."

Riley pried her hand from Becca's and fled the house as fast as she could.

Later that night, while Riley tried to distract herself with homework, Becca texted her.

You know anything about Ouija boards?

No. Why?

What if we talk to Mariah and tell her to say hi to my mom?

I don't think it works like that.

Riley really didn't know how any of it worked, but her gut was telling her *no, no, no*. There was a long pause while Riley waited for Becca to say something else. Just when she started to think her friend had fallen asleep, her phone buzzed again.

Can we try? She's still crying.

No, no, no her gut repeated.

But this had all been her fault. Shouldn't she try to fix it, make Ashley feel better?

Yeah, sure. Where do we get one?

Leave that to me.

She should have said no.

CHAPTER 5

Riley lay awake next to Jade, staring at the dark ceiling of the Hyssop Room. The chorus of rhythmic breathing and soft snores should have been enough to lull her to sleep. They'd stayed up talking for a few hours before everyone covered the bathroom counter with an absurd number of toiletries, changed, and drifted off. Riley suspected Brie had passed out before her head hit the pillow. Sleeping without worrying about tending to her kids for two nights was likely a vacation in itself.

Riley, however, was wide awake. Wired. The maybe-ghost-boy, memories of Rebecca, fear that the beds were going to start levitating and blood would start pouring from the walls … all of it kept her from sleeping. Her heart slammed in her chest so hard, she was surprised Jade couldn't feel it.

The only real "experience" Riley had with paranormal anything before the arrival of Mariah was when she'd watched some old-ish movie called *The Craft* late one night with Becca. For days afterward, Becca had run around trying to use magic to change her hair color. Riley, however, had been hit with a deep sense of "don't screw around with things you don't understand."

A couple weeks after the Mariah episode—long enough that Riley hoped Becca had forgotten about the whole thing—Becca pulled her aside in the hall at school and said, "I got it. Taylor's older sister had one hidden in her closet. Can you meet me at my house tonight?"

It. The Ouija board.

Becca had scurried off when Mrs. Romero headed in their general direction.

No, I can't, Riley had wanted to say. But she would have looked foolish saying that to a bank of lockers, so she ended up at Becca's house that night even though her gut still told her not to.

After school, Riley hopped online to research Ouija boards. The more she read, the louder her mind screamed at her. *No, no, no.*

Gateway. Demons. Unpredictable.

Several people said that even if something nasty came through, as long as you forced the little plastic thing—the planchette—to "goodbye," it shut down the connection and kept the creepy stuff from haunting you.

An hour later, she ran into the living room to tell her parents she was going to have dinner at Becca's.

"Oh, is that my daughter?" her father asked from the couch, a bowl of popcorn between her parents as they watched the local evening news. "I was starting to forget what you looked like."

"Ha ha," Riley said. "I'll be back after."

"Homework done?" her mom asked.

"Most of it." *None of it.* "I'll finish when I get back. I need help on algebra again."

"It's a date."

Riley dashed across the street. She let herself in, like usual, called a hurried hello to Ashley, and took off up the stairs. Ever since the night Mariah showed up at the dinner table, Ashley watched her closely, as if she expected Riley to strike up a conversation with her deceased daughter at any moment. Riley hadn't seen the little girl since, but had woken up out of a dead sleep a few nights, vague dark shapes bleeding back into the shadows as her eyes adjusted.

"Geez!" Becca yelped from her spot on the floor, a hand to her chest as Riley came barreling through the door. She looked like a mini version of Ashley. "I thought you were Mom."

"Should I lock the door?"

Becca painstakingly took the Ouija board out of its box and laid it on a white towel she'd spread out on the floor. The planchette was placed delicately on top, as if it were made of glass. "Yeah, lock it. Mom is making lasagna from scratch, so she won't be done for a while. I think I saw her get the pasta press out. Who makes pasta by hand?"

Riley locked the door, but just stood there, bunching up the bottom of her shirt in her fists. The board looked innocent enough.

"C'mon, you chicken!" Becca said, still focused on the board.

A gulp of breath puffed out Riley's cheeks. She took her spot across from Becca.

"Okay, so Taylor said what you have to do is ask, like, basic questions: what's your name, how old are you, when did you die … they have to answer one letter at a time, so it can't be anything too hard."

"She was just a baby," said Riley, staring at the thick block letters spelling out the alphabet. "How can she spell stuff when she wasn't even old enough to talk yet?"

"You didn't see a little baby though, did you?"

No, Riley definitely saw a toddler. Could *toddlers* spell?

"Let's just try it and see what happens."

The girls sat cross-legged, leaned forward, and lightly placed their fingers on the planchette. Riley bit her bottom lip.

Nothing happened.

"You gotta ask stuff!" Becca whisper-hissed.

"Why me!"

"You're the one who made contact!"

"This is stupid!"

"Ask!"

"Ugh! Fine." Riley cleared her throat, trying to remember the things she read online. "We would like to speak to Mariah Green. Are you here?"

"Oh, that's good," Becca said, gaze zeroed in on the planchette.

Riley held her breath for so long waiting for a response, she was worried she'd pass out. Then the planchette slowly started to inch its way across the board.

"Are you doing that?" Becca asked, eyes wide.

"No! Are you?"

"No, I swear!"

YES, the board said.

"Oh god oh god oh god," said Becca. "Ask something else."

Riley swallowed, sure pools of sweat would soon form below her hands on the board. "What's your name?"

Slowly, it spelled out: **M-A-R-I-A-H.**

"Oh god oh god oh god."

"Are you okay?"

YES.

"Can you show yourself to your mom, like you did with me? She wants to know you're okay, too."

There was a long pause and Riley shared a look with Becca. Then the planchette started to move again.

NO.

"Why not?" asked Becca. "Just show up and wave at her like you did with Ry."

NO.

Becca took her hands off the planchette and put them on her hips, like a mother about to scold a child. "She misses you."

MISS HER.

The planchette had moved with only Riley's hands on it, and faster than it had with them both. Riley's mouth dropped open after the first letter.

"I have an idea." Becca lightly touched the planchette with the tips of her fingers again. "Taylor was saying she watched her sister and her friend do it once, and when it got boring, they sort of … egged it on? They were kinda mean to it, you know? Pushed it to answer."

This was the exact *opposite* of what Riley read one was supposed to do. Before she could say that, Becca spoke.

"Hey, Mariah, I know you were born before me, so you're technically the older sister, but I'm the one *here*, okay? I'm the one who has to see Mom so sad. So how about you give us something we can use as proof you were here." Her voice got stronger, more confident. "We need proof or she's not going to be able to get past it. Go on! Prove you're real and this isn't just Riley screwing around."

"Hey!"

"It's just to get her to talk," Becca whispered, as if that would keep Mariah from hearing her.

Something in the corner of the room hit the floor and the girls yelped, pulling their hands away from the planchette. A two-shelf bookcase holding most of Becca's art supplies had toppled over. Pens, crayons, colored pencils, construction paper, glue, glitter, and googly eyes littered the carpet. Riley felt like the floor was watching her.

"What's going on up there?" Tony called from downstairs.

Riley and Becca stood side by side, hands clasped. Riley couldn't remember when they'd gone from sitting to standing.

They yelped again when someone banged on the door. The doorknob rattled. "What are you two doing?"

"Girls, open up."

Both her parents were there now. The girls looked at the door, then each other, then the board. They scrambled forward without discussing it; they needed to stash the board.

When they were a mere foot away from it, the planchette flew across the room and smacked into the wall.

They both came up short. Riley slapped a hand over her mouth. "Oh god oh god oh god."

Riley lowered her hand. "We have to force it to say goodbye."

"*What?*" Becca asked.

"I read about it before I came over. We have to force the planchette thing to 'goodbye' to make sure we're not haunted."

The doorknob rattled again. "Open up! *Now!*"

"One sec, Mom!"

"If you don't open this door in the next five seconds, I'll get a screwdriver and take this door off its hinges and not put it back on till you're 35." That was Tony.

"I'll get the board; you get the planchette," whispered Becca.

"Why do I always get the worst jobs!"

Becca lunged for the board like it was a wild alligator she needed to wrestle into submission. Riley darted to the other side of the room where the planchette—hopefully—was lying on the other side of Becca's bed. It had bounced off the closet door before hitting the ground.

Crawling across the bed, Riley peered over. No planchette. "*Crap.*"

Hanging halfway over the edge of the bed, she lifted the side of the comforter. The planchette sat directly under the bed. Steeling herself, she reached for the plastic triangle. The moment her hand touched it, Becca let out another startled yelp as something else crashed in the room.

"That's it! I'm getting the screwdriver!"

Riley hurriedly righted herself and whirled around.

Becca stood in the middle of the room, hands clasped to her mouth as she stared at the wall. Written hundreds of times—in what looked like black crayon—was the name **Mariah**. Over and over and over. It looked like little kid writing; the letters not quite all the same size. But it started at the top of the wall—higher than either of them could reach—and went all the way across and down.

"What the hell, Becks?"

Not taking her wide eyes off the wall, or her hands off her mouth, Becca shook her head.

Seconds and eons later, there was a commotion at the door. Riley looked over just as the door was lifted up and out and Ashley ran in, only to come up short and gasp when she saw the wall covered in sloppy black letters.

"What the ..." Tony muttered.

Riley scanned the room, shocked that books and Becca's desk chair and clothes were thrown all over the room. Like a mini hurricane had swept through. Or a child just had an epic tantrum.

Tears in her eyes, Becca turned to her parents. "I don't know what happened. We thought we could talk to her."

It was then that Tony saw the Ouija board on the floor. His gaze snapped to the planchette in Riley's hand. "Was this *your* idea?"

"No ... I ..."

"It was my idea, Dad. I thought we could—"

"Enough!" Ashley snapped, snatching up the board and yanking the planchette out of Riley's hand. "I don't know what the hell is going on here, but it stops now. Riley, go home. I'll be calling your parents within the hour."

"You …" Riley tried. "You have to force the planchette to—"

"*Now*, Riley."

Raising her brows in Becca's direction, her friend nodded.

"Move it to goodbye," Riley said, walking to the door. "I'm … I'm really sorry, Mr. and Mrs. Green. Honest."

She ran home.

Riley received a lecture that lasted half a lifetime from her parents later—mainly from her mother. Not for "playing a cruel joke," as Ashley had claimed, but for opening doors that weren't supposed to be open when she had no idea what she was doing.

The Greens experienced weird things every night after that. The final straw came when Becca woke up screaming, covered in scratches on her back and arms even though she'd been sleeping on her back. The family moved within a month. Riley and Becca tried to keep in contact, but Becca's parents eventually forbade them from communicating. Ashley monitored Becca's internet use and phone, blocking Riley anywhere she could.

By the time Riley started high school, she had no idea where Becca lived. Her cell phone number was changed. They hadn't talked since.

Jade let out a soft snort then, pulling Riley back to the present. Jade shifted on the bed. Seconds later, her rhythmic breathing resumed.

Ever since Riley's experience with Mariah Green, she'd avoided actively calling on her sensitivity. It was all too unpredictable. Not just the spirits or energies, but how living people reacted to it. She didn't want anything that happened this weekend to ruin her friendship with Jade.

Avoid, avoid, avoid.

She knew the circumstances with Rebecca were vastly different than the circumstances now, but she couldn't help worrying.

She also couldn't sleep. It was just after midnight, according to her cell. Perhaps she could get a nightcap from the kitchen. Was the kitchen still open? It wasn't like she could just pop over to a convenience store.

Sighing, she crept out of bed, rummaged through her luggage, and pulled out a hoodie. Grabbing one of the keys off the table by the door, she let herself out of the room.

The hallway was deathly quiet.

Flames danced in their glass enclosures as she made her way down the stairs. Angela wasn't manning the reception desk anymore. The investigation team and their bag of ghost hunting gear was gone.

But, lucky for her, Michael and his companions were still in the lobby. His sister and her wife sat together on a sofa, busily looking over a book. Michael warmed himself in a chair by the fireplace, a mug in hand. Another chair sat beside it, the armrests touching.

Riley plopped into the open chair. Michael gave a start.

"Sorry," she said, tamping down a smile.

He smiled as he recognized her. "Well, hello, fellow skeptic. Riley, right?"

"Good memory, Michael."

The smile turned to a grin. He took a sip from his mug. "Couldn't sleep?"

Riley shook her head. "I'm a bit of a night owl."

"Ah," he said, nodding. "A party girl."

"If you call binging *Tiana's Circle* for the third time a party, then damn straight."

He laughed. "Can't say I have the foggiest clue what that is. Granted, my old ass is rarely hip to what the youths are into these days."

Riley snorted unexpectedly, startling the pair on the other side of the room. They smiled at Riley and waved, then went back to their book.

Michael, when he smiled, had a dimple in one cheek.

"You can't be *that* old," said Riley. "Though only geezers say *foggiest clue*."

"I'm pushing thirty-one."

"Five-year difference … yep, definitely a geezer."

Michael sat up a little straighter and leaned toward her just a smidge. "You're twenty-five? I swear I thought you were seventeen."

"Ha!" she said. "I get that a lot. Young face."

"Well," he said, reclining in his chair again, "at least I don't have to feel like a pedophile anymore for thinking you're gorgeous." He flushed. "Christ, did I really just say that out loud? I think I said that out loud."

Riley flushed too. "You definitely said that out loud."

Michael sat there holding his mug with both hands, staring into it as if he hoped he'd fall in and drown.

"What on Earth is in that cup of yours and can I have some too?"

That broke the spell and he focused on her again. "I raided the kitchen and made myself a White Russian."

"Well, aren't you fancy."

"Want one?"

"*Yes.*"

"C'mon." He walked toward the pair across the way so he wouldn't have to shout. "I'm gonna take Riley into the kitchen and make her a drink." He kept moving, waving over his shoulder for Riley to follow him.

"Literal or euphemism?" one of them asked.

"The latter, if he plays his cards right," said Riley.

Michael stumbled over the edge of a rug, almost spilling his drink.

The ladies both laughed. Michael arched an eyebrow at her.

"Literal, old man," said Riley. "Don't get any ideas."

"Too late."

Michael led her past the dining table and through the double doors at the back of the room. The place was pitch black until Michael flipped on a switch.

Two refrigerators sat against the wall directly opposite the doors she'd just come through. The wall to her left had gas-burning stoves, low cabinets, and a ton of counter space. A large steel island took up a sizable chunk of the room. Sparkling pots and pans hung from the bar above the island, and even more hung below it.

Her father would love this kitchen. The man fancied himself a chef mainly because he'd watched an ungodly amount of the Food Network and owned nearly every appliance and cooking utensil one could imagine. The industrial kitchen was all stainless steel, every surface gleaming under the fluorescent lights.

Riley let out a low whistle.

"Right?" said Michael, heading for the fridges. "Guess they need the big guns for when they host large events."

Resting a hip against the island counter, she said, "I feel like I shouldn't even breathe in here."

Michael collected the necessary supplies, then placed the mug, milk, coffee liqueur, and vodka on the counter next to her. He mixed the drink with the ease and speed of a professional.

"I'm very impressed right now."

"Don't be," he said, sliding the finished product toward her. "I was a bartender for, like, five years. It helped put me through college."

She took a sip. "Oh, that is good."

"I'm glad," he said, then flushed again. "I'll, uh ... just put this stuff away."

She smiled to herself as she took another sip. When he was done and heading back toward her, she said, "So what was this bet you lost?"

He groaned. "I was hoping you'd forget about that."

"Are you kidding? That's the kind of stuff I latch onto."

"Good to know." He huffed, then rested his hip against the counter, too. "It's ... it's embarrassing."

"If you're trying to get me to be *less* interested, you're one-hundred-percent going in the wrong direction," she said.

"Less interested in the story or in me?"

"Man, get one White Russian in you and you're unstoppable." She winced. "That sounded dirtier than I intended. But ... both."

His dark brows shot toward his hairline. "Well, in that case ..." He walked around to her other side, then hopped up on counter, his legs dangling off the side. He patted the spot beside him.

Riley managed to hop up next to him without spilling her drink. Though she was warm in her hoodie, her pajama pants were thin and she shivered as the cold metal touched the backs of her legs.

"So," Michael said, "my sister, Donna, is a year older. We've always been a bit competitive—over nearly everything—and we have this really dumb tradition that we'll challenge each other to eat something particularly offensive at every major holiday gathering. Whoever spits it out first, can't swallow it, or vomits first, loses the bet."

"Classy."

"You know it," he said. "It started when we were kids. 'I bet you I can eat three hot dogs in thirty seconds.' But then, as we got older, we did food challenges *for* things. We had to share a car in high school, so if we both had dates, we did a food challenge to see who got the car for the weekend and who had to hoof it or bum a ride.

"Then, once we were adults, we started doing food challenges to force each other to do things we'd never do on our own. She made me go to one of those paint night events, you know?"

Riley nodded.

"I was the only guy there! But it was actually pretty fun."

"What'd you paint?"

"Bunch of trees … sunset in the background. Didn't turn out half bad."

"What kind of stuff have you made *her* do?"

"Well, the most memorable one was about five years ago. I won the Curdled Milk Challenge—"

"Gross!" Riley said, laughing.

"Oh, you have no idea. It took me years to put milk in my cereal again," Michael said. "Now, my sister can drink me under the table in most circumstances, but she hates bars. Gay bars, straight bars— doesn't matter. Not her thing. So I made her go on a pub crawl with me for St. Paddy's Day."

"Ugh! The green beer!"

Michael nodded sagely. "We were on about bar four of seven when I turn around and Donna is gone. We're both well passed buzzed at this point, so I was a little worried. I finally find her chatting up some girl named Carla who also had been roped into a pub crawl that night by *her* brother. She and her brother hung out with us for the rest of the crawl. A little over a year ago, Donna and Carla got married."

"Damn. You're a matchmaker."

"Right? I'm pretty amazing."

"Calm down, tiger."

He laughed.

"So what challenge did you lose to get sucked into a paranormal investigation?"

"The Ghost Pepper Challenge."

"Oh no."

"*Yeah*, it wasn't pretty. The whole family got together a couple months ago to celebrate Donna and Carla's anniversary, so of course there was a challenge issued. She totally had this all planned, though. She's sneaky like that.

"She said whoever could handle the ghost pepper better would be the winner. Now, we're both fan of spicy foods but hadn't ever tried ghost peppers—and they aren't even the hottest peppers in the world!"

"Who judged who handled it better?"

"My family at large. They're the worst people: none of them warned me about how bad it would be."

"They probably gave up a long time ago about you ever possessing a modicum of sense."

Michael knocked into her gently with his shoulder. "Modicum. Impressive." The dimple reappeared with his smile. "I'm also deeply offended by the insinuation, but I'll allow it. Also, for the record, I'm now more of a *reformed* idiot."

Smiling, she bumped him back and took another sip of her drink.

"Okay, so, the plan was to just take a bite of the pepper and see who lost control of their bodily functions first. Someone was standing by with cold glasses of milk. But because I'm an idiot—" he shot her a pointed look, "—I ate the whole thing, thinking they couldn't be as hot as everyone says. But, oh … holy … *shit*. I immediately started sweating. It felt like my face was literally on fire. I'm tearing up, snot is running out of my nose, the inside of my ears start to itch.

"I lunge for the milk within seconds, gulping it down in record time. I run for the kitchen and start shoveling bread into my mouth. I'm gagging on it given how fast I'm trying to eat the stuff. Donna comes barreling in seconds later, and we're laughing so hard we're crying, but also cursing each other out at the same time.

"I would burp and it would bring all the spice back up and I'd go scrambling for more bread or milk or water. I'm not even going to tell you about the following twelve hours and what that horrible little pepper from the pits of hell did to my intestines, but just know it was horrible. Worst thing I've ever done."

Riley had been reduced to giggles almost immediately. She put down her mug and wiped at her eyes. "My god, you're such an idiot."

Michael smiled at her. "Reformed, Riley. Reformed."

She blew out a calming breath. "How long did it take before you—"

"Until I no longer felt like Mount Vesuvius was erupting every time I used the bathroom?"

Riley let out another undignified snort that set them both laughing.

"I was out of commission for twenty-four hours."

"And Donna?"

"Maybe a little less? She was smart enough to only eat half the pepper. But it destroyed us both."

Riley shook her head, smiling to herself as she watched her feet dangling above the tile floor.

"At the risk of sounding cheesy as hell …"

"Uh oh." She glanced over at him.

"It was all worth it to hear that snort."

She elbowed him.

"What about you?" he asked. "Brothers, sisters?"

"Nope. Only child. Two really awesome parents who are still together. Jade is the closest I've got to a sibling."

"And she's really into all this … stuff?" He waved a hand in the air, indicating the paranormal in general, she supposed.

"Yep. All four of my friends are. Huge fans of the show, too."

"But not you?"

Riley had been having such a nice time with him, she didn't want to sully it with talk of her sensitivity … gift … ability … whatever. "Willing to keep an open mind."

He narrowed his eyes at her a little. "You're really going to give me the same generic answer you gave the group? I thought we got past that. I told you of my intestinal woes."

She smiled despite herself, but didn't say anything. She chewed on her bottom lip, gaze focused on her dangling feet.

"Hey, sorry if I said something to upset you," he said when she stayed silent. "I … I like you. Just trying to get to know you, is all."

"You didn't say anything wrong. You've been perfectly lovely, actually." She hopped off the counter. She shivered a little at the feel of the tile beneath her socked feet. "I should probably get to bed, though."

He stared at her for a moment, his hanging feet crossed at the ankles and his fingers wrapped around the lip of the counter. That single dimple made an appearance as he angled a half-smile at her. She, just for a moment, considered telling him about Becca and the weird experience out on the patio earlier. But how much of that desire was simply because he was easy on the eyes? Like gorgeous criminals who got lighter sentences because it was harder to punish beautiful people.

"Thanks for the drink."

His shoulders sagged. "Of course." Hopping off the counter too, he placed her mug in the sink with his. "I should probably go to bed, too."

They pushed open the double doors to the kitchen. Donna and Carla were still poring over the same book, talking in low tones.

"Oh, the light," Riley said, grabbing one of the doors just before it shut and pulling it back open. As she reached for the light switch, something flickered in her peripheral vision.

Sitting on the island on the edge closer to the door—the opposite side from where they'd been sitting—sat her mug. The same one she'd watched Michael place in the sink before they headed for the door.

"You okay?"

Riley jumped. Flicking off the light, Riley closed the door and smiled at Michael, who stood a few feet away.

"Yep, everything's great."

She told him goodnight, waved to Donna and Carla as she speed-walked across the lobby, and hurried back to her room.

CHAPTER 6

Riley woke with a start, sitting upright in bed. Where was she? The droning whir of a blow dryer started up again.

"She lives!"

That was Pamela, standing beside the other bed, her suitcase open. She still wore pajamas but her hair and makeup were done. Pamela never wore much makeup, but her eyeshadow game was always on point, regardless of the occasion.

"I forgot you sleep like the dead," Pamela said. "Stay up late?"

Riley swiped a wayward lock of hair out of her face. "I, uh … couldn't sleep so I went downstairs and that guy Michael and I talked for a bit."

Pamela threw a shirt at her head. "Shut up!" Bounding over, she plopped on the foot of Riley's bed. "Dish!"

The blow dryer turned off.

Riley laughed. "We just talked! And he made me a White Russian."

"Who made who a White Russian?" asked Jade, poking her head out of the bathroom. Brie appeared to be the one manning the blow dryer. Riley wasn't sure where Rochelle was.

When Riley told Jade about Michael, she scurried over with the same enthusiasm as Pamela. "What *happened*?"

"Y'all need to relax," Riley said. "It's not like I've never talked to a guy before."

Jade and Pamela shared a look full of smirking mouths and arched brows.

"What!" said Riley.

"Honey, you've not only been a homebody for six months, you've been a *celibate* homebody," said Jade, patting Riley's knee.

"My god that sounds incredible," Brie said, wandering over from the bathroom. Her shiny hair fell in a cascading sheet of brown just past her shoulders.

"If you *wanted* to be celibate, you know I'd support that. But I've seen you flirt, girl—you're incorrigible. You don't flirt like a girl who doesn't want a snake in her grass."

Riley and Pamela cracked up. One of Jade's favorite pastimes was coming up with sexual euphemisms. They almost exclusively featured wildlife.

Just then, Rochelle came into the room with two plates heaped with donuts. "The Skinny Jean Quartet totally hates me right now." Then she glanced at Brie. "Oh. Can vegans eat donuts?"

"Yes, but likely not those," Brie replied. "You ladies dig in; I'll be fine."

While everyone got ready—taking intermittent breaks to wolf down donuts; Brie whipped out a nut bar of some kind—Riley was grilled about Michael.

Luckily, they'd all been awake for a couple hours before Riley got up, so she was able to duck into the shower after several minutes to escape. By the time she emerged again, conversation had shifted to the evening's first investigation.

As she followed the girls out of the Hyssop Room and down the stairs, Riley dreaded seeing Nina. Dreaded what she had in store for the group's skeptics.

Angela the receptionist flitted about the room, talking to the three groups. Michael, Donna, and Carla sat in the same places they'd been last night. If not for their change in clothes, Riley would have thought they'd been there all night.

A row of additional tables rested along the wall near the main dining table. Dishes and silverware were stacked on one end, followed by the remnants of breakfast: a basket with a red-cloth lining that now only held a couple of apples and a banana, a small tower of mini cereal boxes, two coffee dispensers, and a carafe of ice water sweating onto a wide, wooden coaster.

Towering green pines stood beyond the large bay windows. A fluffy-tailed squirrel scampered up a trunk and disappeared into the branches of a nearby tree. She imagined the forest was alive with bird song and babbling creeks and humming insects. The world beyond the ranch house's walls seemed safer than whatever might be lurking behind doors and under their feet.

Michael's chair faced the windows, so he wouldn't have seen her come downstairs. He glanced over his shoulder then, scanning the room. A contagious smile broke out on his face when he locked eyes with Riley.

"*Damn*," Rochelle whispered, the only one in their group not currently discussing *Paranormal Playground*. "Get your ass over there right now. When a man that hot looks at you like that, you run, princess. You do not walk."

Riley's attention snapped to Rochelle. "Oh, that's not fair! You can't quote *Tiana's Circle* at me!"

"Can and did!" Then she dramatically nudged Riley towards Michael.

Stumbling over her own feet, she drew the attention of several guests.

Michael saw it and offered Rochelle a thumbs up. Riley headed his way, glaring at the traitorous girl behind her. Rochelle blew her a kiss.

Riley plopped herself into the chair beside him.

"Good morning, Riley," he said, aiming an overly sweet smile at her.

"Good morning, Mr. Roberts."

He laughed. "Oh, so we've gone from swapping stories to issuing formalities?"

Riley really didn't want to like this guy. "I'm sorry I rabbited on you last night."

"So you admit you fled," he said, turning toward her. Lowering his voice, he added, "Honestly, did I say something to upset you?"

"No. It's me, really."

"Ah, *that* classic line," he said, sitting back.

"Get it a lot?"

He smiled. "Haven't gotten much of anything lately."

"Same." Her cheeks burned. *Why* had she admitted that?

"Why not?"

"I could ask you the same thing."

"Well," he said, leaning toward her again; she mirrored him. "My last serious entanglement was almost two years ago, and it ended because I caught her with one of her students."

Riley's mouth dropped open.

"Shit, wait. I should clarify—she worked at a college. So the student was legal, at least."

"That's *slightly* less shitty."

"Slightly," he said. "Did I mention I'd recently bought a ring?"

"Damn."

"Yeah. Sort of swore off dating for a while."

She bit her lip. Casey hadn't actually cheated on her—yet. But one night she'd used his computer to order pizza—her laptop was in her bag in a different room entirely and she'd felt lazy. They knew each other's passwords, so she keyed his in and found that he'd signed up for one of those "cheat discreetly" websites. The idiot had forgotten to log out of it, much less minimize the page, and Riley had seen his profile-in-progress.

"My girlfriend is always too busy working to spend the amount of time with me I need. Plus I have needs and curiosities I want to explore that she's unwilling to try. I love her well enough, and she's marriage material for sure, but daddy needs to play."

After reading that, and nearly throwing up in her mouth, she'd packed up her stuff while he was at work a day later. Her note on the counter simply said, *"Enjoy playing with yourself, Daddy."*

Casey mostly definitely had been a terrible boyfriend. Inconsiderate. Stingy. Verbally abusive when drinking. Passive-aggressive when stone-cold sober. But Riley had known him since freshman year and the good memories often helped crowd out the bad.

But when she'd read that profile, it was as if the world stopped spinning for a moment and the clarity of her situation snapped into place. She'd been lying to herself for years about the relationship. And what for? She couldn't see herself marrying Casey. So she'd left.

And turned into a celibate hermit.

"Riley."

Her attention focused on Michael, his dark brows pulled together.

"Did I zone out again?"

"Happen often?"

"Just lately. I sort of suck at human interaction."

He smiled at her. He had a great smile.

She needed to get her mind *off* that smile. "So what made you want to try dating again?" Maybe someday she'd want to get back on the wagon.

"I met you."

They stared at each other for a solid five seconds, then burst into laughter.

She swatted at his arm. "You're so corny!"

"You almost bought it! For like a split second." Sighing, and still slightly laughing to himself, he said, "One day I just decided I needed to stop feeling sorry for myself. I loved that girl. I really did. But I had to let myself mourn the life I thought I was going to have, and then just … try again. It was too depressing otherwise."

"And dating itself isn't depressing?"

"Touché. I guess I'd rather try and fail than wallow in self-pity?" He shrugged. "I have some *really* good first-date stories."

"Maybe you can tell me some of them later."

"As long as you promise not to run away again."

"I make no promises," Riley said. "But I'll try to suck less at the whole, you know, talking thing."

"I'll take it."

Michael had just started telling Riley about his room—the Crabapple—when Jade crept over and stood in front of them. They looked up.

"Sorry to interrupt." Offering Michael one of her award-winning smiles, she held out a hand. "I'm Jade, by the way."

Michael shook it. "Ah, the best friend who threatened Riley's life should she not attend."

"That's me!" Glancing at Riley, she said, "Since there's still over an hour before the team gets here, we thought it might be nice to cruise the grounds. There's a hiking trail not far from here." Smiling at Michael again, she added, "But if you'd rather stay *here* …"

Before Riley could get a word out, Michael said, "We can talk later."

"I swear I'm not running off this time," she said, standing up.

He just smiled. "Have a nice time, ladies."

Jade hooked her arm around Riley's and dragged her out the front door, the other three girls hot on their tail.

"*Daaamn*," they all said in unison when they were outside.

"Shut up," Riley said, laughing, knowing Jade was behind the group reaction.

"You know I'm not usually attracted to white boys," Jade said, her arm still looped through Riley's as they headed to the trail, "but if I wasn't already happily in a relationship, I'd totally let that fox into this hen house."

The hiking trail had been carved, and maintained, by the horses from the dude ranch on the other end of the property. Though littered with clumps of horse poop, the trampled ground provided a nice stroll. They walked in a single-file line, Jade leading the charge.

The air was a little nippy, but the sun shone bright in the cloudless blue sky. The crisp scent of spruce and flowering plants helped clear Riley's head. The place was beautiful. She could see why Porter Fredricks had bought the place to try and strip it of its awful past.

Riley tried to focus on the present: the smell of trees, the sound of twittering birds, and the rustle of wind through the leaves. It was possible that after tonight, if the place was truly as haunted as she feared, the beauty of it all would pale to the fear it brought her.

A faint trace of music drifted past her. A piano, maybe? She stopped so suddenly, Pamela almost crashed into her back.

"What's up?" Pamela asked.

Riley's head cocked to the side, gaze focused past the trail they were on and into the denser forest beyond. "Do you hear that?"

Rochelle, Pamela, and Brie were huddled behind her now, clearly straining to hear something.

Jade backtracked. "Hear what?"

"It's like … an orchestra now. But far away?"

"What, like a clan of musicians have set up in the forest to play an impromptu concert?" Then Jade gasped. "*Ghost* musicians? Has anyone read reports about that? Music in the woods?"

All three women behind Riley shook their heads.

Then the music abruptly stopped. "It's … gone." Goosebumps sprang up on her arms.

Pamela and Rochelle gave full body shudders.

"Way to creep everyone out, Ry," Jade said, smiling, then turned and kept walking.

Hushed conversation resumed behind her, but she could tell everyone was straining to hear what she had. Riley didn't hear it again.

Once they'd made it back to the trail mouth just before noon, Riley spotted the team out in the small parking area.

Rochelle walked beside her. "Oof, that guy does something to me."

"Which one? Derrick?" It was a shot in the dark; Riley wasn't entirely sure which one had the "sweet goatee" and which sported the "luxuriant mustache." She hoped it wasn't the mustachioed one.

"No. Xavier."

Biting the inside of her cheek, Riley eyed the team leader. He had a dad bod and almost no hair. "He's, like, *twice* your age."

"Don't judge me," she said, gaze focused on Xavier. "I have a thing for mature gentlemen."

Riley snorted.

As their group passed the team, Nina looked over and immediately sought out Riley's attention. Gaze focused on the ground ahead of her, Riley trudged right by. She knew she was being childish, but this was how she rolled.

"Hey, ladies!" Xavier called out, then made a dramatic show of checking his watch. "Guess it's about that time, eh?"

Rochelle swooned beside Riley, the girl letting out a guttural grunt that was one-hundred-percent embarrassing.

"Pull yourself together!" Riley hissed at her.

"Look at his ass, though."

"Oh my god. He doesn't even *have* one. It's like one of those concave asses."

"Exactly."

Riley laughed. "You're so weird."

"Thank you."

At ten past, the whole group gathered near the dining table again. The goateed guy pulled items out of the two duffel bags, while the mustachioed one laid them out in neat rows on the table's surface. As they did that, the group of guests stood huddled around Xavier and Nina.

"Since there have been so many instances of the little boy—" Nina fluttered her lashes at Xavier, "—in the kitchen at night, that will be one of our prime EVP locations."

Michael slowly inched his way toward Riley from the edge of the group. She'd been watching his movements from the corner of her eye. As he got closer, Riley took a couple steps back to stand beside him.

"How was your walk?" he whispered.

"It was nice," she said. "You excited for tonight?"

His gaze roamed her face for longer than was considered a casual glance, and she bit her lip. "Should be interesting. I can't decide if I want this place to be haunted or not."

Riley knew how he felt.

"Now, since each of us has a different specialty, we'll be rotating you between leaders tonight," Xavier said, drawing Riley's attention back. "But whatever smaller group you're put into tonight will be your group for the entire evening. Some of you will be paired with people you don't know for the sake of creating even groups. There are twelve of you, and four of us, so each group will have three."

"Your math skills are quite impressive, boss," said Goatee Guy from where he and the mustachioed one were still arranging equipment on the table.

"Mario is the resident smart ass; I apologize in advance," Xavier said, though he was trying not to smile. "Groups are as follows ..."

Riley was paired with Michael and Pamela. Donna and Carla were paired with the guy who got handsy with the dowsing rods. The remaining three of that group stayed together. Which left Jade paired with Rochelle and Brie.

Riley had a sneaking suspicion Nina was behind her group, at least; she wanted the two skeptics together. That, or she wanted a skeptic paired with the person who had the best chance of *actually* experiencing something. She probably liked the extra challenge.

Equipment tutorials followed. They listened to EVPs as a group, the majority of the listeners gasping and oohing and ahhing at the disembodied voices.

"Did you catch that?" Xavier would ask, then rewind and play the sound over and over. The guesses called out rarely matched what

Xavier claimed the spirit said. It mostly sounded like gibberish and static to Riley.

Huddled around a small camera, several people—Jade and Brie included—almost lost their minds over the apparent proof of an apparition. All Riley saw were shadowy, vaguely human-shaped figures that flitted across the end of dark hallways.

By the time they wrapped up the lesson, Riley's stomach growled something fierce.

"Your late lunch should be served soon," Xavier said, as if he'd heard it. "We recommend trying to take a nap, as the real work of the investigation will start at midnight and often runs until at least five or six a.m. You'll be on a vampire schedule the next two days. If you have any further questions, feel free to come ask. Enjoy your lunch and we'll meet you back here around ten."

The tables along the wall had a metal tub full of iced drinks, two large salads bowls with tongs poised on the edges, and half a dozen platters covered in sandwich fixings.

Riley finished crafting a sandwich roughly ten feet high and was about to follow Jade to the dining table when she heard, "Want to eat on the patio?"

Michael.

"Yes, she does," said Jade.

Riley, mortified, watched Jade's face, whose gaze was clearly fixed on Michael over Riley's shoulder as he walked toward the front door. When her friend's attention shifted back to her, Riley whisper-shouted, "I can speak for myself!"

"No one is debating your ability to form words, babe," Jade whisper-shouted back, holding a plate with a considerably smaller sandwich than Riley's. "I'm questioning your ability to not screw this up."

"How dare you."

Louder, Jade said, "She's right behind you!"

"You're the worst."

"This is what sisters do," Jade said. "Now get out of here. He just walked outside."

Riley threw her head back and groaned. "He's going to want to *talk* about stuff."

Jade faced her head on, raised an eyebrow, and cocked her head.

"Fine. I'm going."

As Riley headed that way, she caught part of a conversation between Donna, Carla, and Brie, who were clustered around the end of the table. The couple were vegetarians and asked Brie about her opinion of quinoa burgers.

"I have this amazing recipe using sweet potato as a binder—totally to die for," Brie said, her deadpan delivery as lacking in emotion as ever.

When Riley stepped outside, she found one of the Skinny Jean Quartet couples sitting outside too, but Michael had claimed a table and chairs on the other end of the wraparound wooden deck. It wasn't far from the spot where Riley had felt something—or some-*one*—yank on her jacket.

Blowing out a breath, she placed her food on the small, round table.

"Do you plan to eat that or use it as a pillow?"

Without replying, she placed her hand on the top slice of bread and pressed down. Mayonnaise and mustard trickled down the sides. She then took a very large bite and angled a smile at him with bulging cheeks.

"Man, you're lucky you're so damn adorable …"

She just barely managed not to choke as she laughed, hand over her mouth. Washing it down with a swig of soda, she sighed contentedly as her stomach settled.

Shaking his head, Michael tucked into his side salad.

"So, Mr. Roberts," she said, wiping a blob of mustard off her thumb, "do you believe in ghosts?"

She wanted both to catch him off guard and to get this conversation over with. If he thought people who believed in "the other" were insane, then they clearly had no future and Jade would stop harassing her and Riley could return to her hermit, celibate life in peace.

"Zipping right on past the small talk, are we?" He sat back, his mouth bunched up a little in one corner as he thought. "Yes and no."

"All that time for a noncommittal answer!"

"Don't rush me, woman," he said, tossing his wadded-up napkin at her.

It hit her in the nose. Laughing, she lobbed it back.

Snatching it out of the air, he kept it in his fist, absently worrying a piece of the napkin between two fingers. "I say yes because I've heard enough stories from my family over the years to think there're lingering energies or what-have-you. I can't say those things are ghosts, exactly, but I believe there's some other, I don't know—force?—out there."

"And you say no because?"

"Because I haven't experienced anything personally."

Riley nodded, attention on her food, not him.

"What about you?"

She knew he would ask. It was a logical counter question. But she'd never told anyone other than the Greens and her parents about Mariah.

"I'm a reluctant believer," she said before she had a chance to think about it. She kept her focus on her plate, picking apart a corner of her bread like a shamefaced little kid. "I've experienced enough weird stuff that it's impossible *not* to believe. But I'd much rather pretend this kind of thing didn't exist."

She fell silent, knowing she probably had an expression akin to "Every person I've ever loved has perished simultaneously," but she didn't know how to control that.

He reached out and gently touched her elbow. "Hey, what's up?"

"You're going to think I'm nuts," she said.

"That ship already sailed, sweetheart."

She snorted.

Just tell him. You have to tell someone. Might as well be a stranger, right?

Blowing out a deep breath, she told him about seeing Mariah as a kid—minus the bit about the Ouija board and the creepy things that followed. One step at a time.

"That's … amazing," he said when she finished.

Biting her bottom lip, her gaze flicking to him. "That's not the word I thought you'd use."

"It's actually pretty similar to something that happened to my cousin," he said. "Ever since she was little, she's talked about voices in her head. Her parents worried it was schizophrenia and had her tested, but there was no medical explanation for what she said was happening. And, aside from the voices, she didn't act like someone with schizophrenia.

"As she got older, she would tell certain people what the voices said, and her parents eventually figured out she was hearing spirits. She was eight and knew things very few people knew; things an eight year old definitely couldn't have known.

"She helped find a long-lost ring that disappeared in our grandma's house fifteen years before. My deceased great-aunt—who none of the children in the family met, since she died when my grandma was a teenager—was the one who told my cousin where to find it."

"Wow," Riley said. "Are you close to your cousin?"

"I don't see her that often. She lives in England. Works as a professional psychic. Medium? Which is the one where you talk to dead people?"

"Medium."

"Okay, yeah, that one."

"That's pretty cool," she said, her stomach in knots. "I've never told anyone outside my family about Mariah."

His eyes widened. "What made you tell *me*?"

"I don't know."

"Well, I'm flattered, for what it's worth."

She managed an awkward shrug.

They talked about mundane things after that. Jobs. College. Family. He worked at an advertising firm and had majored in mass communications.

"How do you like being a waitress?"

"Eh. It's a job. Not something I want to do forever, but it's good for now."

"What would you want as a forever job?"

"Still trying to figure that out."

When a gust of cool air swept past her and she shivered, she looked around, realizing the sun was setting, the semi-cloudy sky tinged pink just beyond the tips of the surrounding pine forest.

"Whoa, what time is it?" she asked.

He glanced at his watch. "Nearly six."

"Yikes," she said. "I should probably attempt a nap."

There was another one of those just-past-polite stares going on and she flushed. She hadn't blushed this much since her first crush. In elementary school.

"That's likely a wise decision," he said.

Standing, she stretched, her shoulders popping softly. She reached for her empty plate.

A hand on hers stopped her. "I've got it."

Nodding, she nervously pulled her long sleeves of her cardigan over her hands. "Thanks. I mean … not just for the dishes. But … for listening."

He smiled, that single dimple making a brief appearance. "And thank you for letting me."

Lord help her.

"I'll see you later tonight, partner."

"Looking forward to it." He smiled, but she thought it looked a little sad, like he couldn't quite muster a full one.

Maybe he was feeling the same thing she was. That she wanted to say to hell with the ghost hunt and just stay out here talking to him until it was pitch black and they were swarmed by mosquitos.

But she was getting ahead of herself. She couldn't get lost in the first eligible man she'd talked to in six months just because he was nice to her.

And gorgeous.

"Goodnight, Mr. Roberts."

"Goodnight, Ms. Thomas."

She hurried off to her room then, refusing to look back at him, even though she could feel his eyes on her every step of the way.

1960

Though Orin deeply resented that his studies were limited to animals and anatomy books—rather than human subjects as he would've preferred—he devoted himself to learning all he could. He developed a particular interest in anatomists of old. His life changed the day he found a book in a local used bookshop about a Scottish surgeon named John Hunter.

In the early 18th century, John Hunter became the father of modern surgery. Between his curiosity about the inner workings of the human body—and his desire to please his brother, William, who ran a successful anatomy school—John was willing to do whatever necessary to make sure the school—and himself—had a steady supply of bodies to study. John knew the importance of hands-on anatomy. Knew that the only real way to learn about organs and bones and muscles was to have them strewn out before you.

But John Hunter, unless he worked on ailing live patients, exclusively performed his anatomy studies on cadavers. He only had a window of a week—assuming it wasn't in the heart of summer when his studies had to stop, lest he be overwhelmed with the stench of rotting corpses—before the body would no longer be useful. Then he had to go out and fetch more bodies. So much work for so little time with his deceased patients.

While it was admirable that John was willing to pay graverobbers—his "Resurrectionists"—to procure his test subjects, it meant John had little say in who ended up on his dissection table. When he could, he sought out oddities who suffered from deformities—he even got his hands on a giant. He searched for children—teenagers, toddlers, even fetuses. If he was lucky, he'd get a pregnant woman so he could study a child still growing in the womb.

Yet, more often than not, John was stuck with what his Resurrectionists brought him.

How much more could Hunter have learned if he had *living* specimens—specimens he hand-selected for himself? Live patients who could be poked and prodded and broken, then put back together to see the results.

Orin, with a few patients, could learn more from one body than he ever could from the two-dimensional pages of an anatomy textbook. One live patient could provide months of study before they were fully cut open to explore.

Orin would take extensive notes of his case studies, just as John had. Organs and tissues would be preserved, bones and muscles dried. His collection of preparations, thorough notes, and careful drawings would be his legacy. This portfolio of work would make him a shoo-in for medical school. They'd fall over themselves apologizing for rejecting his applications.

When they saw how devoted he was to his craft—how similar to the brilliant John Hunter—how could they possibly turn him away?

CHAPTER 7

Riley crashed through the forest like a thing possessed, swatting branches out of the way and ducking under others. Pine needles whipped her in the face, but she kept moving. She had to find him.

Rounding the side of a massive ponderosa pine, she came to a sudden stop, chest heaving, in the middle of a forked path. Both sides of the fork were crude, the paths shallow.

Which way had he gone? Where was he?

Something crashed behind her. A large body making its way up the curving, equally crude path. And fast.

C'mon, c'mon, c'mon ...

A slight flash of blue in her peripheral vision to her left. His jacket. And she was off again. If she ran fast enough, maybe she'd be deep into the woods by the time he reached the fork. Maybe he'd choose the wrong direction.

Another flash of blue through the trees.

She ran harder.

The ground was hard and dry, and though she tried to stay on the balls of her feet as she ran, she was sure she still sounded like a plodding elephant. The pine boughs slapping her arms as she wove around trees didn't help mask her presence. She hoped she wouldn't step on a fallen pinecone and twist an ankle.

The boughs were a blur of dark green on either side of her, broken only by the white space between trees. Brown, green, white.

Brown, green, white. Then—blue. To her right.

She made a sharp, crashing turn between two pines, swatting away the branches that snatched at her hair like grasping fingers.

A small, startled yelp escaped as she stopped abruptly, almost crashing into the boy. He stood in the middle of a few feet of flattened earth. Like someone had leveled the area for a garden way out here in the middle of nowhere, then gave up before planting anything. Two worn stumps marked where trees once stood.

The boy was a tiny, delicate thing. Like he'd been ill for most of his young life. The undersides of his eye sockets were dark, almost purple, as if he hadn't slept in days. His pale skin was nearly gray in places; the veins in his neck and on the back of his hands stood out like blue rivers. Under his thick blue-and-black-checkered jacket, zipped up to his throat, must have been a thin torso, ribs visible. He wore a maroon knit cap pulled down, almost covering his ears. Wild brown curls poked out from underneath.

Riley's chest heaved. "What're you doing out here?"

The boy opened his mouth to speak, but then his dark eyes widened and he stumbled back a step. Riley's breath caught in her throat as she felt the man behind her—that large body she'd heard crashing through the trees after her. Felt the heat of him.

The boy kept stepping back, back, back, shaking his head. He tripped over something—one of the tree stumps—and fell, squirming on his backside like an overturned beetle. Crying like a wounded animal. The man was suddenly not behind Riley, but in front of her, stalking toward the fallen boy.

She tried to go after him, to knock the man aside so the boy could run to freedom, but her feet wouldn't move. Her shoes sprouted roots, holding her fast to the earth—like she'd become one of the watching ponderosa pines.

The man was like an upright grizzly bear clad in a thick, camouflage jacket. A long, black, rectangular patch stretched along his left elbow. While he wasn't plump, he was tall—at least 6'2"—and wide across the shoulders. She couldn't see his face.

The boy still whimpered, still scooted away. On his stomach now, scrabbling across the ground, his legs and checkered jacket picked up a fine layer of dirt. His foot hung at a weird angle; his stumble over the stump must have broken something.

He was too busy struggling to crawl away to see the man reach under his coat to unsheathe a hunting knife strapped to his hip. Riley screamed until her throat was raw, but no sound came out.

The man lunged forward, grabbing the boy by the ankle and twisting him around so he landed on his back. Another bone snapped, his skull hit the hard ground, and he choked out a cry. Riley kept screaming for him, screaming at the man. No one heard her.

"Hold still," the man said, "and this will be over quickly. You're too weak to keep now."

Then he plunged the knife into the little boy's side.

Riley woke with a yelp in the dark, a hand to her own side. Someone was next to her. No, *hovering* over her. Her chest tightened, her breath came in shallow gasps as she shoved the person away. Stumbling to her feet, she darted away, then whirled around with her hands out. "Don't! Don't touch me!"

Light flooded the room and Riley shielded her face.

"What the *hell*, Ry?"

Riley slowly lowered her arm, blinking. Jade sat on the bed they'd both been asleep in, her curly hair a wild mess.

"Bad dream," she muttered, pulling up the corner of her own shirt to make sure *she* hadn't been stabbed. Her skin was warm from sleep, but unbroken. She tugged her shirt back down and crossed her arms, gaze focused on her toes and their chipping red polish.

"Hey," Jade said softly, wrapping a hand around either of Riley's elbows.

Riley flinched at the touch. She hadn't even heard Jade climb off the bed. Looking up, she met Jade's gaze, then glanced at Pamela, Brie, and Rochelle, the latter sitting bewildered on the couch.

"I'm sorry I woke you guys up," Riley said.

"What happened in the dream?" Rochelle asked. "I hear spirits sometimes try to contact people through their dreams. Didn't that happen to Heidi once in an early episode? She fell asleep in the car and a spirit told her she needed to leave or he'd punish her?"

Riley swallowed hard. The idea that the little boy who'd been killed—of that she had no doubt—in the woods was the same spirit who had tugged on her jacket on the patio left her nothing short of nauseous.

But maybe this was an easier way for him to make contact.

The sound of his spine on hard earth sounded in her head again. *Crack.* The muffled cry out of pale lips as the knife sliced through paper-thin skin.

Her stomach roiled. *Shit.*

Riley bolted to the bathroom to heave up her sandwich. She'd gone from avoiding places even remotely tied to the paranormal since she was a teenager to being totally immersed in it here. Like she'd been flung into the deep end of a pool before learning how to swim.

"Probably not the most helpful thing to say, Chelle," Jade said from somewhere just outside the door. "You know how scared she is!"

"Sorry," Rochelle muttered. "I didn't mean to make it worse."

Riley flushed, then sat on the cool tile floor with her back against the clawfoot tub. The door to the bathroom had been left ajar in her haste to make it to the toilet.

Jade poked her head in. "You all right? Need anything?"

Riley shook her head.

"Want to tell me about it?"

To her horror, tears welled in Riley's eyes. "It felt so real, J."

"Oh, hon," Jade said, coming into the room and closing the door behind her. She sat next to Riley, her back against the tub and her arm flush with Riley's. "Tell me."

So she did, leaving out the part about the tug on her jacket. In all likelihood, Jade would be over the moon that Riley had an "experience," but Riley wasn't in the mood to deal with her best friend's enthusiasm.

"Maybe what Nina said about a little boy ghost being around here just got in my head," Riley said.

"Or maybe a little ghost boy is trying to tell you something."

Riley shivered.

"You should talk to Nina and see if anything similar has happened to her."

Riley didn't want to talk to Nina. "Yeah, maybe."

"It's almost eight. You wanna try to sleep for another hour until we have to get ready?"

"Damn, I only slept two hours?" Riley sighed. "I think I'll head downstairs for a while. I brought a book I can read."

"You sure?"

"Yep. It was just a dream. Thanks for listening." Riley felt like she was saying that a lot lately. "We'll have to compare notes in the morning."

Trying to keep her grin in check, Jade said, "I'm so stoked. I'm guessing I won't sleep much more; I'm like a kid on Christmas morning."

After Riley gave Jade a hug, the two girls crept out of the bathroom. The lights were out. Riley quickly changed from pajama bottoms to jeans, grabbed her paperback, popped a mint in her mouth, blindly finger-combed her hair back into what she hoped was a decent ponytail, and headed out the door.

The lobby was empty.

Riley plopped into the chair she had been sitting in earlier beside Michael. A modest fire crackled in the fireplace.

The world beyond the bay windows was dark again. Riley could make out the silhouettes of the chairs and table they'd sat in earlier. The black forms of trees beyond them.

At least Michael hadn't laughed at her. Or given her a look that suggested he questioned her mental stability. She'd kept it all to herself for so long, she'd forgotten there could be people out there who'd believe her. Who wouldn't go screaming from the room. And maybe she'd needed to gauge the reaction of a stranger before she'd consider spilling her secrets to her best friend.

Perhaps if she knew how Rebecca had fared after moving, if she knew the haunting stopped, she'd feel less leery about it. She'd never shaken the feeling that she'd ruined the Greens' lives because she'd dabbled in things she had no business dabbling in.

Sighing to herself, she pulled her legs up onto the chair, got comfortable, and cracked open her book. She was deep into the sixth book of a spin-off vampire series—the original topping out at fifteen books.

It perhaps wasn't the best choice of book given her reading location, but as always, she got so sucked into the world, the real one fell away.

Until that feeling came back. Not as menacing as the man from her dream, but the undeniable presence of someone behind her. Of being watched.

Her gut told her this wasn't one of the paying guests.

Swallowing, she flicked her gaze up to the bay windows. No reflection of someone standing in the dark lobby behind her. But that didn't necessarily mean she was alone either.

Sliding her bookmark into place, she closed the novel and then turned in her seat. A strangled gasp reverberated in her throat and she scrambled out of her chair, book forgotten on the cushion.

The boy from her dream.

But now … now he looked healthy. No bags under his eyes. No pale, nearly translucent skin. He looked alive—cheeks flushed with color. Perhaps she hadn't seen his reflection in the glass due to his height and the angle of her chair.

She stumbled back until she hit the stone of the fireplace. The crackling flames behind the gate warmed the backs of her legs.

He wasn't wearing that black-and-blue-checkered jacket this time, but pajamas—a T-shirt with a vintage Scooby Doo and his pals adorning the front, and Batman symbols all over his slightly baggy pants. The shirt looked cheap, the image a little off-kilter. Like it had been ironed on and shifted during the process. The tip of Scooby's ear had come loose.

"Hi?"

"Hi," the boy said. "I couldn't sleep."

Riley swallowed again, mouth suddenly dry. "Me either."

"Did I scare you? Sorry. My mom always tells me I gotta make more noise when I walk in a room 'cause I'm too quiet and I scare people."

Riley choked out a laugh, unsure yet if she was amused or terrified. "Where's your mom now?"

"I don't know." He bunched up the bottom of his T-shirt in his hands. "I woke up and she was gone. I'm trying to find her. She sleepwalks sometimes, you know? What if she's lost?"

Kids weren't allowed on the ghost hunting investigations, but they likely were on the dude ranch.

Though her heart thumped wildly in her chest, she inched away from the fireplace and toward the boy. Once she got close enough to see him from head to toe, she noticed he was barefoot. The cuffs of his Batman pants were filthy.

"Did you walk all the way over here?"

He nodded, head lowered. "What if I can't find her? I gotta watch her 'cause Daddy's not here."

"Well, let's see if someone can help." Riley walked past the safety barrier of the chairs and made her way to the receptionist's desk. She moved slowly, still coiled tight as if she expected the boy's head to turn 180 degrees at any moment and start speaking in tongues.

The boy merely watched her, hands still clutching the bottom of his shirt. He turned on the spot where she'd first seen him—so he could follow her movements—but he took no steps closer or further away.

He's just a lost kid. He's just a lost kid.

A flash of him running through the forest to escape some creep. A knife sliding into his side. Had the dream been events of the past? The future? Riley's hands shook.

Focus, Ry!

She rounded the corner of the reception desk. A monitor and keyboard—the computer must have been hidden in one of the cabinets below the desk's surface—a binder with "Jordanville Ranch Guest Services" printed on the front, various office supplies neatly organized in mesh cups and slotted boxes. And a phone.

Riley ran her finger down the small, handwritten labels next to their corresponding numbers. Angela was third. Riley picked up the receiver, shot a smile toward the little boy still standing in the middle of the lobby, and hit Angela's extension.

Though it was only just after nine now, Riley was sure she'd woken the woman up. "Angela speaking."

"Hey, Angela," Riley said, trying to keep the quiver out of her voice. Her gaze flicked up to the boy, still looking very alive and lost and worried. "I have a little boy here who says he can't find his mom. It looks like he might have walked here from the dude ranch. Is it possible for you to contact them and let them know he's here?"

"Oh dear!" said Angela. "I swear this happens a few times a year. It's a wonder the poor things don't get lost in the woods. Give me a few minutes to make some phone calls and I'll hurry over there to fetch him. Can you keep him occupied until I get there?"

"Of course."

"You can whip him up some instant hot chocolate in the kitchen."

"Good idea. Thanks, Angela."

"You bet."

Hanging up, she looked at the boy and said, "How does hot chocolate sound while Angela finds your mom?"

The boy nodded emphatically, his bottom lip sucked under his teeth.

"C'mon," she said, joining him on the other side of the desk.

She reached out a hand to place on his back, then thought better of it. Riley'd never felt particularly skilled with kids.

Riley flicked on the lights and the industrial kitchen gleamed to life. A couple high-backed barstools sat in the corner and she dragged one over to the island counter where she'd drunk with Michael last night.

The boy climbed up onto the chair while Riley rummaged around in the cabinets for mugs—purposefully choosing ones that looked vastly different than last night's—then for the box of instant hot cocoa. After some creative searching, she found both the box *and* mini marshmallows. She held the bag up so the boy could see, and he grinned at her.

After putting a small pot of milk on the stove to boil, Riley turned to the boy, resting against the counter so she had a clear view of him across from her. "What's your name, kid? I'm Riley."

"Pete."

"Well, it's nice to meet you, Pete. What's it like over at the dude ranch?"

"It's okay. There are a lot of horses, so that's pretty groovy. I really like horses. But I guess I'm too small 'cause they only let me ride the donkeys. They're *so* slow! We went on a trail ride and I ended up way behind 'cause my stupid donkey stopped to eat leaves."

Riley laughed. "You'll be big enough in no time."

"Hope so," Pete said. "Being small is only good when I'm playing hide-and-seek, 'cause I can fit in little places like a suitcase and no one ever finds me."

"What other kinds of stuff do you do at the ranch?"

"A lot of nature stuff. Hiking. *Lots* of hiking."

"You said your dad isn't here?"

"No," Pete said, rubbing a finger along the stainless-steel counter and leaving a streak. "He always has to work, so it's just me and Mom."

"You don't sound too happy about that."

Pete kept his gaze fixed on the finger trails he left on the metal. "I just don't get to see my dad a lot 'cause he's always busy. It's like he doesn't like us or something."

"Oh, I'm sure that's not true," said Riley. "You seem like a pretty cool kid to me."

"Thanks," he said, but it didn't sound like he meant it.

Riley turned the burner off and carefully poured the boiling milk into Pete's mug, then added the hot chocolate mix without stirring it in—she'd always liked doing that herself as a kid—and put it in front of Pete. She placed a spoon and the bag of marshmallows on the table.

"If you want to pour half that bag in there, I swear I won't tell your mom," Riley said.

Pete stared at the marshmallows with wide, unblinking eyes.

Riley turned back to the stove to fill her own mug. "Do you live near here?"

He didn't answer.

Turning around, mixing the chocolate powder into the hot milk as she did, she found the bar stool empty. Brow furrowed, she rounded the side of the counter, finding no one. Just then, Angela opened the kitchen door.

"Did you see him out there?" Riley asked. "I turned my back for just a second and he disappeared."

Angela's gaze flicked from Riley's mug, to the untouched one on the counter, and then to Riley's face. "I didn't see anyone. And no one at the dude ranch came with a little boy."

"Who the hell was I just talking to then?"

Angela pursed her lips. "You *are* in a haunted house, Riley."

Rubbing the spot between her eyebrows, she closed her eyes and let out a long breath. "Shit." Then she placed her mug on the counter a foot away from Pete's, her hands shaking badly again. "He looked … he looked so real."

"Are you okay? This kind of thing happens a lot."

"Guests making cups of cocoa for kids who aren't really here?" Riley placed her hands on top of the stool's back. He'd been sitting there, plain as day.

"I meant sightings," Angela said. "It being a little boy is new, aside from what Nina's mentioned."

I need to get the hell out of this place.

"Did you need anything else?" Angela asked, as if seeing dead children was nothing to fuss over. "I need to get a few things ready for this evening."

"I'm fine," Riley said. "Sorry for the trouble."

"No, it's great! This is a new story to add to the website."

Riley stared at the closing door, Angela having already disappeared through it. Had any of that actually happened?

Grabbing the bag of marshmallows, she started to walk back to her own mug when she saw them. The streaks left by little fingertips on the surface of the metal table. As she watched, they slowly disappeared, like the foggy handprint of a warm palm pressed against glass.

Riley put a heaping handful of marshmallows in her hot chocolate, her back to the spot where Pete had been. She'd need the sugar; she sure as hell was never sleeping again.

A *tink* sounded behind her and she turned. She nearly dropped her mug. The spoon swirled slowly in the mug, mixing the powder into the milk and bumping gently against the sides. *Tink, tink, tink.*

Riley stood transfixed as she watched the milk turn from white to tan to brown. Then the spoon stilled in the mug. She held her breath for something else to happen. But it didn't.

"Pete, if that's you," she said, voice wavering and tears welling in her eyes. "I'm sorry for what happened to you."

The spoon gave another *tink*, *tink* against the side of the mug.

There was a hollow feeling in the pit of her stomach. He'd looked so real. How had he ended up here?

Don't get invested, don't get invested, the voice in the back of her head chanted. The more invested she got, the stronger her connection to this place, to Pete, would get. It would open that door she'd been trying so hard to keep closed.

She stared at the melting marshmallows in her mug. The marshmallows Pete had so clearly wanted to eat, and would never be able to again.

The memory of him alive and frustrated about slow, leaf-eating donkeys warred with the sickly boy who'd been in those woods. Who had been chased down and killed like an animal.

Who had he been? How long had he been wandering the grounds, waiting for someone who could see him?

Don't get invested, don't get invested.

But what if she just did a quick internet search? Just to see if she could find him. There was no harm in that, was there? Her true-crime-obsessed self was drawn to the idea of researching him solely out of curiosity. Nothing more.

She hoped Angela's computer had modern internet speeds out here in the wilderness. Lord, what if she needed to use dial-up? Perish the thought.

Just before pushing open the kitchen door, mug in hand, Riley looked over her shoulder at the other mug sitting on the counter. It had moved to the end again, just like last night. Though the hair rose on her arms, Riley felt less terrified now that she knew who'd moved it.

"Enjoy your cocoa, Pete."

Tink, tink.

CHAPTER 8

Angela stood behind the reception desk. Riley wished she could sate her research desires on the privacy of her phone, but lack of reception made that impossible.

The Skinny Jean Quartet loitered in the lobby now, huddled in a little circle before the fire. Riley caught one of the girls elbowing her boyfriend—the dowsing rod guy—before pointing at Riley. The whole group looked at her and then quickly turned away. Which meant Angela had already told them about the "sighting."

Angela clearly couldn't be trusted with secrets.

"Hey, Angela?" Riley placed her folded arms on the counter and got up on her tiptoes to see over it. "Is your computer hooked up to the internet?"

The woman glanced up and smiled wide when she realized who the voice belonged to. "Sure is. Connection is slow as dirt, but it's a connection."

"Do you think I could use it for a little bit?" Riley made a show of glancing over at the quartet behind her, then turned back to Angela, leaning toward her and lowering her voice. "I had a dream about that same boy just before I came down here."

"No!" she whispered back, eyes bright.

Riley nodded. "I'm a little rattled, to be honest. I was thinking I could try to do some research."

Angela subtly cocked a brow. The expression very clearly said, "Research on *what?*"

Riley let herself remember the fear she'd felt in the dream when she was literally rooted in place. How she'd tried to scream for the boy—for Pete—but no sound came out. Tears welled in her eyes.

Angela glanced around, then lowered her voice even further. "I'm not really supposed to let guests use it—viruses and things, you know. But, given your ordeal tonight, if you keep it to an hour …"

"Oh, that would be great," Riley said.

Waving Riley over to Angela's side of the desk, Riley watched as she jiggled the mouse on its nondescript black pad, causing the monitor to flicker on. Wallpaper of the ranch's welcome sign popped up behind the password prompt box. Unfortunately for Riley, the password wasn't something easy like "password" or "1234," but some long, complicated nonsense with upper and lowercase letters and random symbols. The folks here were *serious* about potential viruses.

"I'll be back in an hour," said Angela, gathering up some loose papers and stuffing them into the guest services binder. "I need to get coffee and cookies ready anyway." After awkwardly patting Riley's shoulder, she hurried off with her binder clutched to her chest.

Blowing out a deep breath, Riley positioned herself in front of the monitor and keyboard. She pulled up a search engine and waited for it to load. Slow as dirt, indeed.

Her gaze flicked up. The girl who had elbowed her boyfriend quickly looked away. Riley couldn't tell why the girl was intrigued by her—was she convinced Riley had made up whatever Angela had recounted to them? Or was she jealous it hadn't happened to her?

In her peripheral vision, she saw something on the screen change and she glanced back down. The cursor blinked in the box. What exactly was she supposed to look up? "Little boy named Pete who died"? She didn't know his full name, age, where he lived, his mother's age, or what year it was when he died. It could have been in the 1940s, for all she knew. Though she supposed his style of dress would have looked less modern, even if he'd only been wearing pajamas. Plus, Scooby Doo wasn't around in the '40s.

As she replayed her conversation with him in her head, she remembered he'd used "groovy" un-ironically. Did that make him a child of, what, the 1970s?

She knew "Missing children Pete" would get her nowhere fast, even if she limited it to the state of New Mexico.

"Um … hello?"

Riley snapped out of her thoughts. The leather-jacket member of the Skinny Jean Quartet stood in front of her. When the girl just stared at Riley, unblinking, Riley said, "Hi?"

"Oh! Hi. I … I'm sorry if this is super weird, but Angela said you saw a … *ghost*?" She whispered the last word as if it were a great secret.

"Yeah. Well, I mean I'm assuming that's what I saw."

Eyes wide, she said, "What did it look like?"

"*He* looked like a little boy."

"A boy," she repeated. "Like what Nina said. What did he *do*? Like just float around?"

Riley cocked her head. "We talked for a little bit; I thought he was actually a boy who wandered over here from the dude ranch. Said he was looking for his mom. One second he was there, and the next, he was gone. Like he was never there at all."

The girl visibly shivered. "That's so creepy."

Riley managed a smile. "Isn't that the kind of thing you're here for?"

"No. I mean, yes," she said, shaking her head. "The idea of actually seeing a spirit kind of scares the hell out of me. I mean, what if his spirit's been trapped here even longer than Orin Jacobs' Girls? That happened in the '70s and '80s. Over thirty years ago. What if he's been looking for his mom for even longer than that? That's so sad."

The hollow feeling in Riley's stomach worsened. *What happened to you, Pete?* When *did it happen?*

"Well, sorry to bother you …" the girl said, starting to turn away.

"No, it's no problem. The whole thing just freaked me out a little," she said. "I'm Riley, by the way."

The girl smiled, clearly pleased to be accepted. "Heather." She turned to the three people watching them from the fireplace. "That's Mark, my boyfriend—" the dowsing rod guy waved, "—Sarah, and Dave."

Riley awkwardly raised a hand in greeting.

"Just wanted to say hi, I guess," Heather said. "Not even sure why."

"Nice to meet you. And, uh … good luck tonight?"

Heather laughed, but it was more of a choked sound. She hurried back to her group.

The blinking cursor in the search bar taunted Riley. She chewed on the inside of her cheek. It would be a little pathetic if her one hour of research time was spent gnawing a hole in the lining of her mouth.

Staring at the empty spot where Pete had stood, she could still picture him with his hands bunching up the hem of his Scooby Doo shirt. The shirt with the weird, not-quite-right image. The flopping ear where the picture had detached from the fabric.

Was there a reason why he'd come to her in pajamas tonight,

rather than in the checkered jacket from her dream? Was he trying to tell her something? Give her information, even if it wasn't directly?

On a whim, she typed "Scooby Doo original air date" in the search bar and waited for the internet connection to cough up her results. The show first aired in 1969, but the merchandising part of it hadn't really kicked off until 1973. One such product was iron-on decals.

The year lined up with the era of "groovy," too.

Riley tried "Pete missing child New Mexico 1973." Between the National Center for Missing & Exploited Children website, and one for North American Missing Persons Network, Riley scribbled down half a dozen names. She chose the dates between 1969 and 1975, looking for boys named Peter who had been between the ages of seven and ten when they disappeared. All the boys had gone missing in New Mexico.

After clicking on each one, she was able to knock out the first two—one Asian boy and one Hispanic one, as "her" Peter was white. Some of the photos, enhanced with age advancement technology, offered a picture of what the boys would look like now. But she needed a young Peter.

Peter John Howard was too plump in the face to be the boy who had sat in the kitchen with her.

Peter Jonathan Paulson had tight, blond curls—not the right boy.

Peter Bonney's eyes were too close together.

Peter Vonick … Riley gasped, a hand to her mouth as the image of "her" Peter came up on the screen. His half smile, his dark brown eyes, his shaggy, brown hair that curled a little near the nape of his neck. Scooby Doo's slightly askew head peeked out from the bottom of the picture, where it cut off across Pete's chest.

His profile listed his stats. Age: 9; weight: 65lbs.; height: 53″; hair color: dark brown; eye color: dark brown; race: white; gender: male.

The details of his disappearance stated that he'd been shopping with his mother at a department store and had run off when she wasn't looking. He had been quiet for nearly two minutes before she'd realized he was gone.

Riley wondered when and how this ranch played into Peter's disappearance.

She did a search for Peter Vonick and eventually found listings for both his parents: Janet Wesley and Gregory Vonick. They'd divorced in the 1980s. Riley wondered if the horror of losing a child had been too much of a strain on the marriage. The father, Gregory, had died in the early 2000s, but Janet was still alive and very active in missing children groups, especially in Phoenix where she lived. The woman was pushing 80.

In death, the boy had never stopped looking for his mother, and in life, she had never stopped looking for her son.

With a pit forming in her stomach, Riley keyed in "Orin Jacobs." It was something she'd done several times in the past, but was doing so now with a purpose in mind.

His first victim, Gabriella Ramirez, had been abducted in 1978, five years *after* Pete's disappearance. The dude ranch hadn't opened up at this location until after Orin's death in the '90s. What was a nine-year-old boy doing out here in the woods alone? If he'd gone missing while hiking with his mother, wouldn't his missing person's profile have stated that in his "details of disappearance" section?

Did Pete's spirit hang around the dude ranch and watch the animals? Had he been stuck here so long that the memories of his own life and death blurred together?

Orin Jacobs' six victims had all been girls … but what if *Pete* had been his first, not Gabriella? What if Pete had been the catalyst that started Jacobs' years of kidnapping and torture?

She searched for pictures of Orin next—most of which she'd already seen. Two photos were used almost exclusively in news articles and documentaries. One was Orin's mugshot at fifty-five, after Mindy Cho's escape led to a raid on the property. The other was Orin as a twenty-something guy smiling at the camera. He sat at a small, yellow table with two windows on either side of him. Bright sunlight poured in, highlighting his light brown hair with streaks of gold. A breakfast of eggs and bacon and toast sat on the table, and Orin held a fork like he couldn't wait to tuck in.

Then she found another picture of Orin as an adult, maybe when he was thirty or so, standing beside a much shorter woman— his mother, she assumed. *Did she know what he was?* He was tall—well over six feet. Just like the man from her dream.

Don't get ahead of yourself.

Riley stared at his camouflage jacket. One arm was slung over the woman's shoulder, the other stuck out at a playful angle. They were both laughing. He was wider through the shoulders as an older man. Likely from all the work he would have done daily to keep the ranch in order. And, on his elbow, where his arm was propped up on his hip, stretched an all-black patch stitched with dark thread—just like in her dream.

Shit.

Flashes of news articles and shows about Orin Jacobs' Girls flashed through her mind. Torture. Disemboweling. Mutilation.

According to Mindy, in the one detailed interview she'd given a couple of years after the raid, Orin hadn't been into sexually assaulting the girls. He'd made them strip naked, but not to touch them—not like that, anyway. He sketched them in detail, would hit them and prod them and break bones, but did so in order to see how trauma to the outside affected what was underneath. To see how the body healed itself.

Mindy claimed Orin wanted to be a doctor—they were his "patients"—but he'd been rejected time and time again from every med school he'd applied to. He aired his life's grievances with his victims, knowing they'd never share them with anyone. Because they'd never leave the ranch.

Not until Mindy, anyway.

Riley guessed the med school interviewers sensed the man wasn't well and had no business being in a profession where people's lives were in his hands.

Of course, that then meant he had to *find* patients to study, and used his hands to end their lives. What on Earth the man thought he was doing in the name of science was beyond her.

Riley had a rising certainty that Peter Vonick had been patient one.

Had he lingered here because his body was still buried on the property? The bodies of the five girls had been found and removed. But not Pete—because no one had known to look for him here. He'd been forgotten by everyone except his now-elderly mother.

Riley knew the whole theory—and how she'd come about it—sounded insane. This wasn't something she could go to the police with, not without physical evidence. A creepy dream, a run-in with a ghost child, and an hour-long internet search didn't make her a detective.

But how the hell was she supposed to prove it? And what good would it do? Pete and Orin were both dead.

Don't get invested. It doesn't matter. You can't help him. Don't get invested.

Janet Wesley, Peter's mother, however, was not dead. Maybe such knowledge would bring a grieving mother peace. Or maybe it would shatter her hope that her boy survived after some forty-odd years, not that he'd likely been killed mere days after his kidnapping. But closure was closure, even if it wasn't what you wanted.

"How's it going?"

Riley yelped, drawing the attention of the mostly full lobby. *When did they all show up?* She placed a hand over her racing heart. Angela stood beside her, sans binder. "Pretty much done, actually."

Hurriedly, she closed out her tabs and cleared her search history. It wasn't NSA-proof, but at least Angela wouldn't know the extent of her research—Riley didn't want to talk about it yet, and she surely didn't want Angela speculating about it and then posting her theories on the ranch's website. "Thank you for letting me use this," Riley said, motioning to the computer. "I feel much better even though I'm still jumpy."

Angela reached out to pat Riley's shoulder again but changed her mind at the last moment and struggled for an awkward few seconds, unsure of what to do with her hand.

"Well, I better go meet up with my group." Brie and Pamela—and several others—were helping themselves to the coffee, hot chocolate, and cookies laid out on the serving tables opposite the large dining one.

Riley left her mostly untouched hot chocolate on Angela's desk. The melted marshmallows left a thick, sugary, white skin on the now-cold drink. She had a feeling she wouldn't have an appetite for hot cocoa for a while.

Rounding the desk, Riley headed for Brie and Pamela, but Angela stopped her with, "Oh, and Riley?"

She turned.

"Once you're a little more comfortable, would you like to offer us a testimonial about your experience here? Future guests would love to read it!"

Riley wanted to smack her. "Sure."

Angela beamed.

After exchanging a few quick hellos with Pamela and Brie, Riley hurried to their room.

The door clicked behind her and Jade whirled in her direction. "Where have you been!"

"Whoa," Riley said, taking in the pants, tops, boots—even a pair of heels—strewn across their bed, distracted momentarily from her worries about Pete. "Girl, we're only here for two nights. Why'd you bring half your closet?"

"I was panic-packing. I've been looking forward to this for so long that by the time it actually happened, I came unglued."

"Clearly."

"I told her what she has on now is fine, seeing as we're gonna be in total darkness most of the night anyway," said Rochelle, whose couch was just as littered with clothing and accessories as the bed.

"Not a big fan of taking your own advice?" Riley asked.

Rochelle turned, her cascading dark brown hair falling over a shoulder in perfect, silky waves. "Jade has Jonah. Who is she trying to impress? No one, that's who. *I* have to impress Papa Xavier."

Riley snorted. "Wow."

"Don't judge, I said!"

Cocking a brow, Riley said, "A man worthy of your affections won't care what you wear, for what makes a woman irresistible resides in her heart, not on her body."

Rochelle gasped.

"Why do you sound like you just stepped off the set of a Victorian drama?" Jade asked.

"She just quoted *Tiana's Circle* at me!" Rochelle said.

Jade groaned.

Rochelle turned back to face the bathroom mirror, clad in a dangerously low top. "I want to wear something that will make Papa Xavier want to tear said something off me later. That man does things to my bits."

Riley and Jade exchanged looks and burst into laughter.

"What if he's married!" Riley said.

"He's not wearing a ring …"

Jade shook her head. "Girl, you know that doesn't mean a damn thing."

Rochelle sighed and switched to a black *Tiana's Circle* shirt and black jeans.

Riley changed into a long-sleeved top, mainly for added warmth. And she splashed water on her face. And dabbed on some lip gloss, just in case. Of what, she didn't know.

Jade and Rochelle led the way out of the room as Riley hurried behind them after she switched to her flat-heeled, low-slung boots. She was willing to admit that she was just as bad as Jade and Rochelle when it came to wardrobe freak-outs, just not to their faces.

The sock on her right foot rolled under her heel, which always drove her insane. The door clicked, leaving her in the room alone.

She reached up to rest a hand on the wall so she could fix her sock, but the moment her hand touched the doorjamb, she reared back as a flash of images flitted before her eyes. This room, but not. One bed, up against the wall to the left, rather than two in front of the back wall. A small table and chairs where the couch now stood. There was a sofa here, too, but it was older and threadbare. It looked like a tiny studio apartment, not a bedroom.

Another flash of a prone body on the floor, feet tangled in sheets. Female.

The back of another head now, one with short light brown hair. A large male hand clenched the back of the other person's shirt. Arms and elbows flailed; feeble attempts to get away. A hand gripped the doorjamb, then the fingers lost their grip and were pried away—but not before paint was scraped off by scrabbling finger-nails.

There was a brief flash of the girl on the floor, unconscious by the look of it, then the brown-haired one was dragged away.

Another flash of a battered face, one eye swollen shut, the other one close to it, and a split-open lip. The injuries were so extensive, Riley could hardly tell what she looked like. Pale skin beneath blue and red and purple. Same short brown hair.

Frances.

This all came to Riley in a matter of moments, but she felt like she'd been transported somewhere else. Some*when* else.

Then everything snapped back to the present.

Hands on her knees, she pulled a deep breath into her nose, slowly letting it out. In, then out. In, then out.

Jesus. She wasn't sure how much more of this place she could take.

Had Frances and the other girl tried to escape? No one was certain how many of Orin's Girls had been alive at the ranch at the same time, or if he collected one once he'd killed the last. Mindy had never divulged information about other girls. In her one formal interview, she'd talked about Orin freely, but questions about the others shut her up quick.

This … snapshot … would suggest the girls had gotten to know each other in some capacity. They not only had to fear for their own lives, but the lives of others trapped there with them.

Riley was glad Orin was dead—that was all she knew. Glad Mindy had escaped, and Orin had been caught and died in a cell.

Once Riley had composed herself, she stepped up to the door, not seeing a hint of the scratches left by scrabbling fingernails. Frances' memory painted over.

After she took a few more calming breaths, she braced herself as she pulled open the door. No additional snapshots. She met up with the rest of the girls downstairs, who were clustered with Michael, Donna, and Carla. Brie and the couple were discussing vegan recipes again. Something about smashed chickpeas and pine nut salads.

"Hey," Michael said when they approached, and though he appeared to be addressing the group, his gaze was focused solely on Riley. "You okay?"

"Yeah, I'm fine," she said. "Mostly."

The team strolled into the building. Each member had at least one duffel over their shoulder, while the two younger guys pulled black cases on wheels.

Xavier got right down to business, assigning each group with their starting leader. "Mario's group is in the guesthouse, Derrick takes top floor, I've got the bottom floor—including the kitchen—and Nina is in … the cellar."

The air left Riley's lungs.

A few gasps erupted from the group at large.

"*Surprise!*" said Nina, adding jazz hands for extra flair.

"Why do *we* get to go in if the show couldn't?" Heather and Mark clasped their hands between them near their armpits. It looked like they were holding hands more to keep them from jumping up and down uncontrollably in excitement. Apparently, Heather's fear of potentially seeing an entity had worked its way out of her system already.

No. No no no.

"Most groups get to go in, actually," said Nina. "We just make everyone swear to secrecy. And sign a waiver. Since a lot of the same furniture that was here during Orin's time is in the cellar, the house's owners didn't want to run the risk of a camera crew damaging anything. But with our small, contained groups, we can make sure the room stays well preserved."

While everyone around her muttered their excitement, Riley fought back the urge to throw up again. The cellar sat beneath a large portion of the kitchen. She'd assumed the cellar had been stripped, most of it sitting in evidence boxes somewhere, and the room bleached.

From her perusal of the forum, it was clear the kitchen was a hot spot for paranormal activity. It had less to do with being an oft-traversed place, and more to do with it being above the room where unspeakable things had happened to innocent girls. How many of them died there? How many of them lingered?

Riley blew out yet another slow, steadying breath. Could she could do this? Could she play the "I'm terrified!" card and sit this one out?

She flinched when a warm hand pressed against the small of her back. Michael watched her.

"What's up?" he whispered.

"Nervous."

He watched her a moment longer, then gave a short nod, turning his attention back to the group. Though he dropped his hand, he stayed close by.

"You'll rotate downward. Meaning if you're on the top floor to start, your next location when we switch will be the first floor. Then outside to the oldest guesthouse, and finally to the cellar." This elicited at least three squeals from the group.

Xavier started pairing groups off with their first leader of the night.

Please don't start in the cellar, please don't start in the cellar.

"Riley, Pamela, and Michael, you'll start with Mario."

Which meant the cellar would be next.

"That's kind of a bummer," Pamela whispered to her. "It would have been better to end up in the cellar with the later groups. The witching hour is from two to three a.m., right? We won't be in there during the peak hours." Then she offered Riley a strained smile. "But that might be better for you, right?"

Riley wasn't sure how to respond to that.

From across the room, Nina caught Riley's eye and the other woman smiled. A small, smug smile, like she knew something Riley didn't.

Dammit.

CHAPTER 9

With Mario, the goatee guy, leading the way, duffel over one shoulder and one of the wheeled black boxes pulled behind him, Riley, Pamela, and Michael stepped out into the cool night air. Riley tried not to think about what could be lurking in the dark forest to their right. Tried to ignore the skittering of things in the underbrush.

The paved road they'd driven in on split off several yards away from the front entrance to the house. To the right was the little parking lot for the guests; to the left was the road that led to the guesthouses. Angela and Wilbur, the maintenance guy, stayed in one guesthouse during the weekend, and the team stayed in the other. The team's house was much newer—added by Porter during his renovations—so it was left out of the investigations.

The little one-story, cottage-like house blended in with the shadows, a hulking dark shape surrounded on two sides by the silent, watchful trees. The structure *felt* older, maybe even built before the larger main house had been constructed. It reminded Riley of a pioneer log cabin.

Solar-powered lanterns wedged into the ground ran along either side of the path up to the short, two-stair climb to the front porch. The lanterns didn't provide light so much as another set of creepy shadows. Riley wondered where Angela and Wilbur were while groups wandered through their building all night.

Stairs creaking underfoot, the group climbed the steps, Michael helping Mario carry the black case onto the porch.

"This little house was built back in the 1950s. There have been some modern touches added, but all this—" Mario knocked on a beam, "—is the original wood."

"They stayed in the main house during the episode," Pamela said, a hint of disdain in her voice. "Does this place have a specific connection to Orin's Girls?"

They weren't all girls, Riley wanted to say.

"Rumor has it that Orin's mother lived here until she died of natural causes in 1972," said Mario. "She lived in this house while Orin lived in the main one. The Jacobs were well off, thanks to the wealth built up by Orin's father—who died of alcohol poisoning when Orin was a teenager—while this place was a thriving cattle ranch. They owned the land and house outright, and after Orin's mother passed away, Orin sold off the cattle—likely because he wanted as few people here as possible when his … interests changed."

Pete had been taken in 1973. Had Orin waited until his mother died to start his rampage?

"No evidence of the girls was found in the guesthouse, but there've been reports of Orin's mother still wandering the halls here."

Pamela's chest puffed up at the news.

"Since no EVPs have ever occurred here, we're going to focus on that less. Keep a recorder with you, but we'll be looking more for heat signatures, as well as setting up cameras to hopefully capture the apparition of Mrs. Jacobs."

With that, Mario pulled open the slightly askew screen door, then turned the unlocked knob on the heavy wooden one, swinging it open. He strolled inside, his case's wheels offering an unsteady rhythm on the old floorboards.

The small house had a kitchen, a bathroom, a tiny dining/living room area, and two bedrooms. It felt rustic—wooden walls, wooden furniture, red-plaid blankets draped over the back of the sofa; that overly cluttered look Riley associated with cabins. Luckily, there weren't any mounted animal heads on the walls. The last thing she needed was Bambi's ghost prancing into the kitchen and giving her a heart attack.

Mario explained where apparitions of the woman were usually seen: either in the hallway, drifting from one bedroom to another, or sitting at the small table by the windows in the dining/living room area.

A flash of Orin's smiling face sprang up in Riley's mind. Was this the same table where he'd had his picture taken just before breakfast?

"You three decide where to set up the cameras and tripods and we'll get started," Mario said.

They chose one of the bedrooms, with the camera facing the open door of the room opposite. If an apparition appeared, they might get a front shot of her. The second was set up to encompass the entire dining/living room area, rather than just the table.

After hitting the record button on both devices, they huddled together in the kitchen. They were each given a cassette recorder for EVPs—Xavier swore by the older technology—and a choice between an EMF reader or an infrared thermometer.

"There are very few appliances in here, and I'm guessing most of you aren't carrying a cell phone given the lack of reception," Mario said, "so there's less chance of equipment—save the cameras—throwing off the electromagnetic field readings as much as it does in the main house. So if you'd like to get some experience with the EMF readers, that's what I'd choose."

Pamela and Michael both went for the EMF; Riley chose the infrared thermometer that had something called a K-probe. All she knew was that it was supposed to help you figure out where abrupt cold spots originated, following the theory that spirits had to pull energy from the outside world to manifest themselves. Riley thought of the cold spot she'd felt just before something tugged on her jacket. Had that really been Pete?

"We'll start in pairs," said Mario. "Riley and Michael, me and Pamela. That way, each group has an infrared meter between them. Wander the rooms, get a feel for them, ask questions, and *listen*. Ghost hunting is a lot like fishing: a whole lot of patience and waiting."

"I'd like to start down the hall, if that's all right with you," Pamela said.

"Lead the way."

The pair walked off, Pamela's EMF reader held out in front of her.

Riley felt Michael watching her. "Where would you like to start?"

Brow furrowed, he stared at her like he wanted to say, "Why don't you tell me what the hell is wrong with you right now?" Instead, he said, "What if we sit at the table where they've seen her and see if she joins us?"

Her stomach flopped. "Sounds good."

Michael made a grand show of pulling out a chair for her. Of course, it was Orin's spot from the picture. The round, wooden table was painted white, and when Riley rested her arms on the surface, it tottered slightly.

The table from the photo had been yellow, and not wooden, from what she could recall. Different table. Orin hadn't sat here. Unless this table had been purchased later, of course. Maybe—

A hand on her arm made her jump.

"The zoning out thing is getting a little worrying." Michael lowered his voice; she leaned in to hear him. "Are you going to keep blaming that on a lack of social skills?"

Riley was very aware of the camera in the corner. "For as long as you'll accept it."

He smiled, though she could tell he'd tried to fight it. "What should we ask Mrs. Jacobs?"

Turning on her tape recorder, she placed it flat on the table. "Are you here, Mrs. Jacobs?"

The little light on the recorder flickered in time with her voice, then stopped.

"Do you know what your son did, Mrs. Jacobs?" Michael asked.

No response from the recorder. Riley wasn't even sure that was how these things worked.

They tossed a couple questions back and forth. The room felt no different than when they'd entered it. The only sound was the vague murmur of voices from down the hall.

"Maybe we need to try harder to get a *feel* for the room." Placing his hands on the table, fingers splayed and his EMF reader lying between his palms, he closed his eyes. "I'm ready to feel you, room. Let me *feel* you."

He looked so impossibly serious, Riley laughed. An abrupt, startled laugh that made Michael crack open an eye. She tucked her lips between her teeth. "You're not *feeling* the room, Ms. Thomas."

Riley fought as hard as she could to keep the laugh in this time.

Her eyes watered; her nostrils flared. It was that horrible feeling where you were desperate to laugh in a location that didn't call for it in the slightest. And now she could barely contain it.

He opened both eyes now. "For *shame*, Ms. Thomas!" he whisper-shouted at her.

A hand went to her mouth to keep it in, her shoulders shaking. When a snort escaped, Michael slipped into silent hysterics and the two speed-walked outside onto the porch, and down the lantern-lit path before cracking up.

"You're horrible!" Riley said, wiping her eyes. "Pamela is going to hate us."

Michael had a hand to his side like he'd pulled something. "No disrespect to the spirit world, but I had to get that look off your face."

"I might have needed to release a little tension."

"Do you feel any better?"

"A little, yeah."

"Good. But, uhh—" he shot his thumb behind him toward the dark main house, "—what are we going to tell them?"

"The footage will prove later that we're basically eight-year-olds," Riley said. "But for now, we can just tell them I got scared and you came out to make sure I was okay." She sighed. "On the way up here, I told them this stuff freaks me out. Pamela will buy it."

"It *does* freak you out, though."

"Yes. But they don't know why."

Why had she'd confessed all this to Michael and not Jade? Jade loved all things paranormal. But Michael didn't know her. If she didn't want to see him again after this weekend, she didn't have to.

"Because of that little girl? Mary?" Michael asked, redirecting her attention.

"Mariah."

"Right. Mariah." His mouth bunched up on one side. His thinking face. "But you're all *here*. Seems like if anyone would believe you, it's them. They're already believers."

Logically, Riley knew that. She did.

She thought of Heather and her friends in the lobby. How they'd looked at her like she was a foreign creature for experiencing the very thing they had come to experience.

"I think part of the appeal is the unknown," said Riley. "There's evidence—like those videos they showed us earlier—but it's faulty at best. People are intrigued by the idea of lingering spirits because of what that could mean. Because of how it makes us think about our own mortality. People like to be scared by the 'what if.'

"But as soon as someone who's experienced this stuff talks about it, people look at them differently. Are they making it up? Are they delusional? Are they seeing something that's explainable, but putting a paranormal spin on it that doesn't exist?

"As much as they all believe it, I don't want to run the risk of telling Jade and having her look at me like I've lost it." Riley's cheeks flamed. She hadn't intended to say that much when she started. "Sorry."

"For a person who's so inept with human interaction, that was surprisingly well-said."

Lightly smacking his arm, she laughed. "Shut up."

"I don't think you've lost it, by the way," he said. "Remember the clairvoyant cousin?"

She managed a small nod. "Thanks."

With a sigh, he said, "We should probably go back, huh?"

She followed him inside.

The investigation of the guesthouse had been wholly uneventful, sighting-wise. Pamela and Mario had moved back into the main part of the guesthouse when Michael and Riley returned. Pamela had arched her brows in question, but Riley just shook her head.

Since Mario would be camped out in the guesthouse all night, he'd bid them a happy hunt in the cellar, then gone about checking tapes and batteries. All the equipment stayed in one location, so after they deposited their thermometers, EMF readers, and tape recorders in Mario's care, the trio left the small cabin and made the trek back to the main house.

"How'd it go?" Riley asked Pamela.

"It was a little disappointing not to see or hear anything," she said, "but Mario gave me a lot of really helpful tips on using the equipment. I'm super excited that we get to go to the cellar next."

Riley's stomach was the exact opposite of "super excited." Whatever relief she'd felt earlier was gone entirely now.

"On a scale of one to ten," Michael said to Pamela, "how excited are you?"

"Twenty-five!"

Riley couldn't focus on anything they said after that. The crunch of gravel under her feet sounded too loud. Blood pounded in her ears. What waited for her in the cellar? She could get out of this. She knew that. Michael and Pamela could tell Nina that Riley couldn't attend for personal reasons and that would be the end of it.

But maybe she'd see Pete again. Maybe he could tell her where to find his body—bring closure to a family who'd been grieving and wondering for years. Decades.

Sighing in resignation, Riley followed them into the lobby.

Angela popped up from behind her desk when they walked in. Napping? Reading a book? Glancing down at something for a moment, she then angled a smile at the trio. "Oooh, the cellar."

Pamela did a little jig.

"Follow me," Angela said, walking straight back from her desk, then turning right at a pillar, and toward a nondescript door in the wall of the staircase. Once they were all behind her, she opened the door with a flourish and gestured them inside. The door didn't make a peep as it swung open.

Pamela confidently strolled in first, then Michael, and Riley brought up the rear. In the narrow hallway, Riley's shoulders almost touched the cream-colored walls. Michael's did. A single, bare, low-watt bulb in the ceiling provided the only light.

"Good luck!" Angela called out, shutting the door and taking more of the light with her.

The hallway banked left for a short distance, then ended at another door.

In through the nose, out through the mouth. In through the nose, out through the mouth.

"You guys ready?" Pamela asked, glancing over her shoulder. She looked like a little kid who'd just been told she could go into a candy store and pick whatever she wanted.

"Go for it," Riley said. "But ... just ... if I wig out in there, I'm going to bolt, okay?"

Pamela's cheerful expression slipped a bit, clearly having forgotten, again, that Riley was a chicken shit. "Okay."

Michael offered Riley a tight-lipped smile. She couldn't quite read it.

Pamela opened the door, revealing a set of dark cement steps.

A wooden railing ran along either side of the wall. The lighting was weak here, too. The dancing shadows on the wall hinted at candles more than anything electronic.

"C'mon down," Nina said, suddenly appearing at the base of the steps, surrounded on two sides by walls; the space at the bottom of the steps was more of a short landing. "Just take the stairs slowly; they're steeper than they look."

Once Pamela reached the bottom, she turned left and disappeared from sight. Riley heard her say, "I can't believe we're finally here."

When Riley was two steps from the bottom, Michael reached the ground floor and vanished around the corner.

Nina stood in the little alcove, waiting for her. The woman backed up a step when Riley reached her. Taking a deep breath, Riley turned to face the room, bracing herself to find a space filled with angry ghosts and torture devices and blood-spattered walls.

It stood largely empty.

The room was far deeper than she expected, even larger than the massive kitchen above it. Muted-red bricks made up the walls, the floor the same dark cement as the stairs. Three walls were lined with wooden shelving, presumably to hold wine or jars of food. Riley tried to picture it as the world's largest pantry, filled with drying herbs and bags of onions, potatoes, and garlic, cans of non-perishable food, and cases and cases of water. The kind of place that could be stocked to the gills for the zombie apocalypse and keep a family fed for a year.

Though the shelves were empty now, save for the occasional thick candle perched on curving metal stands, Riley had flashes of what used to be here—just like she had when she'd touched the doorjamb of the Hyssop Room. How was she receiving snapshots without touching anything? Why did the rules of this ability she didn't understand keep changing?

She saw shelves packed with old books. Massive tomes, several with loose sheets poking out. Displays of tools lined shelves and tables—scissors, scalpels, forceps, saws, knives of all lengths, and a variety of glass syringes that looked like they'd come straight off the set of a horror movie. A black, plastic apron hung on a wall, reddish water dripping from one edge.

Riley followed the thin stream of pink as it wove its way over the bumps and curves of the uneven floor. Watched as it snaked its way into the cracks in the cement, staining them. Watched as the stream disappeared into the large, round floor drain in the middle of the room. Two enormous steel tables sat end to end. The surfaces gleamed, reflecting the lights from the small bulbs running along the space where wall and ceiling met.

Was it bulbs or candles lighting the room?

She glanced back at the wall. The apron wasn't there. There was no pink water. There were no books or primitive-looking medical tools.

Breathe, Riley.

She realized then that Nina had been talking for some time. On one of the steel tables lay three cassette recorders and four sets of dowsing rods. The rods were L-shaped copper bars, the handle side not much longer than the width of Riley's hand, the long side triple that. Riley had only ever seen them on shows like *Paranormal Playground*—a non-electronic way to pick up the presence of ghosts. Spirits could cause the rods to swing in or out to signify a yes or no to a spoken question. It had to be less energy-taxing than manifesting as an apparition, Riley guessed.

Since she had originally only taken a few steps into the room before she stopped, she inched her way toward the others now. One step and then another. Lord, how she didn't want to be in here.

This room, unlike the guesthouse, had a *feel* without effort.

She'd only made it five or so more steps before it felt as if something heavy, like a boulder, dropped onto her chest. It crushed her lungs. She gasped for breath, but couldn't suck any air in. As if the air was molasses. Something thick and clogging and a thing that shouldn't be in lungs. A thing that stopped lungs altogether. Riley gasped again, her attempts coming in short, quick bursts. She'd suffocate.

Run run run! her mind screamed at her. Everything in her told her this thing, this energy, was wrong. Unnatural. Did the thing want her out or was her body trying to force the flight response? *Run, flee, get out while you can.*

Hands clamped onto Riley's elbows and she flinched away, but her wild, darting eyes found the startling green ones of Nina.

"*Breathe*, Riley," she said.

"I ... can't ..."

"Yes, you can," she said, voice firm but not unkind. "Don't let it force you out. Breathe."

Riley closed her eyes, pushing out the worried sound of Pamela asking if Riley was having a panic attack. She'd never had a panic attack before, so she couldn't say this *wasn't* one.

"You okay, Riley?" That was Michael.

She didn't know how to answer that.

Giving Riley's elbows a squeeze, Nina said, "In and out through your nose. Slow and steady."

Riley slowly pushed her breath out through her nostrils, the tension easing in her chest a little.

"In. Fill your lungs."

She did. Again and again, until she could breathe normally. Opening her eyes, she met Nina's gaze. "I think I'm okay."

Slowly letting go, Nina took a step back. "The same thing happened to me the first time I came down here. I was alone, desperate to see the place. That feeling hit me—like something shoving me in the dead center of my chest and screaming '*Out!*'"

"Yes," Riley gasped.

"I bolted out of here seconds later," she said. "Took me two weeks to come back in."

"Why did you?" This was the first and last time for Riley. Without a doubt, something was in here with them. Watching. Circling. Assessing.

Riley couldn't tell if it didn't like the interruption or if it was simply malicious. Goosebumps broke out across her skin. The presence of something lurked behind her. Ignore it. Ignore it. She whirled around. Nothing.

She took several more steps into the room, closer to a silently watching Michael. Was the thing herding her further into the room? Glancing at Pamela and Michael, she could tell they were only concerned about whatever in the hell was happening to her. Didn't they feel it?

The crushing feeling had been replaced by this lingering presence. The creator of her maybe-panic-attack.

"I came back," Nina said, "because if you don't let the spirits call the shots, then you always have the upper hand." She watched Riley for a moment. "Do you sense it?"

"Yes," she said. "God, you do, too? The … entity or whatever?"

Nina nodded. "He's always here."

"He?"

"Orin."

Riley's mind filled with the memory of her dream. Of Pete trying to crawl away from the looming figure of Orin in that camouflage jacket. How could he have seen Pete's sweet, innocent face—a boy who loved Scooby Doo and his parents—and thrust a knife into his side? Had he let the boy bleed out there in the forest? Had he brought the body back here to cut him apart like a piece of livestock, Pete's blood oozing across the table's surface before dripping into the floor, snaking its way into the floor drain?

Bile rose up in Riley's throat, hot and acidic.

"Let's try something," Nina said. "Everyone pick up a pair of dowsing rods. Hold them from the shorter end and try to hold them steady. The most comfortable position for me is to keep my bent elbows flush with my sides, so my arms are at ninety-degree angles."

Taking the rods from Nina with a bit of skepticism, Riley's hands shook, the rods slowly swinging toward each other and away. They all looked rather silly, she thought, metal rods pointing out in front of them like over-sized, ineffective copper guns. Riley stood near the head of the table, Michael to her left, and Nina and Pamela to the right. Nina had turned on the EMF detector and hit the record button for possible EVPs on the cassette recorders.

"We'll start with simple yes or no questions," said Nina. "The rods will swing toward each other for yes, and apart for no. Try not to move your wrists. Hold as still as you can while keeping relaxed. Holding too tightly or too loosely can cause fluctuations." Blowing out a slow breath, Nina asked, "Is today Saturday?"

All four sets of rods slowly swung inward.

"Did it rain today?"

They all slowly swung out.

Dowsing rods held a similar stigma to Ouija boards, as both could easily be manipulated with the slightest movement. Someone could know the answer to a question and subconsciously move their hands just so to get the desired response. Riley didn't think anyone here would purposefully cheat, but the mind could easily trick itself.

"Is my son's name Warren?"

Riley's rod swung out. Michael's didn't move much at all. Pamela's swung in, just slightly. Nina's swung out.

On and on it went like this, questions with obvious answers getting unanimous replies. Less obvious ones getting mixed responses.

"Okay, now just Riley and me," said Nina.

Michael and Pamela glanced at each other and shrugged. Then they placed their dowsing rods on the metal table with clinks that sounded too loud in this quiet room.

The presence still circled. Watching. Waiting.

"Each of you grab an EMF reader. Michael with me; Pamela with Riley."

They did as instructed, while Riley and Nina continued to hold the rods. Riley's arms started to get shaky.

"Now, each of you keep your EMF reader trained on your partner and take note when—*if*—there are spikes in the electromagnetic field as the rods respond to questions."

Riley shot a glance over at Pamela, who nodded. Her expression implied that she took this very seriously, like she'd just been given the nuclear codes and had sworn to protect them with her life.

"Riley?" Nina asked. "I want you to ask the questions."

"Why me?" It was like she was thirteen again.

"He's never responded to anyone in this room like this before. Only me. And never this strongly."

Blowing out a slow breath, all she could see was the overturned craft bookcase in Rebecca's childhood bedroom, the word "Mariah" written over and over. The Ouija board planchette's flight across the room. The horrified looks on Rebecca's parents' faces.

But then the image of Pete popped in her head. Of him looking wide-eyed and scared, unable to find his mother. The way he'd bunched up the bottom of his Scooby Doo shirt in his hands.

"Was Gabriella Ramirez your first victim?" It was out of her mouth before she realized she was going to ask it.

Nina, Pamela, and Michael all seemed startled by the question.

Riley willed her hands not to shake, either from fear or muscle strain. Several seconds ticked by with no movement, and when Nina opened her mouth to presumably tell Riley to ask another question, Riley shook her head. *Just give him time.* A hesitation laced the silence.

Ever-so-slightly, the rods swung outward. Nina's didn't move.

"Whoa," said Pamela, "the meter just fluctuated like crazy."

"Keep going," Nina said.

"Did you kill Peter Vonick?"

Riley could feel the eyes of her companions on her, but she kept her focus on the rods in her hands. The rods shot inward with such force, they clacked together. *Shit.* "Why?" she wanted to ask. "Where is he?" But she was limited to yes or no questions.

Suddenly switching her dowsing rods for one of the still-running EVP recorders, Nina said, "Ask a series of questions and give up to twenty seconds for him to reply."

Riley's hands sweated, but didn't put the rods down; she was too scared to move.

"Why did you kill them?" Pause. "Where is Pete's body?" Pause. "Why was Pete first?" Pause. "Why are you still here?" Pause. "Are you stuck here?"

"Provoke him," said Nina.

Riley's attention snapped to her. "Are you serious?"

"Don't do anything you're uncomfortable with," Michael said.

Riley had almost forgotten anyone else was there. Her stomach knotted. She wanted this to be over. She hated the idea of a second night of this. Hell, she still had two more locations to go after this one.

"Take your time," Nina said.

There wasn't much Riley knew about the middle victims. She knew Gabriella's name because she'd been the first. And she knew Mindy's because she'd been the last.

"How did Mindy escape?"

"Tougher," said Nina.

Riley wanted to whack Nina over the head with one of her dowsing rods. Perhaps Nina was jealous. She'd been trying to get this spirit to interact with her for months, and all Riley had done was stroll into the room once. Well, *stroll* was generous.

"Why did you *let* Mindy escape?"

The wooden handles of her dowsing rods seared her hands and she yelped, letting them clatter to the cement floor. Two red, puffy lines ran down her palms.

"We need to get out of here," Riley whispered, so low she wasn't sure anyone heard her.

Goosebumps broke out across her skin again as the temperature plummeted. The room, a little chilly before, now grew frigid. The string of round bulbs lining the ceiling flickered.

Nina looked up, a twisted kind of joy on her face. The kind of thing she'd been waiting for.

A bulb popped and Pamela shrieked. Then another. And another. Shattering in quick succession like a smattering of gunfire.

Nina finally came to her senses. "Calmly get to the lobby!" she told them but her tone was anything but calm. Pamela took off like a cheetah. Michael tossed his EMF reader on the table, hurrying to

Riley who stood paralyzed while the bulbs above continued to pop, glass raining down on the shelf tops.

That heavy feeling in Riley's chest was back. That rooted-to-the-ground feeling from her dream. Sleep paralysis, but while waking. *Oh god oh god oh god.*

The thing—Orin, if that's who this was—was pulling in all the energy from the room it could. The heat from the air, the electricity from the bulbs, and the batteries from the meters on the table, the red battery indicators flashing on their screens before they went black.

Michael had hold of her hand. Was he talking to her? Riley was too lost in the crushing weight on her chest, lost in the darkness as the last of the bulbs exploded. Something behind Michael twitched. Nina? No, it didn't move like Nina. It was too tall.

Riley stumbled back, able to move again, and her lower back smacked into the table, reaching behind to steady herself. The moment her hand touched steel, her mind filled with image after image. Like a film reel being played at triple speed. A lifeless hand hung off the side of the table, blood dripping from dark fingers; the glint of light off a shiny cleaver as it was hoisted into the air before a strike; a girl curled up in a corner, back against the wall, her skin a sea of blue, purple, and yellow-green bruises; the slice of scalpel through flesh and the welling of blood.

Riley pitched forward and threw up.

Someone's hands landed on her shoulders and she struggled away from them, swatting in the dark at things she couldn't see.

"Riley, it's me!" *Michael.* "Take my hand. I know where the stairs are."

Riley let him slip his warm fingers between hers, her scalded palm aching at the contact, and then he was dragging her to the steps. He swung her around in front of him and put his hands on her waist.

"Go! I've got you."

She scrambled for the wooden railing and used that to get up the steep stairs. She tripped a couple times, pitching forward, but Michael always managed to catch her. When they reached the narrow hallway, the bulb blown out here, too, Riley bolted, hands out. It was a straight shot to the door. Michael pounded along behind her. When her sore palms hit the wall, she yelped in surprise. Groping wildly for the doorknob, she found it and wrenched the door open.

A sobbing Pamela, and Nina, trying to console her, stood in the lobby. A few others loitered around—the group scheduled for the main part of the house—worried expressions pulling brows and mouths down. Angela flitted about the group, trying to figure out what had happened.

All the lights in the lobby burned bright.

Riley ignored everyone, the churning of her stomach and the acidic burning in her throat telling her she very well might throw up again. She sprinted outside.

"*No*," she heard Michael say behind her. "I've got her; give her space."

Riley didn't stop until she was halfway down the path that led off this horrible property. Hinged forward, hands on her knees, she willed the spring night air to cool her flushed skin. Her stomach convulsed, but she swallowed down the burn of acid.

She stood to full height when the ache of her hands against the rough material of her jeans was too much to bear.

Michael watched her from several feet away—giving her space, as he'd told the others to do, but letting her know he was still nearby. She knew if she adamantly demanded he go back inside and leave her alone, he would.

Wiping a hand under her nose and across her mouth, she looked at the house behind him. "I can't go back in there."

"Then don't."

Her gaze dropped to his face. "And what, sleep outside?"

"There are half a dozen cars in that lot. You want to leave? You tell me where to find your stuff and I'll drive you out of here myself. Even if it means hotwiring one of those things."

Riley sniffed. "You know how to hotwire a car?"

"I don't have the foggiest clue."

"You and your foggy clues." Then, rather abruptly, she burst into tears.

"Aw, shit," he said, taking a step forward with his hands out, placating. "I was trying to be funny. You know, lessen the drama? Instead of dealing with anything too serious, I crack jokes. I'm starting to see why all my exes left me; I'm terrible at dealing with emotion."

Riley let out a choked laugh. "That was very informative. Also, you're old as hell."

"True."

She proceeded to lose her shit for the next ten minutes, while Michael waited patiently. Every time she thought she was okay, that she could get through the weekend as long as she stayed out of the cellar and opted out of the rest of the investigation, her breath would come in rapid gasps. If anything she'd experienced tonight had been close to a panic attack, it was this.

"I can't go back in." She heard the finality in her own voice and blew out a shaky breath, hands on her hips, eyes focused on the ground. "Jade is going to be so disappointed."

"Riley," Michael said. "Riley, look at me."

She did.

"I have no idea what the hell happened in there, but Nina got her damn wish: I'm a believer now. But I'm not staying here."

Riley managed a slight nod.

"I'll go talk to Angela to figure out where Jade is. I'll send her out here to talk to you and you two can figure it out. If she wants to stay the rest of the weekend, I'm happy to drive you home. But I'm getting the hell out of here either way."

"Thank you," she managed.

He took off for the front door.

Her attention suddenly snapped to one of the windows on the top floor, at a spot above the bay windows. Given the layout of the lobby, Riley couldn't process how someone could be watching her from up there.

But then she remembered how often spirits were said to inhabit the used-to-be spaces of a building even after it was remodeled. Residual hauntings. The phantom sound of feet traveling up stairwells that no longer existed. The slam of a door that had been painted shut or removed entirely.

The face of a young boy watching her from a room that was no longer there.

"I'm sorry, Pete," she whispered, knowing that even though he was long dead, she was still leaving him behind.

CHAPTER 10

Riley paced, somehow more comfortable surrounded by a dark, cold forest than inside a warm house. Every time she closed her eyes, the flash of images from the cellar assaulted her. She felt the massive black figure looming in the dark. She heard the bulbs shatter.

While Riley was sure Orin was trapped in the cellar, she couldn't imagine sleeping in that place another night. Could Orin get to her in her sleep like Pete had?

This was why she avoided places with known paranormal activity. If she avoided them, nothing could come knocking. Nothing could prod at her defenses.

"Oh my god, Ry."

Jade hurried toward her, the rest of the girls on her tail. Riley's bottom lip quivered at the sight of her best friend, but she kept herself together.

Pamela, whose skin looked translucent, stood a little ways off from the group, her perfect eye makeup a smudgy, runny mess.

Craning her head to look between Jade and Brie's shoulders, Riley made eye contact with Pamela. "Why are you all the way over there? I'm not contagious."

Pamela's eyes welled with tears. "You must hate me."

The three girls parted so Riley could make her way to Pamela.

She took the other girl's downturned face in her hands, then tipped it up. Pamela's gaze only met hers for a second, then flicked back down to the ground.

"Why would you think I'd hate you?"

Pamela sniffed. "I just … left you in there. I was so scared. I wasn't thinking. What if something happened to you?" She choked back a sob. "I liked it better when this was all just a TV show."

"I know the feeling." Riley pulled Pamela into a hug.

Once her friend calmed down, Riley slung an arm around her shoulder and turned them to face the others.

"I'm gonna start talking," said Riley, blowing out a long breath. "Let me finish before you start asking me stuff."

She told them everything. From Mariah, to the Ouija board, to Pete, and finally whatever the hell happened in the cellar.

After she finally stopped, her mouth parched, she expected to be bombarded by questions. But they just stared at her, slack-jawed.

Jade stepped forward and slugged Riley in the shoulder.

Pamela yelped and scurried over to join the others.

"Ow! Jesus! What the hell?" Riley said, hand on her sure-to-be-bruised arm.

Jade pulled her into a hug so tight, Riley's back cracked. Pulling out of the embrace, hands on Riley's shoulders, Jade shook her, hard. "Why didn't you tell me any of this sooner!"

"Because I'm a chicken shit."

"Do better than that."

"Because I didn't want to lose you like I lost Rebecca."

Frowning at that, Jade hugged her again. "You're so stupid."

Riley hugged her back. "Love you too."

"What do you want to do?" Jade asked, letting her go.

"Go home?" Riley quickly added, "But I don't want you to

feel like you need to leave too just because of me. From what I know about hauntings like this, the chance of that thing leaving the cellar is likely slim. Plus there aren't any reports that he's ever done it before. You'll likely not experience stuff on the same level I did because—"

"—we're not special enough," finished Rochelle, but she was smiling.

Riley shrugged. "Yeah, something like that. I swear I won't be upset if you guys want to finish out the weekend here, just stay out of the cellar. I assume they'll close it off for at least tonight anyway because of the glass."

"Angela said it's closed for the rest of the weekend," Pamela said.

"Good." Her friends shifted anxiously, shooting looks at each other out of the corner of their eyes. But no one said anything. "I honestly won't be upset if you all stay. You've been waiting to get in here for such a long time."

Jade pursed her lips. "You say the word and we'll caravan out of here."

"Stay. Really."

After a few more seconds of silence, Brie said, "How would you get home? It's not like we can call you a taxi without it costing you a small fortune."

"Michael said he'd drive her." Jade waggled her eyebrows.

"This is so not the time to worry about my love life," Riley said, rolling her eyes.

"Maybe the reason for this whole thing was the universe shoving the two of you together," Rochelle said.

"No more *Tiana's Circle* for you."

Rochelle grinned.

"I think we'll stay, but we promise to skedaddle if things get hairy," said Jade. "Well, hairier."

Riley figured on some level that her experience would make them even *more* keen to stay. Plus, there were no refunds. Riley couldn't care less about her own loss of money.

She explained the energy theory—that a spirit would pull in energy from any sources it could to manifest itself. "The good news is that whatever's down there still wasn't able to fully manifest beyond taking shape as a shadow-person. And I really do think he's trapped there. So just … be safe."

Wringing her hands, Pamela looked over her shoulder at the house, then back at Riley. "Can I go with you? I don't … I don't think I can stay here either. I keep thinking that … thing … is behind me."

"Of course."

Brie and Rochelle hugged Riley, then headed back inside.

"I'll go get our stuff," Pamela said, before hurrying after Rochelle and Brie.

Shifting her attention to Jade, Riley said, "Please, please be safe."

"We will. You be safe, too." Jade blanched suddenly. "What if Michael is a psycho?"

"You were practically planning our wedding like ten seconds ago!"

"I just needed to say it," Jade said, waving her hands dismissively. "Call and leave a message here when you get reception back, okay?"

"Okay."

Riley watched her friend disappear inside.

Some twenty minutes later, Michael walked out, a duffel over his shoulder, her bag in one hand, and a book in the other. Pamela was on his heels, backpack strapped on.

"You two ready?" Michael asked.

Riley nodded, shouldering her bag. Pamela offered her a small smile.

"I'm guessing this is yours?" The book Michael held was the one she'd been reading when Pete showed up. She'd forgotten all about it. "It was on your chair."

"Thank you," Riley said, cradling it to her chest. "So how are we getting out of here?"

"We're taking my sister's car. They're gonna hitch a ride back with your friends. They really hit it off with Brie."

He led them to a white four-door sedan and opened the trunk for their bags. Pamela let herself into the back and wrapped her arms around herself.

After getting situated in the passenger seat, Riley turned to glance back at Pamela. "You okay?"

Pamela's eyes were lined with silver again, moments from losing it. "I'll be better when we get the hell out of here. I'm never watching *Paranormal Playground* again. Lying bastards. This place is haunted as hell and they had no idea."

It had been a long time since Riley had roomed with Pamela, but she had very few memories of the other girl sounding this … venomous. But people reacted to this kind of thing in very different ways.

Michael slid into the driver's seat.

Something occurred to Riley then. "Where do you live?"

"Florida."

"*What?*"

Michael laughed. "The look on your face! I live in Los Lunas, about half an hour outside Albuquerque."

"Not funny! I was actually really worried you lived far from me."

"Aw!"

She fought a smile and lost. "I mean because I don't want it to be out of your way. Pam and I live in Albuquerque."

"I guess that makes sense." As he maneuvered the car out of the tiny parking lot, Riley's leg started to bounce, just as nervous now to leave as she'd been to stay. He placed a hand on her knee for a moment to still it. "Why don't you find something for us to listen to? I grant you full access to the radio."

"You're going to regret the hell out of that."

From the backseat came Pamela's soft, faraway voice. "They'll be okay, right?"

Riley turned in her seat again, her friend's gaze focused on the house to their left as Michael made the slow drive along the gravel-covered driveway. With Pamela's face cast in shadows, her smudged makeup looked even darker below her eyes, as if she hadn't slept in weeks.

It reminded Riley of the dark smudges she'd seen under Pete's eyes, in the dream where he'd been running from Orin.

"Yeah, they'll be fine," Riley said, though she could hear the lack of confidence in her own voice.

"They're in good hands," Michael echoed. If he thought his sister and sister-in-law were in any real danger, he wouldn't leave them behind just to get two virtual strangers to safety, would he?

Pamela nodded, but didn't say anything. She slunk down a little more in her seat and closed her eyes.

Sighing, Riley turned back in her seat. "It feels like I was here for a week," she said, staring out the window at the dark forest beyond the blank backside of the welcome sign. Then, rather abruptly, she asked, "You're not a psycho, right?"

"Wait, what?"

Staring at his profile, she took in the day-old scruff on his face. "I barely know you."

"True," he said. "We have roughly four hours to fix that. And, no, I'm not a psycho. I don't think."

Four hours. The dashboard clock read two in the morning.

When they pulled out onto the two-lane road masquerading as a highway, some of the tension in her chest eased. Soft snores emanated from the back seat. Back in college, Pamela had been a fairly heavy sleeper.

Riley flicked on the radio and hit scan. Either static, Christian ballads, Spanish language programs, or opera. She hit the power button.

"Why don't you tell me about what happened in there."

Riley really wasn't in the mood to recount it again, but he'd been in that cellar, too. He'd gotten the firsthand evidence of the paranormal he claimed he'd needed and was probably confused as hell. Glancing behind her, she confirmed Pamela was still asleep before she told him about her dream and her run-in with the same boy in the lobby. Michael stayed quiet, hands kept firmly at ten-and-two on the steering wheel.

"So that kid you asked about—Peter V-something—"

"Vonick."

"Yeah, him. You *saw* him?"

"Plain as day."

"If you were seeing him right now, would I see him too?"

"I don't know. No one could see Mariah but me," she said. "He might have shown up when he did because I was alone."

"Hm." After a long pause he said, "Do you really think that was Orin?"

Riley shook her head. "I don't know that either. It kind of reminds me of the Ouija board fiasco. Something about the spirit felt … off. Well, you know, other than the obvious. I mean, Mariah was a baby when she died. How would she know how to spell her name?"

"*That's* the thing you wonder about?"

Face flushed, she managed a laugh. "Is that stupid? It's not like I know how this all works."

"No, not stupid," he said. "I guess I wonder if she was just a baby when she died, and it was a fluke that killed her, why all the hostility?"

"Yeah! That's kinda what I mean. The haunting felt … older? Like maybe it used Mariah to manipulate us?"

Michael nodded. "Maybe. You said the board is like a door to the other side, right? Maybe it knew it could lure you in with Mariah—maybe it wasn't her, maybe the thing just *pretended* to be her—and then planned to use you guys to let it out. You were just kids and it used that to its advantage."

Whatever had haunted the house had been violent toward Becca. Why would the spirit of a two month old be vengeful?

Michael's theory sounded good. Hell, it even made her feel a little better. But there was no way to prove that's what happened. And at the end of the day, Tony and Ashley had quit their jobs, packed up Rebecca, and moved to a different house to escape what Riley never should have let happen.

"Did this *thing*—Orin—feel old, too?" Michael asked.

"Kind of? They both seemed … angry. Like they're both trapped and pissed about it."

"What traps a spirit somewhere?"

"A violent death. Some say their remains can bind them to a place. Others say a connection to something or someone still alive …"

"Unfinished business?"

"Ha. Yeah. That's what Hollywood always claims, anyway." Riley chewed on her bottom lip, trying to recall the questions she'd asked Orin. The one about Mindy being *allowed* to escape had set him off. "I don't even want to know what kind of unfinished business Orin has."

She examined her hands. The two lines of puffy skin from where the dowsing rod handles scorched her palms had mostly faded now. Her hands were a little sore and tender to the touch, but the heat and swelling was gone.

Orin must have been angry that Mindy not only escaped, but ratted him out. He likely assumed a young girl lost in the woods wouldn't last long on her own. She'd either die from the elements or come crawling back when she got hungry. Police showing up in her stead must have been quite the shock. Was that the source of the anger? The memory of being blindsided?

Even so, Orin's agitation had begun the moment she'd entered the room. It felt like he'd been circling her and the others, like a mountain lion slowly sizing up prey. He'd been … territorial. The cellar was where he'd done all his "work," as Mindy had called it once. He didn't like strangers invading his space.

Riley told Michael this theory.

"That makes sense. He seemed pretty pissed."

None of this made her feel better about Pete. He was stuck too—his body still somewhere on the property.

"Can we talk about something else?" she asked.

"Anything."

They were still on the two-lane highway, the road curving periodically. His brights carved through the still night air.

"Did your exes really jump ship because you're emotionally unavailable?"

His laugh was sharp and quick. Pamela offered a snort from the backseat, but she was still asleep, head lolling against her chest. They grinned at each other.

"I've been told this is a problem, yes," he said.

"Why?"

"Because I'm a guy?"

She shot him a look. One he saw in his peripheral vision, even in the dark, given his smile. "The only person in my immediate family—my mom included—who was any good at talking about feelings was Donna. And I think that was partly because she had to deal with the reality that her feelings were different from the quote-unquote normal ones her friends had. We didn't really start getting better about talking to each other until Donna came out, really."

"How did they take it?"

Michael shrugged. "I think we all knew; it wasn't really a shock to us or anything. She fared pretty well in high school, considering, but totally blossomed in college. I think seeing how well she was doing—just coming into her own as a person, you know? Seeing that brought us all closer together. She was happier, so we were happier. We made time for each other. And just … talked more. Funny how talking makes things easier."

"Hey! So you were giving me hell about *my* social interaction issues when you're even worse than I am?"

"I was hoping you'd be so dazzled by my good looks that you'd overlook my flaws."

She rolled her eyes. "Okay, Edward Cullen."

"Who?"

Riley laughed. "Nothing." She stared at his profile for a second. He didn't seem like a psycho. "Thanks for getting us out of there."

"No problem. I was leaving one way or another—I'm grateful for the company."

They talked shows and movies. Michael went on a long diatribe about why *Tombstone* was the best movie ever made.

"What is it with guys and that damn movie?" Riley asked, then got an earful she didn't expect.

She tried to sway him on the brilliance of *Tiana's Circle*, but it seemed to be a losing battle.

"Did you know that when you get super passionate about something, your hands flail all over the place?"

Suddenly self-conscious, she shoved her hands under her thighs.

"Don't stop; it's adorable."

"Patronizing!"

He laughed. "Please bear with me; I'm at that stage where everything you do is the cutest thing I've ever seen. It's the cutest it's ever *been*."

"You're not as bad at expressing feelings as you claim," she said. "But you're still super corny."

"What can I say? You make me want to be a better man."

Eyes wide, she slowly turned toward him. When they made eye contact, he cracked a smile and they both burst into laughter. Then quickly clapped their hands over their mouths to keep from waking up Pamela.

"Oh my god!" Riley whisper-shouted. "I swear you meant that one. I was thinking, okay, this is it: he *is* a psycho."

Michael was still silently laughing.

"You and your terrible movie one-liners."

"You keep buying 'em—for at least the first five seconds—so I'm gonna keep selling 'em."

"You know, I totally swoon whenever I hear that kind of stuff on screen."

"I *knew* it."

"Shut up," she said, laughing. "Let me finish. I always swoon, but I always think, too, if anyone said that kinda thing to me in person— the 'you complete me' stuff—I would feel super uncomfortable."

"Right! I keep thinking that if that's the kind of thing women want to hear, it's no wonder I'm single. I don't talk like that. And if I did—as was just demonstrated—I couldn't keep a straight face." After a slight pause, he said, "For what it's worth, I really do think you're adorable. It's … kind of upsetting how adorable, really."

She bit her bottom lip and flushed slightly. "I think you're pretty cute, too."

"Sweet!"

"Ugh. I take it back."

"Nope."

Reception didn't return until they'd been on the road for over an hour. Pulling up the website for the ranch, her stomach clenching at the sight of the welcome sign's picture, Riley hit dial.

It went to voicemail and she left a rambling message asking Angela to have Jade call her in the morning.

Soon after, her phone started to bling with emails and texts she'd received while reception was out. Then both Michael's and Pamela's phones did the same from somewhere in the back.

The texts were mostly from co-workers who had forgotten she was gone for the weekend—Riley never went anywhere—asking if she could take an extra shift. Two were from her parents. "Be safe!" from her father, and "Call me when you return to civilization" from her mother. She'd tell her parents about her run-in with the paranormal later. Her mother, especially, would want details and Riley wasn't ready to go through it all again. She dropped her phone back into her purse.

They had just wrapped up a truly horrible rendition of a Johnny Cash song neither one of them really knew the words to, when Pamela spoke, her voice groggy. "Can we stop somewhere so I can pee? Also, y'all are *terrible* singers."

Michael and Riley laughed.

Turning to glance at Pamela, Riley said, "How you feeling?"

"Better," she said, rubbing the heel of one of her palms against her eye. "Just really need to pee."

"I'll stop as soon as possible," Michael said. "We can get snacks! Whatever you ladies want. I'm buying."

He pulled off the highway twenty minutes later. While he pumped the gas, Riley and Pamela went inside the attached convenience store.

"Girl, he's super into you," Pamela said after leaving the restroom and joining Riley before a display of chips and popcorn.

A bell above the door chimed and Riley tore her attention away from the Doritos. She watched as Michael scanned the small shop, then spotted them. His face lit up when he made eye contact with her. Her stomach flipped.

"Circumstances are weird as hell, granted," Pamela said, voice soft. "But *damn.*"

"Shh!"

Laughing, Pamela headed for the coffee station to join Michael. Once they were loaded up on chips, candy, and caffeine, they were off again.

Riley linked her phone to the car's Bluetooth and showed Michael the true danger in granting her full access to the radio.

After a steady diet of boyband jams for forty-five minutes—to which Pamela matched her note for note—he groaned and hit the power button.

Riley laughed. "You lasted longer than I thought you would."

"I hear that a lot."

Pamela cackled.

Riley almost shot water out of her nose. "You have impeccable timing."

He grinned. "You ladies feeling okay?"

"Yes. I'll feel even better when I hear from Jade," said Riley.

"We'll hear from her in the morning, I'm sure," Pamela said. "She'll be worried about us too."

Around five, Riley stifled a yawn. They were still an hour outside Albuquerque. Pamela had fallen asleep in the back again, which was a feat in itself given how much coffee and chocolate she'd consumed.

"You can't fade on me now!" Michael said. "Have any plans for the weekend? Well, I guess you wouldn't, since you were planning to be at the ranch. Ha. That was a dumb question. I meant—"

Riley saved him from himself. "No plans other than sleeping. I have a shift on Monday."

"Think maybe we could grab lunch or something tomorrow?"

She tried very hard not to smile. "Are you asking me out?"

"Yes?"

"You're not sure?"

"I'm only sure if you say yes."

Without hesitation, she said, "Yes."

"Then I'm asking you out."

"I'm okay with pretty much anything but dim sum, given my current profession."

"I can work with that."

When the distance to Albuquerque got shorter and shorter, Riley gave him directions to Jade's house, where she and Pamela had both left their cars.

Birds chittered in Jade's fancy-pants garden, flitting between the bright flowers opening their petals to the early morning sun, and splashing in the fountain.

Riley gave Pamela a shake to wake her up. "We're back. You okay to drive yourself home?"

Pamela, bleary-eyed, nodded. Michael helped them get their things and stood outside his car while Pamela and Riley walked up the driveway to their cars. Hopefully their skulking about the drive-way at the crack of dawn didn't wake Jonah.

Standing outside Riley's car, Pamela shot a look toward where Michael loitered outside his own, gaze focused on his phone. Then she jutted her chin at Riley. "What's going on with you two?"

"I don't know," she said. "We're going out tomorrow."

Pamela squealed. "Oh, thank god."

Riley flushed. "You sure you're going to be okay?"

Shoulders drooping a little, Pamela said, "Yeah. I'm assuming I'll have nightmares for the next six months, but I'll be okay. Are you? I mean … that had to be even scarier for you."

"Nightmares for me, too," Riley agreed. "If I ignore it all for long enough, my connection to the place will fade. The distance helps, too."

Pamela nodded, but Riley didn't know if anything she said actually made any sense to her.

Riley pulled her friend into a hug. "If the nightmares get really bad, call me."

"Same goes for you." She glanced over at Michael again. "I'm leaving now. Go make some bad decisions." With that, she wiggled her eyebrows.

"You're as bad as Jade!"

Laughing, Pamela climbed into her car.

Riley waited for her friend to back down the driveway before she headed toward Michael. The Jeep pulled up to idle parallel to Michael, and Pamela reached across her passenger seat so she could roll the window down.

Riley hadn't reached them yet, but she heard, "Thanks for everything, Michael! Also, if you hurt her, I have your license plate number, and you better believe you'll have four super pissed-off girls ready to tear your face off."

"Pam!" Riley said, half horrified, half amused, deciding not to point out that the car actually belonged to Michael's sister.

Michael laughed. "I would expect nothing less."

Waving cheerfully, Pamela drove off.

Riley reached him, shaking her head. "Sorry about that."

"No need to apologize." Resting a hip on the car's bumper, he assessed her. "Do you need me to follow you back to your place or anything? Pamela slept a little, but you're running on fumes."

"So are you," she said. "And you have farther to go."

"I got one of those probably-should-be-illegal energy drinks. They make me feel like I'm on crack. I'll chug one of those before I head home."

"Can't possibly be a good idea," she said, laughing.

He smiled, his gaze dropping to her mouth for a moment. God

help her, what if he wanted to kiss her? She was ninety-five-percent sure she smelled like a sewer. And she'd tossed her cookies earlier because she communicated with *dead people*!

Why in the *world* did he want to see her again?

"You should probably give me your phone number if you want this date to happen," she said.

"Oh, right." The tips of his ears went pink as he grabbed his phone out of his back pocket.

She smiled to herself.

After giving him her number, he called her cell so she'd have his number too.

They exchanged a quick hug.

"Text me when you get in so I know you made it," she said.

"Will do."

Thankfully, she lived close to Jade, as she started yawning so hard on the drive to her apartment, her eyes watered, blurring her view of the road. Getting her belongings and herself up the set of outdoor stairs and into her apartment happened in a blur. Sometime in there, Pamela texted that she'd made it home.

Riley didn't have the energy to change, let alone make it to her bedroom. It was a miracle she'd made it inside and locked the door behind her.

Something made an awful racket. She woke with a start when she realized it was her phone.

For a moment, she had no idea where she was. Her mouth felt dry and tasted like an old shoe. It took her eyes a moment to adjust to the light.

She was in her apartment. She'd fallen asleep on the couch. She *really* needed to brush her teeth.

Her ringtone started up again and she lurched for it. The ID was a number she didn't recognize, but the location said, "Silver City, NM."

"Jade?" she asked, worried she wouldn't answer in time.

"Thank the lord!" Jade said.

Flopping back on the couch, she pulled her legs into her chest. "You're okay?"

"Yep! Nothing weird's happened since you left, really. There were a couple thumps from the cellar about an hour later, but that was it. Xavier claims at least one of the groups got an EVP in the kitchen.

"With you, Pam and Michael gone, Nina got paired up with Xavier. Learned all kinds of things for my future as a paranormal investigator, but no major happenings aside from what happened to you."

"You realize how white girl it is of you to stay, right?" Riley asked. "White folks live for haunted houses."

Jade cackled. "Girl, I know! I don't know what the hell is wrong with me. No sensible person would stay after what you all saw."

With a smile, Riley asked, "So you don't hate me for leaving?"

"Stop with that mess already, okay? How's Pam doing?"

"She's good. She got home before I did."

"Phew. She was a little nervous about joining you guys, you know. She didn't want to be a lady-boner-block."

"Stop trying to make that a thing! It has to rhyme!"

"That's the best I've come up with. Clam jam sounds like something you need ointment for, and nothing rhymes with 'vagina'!"

Riley snorted.

"Man, I just got some *seriously* weird looks." Then, softer, she said, "So. Michael. Give me the deets."

"We're getting lunch later."

"Is he in *your apartment* right now?" she hissed. "Did you let that arctic wolf into your den?"

"You're ridiculous! No. He's not in my apartment *or* my den. He's a nice guy and I like him."

"I'm so happy!" Jade chirped, then let out a long sigh. "And *you're* probably exhausted. I'll call you tomorrow morning before we leave. I want details on the date!"

"Good*night*, Jade."

"Night, hon!"

When Riley ended the call, she saw she had several texts from Michael that had come in around half-past six.

Hey. Made it home in one peace. Energy drink kept me awake and allowed me to taste sound. Hope your sleeping.

Followed by: piece* you're* I swear I can spell.

Followed by: This is Michael, btw.

Followed by: Michael Roberts.

Followed by: I'm guessing you figured that out.

Then, ten minutes later: Please still go to lunch with me.

Even after crawling into bed, she was still smiling.

CHAPTER 11

Riley woke again around noon, thanks to the distant rat-tat-tat of a jackhammer in the street outside her apartment complex. She stared at the ceiling. Thoughts of both Michael, and the Jordanville Ranch kept inching their way into her mind. Both lines of thinking filled her with nervous energy, but for totally different reasons. She batted them back.

Maybe she could finish her third viewing of *Tiana's Circle* …

Jade's words came back to her: "Don't you usually take Thursday nights off to watch your shows?"

Her shows. Was that *really* all she did anymore? Why hadn't Jade intervened sooner?

But she'd tried, hadn't she?

Riley threw back her comforter and took the longest shower of her life. She brushed her teeth, gargled with mouthwash, then brushed again.

As she was up close and personal with her reflection, examining the state of her pores, something shifted in her peripheral vision. Something dark, like a cat zipping past. But Riley didn't have a cat.

Stepping out of her bathroom, she gave a quick scan of her bedroom. No movement. She waited, listening. Saw nothing. Heard nothing.

It was just a lingering creepy-crawly feeling, courtesy of the ranch, she told herself. She went back into the bathroom to continue scrutinizing her face.

When she felt semi-human again, she replied to Michael.

You pick a place for lunch yet?

He immediately replied with, How do you feel about pizza?

I feel great about pizza.

I knew I liked you. What time are you free?

Now. She texted him her address.

Leaving in 10!

Riley never wore much makeup but given the vomiting in the cellar and the freak-out over the haunting, she needed a little something extra to help decrease her disaster-status. Plus, she'd just accepted that she wasn't living her best life, but the life of an eighty year old. Mascara to the rescue.

Though her eyeshadow game wasn't as strong as Pamela's, it helped hide the less-than-six-hours-of-sleep under-eye bags she was rocking. After changing nearly ten times, she finally settled on a black tank with a white, off-the-shoulder top over it, jean shorts, and sandals. She left her hair down, curls mostly behaving.

I'm out front, Michael texted.

Be right out!

Breathe, Riley. It's only pizza.

Michael was leaning against his passenger side door when she walked out of the pedestrian gate a few feet from where he was parked near the apartment call box.

He gave her an elevator scan without moving away from the car and she felt suddenly exposed. "Hey, gorgeous."

"Hey," she said, walking up to him, reminded of high school. Of how shy and nervous she'd been any time a guy came to pick her up.

Granted, there hadn't been any guys as hot as Michael in high school. Except for Mr. Kirk the English lit teacher, but that was another matter entirely.

Michael wore jeans and a just-tight-enough gray shirt. His short brown waves were slightly out of control, and he'd left the day-old stubble unshaven. "You ready to have your mind blown?"

"This better be some damn good pizza."

The hole-in-the wall restaurant had a gaggle of people waiting out front for their carry-out orders. Inside, the dozen tables were almost all full, and a small line formed at the door shortly after Riley and Michael scored the last table at the back. All fifteen barstools were full, too, a soccer game playing on a single screen up in the corner opposite Riley's table.

Michael ordered a pepperoni and sausage pizza and a side of cheesy garlic bread, then told her to wait to experience nirvana.

Riley let out a completely embarrassing groan after the first bite. Michael lit up like a Christmas tree.

"Ha! I've impressed you!"

A bark of laughter sounded to Riley's right.

"You say you impress her as if you cook the thing yourself."

Michael, whose back faced the restaurant, stood up suddenly, arms out. "*Tony!*" he said, dragging out the two syllables in an elongated drawl Riley swore she'd only heard in Italian mob movies.

"*Mikey!*" Tony replied in an identical fashion.

A sixty-plus-year-old short man emerged from behind a pair of swinging doors. He embraced Michael in a bear hug, only coming to Michael's chest. He wore a stained white T-shirt and black pants—his protruding belly hanging a bit over the top—and sported a sparse comb-over.

"Paul came back to tell me he saw you come in," said Tony. "Haven't seen you in a while. Where you been?"

Michael angled his head in Riley's direction.

Tony glanced at her, where she was still seated in the booth. "Oh ho! What have we here? You bring a girl here for once?"

Michael smiled at her. "Tony, this is Riley. Riley, this is Tony."

Riley stood and held out her hand, oddly pleased Tony was surprised to see him there with a date. "Nice to meet you."

"Get in here," he said, pulling her into a tight hug. He smelled like flour and garlic.

"I'm trying to get this girl to like me, Tony. Don't tell her anything embarrassing."

Tony pulled away, but held fast to her hands. "Mikey is a good guy. But between you and me—" he shot a look at Michael over his shoulder and made no attempt to lower his voice, "—I've seen him try to pick up women here. He's *very* bad at it."

Riley laughed. "Oh? Do tell."

"All right, all right," Michael said from behind them.

Tony laughed and deposited a kiss on the back of either hand. "You need anything, you let me know. Mikey's like family. Like the extra son I never wanted." He made a dramatic show of dodging while Michael pretended to give him a swift kick in the rear.

With a final wink to Riley, Tony ducked back through the swinging doors.

"He's fun," she said, sitting back down.

Riley tried very hard not to make obscene noises while she polished off the rest of her pizza. "I would like more information on your failed attempts at hitting on women."

He wrinkled his nose. "The one time I had a drink thrown in my face just happened to be when Tony was watching …"

With a gasp, she asked, "What did you say!"

"Nothing!" he said, hands up to show his innocence. "I just used the 'If I told you that you had a nice body, would you hold it against me?' line and she was not amused. She was also close to twice my age."

Riley was caught between amusement and horror. "Oh my god."

"My only defense was that I was twenty-two and the world's largest idiot."

"Was?"

He tossed a wadded-up napkin at her. She'd learned from last time, though, and swatted it back effortlessly, beaning him square in the forehead.

Smiling at her, he said, "How long do I have you for?"

"I'll let you know when your time's up."

They went to an open-air flea market in Albuquerque, wandering around for a couple hours. They looked at handmade jewelry, painted ceramics from Mexico, clothes, and somehow managed to eat more. Riley polished off half a bag of caramel popcorn before thrusting it at Michael and telling him never to let her eat again. Half an hour later, they each had an ice cream cone.

A long stroll through Old Town Albuquerque ended at yet another restaurant sometime after seven. Riley told him about the time she'd locked herself in her parents' car when she was three and had to be rescued by the fire department; he told her about the one and only time his father participated and won a food challenge because his spleen ruptured. The Chicken Wing Challenge hadn't caused the rupture, but Michael and Donna had felt so bad for him that they gave him a pity win and the pair agreed to watch the Golf Channel all day.

A waiter stopped by the table, interrupting Riley's very detailed account of the guy she'd seen last week in the grocery store who had a ferret poking out of his fanny pack.

"Just wanted to let you folks know we close at ten …"

It was 9:55.

"Yikes when did that happen?" Riley asked, then stifled a yawn.

"I think maybe my time is running out," he said, watching her from across the table.

"Just a little behind on sleep." Another yawn seized her.

"I'm taking you home now," he said, laughing. "At this rate, I'll have to carry you inside."

Leg bouncing, Riley watched the passing scenery, now muted shades of blue and black. Why was she nervous *now*? They'd been together all day.

She buzzed them through the gate and he pulled into a guest spot. Parked. They didn't move. Should she invite him up? She should probably invite him up. Even though the date had lasted nearly ten hours, she wasn't sure she was ready to say goodnight to him yet. But she needed to sleep, too.

"Is it too much to ask if I can see you tomorrow?"

She glanced over at him. He seemed tense, shoulders rounded.

"Not sick of me yet?" she asked.

"Not even a little bit," he said. "But, uh … this is going to sound really stupid but—can we take this kind of slow?"

"Yes!"

He laughed, straightening. "Yeah?"

She nodded.

"Okay. I just … I *really* like you, Riley. It's actually scaring the shit out of me. And I just don't want to screw up."

"Who told you that you couldn't express your feelings?"

His mouth quirked up on one side. "Every girlfriend I've ever had. And … uh … most recently, my therapist."

Oh. *Oh.*

"And that same therapist said I should be really transparent with the next woman I'm interested in …"

When he paused for longer than seemed necessary, she wondered if he sought permission to continue. "Transparent about what?"

"So. Uh. When Kim, my ex-fiancée, and I broke up—you know, after her whole affair with a student thing—I did *not* take it well. Eventually, thanks mostly to Donna, I went to talk to someone. Which I'm still pretty shit at. My family's gotten better at talking in general, but I still had a really hard time with all of it. I'd say I was fine when I wasn't."

"How long have you been going?"

"I went weekly for about a year. I've scaled it back to once a month." His shoulders were rounded again, gaze focused on his lap. "I wouldn't have gotten through it without a significant drinking problem otherwise."

Unsure of how to react to this, Riley reached out and gently placed a hand on his back. "I'm really glad you went."

He flinched slightly, as if startled, but nodded. "Me too." Sitting straighter, he focused on her, rather than addressing his lap. "I just … I wanted you to know. People hear 'therapy' and get a little creeped out."

"I'm not creeped out. I get visited by *dead people*, remember?" she said. "I want to see you tomorrow."

His smile made her stomach flutter. Lord was she in trouble.

Walking her to the base of the stairs, he kissed her on the cheek. "I'll call you in the morning, okay?"

All she could manage was a nod.

"Night, Riley."

"Night, *Mikey*."

"Don't."

Grinning, she hurried up the steps without tripping. The night had definitely been a success.

CHAPTER 12

After a long, hot shower, her hair wrapped up in a towel, Riley suddenly felt wide awake, wired after her conversation with Michael, and the memory of the soft, warm kiss on her cheek. She sat on her couch with the next episode of *Tiana's Circle* loaded and ready, but she couldn't get herself to hit play. If only Jade were there to grill her about every little detail of the day.

A very small part of her wished she was still at the ranch so she could talk to all the girls about it. Too bad the place was four hours away and crawling with spirits. If it wasn't already so late, she'd call Pamela.

Something quick and black darted in her peripheral vision, just as it had that morning. But when she turned her head, nothing was there.

The memory of Pete watching her from the top window twisted her gut. Her time with Michael had been a welcome distraction, but it was all coming back to her now. Riley had been lucky enough to have a way off the ranch, but Pete didn't. In life *or* death.

Another quick dash of the dark not-cat. Riley pulled the towel off her head, her damp curls falling against her shoulders. Nothing.

The temperature in the room plummeted abruptly. Goosebumps raced across her skin.

"Hi."

Riley shrieked, leaping to her feet with a speed that surprised even herself. Behind her couch stood Pete himself. Her heart slammed in her chest. "Oh my god, kid. You can't sneak up on people like that." Then her brain caught up. "How are you *here*?"

He wore his Scooby Doo shirt again. A pair of beat-up white sneakers peeked out from the hems of his jeans. His hair wasn't tamped down by the maroon beanie this time, his dark curls wild. The image of him flickered then, like an electrical glitch. Then he solidified again. "I followed you."

Riley placed a hand on her forehead. He *followed* her? "How?"

"I didn't want you to go. You're nice." His voice was quiet when he said, "Orin's not nice."

Riley blew out a slow breath.

"I don't like it there," Pete said, chewing on his bottom lip. "Can I stay with you?"

How was she supposed to tell him that she could hardly take care of herself, let alone a kid? She shook her head. *He's not alive*, she reminded herself. No matter how real he looked standing there in her living room.

His image flickered again. There, not there, there, not there.

"Pete?"

Gone.

Riley quickly rounded the couch, as if she expected to find him squatting behind it. Some ghostly version of hide-and-seek. She checked every room, but he was gone. Into thin air, just like Mariah.

Flopping onto her couch, she covered her face with her hands. The temperature had returned to normal at least. This couldn't really be happening, could it? She'd moved out of her *last* apartment because it was haunted. She really liked this one. And breaking her lease—again—would be a pain in the ass.

Don't get ahead of yourself.

Heart thumping, she pulled in a long breath through her nose, then let it out slowly. Just as Nina had told her to do in the cellar. In … *out*. In … *out*.

Gradually, she took her hands away from her face and scanned the living room. No little ghost boys. Maybe she'd imagined it. But she knew she hadn't.

Unable to stay idle for long, she snatched up her phone and opened the browser. "Can a ghost follow you home?" she asked her search engine.

It didn't take long to get the answer. Sometimes ghosts tagged along with those sensitive to their presence. Sometimes they piggybacked with people who took items of importance to the victim from a location. She hadn't taken anything. Perhaps what Pete had told her was true: he didn't like the ranch, so he'd followed her. Easy as that.

Sighing, she did anther search and found his missing persons' photo again. The wild mop of curly hair tamped down by a maroon beanie, and the half-smile that lit up his eyes.

Obviously, she couldn't let him stay with her indefinitely. He couldn't go from being trapped at the ranch to being trapped with her. He needed to move on—or whatever it was that ghosts did. Maybe his dad was waiting somewhere for him.

But in order to find his body and free him, Riley would have to return to the ranch. Her stomach churned at the thought. Guilt or not, could she deal with another run-in with Orin's ghost? And where in the hell would she even look? Out in the woods, in that clearing she'd seen in her dream? Buried somewhere near the dude ranch, since Pete seemed to spend a good deal of time there too? *In the house?*

For all she knew, he'd been buried under the concrete floor of the cellar.

Though her gut told her Orin hung out in the cellar exclusively, it didn't mean he couldn't move locations if he wanted to. If Orin popped up in her apartment next, she'd break her lease and go on the lam. Being haunted by a serial killer ghost was above her pay grade.

The cellar had been the place of Orin's prized "work," and while the physical evidence of that had been taken out, he still felt the need to protect it. She hoped he'd stay there.

The memory of her dream came back to her. It made more sense to her now. Her chasing Pete, and Orin chasing her.

Knowing she would likely regret it, she swapped her phone for her laptop, then typed "Orin's Girls" into the search bar. Of the five bodies recovered, none had been found in the cellar. All manner of tools had been found, though: knives, scalpels, rib spreaders, bone saws. The bodies, however—minus various organs—had been buried outside.

Given the varying level of decomposition of the bodies, it was assumed he'd buried one girl a year. A year of torture and mutilation before he put them in the ground.

Most of the girls were runaways. One hadn't been identified; she'd been decapitated before she was buried, her head never found. It was speculated that she'd been killed three years before she'd been discovered. The body had been so decomposed, they hadn't been able to gather any identifying information.

Jane Doe, ten to twelve years old. No pictures.

All investigators had to go on when it came to figuring out what had happened in the cellar were the tools in the cellar and the five bodies out back. In the short video of Mindy not long after her escape, the girl had looked around repeatedly, as if she was sure Orin was out there in the crowd, ready to snatch her up and drag her back. It reminded Riley of Pamela, shooting looks over her shoulder, sure his ghost still lingered there.

Had Mindy been too scared to speak about the others even though Orin was in custody with no hope of being released? Yet, even after his death, Mindy still didn't talk.

Orin, however, had reported several times that he'd had an accomplice named Hank Gerber. Swore up one side and down another that if he himself was to be arrested for kidnapping, then Hank should be too. No Hank Gerber who even remotely matched Orin's description had ever been found, of course. Orin pleaded guilty to the kidnapping charge but claimed he hadn't meant Mindy any harm—said that he'd hoped to adopt her one day.

Then, nearly a week later, an anonymous tip came in telling police Mindy hadn't been Orin's only victim and that they wouldn't be surprised if there were bodies in the yard. Sure enough, when they went back with cadaver dogs, they found a small graveyard.

Reports said Orin clammed up altogether then, other than to say he wasn't guilty. It went to trial. The surviving family members wanted the death penalty.

Orin said nothing during the proceedings, merely sat there and watched with a constant little smirk on his bearded face. His years in prison had softened his muscles. He looked like an old man. Someone's creepy grandpa.

He obviously had buried Pete Vonick somewhere else, since they didn't find him with the others. His little secret. His reason for smiling to himself like he was a cat who'd just caught the canary. Maybe that was where part of his spirit's anger had come from, too. Maybe the secret of Pete's death kept Orin tied to that house as much as

Pete's body tied the boy there.

If she found his body, perhaps it would release them both. Perhaps Orin didn't want that to happen.

But Riley was still stuck with the how of it: how could she prove to the police that Pete was Orin's first victim, especially when the boy didn't fit Orin's pattern of young girls with few family ties? Pete had been taken five years before Gabriella, snatched out from under his mother's nose, and the hunt for him went on to this day. His mother gave talks about child abduction even now.

Had it been too close for Orin? Had Pete been a reckless grab that almost got him caught before he really got started? The first kill was often the sloppiest. The kill with the training wheels still on. When it had come time to nab Gabriella, Orin had been ready. Practiced.

Riley did a search for Mindy Cho next. She'd been sixteen when she was taken and had been a runaway for nearly a year before that. Mindy's mother had passed away when Mindy was a baby, which left the girl in the care of her only local family: an abusive father. Her extended family was scattered between Los Angeles and South Korea.

Mindy had run away to escape her father. Then was snatched up by someone even worse.

Mindy had done a total of two interviews after Orin's arrest. One decidedly less formal than the other. Riley pulled up the first one on her laptop. In it, Mindy was outside the police station, being ushered out by her court-appointed lawyer and a woman from Child Protection Services. The girl and two women were swarmed by journalists, questions flying at her from all sides. Flashes went off, microphones and recorders shoved in her face. Mindy's haunted gaze darted here and there and over her shoulder, like a mouse in a meadow, knowing a hawk circled overhead.

The video was only thirty seconds long, and in half of it, Mindy remained silent. Silent and scared and shielded by the bulldog women who looked ready to tear the heads off the reporters. She was just outside the open door of the waiting car when she looked up, glancing past the car's roof and the reporters. Her eyes went even wider. Then she lurched away from her protectors and grabbed the lens of the camera focused on her.

Riley, as always, sat back as Mindy's entire face took up the screen. A gaping mouth, a flaring nostril, tear-clumped lashes. "He's out there," Mindy said, pulling back slightly, staring at the camera. Staring at Riley. "You didn't find him. He's still watching. He'll still find me."

Someone yanked Mindy away from the camera—the shot a blur of flashes and limbs for a few seconds before the lawyer and CPS woman yelled at the frenzied reporters. Mindy had just thrown chum in the water.

"Who are you talking about, Mindy?"

"Did Orin have help?"

The girl froze, wide eyes focused past the car. Scanning, watching, searching.

Her bulldog protectors all but shoved her into the car, scrambling in after her, and then the car peeled away from the curb.

Riley searched for the second interview, the formal one from two years later when Mindy was eighteen. She wore makeup, a pristine white silk blouse, and black slacks. Jet-black hair brushed to shining hung stick-straight over one shoulder. Freckles were scattered across most of her face, as if someone had blown a fine mist of cinnamon on her cheeks and nose.

The pair were in a dark-wood-paneled room, the camera facing them as they sat awkwardly across from each other at a weird angle in uncomfortable-looking blue chairs—the wall behind them was mostly windows, partly covered by soft, gauzy curtains that pooled on the floor. On either side of the windows stood three-foot-high stands that looked like a cross between a stool and a side table. A small, elegant white vase sat atop each one.

It was from the late 1980s, so the quality of the video was pretty terrible and grainy.

Riley had always hated this video.

Mindy sat with her legs crossed, folded hands propped on her knee. The small smile on her face twitched occasionally, as if her cheeks hurt from the effort. Given that Riley knew Mindy ended up in a psychiatric hospital three years later, she could only imagine the mental state the girl had been in then, trying to look calm and professional on the outside, while falling to pieces on the inside.

After a few pleasantries, where the woman thanked Mindy for letting them into her home, they went through a series of benign questions, like how her classmates at Desert Crest High School reacted to the news of both her kidnapping and return. Then, rather abruptly, the woman dove into the heart of Mindy's personal hell.

> **Interviewer:** You said you were drugged? A rag soaked in chloroform, was it?
>
> **Mindy:** Yes.
>
> **Interviewer:** How scared were you when you woke up, realizing you'd been kidnapped?
>
> **Mindy:** I was terrified.

Interviewer: You must have feared for your life.

Mindy: Yes, I did.

Interviewer: You thought you might die there.

Mindy: Yes.

Riley blew out a breath, fast-forwarding a bit. At one point, the pair moved the interview outside for some inexplicable reason. They walked side by side, slow as molasses, down a sidewalk through what Riley could only guess was a park. Mindy's tiny heels clicked as she walked a little unsteadily.

Interviewer: When you were finally able to leave the police station after hours of interrogation, how relieved were you?

Mindy: I was happy. But I was also scared because I didn't know what was waiting for me out there.

Interviewer: Out in the world, you mean?

Mindy: Yes.

Interviewer: Because even though you were free, you didn't want to return to your abusive father.

Riley noticed Mindy's jaw and hands clenched here, just for a moment.

> **Mindy:** Yes.

> **Interviewer:** You must have felt deeply worried about your future.

> **Mindy:** Yes. I had family in California—my mom's sister and her two kids. But my father always tried to keep me isolated. I didn't know if they'd want to help me. I didn't know if my father would let them.

> **Interviewer:** You didn't know then that your father had died from an accidental overdose the same year you were taken, did you?

Mindy's eyes welled up.

> **Mindy:** No.

> **Interviewer:** Your father left you everything he had—including your childhood home—in his will, didn't he?

> **Mindy:** Yes.

> **Interviewer:** Did that surprise you, given your relationship with him? Especially since he had

no way of knowing whether or not you were alive?

Mindy: It did surprise me. But I also knew he loved me. He was a sick, sick man who never got over losing my mother—the love of his life.

They walked a little farther, then stopped by a bench, a tree heavy with purple flowers hanging over it. They sat. But it was at an awkward angle again, turned slightly toward each other so their knees almost touched. Like they'd been told to look like a pair of chatting friends, but also to offer decent angles for the camera. Decent in the way that nothing Riley saw from the '80s ever seemed to be.

Interviewer: Now, I must ask you about something that's caused quite a bit of speculation amongst those following your case closely.

Mindy sighed here, squaring her shoulders as if she'd been waiting for this.

Interviewer: When you were led out of the police station toward the press waiting for you, you said he was still out there. That *he* would find you.

Mindy flushed, her reddening skin a stark contrast to her white blouse. She nodded.

Interviewer: Who were you referring to? Surely you knew Orin was no longer out there; he was in custody.

Mindy: I … I wasn't thinking clearly that day. I was so distressed.

Interview: From your trauma.

Mindy: Yes. I was so distressed from my trauma that I don't even remember saying that.

Here, Mindy looked over at the camera, breaking the fourth wall as she spoke directly to her rapt audience.

Mindy: There was no one there other than Orin. I was just scared he might escape jail somehow and come for me. I know now that it was just my fear talking.

She looked back at the interviewer.

Mindy: I've gotten help, you know, mentally, and I'm working through all the things that were real, and all the things my mind made up.

Interviewer: Things your mind made up to assist with your trauma?

Mindy: Yes. My doctor calls them coping

mechanisms. But there was no one else. Just Orin and me.

Interviewer: And Janay, for a time.

Mindy nodded, her smile slightly more believable, but still strained.

Mindy: Yes. Just us.

Interviewer: What do you make of Orin's claims that another man, a Hank Gerber, was there?

Mindy flinched.

Mindy: He lied. Orin lied.

Riley hit pause, her stomach in knots. "No, *you're* lying," she whispered to herself. When Riley first saw the video, she'd assumed Mindy had wanted to show the world how adjusted she'd become. That she was better.

Now, Riley got the distinct impression Mindy had spoken the truth originally, and this cleaned-up version of Mindy was put in front of the camera to dispel the rumor she started. The question now, was: who had coerced her into changing her story? Orin had been on death row at this point; Riley highly doubted he could have contacted her.

Was the myth of Hank Gerber not truly a myth?

Something fell behind her—somewhere in the back of her

apartment. She yelped, dropping her laptop onto the couch and turning around, her knees on the cushion. She waited, straining to hear something else.

Thud.

This was a softer sound. Muted.

While one part of her brain yelled, "Intruder! Call the police!" the other part of her brain knew the sound was likely the work of a less corporeal guest.

Reluctantly, she got up and crept toward her bedroom, carpet soft and quiet beneath her bare feet. "If this is you, Pete," she whispered, "we're going to have to discuss this whole haunting thing. If this is you, Orin, I'm going … well, I don't know what I'm going to do."

Standing outside her bedroom with her back to the wall, the memory of being ten and investigating a curious noise rose up in mind. Taking a deep breath, she darted into the room and flicked on the light.

Empty. Her closet door—which she always kept closed—stood open. And her unpacked duffel bag from her ranch trip lay in the middle of her room, contents spilled out across the floor.

She crept toward it, gaze darting back and forth, searching for any sign of ghostly visitors, but found nothing. Squatting before her clothes, she was moments from shoving everything back into her bag when a chill raced down her spine. She yanked her hand away.

Poking out from underneath a pair of jeans was the edge of a maroon-colored knit cap, though the color was muted thanks to a layer of grime. Carefully, she pulled back the jeans to reveal the beanie. Pete's beanie. How in the ever-loving hell had *that* gotten into her bag?

She snatched it up, ready to wave it around like a disappointed parent and demand an explanation from her new roommate, but she was hit with a burst of images before she could get a word out.

A picture of an alive-and-well Pete, laughing as his father held both of his hands and spun in a circle, filled her mind. Pete cackled like he was on the world's best rollercoaster, his eyes squeezed shut. His mother stood nearby, grinning as she watched her two favorite people in the world.

Riley dropped the cap, stumbling back, a sob choking her. She sank to her knees, hands in her hair.

When the temperature dropped, it wasn't as shocking as it had been the first time. Not as cold.

Tears streamed down Riley's face by the time she looked up at Pete, wearing the same clothes as before, but with his wild curls held down by the beanie now. The same beanie sitting on her floor. The image of him was fainter. Not quite transparent, but not quite solid either. He had the decency to look shamefaced.

"Did you put that in my bag?"

He nodded emphatically, but didn't speak, hands bunching up the hem of his shirt. Scooby Doo's slightly detached ear flapped a little, as if he took responsibility for this too.

What did he want from her? What did he expect her to do? Her stomach roiled.

"Do you want me to free you from the ranch?"

He nodded.

"And I have to find your body in order to do that?"

Another nod.

"You know this would be a whole lot easier if you just told me where to look."

The temperature slowly started to drop as Pete tried to pull more energy into himself, just as Orin had done. But the colder it got, the more Pete's image flickered. The room grew frigid, Riley's breath puffing in front of her face in white clouds.

Pete opened his mouth, then flickered out of view altogether, abruptly taking the cold with him.

Chin dropping to her chest and shoulders slumped, Riley groaned. "Of course."

She shoved her clothes into her bag and tossed it into her closet, closing the door with a satisfying click. Walking back to the beanie on her floor, she wondered if Pete would be offended if she kicked it under the bed and out of sight. Who knew how many memories were locked up in that one article of clothing?

Grabbing the blanket she had folded at the foot of her bed, she used it like an oven mitt to place Pete's beanie on her dresser, keeping her hands from making contact. She felt like a fool, but she didn't want to risk being blindsided by another memory. Her nerves couldn't take anymore.

After a glass of wine, she started to relax a little, her thoughts dulling. If she ended up sharing an apartment with a dead nine-year-old boy, she'd surely have to become an alcoholic to cope. Tucking the half-full bottle under her arm, she wandered back into her living room.

Her laptop still sat on her couch, the screen black. A swipe of her finger along the mouse pad brought her computer back to life. After keying in her password, the screen filled with the paused image of Mindy's face, false smile frozen on her face.

Riley poured herself a second glass of wine. Stared at Mindy's face. Slowly drank down her glass. Her mind was ... fuzzy now. She liked fuzzy.

"I wonder if *you'd* know where Pete is buried," she said to Mindy. "Did Orin tell you not to tell? Did the mysterious Hank Gerber swear you to secrecy?"

Something darted in her peripheral vision and she whipped her head in that direction. Her vision swam a little with the sudden movement. Probably shouldn't have more wine.

"Oh, fuck it," she said, pouring the rest into her glass. She gulped down half of it and placed the glass on her coffee table, almost missing it and spilling red wine all over her beige carpet. Her vision swam a little again. "What are you hiding, Mindy?"

Riley had slipped passed buzzed territory and was quite sure this was the time to put the computer away and go to bed, but she suddenly couldn't shake loose the idea of contacting Mindy.

The problem with stalking Ms. Mindy Cho, however, was that her social media was either non-existent or well-hidden. And, even if Riley found her, could she really contact a traumatized woman some thirty years after the worst time in her life and ask her if she knew how to find the body of a dead boy? A boy Riley knew about solely because she had been contacted by his spirit … a spirit who was taking up residence in her apartment now because he'd used his ghost skills to slip his beanie into her bag.

Riley polished off the wine in her glass. Frowned at the empty bottle laying on its side beside the couch. She almost toppled off the couch as she reached for it, then laughed as she pushed herself back to sitting.

Something hovered just out of sight again, but she didn't dare look at it. Maybe it was just her hair. Maybe it was Pete.

Number one item on her to-do list tomorrow? Buy more wine.

Her wobbly gaze shifted back to her computer. Riley wondered how many whackadoodles had tried to get Mindy to talk to them over the years. Why would Riley's attempt be any different?

Mindy was still frozen on screen, her eyes downcast.

Riley sank into her couch, heels of her hands pressed against her eyes. She really needed to go to bed. Hopefully the wine haze would help her sleep and keep her from waking up every two seconds, paranoid about being watched.

But her sluggish brain kept on trucking.

What if Mindy had gone back to Korea after all this? That would put a serious damper on Riley's current plan. Maybe the airing of the Jordanville Ranch *Paranormal Playground* episode had been the final straw for Mindy, and she'd fled.

Riley sat up. Too fast, much too fast. She blinked away the spins.

The *Paranormal Playground* episode. Mindy had made a public statement about her distaste for the show.

Slowly, oh so slowly, she pulled her computer back into her lap.

A search for Mindy's statement took Riley to YouTube. Mindy had made the video herself, in what looked like her living room. Thanks to both *Paranormal Playground*'s popularity and the two stars issuing a response statement before the episode, Mindy's video had gone viral. The local news showed it a day before and after the episode, which gave Mindy's video an added boost in views.

Mindy, now in her mid-to-late forties, sat before the computer wearing a plain black T-shirt. Her pretty, slightly round face was devoid of makeup, and her black hair, showing the faintest hints of gray at the temples, was pulled back in a ponytail. Her freckles seemed to have faded over the years. Her eyes drooped a little. Riley wondered if she'd been having a rough day when she recorded this, or if this was just what life had done to her.

"For those of you who don't know me, my name is Mindy Cho, and I was the sole survivor of … of Orin Jacobs. I have tried for a year to get the producers of *Paranormal Playground* to not feature the ranch where I was held captive. It's a novelty for most, but this was my *life*. All I can ask now is that people boycott this episode. Of all the shows they've done, this one is the *only* one where the victim of a crime committed at one of the locations is still alive. Please don't let them monetize the worst years of my life."

Mindy continued, but Riley's attention had zeroed in on the room behind her. The webcam faced what looked like a backyard beyond the wall of windows. Cream-colored curtains were drawn open, letting in what looked like afternoon light. And on either side of the windows were two dark-wood stands, each topped with small white vases.

"Oh shit," Riley whispered to herself, sobering slightly.

As of the recording of the video, some two years ago, Mindy still lived in her childhood home.

Riley had to hope she was still there. And was willing to talk.

CHAPTER 13

Riley awoke on her couch, cheek resting on a patch of dried drool. After slithering to the floor and plugging in her dead cell phone—which had somehow ended up *under* her couch—she popped two aspirin before showering. It was the first day in a while that she'd felt really rested, headache notwithstanding. Thank you, Merlot.

In the middle of brushing her teeth, she heard her phone come to life—ping after ping to alert her to missed calls and unread texts. Both her mother and Jade had called. Her mother no doubt wondered how Riley's trip had gone, as she would have been heading back home by now had she stayed. Two missed texts from Michael.

Morning, sunshine! was sent at ten.

Afternoon, sunshine? at 12:15—twenty minutes ago.

She fired a quick text back: **Hey, sorry, just woke up a little bit ago. Text me your address. Will be ready in 20!**

No rush. I'm ready when you are.

Both Jade and her mother left voicemails. Jade said everything had gone fine and that they'd be heading back to the city within the hour. They wouldn't be in town again until well after two. Riley's mom was just checking in and wanted Riley to call her when she could.

She sent her mom a text: **I'm fine. Long weekend. Met a**

guy! Will give you details soon!

That's great, honey! She added the toothy emoji that usually meant "everything is a trash fire but I'm trying—and failing—to stay positive." Her mother's emoji skills were hit and miss.

After deciding on her favorite *Tiana's Circle* shirt and a pair of shorts, Riley braided her hair, slipped on some flats, and texted Michael. Just before walking out the door, she gave her apartment a quick once-over. "Don't break anything while I'm gone, Pete."

Michael lived in the back unit of a duplex. He texted to tell her to pull into the long driveway behind his car. Riley had just parked when Michael emerged.

He wore jeans and another just-tight-enough shirt, this one blue. Damp hair curled slightly at his neck, like he'd just gotten out of the shower. Despite all the time she'd spent with him yesterday, the sight of him still caused a nervous flutter in her stomach.

"Hey," he said.

"Hey yourself," she said, walking up the two steps to his porch.

"Wanna come in for a few? I need to feed the cat before we head out, otherwise he'll shred the furniture."

"You have a *cat*?"

"I inherited the cat from my ex. I sort of grew attached to the furball, and when I told her it was over, I told her I was taking Baxter too. Kim didn't put up much of a fuss."

"I should hope not." She followed him inside.

The duplex was a two-bedroom, one bath—and though it was small, he'd done creative things with the space available. His dark brown sofa sat in the middle of the living room slash dining room area, surrounded by wraparound, low bookshelves. A shorthaired orange and white cat sat perched on the sofa's arm. His tail twitched, then curled around his feet. Michael wandered past the couch and the small dining table with four high-backed stools, turning into the kitchen.

Baxter mewed, stood, and stretched, butt arched in the air in the way only cats could. He hopped to the ground with a muted thud, walked over to her and, quite dramatically, flopped onto his side.

Riley laughed, bending down to give his belly a scratch.

"Well, I'll be damned," said Michael, walking into the room with a fork and a small bowl in his hand. "He doesn't even let me do that."

Baxter's eyes closed and he purred so loudly, Riley could feel the soft vibration in her flats.

"C'mon, you flirt," Michael said, clinking the fork against the side of the bowl.

Baxter perked up immediately and scampered after Michael, back into the kitchen.

A low, dark-wood TV stand stood against the wall near the front door, a slightly obscene-sized flat screen resting on top. The bottom of the stand held row after row of DVDs on one side, and a gaming console and a slew of games on the other.

A framed, vintage map of the world hung on the wall near the dining table. Two bookshelves sat on either side. He had a mix of memoirs and biographies, as well as an eclectic assortment of fiction.

Riley was in the middle of perusing his fiction titles when she felt his gaze on her. A decidedly better feeling than being under the watchful eye of a spirit. She looked over to find him leaned against the doorway of his dining room.

"What?"

"Nothing," he said. "I just like looking at you."

"You are *so* corny."

"And you like it," he said. "I'm corny a good sixty percent of the time. You spent *hours* with me yesterday and yet here you are again."

She couldn't argue with that logic.

"How do you feel about arcades?"

"The same way I feel about pizza."

He grinned.

To Riley's utter delight, Michael was absolutely abysmal at air hockey. Every time she sank a shot, he let out an involuntary grunt like an old man upset that his lawn had been invaded by teenagers.

After several hours of driving games, shooting games—Michael gunned down zombies with a fierce accuracy she'd never seen the likes of—and a rematch at air hockey, they wandered next door to a fifties-themed diner and gorged themselves on burgers and fries.

"My buddies and I used to come here back in high school. We'd spend most of our money at the arcade, then pool our remaining cash to get food here," he said, polishing off the last of his fries.

"Were you as bad at air hockey then as you are now?" she asked.

Glaring, he said, "I'm not *bad* at it. You, dear lady, are an air hockey hustler."

She laughed.

After a moment, he asked, "So did you sleep in until noon today because you were just that tired or were you out partying all night?"

Though he'd clearly meant it as a joke, the question caught her off guard and her hand stilled on its way to reaching for her last fry. Would she scare him off by telling him a ghost had followed her home?

"Oh," he said. "Do tell. What level of debauchery are we talking here?"

"Defcon level two." She popped the fry in her mouth. "I was deep in an internet wormhole until three."

His eyebrows shot toward his hairline. "What kind of wormhole?"

"I get kind of obsessive about true crime stuff. I spend a lot of time reading up on local cases, watching documentaries about serial killers … I think it's because of the medium thing. I want justice for the dead or whatever, even if them swinging by to say hello scares the crap out of me," she said. "I've seen the Orin Jacobs episode of *Dateline* four times."

"Whoa."

Biting down on her bottom lip, she kept her gaze focused on her empty plate. "Last night's wormhole was mainly Mindy Cho."

"What'd you find?" When she glanced up at him, he had a slight smile on his face. "Gonna take more than that to scare me off."

"Pete the ghost moved into my apartment. I got semi-drunk on wine to deal."

Michael nearly choked on his soda. "Wait, are you serious?"

She told him about the two sightings, as well as the beanie that had appeared in her belongings.

"How … how is that even possible?"

"Hell if I know." Tears inexplicably welled in her eyes when the memory of a laughing, spinning Pete filled her mind again. She had to help him. Had to reunite him with his father. But it all scared her so damn bad.

Michael reached across the table and placed a hand on hers. When she finally made eye contact with him, he offered her another small smile. "I'm still not deterred." Giving her hand a squeeze, he said, "Tell me what you found out about Mindy."

"I think she might still be in Albuquerque. I just have to find her. I figure I can start with the phonebook—those things still exist, don't they? There might be a landline at her house—maybe there's still a listing under her father's name. I swear they never update the listings. Shouldn't be too many Jinwoo Chos."

Just before bed last night, Riley's searching had turned up Mindy's father. But she'd found little about the man himself.

Michael was quiet for a moment. "Okay, let's say you can track her down. What would you say?"

"Ask her if she knows anything about Peter Vonick. Maybe the name will jog a memory. Maybe Orin talked about him." She chewed on her bottom lip. "There's something so off about that interview. There's something she's not saying."

"Do you think she'll even talk to you? If she's been quiet for this long, why would she talk to a stranger now?"

"No clue," she said. "But it's the only idea I've got. And I was wine-drunk when I came up with it."

Michael laughed. Then he fell silent, clearly mulling it over, given the way his mouth was bunched up at the side. "Want me to help you?"

She perked up. "Really?"

"Really." He checked the time on his phone. "We've got about an hour and a half to kill before the next thing."

"What next thing?"

"The next thing is a secret," he said. "But if you wanna head back to my place for a little bit, we can try to find Mindy or her dad in the White Pages—that thing is digitized by now, I think."

When they got back to his house, Baxter greeted them at the door. Riley put her purse on Michael's small, oval coffee table and plopped down on the couch. The cat promptly jumped into her lap, curled into a ball, and started purring.

"Geez," said Michael, sitting next to her once he'd snagged his laptop. "He largely ignores me unless there's food involved."

Riley gave Baxter a scratch behind the ears. He turned his purr up to a level ten.

While Michael searched for Jinwoo, Riley tried to hunt down Mindy. Riley looked up Melinda Cho, too, realizing Mindy could be a nickname.

Michael turned up four Jinwoo Chos in Albuquerque, but only one had an address listed.

Riley found eight Mindy Chos and three Melinda Chos. Few of them had addresses listed either, and of the ones who did, none matched the one Michael found. They then compared listed phone numbers, hoping the listing hadn't been updated since Mindy's father died. But no luck there either.

After calling all four of his numbers and striking out—all four Jinwoos were still alive—Michael took the second half of Riley's list while she worked through the beginning.

They collectively settled on, "Hi. I'm doing an article about Jordanville Ranch and hoped you could answer a few questions about Peter Vonick." If she had no clue what the Jordanville Ranch was and/or had never heard of Pete, it likely wasn't their girl. If she hung up or hesitated for a long time, she likely was.

They both left messages when no one answered. One of the last numbers Riley dialed had a voicemail message that said, "This is Mindy Cho. Sorry I missed your call. Please leave a message after the beep. If you're calling about anything to do with the Jordanville Ranch, *Paranormal Playground*, or that serial killer, just hang up now— you've got the wrong Mindy." Riley hung up.

They'd just worked through the entire list, feeling no more enlightened than when they started, when Michael glanced at his watch. "Oh shit. We should probably head out or we're going to miss the thing."

"What thing is this thing?"

Michael shut his laptop, deposited it on the coffee table, and stood up. "Baxter! Unhand her. We must get to The Thing!"

Riley rolled her eyes and gently placed Baxter on the couch. He curled back into a ball and continued dozing.

After grabbing a duffel bag out of the bedroom, he said, "This is for The Thing."

"You're so weird."

The Thing turned out to be a movie in the park, and the duffel held two blankets, a couple bottles of water, and a few random snacks.

A handful of families were spread out in the grass when they arrived. Kids ran around screaming and laughing, enjoying the late springtime air, most heading to or from the playground on the other end of the park. Riley didn't see a screen anywhere, but the park was flush with the backside of a large building, its back wall a pristine white.

After they set up near the back of the group, the sounds of kids playing a near-distant hum, they plopped down on the blankets.

"I used to come here all the time as a kid," he said. "Parents were big on family outings that didn't require a ton of talking." He handed her a bottle of water.

Taking it, she said, "I've never done this before. Well, my parents and I went to the drive-in a couple times."

"The only problem with this place is that they never announce the movies beforehand. So sometimes you get a super recent one, sometimes a real old one, and sometimes, if you're lucky, you get an indie one from a local studio. I saw one once that actually ended up at Sundance."

"I'm mildly impressed again."

"Mildly. Ha," he said, bumping her shoulder with his. "They usually play two: one PG for the families, then a PG-13 or R for later. The audience shift from families to twenty-somethings is kind of funny. The food trucks should be showing up soon, too."

"How often do you come here?"

He shrugged a shoulder. "Most Sundays. Sometimes I can get my buddy Jupiter to come, but he spends most of his time hitting on whatever unfortunate girls happen to be nearby."

"Hold up," she said, turning to him. "You have a friend named *Jupiter*?"

He laughed. "His parents are a little … strange."

"So when Jupiter isn't with you, you come by yourself?"

"Are you fishing for information about any potential lady friends, Ms. Thomas?"

"You asked about my partying habits!" she said. "I just … seems like it could get kind of sketchy here at night alone."

"I'm an old-ass white guy," he said. "No one is going to look twice at me."

An elaborate series of horns blasted from somewhere on the other side of the playground. This was followed by an elaborate series of shrieks from the children, and then a mass exodus of tiny humans toward the parking lot.

Riley arched a brow in Michael's direction.

"There's a local dessert shop that makes ice cream sandwiches with fresh-baked cookies," he said. "Want one?"

"I would like seven," she said.

"I'll be back!"

"Nothing with nuts!" she called after him. "Or raisins!"

He jogged toward the other end of the park but shot a thumb into the air to acknowledge he'd heard her.

Figuring she had ten to fifteen minutes until he got back—given the insane line that had already formed—she quickly fished her phone out of her bag and called Jade.

"Girl!" Jade said by way of greeting. "Why haven't you called me!"

"I'm calling you now!"

"Tell me everything."

"You got home okay? And Donna and Carla? Jonah didn't starve?"

"I'm home safe and so is everyone else. Jonah is alive but he asked me not to leave him, like, ever again. I left him *twelve* prepared meals to last him three days and he ate all of them by breakfast yesterday. I don't know how that's even possible." Jade sighed loudly. "Now! Give me what I want."

"He's currently getting us ice cream sandwiches before we watch a movie in the park."

"Oh my lord."

"I know." Riley told her about the ten-hour date yesterday. "He's kind of fantastic."

In a voice subdued for Jade, she said, "I'm … I haven't heard you this happy. Like ever. Even before or, hell, *during* stupid Casey 'Daddy Needs to Play' Donovan."

Riley looked down, suddenly feeling sheepish—she wasn't sure why. She pulled out a blade of grass poking between the two blankets.

"I'm so glad I forced you to experience the scariest moment of your life if it means I get to eventually go to your wedding."

"Slow your roll."

"My roll will not be slowed. You deserve someone great."

After a few minutes of catch-up chit chat, Riley saw Michael returning with their sandwiches. "Oh, he's almost back. I'll call you later."

"If you let the hound into the foxhole, just make sure you use protection!"

"Oh my god. Bye, Jade." Riley hung up.

"Everything okay?" he asked as he sat beside her.

She took her sandwich from him, two slightly-warm chocolate chip cookies with a generous helping of vanilla ice cream in the middle. "If I keep seeing you, I'm gonna need to start going to the gym."

"You want me to take it back? I'll eat both."

She cradled the dessert from his grabbing hand. "Don't you dare." He watched her as she took a bite, careful not to send ice cream everywhere. "Oh hell."

"I know," he said, smiling.

"And everything's fine. I was just talking to Jade. Everyone made it back in one piece."

"Good. I got a text from Donna earlier. They're gonna take Carla's car over to my place to pick up Donna's."

"Thank them again for supplying the getaway vehicle."

"Already done."

The movie started about twenty minutes later, the park nearly full. It was an indie sci-fi movie about an alien invasion. Riley wasn't sure how well a PG independent sci-fi film would go, and after about half an hour, she had her answer: not well. The acting was so bad, Riley honestly couldn't tell if it was a spoof or not.

During a terribly choreographed fight scene, Riley did everything she could not to laugh. Michael seemed riveted, so she kept her opinion to herself. He saw movies here all the time; maybe this was some really deep, artsy movie she just didn't "get." For all she knew, it could have been full of biting subtext she was too slow to pick up on.

Michael leaned toward her, his hot breath whispering past her ear. "This is the worst movie I've ever seen in my life."

Riley choked back a laugh.

They stayed close, sides flush, and offered their own commentary. When a scene looked particularly tense, they supplied their own dialogue.

Riley offered a line that so surprised Michael, he let out a sputtering laugh that earned them a scowl from a nearby family. Their kids seemed to be enjoying the movie, while the mother busily played a game on her phone.

"Wanna go for a walk until the next one?" Michael whispered to her.

By way of answer, she grabbed her purse and scrambled to her feet.

When they were out of earshot, Michael said, "Holy shit. I'm sorry. It's like they took all their worst ideas, threw them in a hat, then said, 'You know what? Fuck it. Let's do all of them.'"

"Someone was killed by a sentient umbrella in the first fifteen minutes!"

"Someone paid to make that. They spent actual money, edited it, watched it, and went, 'Yes, we are ready.' I wonder what got cut." Michael laced his fingers through hers. "Hopefully the second one isn't as bad."

"I mean … how could it be worse?"

It was, in fact, worse, as the second movie was a rather racy sequel set on Mars. When the alien queen declared that she "would show the humans how one truly experienced bliss" before using her alien powers to literally disintegrate the clothes off an unsuspecting man, Riley flopped onto her back with her hands clasped over her mouth, trying to keep herself together. She heard the sounds of the human man's rapturous pleasure and kicked her feet in delight at the sheer horror of it.

Michael laid down next to her, propped up on his side. He looked from the screen to her and back again. His mouth dropped open. "She just sprouted three extra hands."

The man on screen let out a sound somewhere between a moan and a scream and Riley lost it again, hands still over her mouth, body shaking. Tears leaked out the sides of her eyes. The rest of the audience—the younger, more hip crowd—seemed to be laughing just as much as she was, at least.

Riley lowered her hands, her head turned toward Michael. "Is it all a joke?"

His mouth still hung open. When there was a collective gasp from the audience, he too winced. He looked at her, eyes wide. "My god."

She cracked up. "I don't think I want to know."

"You don't. I … I can't tell if this is horrible or ingenious."

"Fine line, I guess." Biting her lip, she smiled softly at Michael's profile.

This evening had been what she needed. Something to get her mind off the fact that a nine-year-old ghost boy now haunted her apartment.

With his head still propped up on his hand, Michael asked, "Are you having fun even if this is a crime—I think—against film?"

The dim lighting, only punctuated periodically by the flicker of the movie, cast soft shadows over his face. Why'd he have to be so damned handsome? "Yes."

"Good." The just-past-casual stare was back and his gaze shifted to her mouth for a moment. "I'm not sure how much longer I'm going to be able to keep myself from kissing you."

She flushed. "Maybe you shouldn't keep fighting it."

He grinned at her, scooting closer so his chest was pressed to her side. Reaching out his free hand, he caressed the side of her face with his thumb, his palm cupping the back of her head. He stared at her for only a moment longer before he lowered his mouth to hers.

He smelled like soap and grass and tasted like chocolate. One of her arms snaked around him, her fingers in his hair. He adjusted himself so their chests were pressed together, one of his legs tangled up in hers.

Their mouths parted and his tongue glided against hers. He let out an involuntary groan that was far sexier than his I-just-lost-at-air-hockey-again groan, and it sent a spark of heat down her body.

They broke apart for a moment, her arms around his neck, and one of his hands resting on the bare skin of her hip. She hadn't registered his hand sneaking under her shirt. They breathed heavily, foreheads pressed together.

"Have I mentioned that I like you?" he asked, thumb sweeping slowly back and forth across her side. It felt like her skin was on fire.

"I think I figured it out," she said.

Someone very loudly clearing their throat caught Riley's attention. She managed to turn her head, despite the weird position she was in, and lock eyes with an irate woman who'd stuck around despite the drastic shift in the audience's average age.

"Get a room," she mouthed, then proceeded to whisper to the woman next to her.

Then the second woman shot them a death glare.

Riley snorted, looking away. "I think we're offending the patrons of this fine cinematic event."

"Maybe we should go," he said, voice soft. He ran a thumb down the length of her jaw, looking at her like it was taking all his willpower not to take her right here in front of the offended old biddies. "If we're going to continue taking this slow, we need to be somewhere where I'm not lying next to you—hell, *sitting* next to you—because you're driving me fucking crazy."

Riley bit her bottom lip, cheeks flushing.

"Not helping," he said with a sigh.

"Okay, tiger, let's go," she said. "Gotta walk it off."

He groaned in disappointment as she disentangled herself from him.

After gathering up their things, Michael offered an, "Evening, ladies," to the grumpy pair beside them.

The women scoffed at his politeness. Riley was fairly certain one of them uttered a "Why, I *never* …" at them as they left.

They dropped their things off at the car, then went on a stroll through downtown Los Lunas. Stores and restaurants started to close for the night, but handfuls of people were still out and about. A pair of rowdy boys ran down the street with ice cream cones in their hands, two adults walking hand in hand behind them. Riley figured one boy wasn't their child, due to the lighter tone of both them and one of the boys. The other boy looked a few years younger, his skin a creamy brown.

Riley and Michael moved at a safe distance behind them, fingers laced together, keeping up a steady stream of conversation that Riley hoped was helping to cool Michael down. That and the light breeze.

They walked past a few bars, a Middle Eastern restaurant, and a couple of little clothing shops Riley was sure she couldn't afford. A busier street was a block ahead, and Michael told her there was a really great coffee shop on the upcoming corner.

Riley's attention kept shifting to the little boys running out in front of them, getting further and further away from the pair. The adults didn't seem worried, but Riley had a sinking feeling in the pit of her stomach. They were getting too close to the busy street ahead.

Her fingers instinctively squeezed Michael's.

"What's up?" he asked, glancing over at her.

But she couldn't take her eyes off the boys. Their excited chatter and gleeful shouts seemed to echo, bouncing off buildings and trees.

When they came to a stop as they reached the intersection, the boys turned to look over their shoulders. Ice cream cones still firmly clasped in their hands, melted chocolate ran over the fair fingers of the older boy.

Riley and Michael caught up with them, the six waiting until the red neon hand flipped to the walking sign.

The woman glanced back at Riley and smiled weakly—just acknowledging that someone was there behind her. Her face was pale, bags under her eyes. Riley had never seen the woman before but felt a sudden urge to ask her what was wrong. To ask her why she looked so miserable.

"Race you!"

Riley's eyes snapped to one of the little boys who now dared the other to chase him just as the walking signal changed. They bolted across the intersection, focused on outracing the other. Focused on licking melted, sticky chocolate off hands. They didn't see the car run the red light.

"No!" Riley called out, yanking her hand free from Michael's and slamming into the pair in front of her.

She came to a sudden stop on the curb, heart pounding violently, holding her breath as the giant SUV zipped through the intersection. Riley waited for the crash of bodies against metal, to see ice cream cones smashed in the street. But there was no sound.

The SUV—with a license plate frame stating that the driver would rather be fishing—blasted through the intersection, and after half a block just … disappeared. Poof. Into thin air.

Riley stumbled back a step, right into Michael who had rushed up to grab her. Swaying, she sat hard on the sidewalk, head in her hands.

Michael squatted before her. "Riley? Ry, Jesus, what happened?"

Those boys weren't there. Well, they had been. Just not today.

Swallowing, she looked up again, eyeing the intersection. And then it changed, just as it had back at the ranch. Two boys running into an intersection too soon, a driver not paying attention, limbs at awkward angles, chocolate ice cream mixing in the street with blood.

"You didn't see them, did you?" Riley asked, attention shifting to Michael's concerned face. "The little boys with the ice cream?"

"What are you talking about?" He placed the back of his hand on her forehead. "You're pale. Are you okay? You look like you've just seen a—oh. Oh! Shit. You saw a ghost."

"Two of them. Two boys."

A strangled sob shifted Riley's attention again. This time to the sad woman who'd been standing in front of her. She hadn't crossed the street.

"You … you saw them? My Henry? You saw him?"

Shit. Why was her … *gift* … flaring up now? Her apartment wasn't safe, and now the outside world wasn't safe either. How could she avoid all this if it kept coming to *her*?

The trip to the ranch had altered something in her. She wanted to turn it back off.

"It was a hit and run." The woman's tone sobered, and her husband—who looked supremely uncomfortable—tried to pull her away, but the woman wouldn't be moved. "My baby and his cousin were run over and left here to die in the street like animals. That bastard ran over my baby and just—" She didn't finish her sentence, choked off by her own sobs.

The man wrapped his arms around her. "She insists on walking down here every night. It's been three months." It almost sounded like an apology.

Riley looked down the street, seeing a flash of the speeding SUV again. Voice hollow and distant, she said, "I saw the license plate."

The couple froze for a moment. The woman furiously wiped her face with her hands. "You were here?"

With an exhausted sigh, Riley told these two broken people about her ability. When doubt crept onto the man's face and pulled his brows together, she told them what the boys had been wearing. What kind of ice cream they had. How one of Henry's shoes had been found in the intersection—she left out the detail that Henry had been hit so hard that his shoe had been knocked clear off him and his body had been dragged several feet before rolling off into the gutter.

Thankfully, they believed her without her needing to get too far into the gory details. She told them the license plate number and what had been on the frame. Maybe police could get a warrant for checking out the SUV and luck out and find blood on the front fender. Thanks to her penchant for *Dateline* and cop shows, she knew all too well that blood hung around even after a good cleaning.

Riley hoped it would help them.

When the couple walked off, holding each other up as they both cried, she looked at Michael's shell-shocked face. "I think I need to go home."

CHAPTER 14

Though Riley's shift at the Laughing Tiger wasn't until two, she sneaked in just under the wire. Every time she'd fallen asleep last night, she'd relived the accident. Sometimes the victim was Michael. But usually it was a twin pair of Petes—one in his black-and-blue-checkered jacket, and one in his Scooby Doo shirt and Batman pajama pants. Over and over and over.

Luckily his spirit hadn't made an appearance all night, though she wondered if he somehow was responsible for her nightmares.

At the end of her shift, half starved, she checked her phone as she walked to her car parked behind the restaurant. It was just after ten and she hadn't eaten since noon. With a bag of leftover food clenched in her hand, she read her texts from Michael—all with some version of "I'm here if you need anything." She also had a voicemail from a private number.

She flopped into her car, the smell of hours-old shumai, sausage rolls, and dumplings causing her stomach to rumble. As the cabin lights dimmed to black, she dialed her inbox.

After a long pause—one long enough that Riley wondered if it was an accidental message left by a telemarketer—the message started: "Hi. This is Mindy Cho returning Riley's call. I, uhh … I don't know how you know that name. If you're friends with Ha—if you're just trying to screw with me, don't worry, okay? Lips are sealed. Just … leave me alone."

Riley's heart hammered in her chest. She'd actually called back! Mindy Cho was still in Albuquerque. She in no way sounded like she wanted to talk, but that was because she'd figured Riley was up to something. And she'd heard of Pete before! That had to be a good sign.

She stress-ate four dumplings in as many minutes.

Calling Mindy back would have to wait until tomorrow. Since the number had come through as private, Riley would have to go through her entire list of numbers again and hope Mindy picked up.

With similar work hours tomorrow, she'd need to get her act together earlier. And she needed to figure out what the hell to say to convince Mindy to give her a chance.

The next morning, around ten, Riley set up her laptop, note-pad, and a mug of coffee on the coffee table. She sat on the floor between the couch and table. One day, she'd actually buy grown-up dining room furniture.

The objective of the call was to convince Mindy to meet her in person; hanging up on someone was a lot easier than literally walking out on them. Even if she was uncomfortable, Mindy might be more willing to tough out a conversation if they were in a coffee shop. Especially if Riley promised to pay.

She scrolled through her call history and dialed the first one. Her heart thrashed around in her chest like a trapped bird. How many calls did it take before one was considered a stalker?

Chewing on her thumbnail, she gave herself a pep talk. *Be polite. Don't say anything too weird. Remember, she's been through a lot and has every right to be skeptical.*

Voicemail.

"Thank you for returning my call, Mindy. This is Riley again. I promise you this isn't a joke. I just want to talk." She rattled off her number, hung up, and tried the next, leaving an identical message.

While she listened to the phone ring during her third call, Pete flickered into view, head cocked as he stood in front of her TV.

Riley yelped and let out series of truly profane curses. "Not now, kid! Really bad timing."

"Uh … you called *me*, lady," someone said in Riley's ear.

Riley's posture straightened, the ghost child wandering her living room momentarily forgotten. *Oh shit. She answered! Shit.* "Uh … Mindy? This is Riley. Riley Thomas? I called you on Sunday about the—"

"Oh. It's you. I told you to leave me alone."

"I just want to talk. Honest."

"Who put you up to this? I'm *really* not in the mood. I've had a real shitty week and I don't need another jackass with a hard-on for serial killers to start blowing up my phone. So what do you want? You've got roughly thirty seconds before I hang up and block your number."

Jesus.

"Does the name Pete Vonick mean anything to you?"

The flickering figure of the boy in question turned at the sound of his own name, abandoning his perusal of her shelf of knick-knacks. A delicate glass fairy figurine her mother had given her when Riley had been around Pete's age had caught his eye.

Mindy didn't say anything. But she hadn't hung up either. Riley's hold on the other woman felt too precarious to drop the "I see dead people" bomb just yet. She scrambled for something else to say.

Something to make Mindy realize Riley wasn't some nutjob, some freak with a "hard-on" for serial killers.

Pete shifted in front of her, pulling her attention to his face. When they made eye contact, a name popped into her head again. *Frances*. The moment she heard it, Pete's image flickered dangerously—like the disrupted signal from a TV's antenna. Then he vanished altogether.

The flash of images she'd seen in Hyssop Room came flooding back. The pair of girls, one with a face beaten so badly the features were unrecognizable, the other sprawled on the floor, legs tangled in sheets.

"When you were at the ranch, were there two of you there at a time? More? Did you ever stay together in the same room?"

Mindy made a sound like she was going to reply, then stopped.

"Did … others try to escape? Had two of you been planning to make a break for it and Orin attacked the other? Beat her up so badly that her eyes swelled shut? He dragged her out of the room while leaving the other girl on the floor."

The sound from Mindy was more like a choked sob now. Softly, she said, "Why are you doing this?"

"Pete … the … Pete died at that ranch, didn't he? Orin killed him. Killed him first. Killed him before Gabriella was even on his radar."

The pause was long and drawn out again, and when Mindy finally spoke, her voice wavered. "Do you know him? Is this some kind of test to see if I'll crack?"

Brow furrowed, Riley cocked her head. "Know who? Pete? He—"

"*No*," Mindy snapped, word sharp and biting, like her teeth were clenched.

Riley desperately tried to remember what Mindy's voicemail had said. Hadn't she asked if Riley had been friends with someone? Someone who knew … "Hank?"

Mindy hung up.

"Shit!" Riley redialed, but it just rang endlessly. Had there been an answering machine and Mindy unplugged it so Riley couldn't even leave another message?

Hank as in … Hank *Gerber*? Riley had thought that was a possibility when she'd been wine-drunk, but the idea had started to lose traction once she'd sobered up. The police had never found a trace of Hank Gerber. Most assumed he'd been a fever dream of Orin's. A scapegoat to help minimize his sentence.

What the hell was she supposed to do now?

"Any bright ideas, kid?" she asked, but Pete didn't reappear. He hadn't been completely solid-looking since yesterday and hadn't spoken since then either.

By the time Riley left for work just before two, Mindy still hadn't called back.

Two days later, Riley lay in bed staring at the ceiling, trying to ignore the fact that Pete had, once again, found a way to drift his beanie onto her bed while she slept. She saw the thing out of the corner of her eye, its grimy maroon fabric lying on top of her clean, baby blue comforter.

Pete was nowhere in sight. How much energy did it take to perform his little tricks? When he wasn't wandering around her apartment, where was he? Charging up his ghostly battery so he could pop in later to scare the bejesus out of her?

Her phone rang, buzzing loudly on her nightstand.

When she saw the call came from a private number, she nearly fell off her bed in her haste to get the thing unplugged and answered. "Hello?" she said breathlessly.

"Am I interrupting something?"

"Oh my god. Hi. You called back."

"How do you know about … about … *Hank*?" She practically whispered the last word, clearly apprehensive to even speak the name.

"Honestly? I don't," Riley said, sitting up in bed now, her legs folded beneath her. "Just hear me out, okay?"

Mindy sighed heavily into the phone, but neither said no, nor hung up.

"I'm a medium … you know, like a psychic? I can communicate with spirits."

"For *fuck's* sake …" Mindy said. "Another one of you? Seriously?"

Riley swallowed. "Other psychics have contacted you?"

"I've lost count."

She was at a loss. Had Pete tried this with others, too?

"You're the first one who doesn't sound totally batshit, though," Mindy finally said. "I … don't get why you're so desperate to talk to me."

"I have reason to believe that the body of Peter Vonick is still on the Jordanville Ranch property. I can't free his spirit unless I find it. Since you're the only person left who has a connection to the ranch from back then, I thought you might know something about him."

"Well, I don't."

Dammit.

"What … what you said about the girl who got beaten to a pulp? And how there was another girl at the property?"

"Yeah?"

"The girl on the ground was me," Mindy said.

"No way." The Hyssop Room had been Mindy's room. "Who was the other girl?"

"That's the thing," she said. "What you described happened, but it wasn't me and another girl. It was me and … and …"

Riley swallowed. "Hank?"

Mindy's breath whooshed through the phone in a rush. "This is going to sound super paranoid, but I don't like talking about shit like this on the phone."

Riley glanced at her alarm clock. Eleven-fifteen. "So let's talk in person. I'm in Albuquerque too. I have to be at work by two, but we could maybe meet around noon?" Long pause. "I'll buy you lunch."

Another pause. "Yeah, okay. Where?"

Riley shot a fist into the air.

They settled on the Redbird Café, about a fifteen-minute drive for them both; they'd meet in the middle. Riley had been there once with Jade—the place had a nice outside patio area where they might have some privacy if the place wasn't too crowded. It usually filled up for lunch, but it was local business people running in to grab to-go orders before rushing back to their offices.

Riley requested a spot outside in the corner. There were a few other occupied tables out there, but the patrons all sat alone, busily typing on phones or tablets with one hand while shoveling food in their mouths with the other.

At a little before noon, Riley got a text from an unknown number.

This is Mindy. Should be there in five or so. Had a hard time finding parking.

Riley programmed Mindy's cell into her phone, then texted

back: **No worries. I'm on the patio. Wearing a black top and slacks.**

Riley's leg bounced under the table.

And then Mindy was there, poking her head out the open doorway to the patio, gaze shifting this way and that. Riley raised a hand in greeting. When Mindy spotted her, she offered a tight-lipped smile, both hands tightly clasping the strap of her messenger bag.

Riley stood as she approached, the heavy feet of her iron patio chair scraping loudly across the cement floor. They both flinched.

Holding out a hand to Mindy, Riley said, "Thanks for meeting with me."

Mindy nodded, giving her hand a quick, firm shake.

The waiter brought them menus.

Mindy looked less haggard than she had in the last video. Her jet-black hair was still lightly streaked with gray, but it was down around her shoulders now. The freckles were less prominent than when she was a teenager, but Riley wasn't sure if that was due to age or makeup. She wore jeans and a T-shirt of a band Riley had never heard of. Mindy pulled the strap of her bag over her head, then draped it on the back of her chair.

"So, a psychic, huh?" Mindy said, folding her arms and resting them on the table after they ordered.

Riley shrugged. "Technical term is medium, but yeah."

"This like your job or something? You lure me in with details no one else knows and then make me cough up cash to talk to the ghosts of the girls who didn't make it? Offer me closure as long as the check I write has enough zeros at the end?"

"*What?*" Riley asked, head reeling back as if Mindy had slapped her. "Do you just not trust *anyone* or have people truly been that shitty to you about all this?"

"Both."

Riley wanted to reach across the table to grab the Mindy's hand. But given how jumpy she seemed, Riley figured that would be a surefire way to scare her off, so she kept her hands to herself. "No. Not my job. I don't want money. I have a nine-year-old male ghost wandering my apartment and I want to help him. And my attempt to do that led to you. Granted, when I came up with said plan, I was wine-drunk."

Mindy fought a smile. "Are you usually wine-drunk when hatching your schemes?"

"I'm usually wine-drunk when ghosts show up unannounced."

The silence that descended on them was long and just awkward enough that Riley's leg started to bounce under the table again.

"I don't really know what to say," Mindy finally admitted. "I just … I don't talk about my time there. Unless it's to my shrink. And even then, I feel squirrely as hell."

"Can you tell me about this Hank guy?"

Mindy flinched at the sound of his name. She tucked her hair behind her ears. Folded her arms. "How do I know I can trust you with any of this? Why should I? I don't know you from Adam."

"Yet here you are." When Mindy didn't reply to that, Riley said, "I just want to help. Hell, if all you need is someone to listen to you, I'm good with that. As corny as it sounds, I feel like I'm here talking to you now for a reason. Maybe this is the universe's way of letting you know it's safe."

Mindy readjusted her shoulders, glanced over one, scanning the sidewalk full of people rushing around on their lunch breaks. Was she still looking for someone after all this time?

"In that video of you outside the police station, you said he was still out there watching you. That you worried he'd find you? Did you mean Hank?"

Mindy visibly swallowed. Then nodded.

Hank Gerber *was* a real person.

The waiter arrived with their food then, and they waited a minute while he came back with a lemonade for Riley and an iced tea for Mindy. Riley low-key wanted to slap the guy for interrupting.

"So ... uhh ..." Mindy said, staring at her newly arrived sandwich. "You asked before if there were ever two girls there at the same time. There were, but never more than two—alive, I mean—at the ranch."

Riley swallowed and nodded. It hit her then how close Mindy had been to being number six. That there could have been others—dozens of others—had she not managed to escape. Who knew how many lives she'd saved by making a break for it.

There was also a sick sense of excitement now—and disgust with herself for being so enthralled by something that had happened directly to Mindy.

"It was me and the second to the last girl—Janay. Orin ... Orin liked her because her skin was so dark." Mindy worked her jaw, like she was somewhere between crying and throwing up and wasn't sure which one would win out. She lowered her gaze for a moment, then looked back up at Riley. "He liked finding ways to batter her to see how she'd bruise in comparison to someone lighter-skinned."

A memory from the night in the cellar came back to her then. The image of blood dripping off the tips of dark fingers. Riley's stomach roiled.

"I think Orin liked to have one 'fresh' girl there as well as a nearly destroyed one. I don't know if it was a psychological thing for the new ones—giving us a taste of what was coming next—or if he just liked seeing the comparison."

"Sick bastard."

"Yeah," Mindy said. "But, uh …" She blew out a breath, rocking gently back and forth in her chair, the pressure of the table's edge against her forearms turning her skin white in two horizontal lines. "One or two girls before Janay, Orin brought Hank to the ranch. He was a runaway too. He was seventeen by the time I was taken, so he must have been thirteen or something when Orin nabbed him?"

"A male victim … like Pete?" But that instantly felt wrong. Mindy could hardly say the guy's name, even all this time later.

Mindy shook her head. "Orin used Hank to lure girls. He started showing up at the shelter where I was staying. He was a good-looking guy, really nice in a kinda understated way? I was in a really bad place mentally and he knew what to say to make me think I finally found someone who got me, you know?"

Riley nodded.

"So when he told me he'd found this cool place we could hang out, have some alone time …" She shrugged. "I went with him thinking we were just gonna fool around. Instead Orin was waiting for me in the dark."

"Jesus Christ." Riley fought the urge again to reach across the table to squeeze her hand. "I swear I'm not judging you. I … just … why haven't you mentioned any of this to the police? What happened to Hank?"

"Ever wondered how I got out?"

The question took Riley a bit by surprise. Very little time in the reports focused on her escape. From the sporadic reporting of it, Riley had pieced it together. Mindy had claimed Orin went to bed at a certain time every night, like clockwork, yet something had upset him that day, and though he tied her to the bedpost like usual, he'd closed the bedroom door without locking it. It was unusual for him to be so careless, so she'd known this was likely her only chance. She'd nearly broken every bone in her hands getting loose, and from there, it had just been a matter of getting outside as quietly as possible before running like hell out into the dark forest.

Riley had never given that part of the story much thought. Of all the things she could have lied about, why would her escape have been one of them? "So how did you *really* get out?"

Mindy chugged half of her iced tea. "I wish we were wine-drunk right now."

Riley managed a half smile.

"Hank let me out." At Riley's confused expression, Mindy said, "He was pissed at Orin." She guzzled down the rest of her tea, then folded her arms on the table. She had a black, leather band around one of her wrists. "Orin wasn't interested in us sexually, which I guess was a small blessing. But Hank was another story. Orin was obsessed with John Hunter, so—"

"Sorry. Who?"

"Oh, right. Sorry. John Hunter was a Scottish guy who lived in London in 1700-something. Father of modern surgery. Had really extensive anatomy records—like crazy extensive for someone from that time," Mindy said. "He needed bodies to study, so he and his brother hired graverobbers."

"Wait, this is real?"

"Yep. They were called the Resurrectionists. John and his brother didn't want details on how the bodies were obtained as long as they got the bodies. Orin idolized the guy."

Riley knew Orin had fancied himself some kind of doctor. "So … what he was doing to you girls was some even more perverted version of that?"

"Yeah. Orin thought John had sold himself short by mostly working on cadavers," Mindy said. "Only problem was, collecting live patients was even more illegal than stealing already-dead people."

"And Hank was the start of his Resurrectionist crew?"

"I think so," Mindy said. "Hank wasn't super into it like Orin was, but he helped him just the same. Hank liked having a roof over his head and food in his belly and the relative freedom to run around in the woods like a damn animal. Orin, on the other hand, genuinely thought his work would help revolutionize medicine."

Riley could hardly process how ten shades of crazy that all was.

A snapshot from her time in the cellar flashed in her head again. "Did Orin have a lot of notes and books on anatomy?"

"*Tons*," she said. "They were stacked all over the cellar."

"And books and notes about John Hunter?"

"Oh yeah," she said. "He was even working on his own biography of sorts on him."

"It seems weird this wasn't ever mentioned in reports," Riley said. "I could see the media having a field day with it."

"Yeah, I thought it was a little strange too. I figured they didn't think it was relevant." She shrugged. "It was even weirder that Orin didn't make a fuss about it. He was the kind of guy who would have wanted to be buried with his life's work. So, considering that wasn't an option, I figured he would have made a request to keep it preserved. Instead he never even mentioned it. But maybe he knew he wasn't getting out again unless it was in a body bag, so why bother?"

Riley thought about that for a while. "You were saying something earlier about how Orin didn't see you all … uh …"

"Sexually? You can say it. So, yeah, Hank saw us—Janay and me, anyway; I don't know about the others—like girls *first*, and patients second. Hormones going into overdrive, I guess.

"Janay was … not doing well for most of my time there, so Hank left her alone. He would talk a lot about how pretty she'd been when he first lured her there; how it was such a tragedy that she wasn't pretty anymore," Mindy said. "So he tried to get *me* to like him. I *hated* him, of course, since he was the reason I was there.

"I think he seriously was upset by that—that I wanted nothing to do with him. But he tried anyway. He had access to all the rooms in the house, except the cellar and our rooms, but he was pretty good at picking locks, so he'd bring me books or magazines sometimes. Or he'd save his dessert and leave it in my room.

"He was the one who told me about Pete, actually—Orin told Hank about him because he was his first 'patient.' Orin was stupid and snatched the kid from a store or something without thinking about it. Killed him too quick because he hadn't figured out what he was doing yet. I guess Hank thought telling me Orin's secrets would make me like him more.

"After a few weeks of Hank's—I don't know, flirting?—I tried to make him think I liked him so I could convince him we should leave together. It kind of worked at first, but he'd get mad if I wouldn't let him do more than kiss me.

"He backed off at first when I told him no, but he got more and more angry about it. There was only so much he could do though, since Orin didn't know Hank had found a way to get into my room even though he was 'strictly forbidden.' If something happened to me, Orin would know Hank did it. And he avoided pissing Orin off if he could help it."

Mindy had been on a roll, but she stopped talking abruptly. She grabbed her glass and sloshed the contents, but all that was left was ice. She crunched down on a piece.

"You all right?" Riley asked.

"Yeah. Just give me a sec." Mindy crunched another piece of ice. Put her glass down. Crossed her arms. "So, uh … one night, Hank let himself into my room while I was sleeping and pinned me down. I woke up and couldn't move my arms. He said if I didn't give him what he wanted … he'd kill me before Orin got the chance."

When Mindy's eyes welled with tears, so did Riley's. She didn't want to hear anymore. But she could tell Mindy needed to get it out.

Mindy wiped a tear away quickly. "He pinned my arms behind and underneath me, holding them there with his hand and the weight of my body, then yanked my shirt up with his free hand. His hands were grabbing at my breasts so hard it hurt—pinching, smashing. He didn't seem to know what he was doing.

"It's like … I knew he wanted me on a base level, but he didn't know what that meant?" She swiped away another tear. "I *screamed*. As loud as I could. Just … I'd managed to avoid anything like that at the shelters. I don't know how I did, because so many of the girls I knew had been raped. I just snapped. I'd never made sounds like that before.

"I lost it so completely that it scared him, and I was able to knock him off me. I was tangled up in the sheets and hit the floor trying to get away. I was literally crawling to the door when Orin came in.

"He figured out pretty quickly what was going on. He grabbed Hank and pulled him out of the room. Whatever you were told by spirits or whatever vision you had about someone getting beaten up—it was from *that* night. It wasn't another girl who had the shit kicked out of them. It was Hank. It was the beginning of the end, that night."

Frances. But … a boy, not a girl. *Francis.*

Mindy tucked her hair behind her ears with both hands. "Orin pulled Hank out and locked the door but didn't tie me up like usual—that part of the story was true. I was too scared to try and leave, though. Plus, I heard Hank screaming downstairs—I was totally freaked out.

"I didn't sleep a wink, and when my door was unlocked in the morning, it was Hank—face a swollen, bloody mess—who brought me my tray of food, not Orin. Orin stood in the doorway watching him. He made Hank tell me that the patients were to be respected and that he'd never touch me inappropriately again.

"Orin took away his keys and restricted his ability to roam the grounds like he used to—he could have picked the lock on my door whenever he wanted, but he didn't. I could tell even then how mad Hank was."

Riley hugged her arms to her body.

"Once a week, Orin made us scrub the cellar. So, a few days later, Hank and I were down there cleaning up—Janay had died the day before—when Hank told me he was really and truly sorry and he was going to get me out. I didn't believe him.

"He even told me he loved me."

Riley's face screwed up.

"I know," she said. "Orin, a couple nights a month, left the ranch. I don't know why. I'm guessing to troll for more kids to snatch. But he was usually gone for hours. Orin was gone that night. A lot of the time, he took Hank with him, but Hank was under house arrest.

"It was still light out when I heard crashes down the hall—Hank had managed to kick his door down. Orin had locked him in too.

"But then I heard him go down the steps, so I figured he'd decided to make a run for it and left me there to rot. I heard the front door open and close. Heard Hank losing his shit outside. He already was a little off, but he *really* went off the deep end after Orin beat him.

"I just lay there waiting. After what happened with Hank, Orin stopped tying me to the bedposts. He felt bad for me, I guess. Which was weird, given everything.

"I woke up out of a dead sleep hours later. It was dark out. Footsteps were pounding up the stairs. I had no idea if it was Hank or Orin, but I was scared out of my mind of them both.

"I was curled up in the corner when Hank picked the lock on my door. His face was covered in this red stuff, his eyes were swollen, and he had scratches on his face like he'd just gotten attacked by a cat or something.

"I got ready to scream, but Hank said, 'No point in screaming when no one can hear you but me. Now's our chance.'

"He told me that he'd 'done something' and needed my help. Last time that little shit lured me somewhere, I ended up at the ranch, so I sure as hell didn't want to help him. But I was thinking maybe Orin came back and Hank ambushed the guy and needed me to help him hide the body or something.

"When we got outside, Orin's car was still gone, so I knew that wasn't it. Hank yelled at me to follow him and then he started running for the forest.

"He was crazed—like worse than I'd ever seen him—and he was muttering to himself about how 'she shouldn't have done that.'"

"She? She who?"

Mindy frowned, gaze focused on the table. "I don't know. I've felt guilty about it ever since."

Riley wanted to ask more questions but told herself to shut up.

"We kept running through the forest, off the path, and I got the worst feeling. He kept looking behind him to make sure I was still there. Said we were close.

"When his back was to me again, I found this small log. When he turned to check on me, I swung, hitting him square in the nose. The bones cracked, he screamed and hit the ground. Blood poured out of his face like a waterfall. I whacked him again on the side of the head and *boom*—lights out. That's when I ran for the road."

Riley's mouth hung slightly open. This all brought Riley back to the same question: why had Mindy pulled back on saying someone else had been out there? The same person Orin had tried to incriminate. Especially if he'd "done" something to someone else.

"Before you get all judgy," Mindy said, "I didn't even know until after I got out what Hank's last name was. He was just Hank when we were at the ranch. Second, I didn't tell police about him in any detail because I was honestly scared I'd killed him. I hit him so hard and then ran—I didn't know what happened to him. What if after everything, *I* ended up in jail? I was a kid and I was scared.

"So after … everything … I really wanted something like a normal life. I just wanted to pretend none of it happened. I was living with a foster family when school started back up. A few days after I started going to school again, I was walking to my foster parents' house when Hank rounded a corner."

"Oh hell."

Mindy nodded, chewing on her bottom lip. "I was so scared, I didn't even think to run. At least his stupid face didn't look perfect anymore, since I'd broken his nose."

Riley offered a faint smile despite feeling sick to her stomach.

"Hank asked if anyone knew about him. I said I'd mentioned him to my lawyer and my lawyer was looking into finding him—

mainly 'cause I'd been scared I'd killed him and my lawyer figured it could hurt my case some if I murdered a kid.

"But my lawyer couldn't tell the police about Hank 'cause I asked him not to and he was bound to that because of client confidentiality. My lawyer couldn't find a Hank Gerber who fit the description anyway. Hank told me to call off the search. I guess some guys who looked like private eyes were following him—but I think he was just super paranoid.

"Hank ambushed me on my walk home several more times over the next few months. Even when I changed routes, he'd find me. I'd ask my foster mom to pick me up for a couple weeks—didn't tell her why—and then the day I started walking home again at a totally different time, he'd pop up. One day he grabbed me and pulled me into an alley—slammed the back of my head into the brick wall. He said people were after him and it was my fault, and if I didn't get them to back off, he was going to kill me. He pulled a pocket knife on me and held it to my throat and said Orin taught him tons of ways to kill a person slowly. I didn't doubt for a second that he was bluffing."

"Jesus." They sounded like two peas in a pod, Hank and Orin. "So … was it *you* who requested the formal interview?"

"Yeah … well, my lawyer. He thought it was a good idea. Said it would help bring me closure. But I'm assuming it was about him getting publicity since he was interviewed, too."

Riley remembered him as a skinny, bald man. "And Hank stopped harassing you after that?"

Mindy shifted in her chair. "Kind of. Still saw him randomly around town, but he didn't talk to me that often. Like he just wanted me to know he was watching. But it was enough to drive a girl crazy. Always worried I'd run into him. Always looking over my shoulder.

Always wondering if it would go from just watching to something … else.

"After high school, I moved to Los Angeles for a little while. I went for college but also to see my mother's family. I think I just needed a change of scenery—needed to get away from Hank."

"What'd you study in school?"

Her shoulders relaxed a little. "Random stuff. I ended up with an AA in humanities. I figured out I loved music, too. I turned into a total cliché and joined a garage band."

Riley grinned. "What kind of band?"

"Rock," she said. "I was the lead singer and played a little guitar. We called ourselves the Crooked Horseshoe."

Riley cocked her head. "Wouldn't that just be a straight line?"

Mindy laughed. "We thought it was edgy."

"I love it."

"We went on a tour across the country for a year or so. Made garbage money, but it was amazing, experience-wise. I just bounced around for a while. Went to Korea for a bit, too."

"I guess if Hank was trying to stalk you, he'd have a hard time tracking you down."

Mindy nodded. "I get occasional blocked calls on my cell. Hang-up calls on the house phone started a couple months ago. Could be telemarketers. But some part of me always wonders if it's him. It happened a lot at my aunt's place in L.A. when I first moved there. It's part of why I panicked when you called. Usually the true assholes— the obsessive people—find my cell number somehow. I'm pretty sure someone doxed me while I was in L.A. I was getting bombarded with calls. I've changed my cell number about a dozen times.

"I rented out the house I got from my dad until I was ready to come back. Which was about two years ago. Just in time for the airing of that goddamn show." Mindy shot her a *look*.

Riley winced. "What made you come back?"

Mindy gave a full body shrug. "I don't know. This place holds nothing but bad memories for me, really. But it's also all I have. Nowhere else ever felt right."

Riley wanted to say there were countless places she hadn't seen yet. But maybe Mindy was drawn here, was stuck in the city, just like Orin and Pete were trapped at the ranch. Something kept her tethered to this place.

"Hank hasn't contacted you at all since you've been back?"

Mindy shook her head.

Suddenly, Riley's phone blared, her alarm warning her that she now only had half an hour to get to work. "Shit." Had over an hour already passed? Neither one of them had touched their food. "I'm going to go pay the bill then pee. I'll be back."

After taking care of both things in under ten minutes, and armed with two to-go boxes, she went back to the patio. Mindy had inhaled her sandwich.

Shoveling her slightly soggy Cobb salad into a box, Riley said, "I can't thank you enough for talking to me."

"Not sure how any of that would be helpful." Mindy stood, both hands awkwardly gripping the strap of her messenger bag again. Her face grew bright red.

"Hey," Riley said. "You okay?"

"I didn't … I really didn't plan to tell you all that," she said, her gaze focused on the tips of her combat boots. "It just kind of poured out and I couldn't stop."

"I'm glad you felt comfortable enough."

Mindy shrugged. "I guess I figured you might know a lot of it anyway, because psychic."

Smiling, Riley said, "Will you keep in touch?"

"Sure."

"I'm not a hugger, but …"

The embrace was fierce, but short.

After collecting her stuff and calling a quick goodbye, Riley bolted for her car.

1980-1983

O rin couldn't pinpoint what it was about Hank Gerber that drew him to the thirteen-year-old boy, but there was an immediate kinship. Orin had never gotten along well with his little sister Beverly and never connected with his classmates. The moment Bev was old enough to leave home, she did so without looking back. Not even after their mother died. Orin thought it might be connected to the time he'd tied her to a tree, but he couldn't be sure.

Perhaps Hank was the brother he never had, or the son he assumed he'd never create. Women complicated things too much. He couldn't possibly bring a woman into his life when his devotion to anatomy was sure to make her jealous. Besides, they were such fragile things. He couldn't have a woman around who fainted at the merest sight of blood.

He knew his methods for procuring specimens were unorthodox. He didn't need the stress of a woman focusing on the *how* of his studies rather than the *why* and alerting authorities.

No, when he became a renowned surgeon, and the general public learned the brilliance of his methods, then he'd be able to devote his time to finding a proper wife.

John Hunter had married, but Orin thought the surgeon's brother, William, came closer to the truth: the lives they led, ones devoted to anatomy and the exploration of biological sciences, were wholly incompatible with marriage.

When Orin needed his carnal itch scratched, he'd drive into town and pay for a prostitute. They didn't care who he was or what occupied his time. They both got what they wanted and then Orin could go back to his house alone with only his patients. Just as he preferred it.

So it was a surprise to even himself when he found Hank—not because he fancied the boy as a patient, but because he thought he might be the start of his team of recruiters. He had admired this too about John Hunter. His idol had his Resurrectionist crew bring him corpses, so why shouldn't Orin enlist the assistance of someone like-minded to assist in his own endeavors?

Orin knew he wasn't the most handsome of men. He couldn't be bothered to keep up his appearance and this got no better as he aged. Young girls skirted around him when he was in public. Women in general gave him a wide berth. How could he procure patients if they were too leery to give him a chance? He'd never really known how to interact with young girls—his failed relationship with Bev was proof enough of that.

Gabriella, the girl in his house now, had made quite the fuss when he'd snagged her. He had followed her down a deserted, dark street—finally alone, for once, rather than surrounded by her fellow homeless deviants—and when he cornered her down the dead-end street he'd chased her into, she screamed and thrashed. The eye she'd managed to land a blow to just before he finally knocked her out had purpled in minutes.

It was the almost-escape of the girl that made Orin consider an assistant.

Hank was a looker and charming to boot, but he'd been scrawny and ill-fed. Orin offered him a place to live and a small wage to help with chores. Hank clearly thought this would be a sexual arrangement—an arrangement Orin was sure the boy had agreed to before. But while he agreed to come back to Orin's house with little convincing, the boy had been clearly relieved when Orin, horrified, had waved off the boy's offer of fellatio. Though the boy had worded it in a much crasser fashion.

After that, the two got along swimmingly. Orin grew frustrated at times—and even worried—when the boy would vanish for hours at time. But he always returned with snared rabbits and slingshotted birds and rodents. Some they cut up and skinned or defeathered to eat, but mostly they dissected the animals together. Hank seemed just as fascinated by the inner workings of things as Orin did.

Orin thought he'd not only started his own Resurrectionist-inspired crew, but also found his own Edward Jenner—the young, like-minded pupil John Hunter had trained. The man who would later create the smallpox vaccine.

Orin's relationship with Hank was destined for things just as great, he knew.

After Hank was given his first assignment—to slowly gain the trust of a blond-haired waif who frequented a shelter in Silver City—Orin was impressed that after only a few conversations with the young Alice, Hank was able to lure the girl to an alley with the promise of drugs and "a little fun." Instead, Orin lay in wait, used a chloroform-soaked rag to incapacitate her, and just like that, they had their first joint patient. The girl, well and truly surprised, hardly had a chance to make a peep of protest.

But Orin could soon tell that Hank wasn't nearly as fascinated with slicing open human patients as he was with their wildlife ones. They worked together to decapitate Alice—Hank holding the body still while Orin hacked through her neck—but Hank's heart wasn't in it. Yet, the boy continued to watch, take notes, and participate when needed. Maybe not as promising as Edward Jenner, but they'd get there.

It was the capture of Janay—the dark-skinned beauty—that

began to cause a rift between the two. Hank often requested to be alone with Janay. Orin refused. He wanted, Orin knew, to sleep with her. But these girls were patients, not prostitutes.

Orin spent a small fortune buying time with hookers for the boy, but his appetite for sex seemed insatiable. Orin started locking the door to the girls' rooms in addition to binding them to their beds, and only allowed supervised time with them after the night he found Hank skulking the halls near Janay's room.

But it was the arrival of Mindy that truly made Orin question his decision to recruit Hank to his cause. Orin could see the way he looked at Mindy was different. The way he talked about her. The way he talked *to* her during their supervised time.

Orin hoped he could squash Hank's desire for her before he had to put a stop to the boy and bury him out back with the others.

CHAPTER 15

Between replaying her conversation with Mindy, and wanting desperately to talk to Michael, Riley managed to screw up three orders. One of which resulted in a passionate lecture from an older couple who felt it necessary to let her know just what they thought of the work ethic of today's youth.

They were lucky she didn't spit in their food when she brought back the correct order.

Days passed in a blur, thoughts of Mindy, Hank, Orin, and Pete—who hadn't materialized since the phone call with Mindy—taking up most of her time.

Her and Michael's schedules conflicted something fierce thanks to him being on deadline for a massive ad project at work, so he didn't have much availability until the end of the week. And Jade, Pamela, and Rochelle were all asleep well before Riley got home from work.

She needed to talk things out with someone before she burst. And Pete the ghost definitely didn't count.

So, left to her own devices, Riley sat in front of her laptop night after night. It took her three nights to finally get up the nerve to search for Francis. Just like with the name Mariah, this one had popped into her head of its own volition. Pete had somehow given her a little piece of the puzzle to put together.

Was Hank's real name Francis? Had "Hank" and Orin concocted an alias for the boy when he'd joined Orin's little demented team?

Riley knew from Mindy that Francis/Hank had also been a runaway and knew the boy had been twelve or thirteen when he'd joined Orin. Which, if someone had reported him as missing, would have happened in the early '80s.

Using the same websites where she'd found Pete, Riley looked up "Francis" and scanned for the years she needed. She got no hits at all on one site, and too many on the other. "Francis Hank" got her two hits. Allison Francis Hank and Francis Hank Carras. Not a Gerber listed anywhere.

Riley swallowed and clicked on the second one, bringing up a page similar to Pete's. The photo at the top featured an extremely good-looking boy; even at thirteen, Riley could tell he would grow up to be a heartbreaker. He had lightly tanned skin, a beaming smile of straight white teeth, and a head of unkempt dark curls.

Biting her lip, she took a screenshot and texted the picture to Mindy with a question mark, hoping it wouldn't wake the other woman up.

A text came through almost immediately. Damn, Sherlock Holmes! How'd you find him that fast? His legal first name is FRANCIS? No wonder he went by Hank. He would have thought that was too girly. And explains why my lawyer couldn't find him.

Guess we can add pathological liar to his CV, Riley wrote back.

His stats were listed as Pete's had been. Age: 13; weight: 110lbs.; height: 66"; hair color: dark brown; eye color: dark brown; race: white; gender: male.

The details of his disappearance listed the date as "June 7,

1980," followed by, "It's believed he ran away from home after a heated argument with his parents. Arguments were not uncommon in the Carras home, but in the past, Francis always returned in a couple of hours. When he was gone overnight, the family knew something was wrong."

She did a search for Francis Hank Carras next.

A year after the raid on the ranch and Orin's arrest, Francis got into trouble with the law too. He'd been caught with a thirteen-year-old girl when he was eighteen and wound up charged with "fourth-degree criminal sexual penetration." Francis was sentenced to eighteen months.

Riley wondered how the timelines of Francis going to jail and Mindy moving to Los Angeles lined up. Maybe the harassment of her largely stopped because he'd been in jail and lost track of her.

From what she could find, Francis wasn't registered as a sex offender. Though, if he didn't commit any other crimes, and even if he *had* been on the list for upwards of twenty years—a punishment on the high end for one of the "less serious" sex crimes—he might no longer *need* to be registered.

She found a social media page which had been updated as early as last week. He'd dropped the first name and was going by Hank Carras. He was listed as divorced, and though there was no mention of kids, it didn't necessarily mean he didn't have any. He was the co-owner of a small, local tech firm she'd actually heard of. Managed to do well for himself despite everything.

There were mostly pictures of himself out with friends—lots of happy, red-faced drunken pictures. Pictures of pretty women with their arms thrown over his shoulders. Clusters of attractive men in bars, all posing with beers in hand. There were also reposts with inspirational quotes and "funny" ones about the horror of Mondays.

He'd gone gray at the temples, like Mindy. And he was devastatingly handsome even at fifty; his boyish good looks hadn't faded in the slightest. What her mother would call a "silver fox."

He lived just outside of Santa Fe.

Had he moved off his twisted path? Had his time in jail set him straight, encouraged him to undo the damage Orin caused? She hoped so. She hoped those smiling women were blissfully unaware of his time with Orin. Of what he'd tried to do to Mindy.

Riley searched for Mindy's social media next. She'd looked for it before but hadn't found it. No profile photos had given her identity away.

Turned out, she *did* have a page, but the picture wasn't of her—it was the logo for her old band, The Crooked Horseshoe. If Riley hadn't seen the shirt on her, she wouldn't have known who this page belonged to. Her location was set to Anywhere, USA, and the majority of the page was set to private. Good girl.

Around noon the next day, Michael sent her a text: Please tell me you're still available for dinner tonight! I miss your face. I'm not sure I remember what it looks like, though. Do you remember me? I'll be the old guy in the lobby sleeping sitting up.

She replied with, **Sorry, who is this?**

He sent fourteen crying emojis in response.

See you tonight. I have things to tell you! If you get super busy like this in the future, I request that you quit your job so I don't have to sit on news like this again.

Done and done.

When she left her apartment later that evening, she was annoyed with the flutter in her stomach. It had only been four days! She remembered another reason why she hated dating: it turned her into a goofy mess.

When she made it to the entrance, she found Michael already there and waiting for her. He paced slowly back and forth in front of a bench flanked by overflowing ashtrays, hands in the pockets of his gray slacks, eyes focused on his shiny black shoes, clearly having driven over directly from work. His dark blue button-down was tucked into his slacks, the cuffs unbuttoned and rolled to his elbows.

Oh lord help me.

"Hey," she said, startling him.

An uncontrolled smile lit up his face when he saw her. *That dimple.* "Hey," he echoed, stepping toward her, arms out. "Hug me, woman! I forget what human interaction is like."

She wrapped her arms around him, laughing. "Don't you work in an office full of people?"

"Shh," he said, squeezing her. "I'm having a moment."

She laughed again. "Unhand me, you weirdo!"

He did and pecked her quickly on the lips. "I missed you."

Grinning, she said, "I missed you too. Now hurry up so I can tell you about the things!"

With a fifteen-minute wait for a table, they plopped down in the lobby and maintained their usual level of conversational ease while they were eventually seated, and then ordered and got their drinks. Michael mostly wanted details on what it was like to have a ghost for a roommate.

"So what is this thing you wanted to tell me about?" he asked once the waitress left.

Riley was torn between bouncing up and down in her seat like an excitable kid and being worried he was going to think she was insane for meeting with Mindy.

"Dude, what is going on with your face?"

"Don't call me dude!"

"Dudette?"

She thunked herself in the forehead with the heel of her palm. He laughed. "I met Mindy Cho for lunch."

His laughed died abruptly and she lowered her hand. "You … you *met* her? How?" Eyes wide, he added, "Why are you just *now* telling me this?"

"It was too much to text!"

"Leave me a voicemail, woman!"

With a snort, she said, "She actually got one of the messages we left."

"No way."

The waitress arrived with their food.

As they ate, Riley filled him in on the details, thrilled to have someone to talk with about it. She'd tell Jade all about it soon enough, but Michael felt connected to this whole thing even more since he'd actually seen what happened to her in the cellar. Pamela was still so traumatized by the experience, Riley hadn't wanted to upset her further.

"It's so crazy to think that house is the same one where she was held captive," he said. "I guess when you hear about these kinds of stories, most people are long dead already, you know?"

She nodded. Now if only she could voice the thought she'd been having since she'd fallen into the Francis Hank Carras wormhole.

"What's that look for?"

She swallowed a large bite of salad. "What look? You can't be tuned into my expressions. I forbid it."

"It's a vaguely guilty look," he said, narrowing his eyes. Then he straightened, pointing his spoon at her. "Please don't tell me you're thinking of trying to find *him* now."

Lips pursed, she tucked into the salad again. "Seriously. It's not fair you can read my face already."

"So not the thing to be concerned about right now. He might be a sex offender. He was only *caught* once." Michael lowered his voice, leaned forward, and added, "What if he has his *own* cellar full of kidnapped girls?"

With a sigh, she put down her fork. After a few moments of thought, she said, "Do you think things happen for a reason?" Before he could reply, she said, "If you use one of your corny-ass lines on me, I will fling the rest of my dinner at your head."

He grunted, lightly knocking his fist against the table. "I had a really good one, too!"

"Don't you dare."

Grinning, he said, "Sometimes, yes, I do think things happen for a reason."

"I think I'm *supposed* to make sure Pete gets put to rest. And not just because he's currently haunting my apartment. I ... I think I ended up at the ranch for a reason." When she saw the goofy look on his face, she said, "And, yes, you were a nice bonus."

"A bonus!" he said in mock-horror. "Second fiddle to a ghost."

Ignoring him, she said, "Pete put Francis' name *in* my head. He wants me to know who he is. And Francis knows about Pete—Mindy said Orin told Francis about him. Maybe I can get Francis to tell me where he's buried."

"Why didn't he tell the police back in the day?"

"No one knew he was there. I mean, Orin and Mindy didn't even know the guy's real name. Plus, Orin wanted Francis to take the blame for at least some of the kidnappings. Makes sense that Francis would want to lie low. Didn't want to go down for something Orin did."

"Or maybe he's just as guilty as Orin, and Francis just happened to get away with it," Michael said.

He had a point. Had Orin just wanted to pin some of this on Francis in hopes of lessening his own sentence somehow? Or had Francis, as Michael suggested, gotten away with it, and Orin tried to rat him out because of some perverted desire for justice?

According to Mindy, Francis had "done something" out in the woods. Riley figured Michael would go into cardiac arrest if she mentioned that part, so she kept it to herself.

"Do you think he could be reformed now?" Michael asked, pulling her from her thoughts.

"No idea," she said. "It looks like he's living a fairly normal life now. Has friends, was married at some point, co-owns a successful business. It's been thirty years; he's had a long time to think about it. Maybe he'd be relieved to have it off his chest."

Michael squinted at her again. "Maybe."

"I can keep it all strictly on the phone. Block my number before I call him or something?"

"Just ... be safe," he said. "You might have more faith in humanity than I do. I assume if the guy was scum as a teenager, he's going to be scum as an adult."

"So says the guy who calls himself a reformed idiot."

"Oh, I'm still an idiot," he said. "But I'm trying to be better about it."

Riley shrugged. "Maybe Francis is trying to be better, too."

After they paid, Michael walked her to her car. They lingered outside it, her back to the driver's side door. Dinner hadn't lasted nearly long enough.

Reaching to grab one of her hands, he ran his thumb over the back. "So when do I get to see you again?"

"You're the one with the fancy-pants job," she said.

"Not anymore," he said. "I'm now a vagabond and ready to be at your service whenever you need me."

She smiled, rolling her eyes. "Sunday? I work all day tomorrow and Saturday."

"Okay."

Riley pulled him into a hug.

When they broke the embrace, her hands slid from around his neck, to flat on his chest. He still had both arms around her waist. When she glanced up at him, his focus was on her mouth. His lips parted slightly and his tongue flicked across his bottom lip.

His gaze found hers. "We're still taking things slow, right?"

Riley nodded.

"Is it still considered moving slow if I kiss you goodbye?"

"Yes."

One of his hands cupped the back of her neck, and his lips were on hers before she finished the word. Though the kiss felt a bit desperate, it was chaste, and over after only a few seconds. Her eyes stayed closed for several moments after it was over, missing the feel of it already.

When she opened them, he was smiling down at her. "I should probably let you go before I embarrass myself."

"Before?"

"Ha ha," he said, backing away and fully breaking the embrace. "I'll see you on Sunday."

"Okay."

He stared at her a moment longer, his smile slipping a little—it reminded her of the look he'd given her in the kitchen at the ranch when she'd told him she was going to bed. "Have a good night, Riley."

"You too."

Normally before Riley took a shower, she ended up in some state of being disrobed—if not complete—while she rummaged for a change in clothes and waited for the water to get warm. Now, with a nine-year-old boy able to appear at any moment, she didn't start to take off a stitch of clothing until she was inside her bathroom with the door shut. Which was ridiculous, she knew, because doors didn't keep spirits out. The kid hadn't taken to snooping, but she didn't want to encourage the possibility. She hadn't seen him at all in over twenty-four hours, actually.

She'd just whacked her elbow on the sink in her tiny bathroom as she tried to pull off her socks in the small space available, when her cell sitting on her counter beeped. The excited flutter in her stomach quickly turned to one of mild dread when she saw it was an email, not a text. And it was from a Nina Galvan, not Michael Roberts.

Dear Riley,

I hope it's okay that I got your email from Angela. I thought you might want to hear these. They're both from our time in the cellar.

Orin answered a couple of your questions. If you have any idea what they might mean, I'd love to hear your theories.

Best,

Nina

She stared at the two attachments to the email. Audio files. Goosebumps broke out across her skin at the mere thought of hearing Orin's disembodied voice.

Curiosity was definitely going to be her downfall.

She turned off the shower, scurried out of the bathroom in just her bra and jeans, hurried back to the bathroom to pull her shirt back on, and then set up her laptop on her coffee table. Remembering how distorted and gravelly the EVPs sounded when the team shared their most "impressive" ones, Riley went hunting for her headphones. She pictured herself playing the files on a loop for half an hour before she even had a guess as to what they said. On *Paranormal Playground*, they often added subtitles to EVPs, as they were largely unintelligible.

Sitting cross-legged on the floor in front of her laptop, she made sure her headphones were snug, then downloaded the files. Her heart thudded so hard in her chest, her body slightly rocked with the force of it.

She hit play on the first one. Blowing out a deep breath, she heard, "Why was Pete first?"

Ugh. Did she really sound like that?

A long stretch of silence after the question. Riley's blood pounded in her ears while she waited.

"Why are you still here?"

"*Dark room*," boomed into her ears in a clear, deep voice.

Riley yanked off her headphones. On her feet in an instant, she let out a sound she usually reserved for successfully flicking a bug off her shirt, thereby narrowly escaping death. She shook out her arms, the hair on the back of her neck standing up.

Orin still hung out in the cellar because of a *dark room*? Like where people developed pictures back in the day?

Riley rubbed her hands up and down her arms as she paced behind the couch, scowling at her computer like she blamed it personally for the creepy shit that just came out of her headphones.

"Now's the time to help me out," she said to her empty apartment. "Any clue what the dark room is, kid?"

Something moved in her peripheral vision to her right and she turned toward it. Nothing. A cold draft swept past her suddenly and she shivered. The air grew colder and colder. Her cell phone's screen lit up, then gave a beep and died, the battery drained. Then her laptop died, the screen going black. Riley rubbed her hands up and down her arms.

"You're creeping me out, kid," she whispered, glancing around the room. Pete had never needed this much energy to manifest before. Why did he need so much now?

A faint outline of the little boy shimmered into view on the other side of her coffee table. Riley could see right through him, like he was made of plastic. His brows were pulled together, his expression pained. Fists balled and jaw tight, he appeared to be doing all he could to will himself into existence.

"Pete … ?"

The image flickered, the outline of him twitching. Then he was gone. Cold air sucked away.

A lump welled in her throat. She couldn't shake the feeling that somehow this little boy was dying all over again. Was it because he was here with her, so far from his body? What would happen if he stayed here too long? Would he just fade away? She didn't want that for him.

Blowing about a breath, she eyed her devices. After plugging them both in and getting her laptop booted back up, she pulled up her email again, where the EVPs waited.

"One more," she said to herself, putting her headphones back on. "Dammit dammit dammit."

She hit play on the second file.

A long silence followed by, "Are you stuck here?"

Riley preemptively pressed her fingers to her lips, the side of one foot tapping rhythmically under her crossed legs.

"*Hank … lied.*"

Riley ripped the headphones off again. What creeped her out more than anything was that this *thing*—because it wasn't the same as Pete's spirit, not even close—had been in the room with her and she hadn't heard it. She knew on an instinctual level that this voice belonged to Orin. That the force that tried to shove her out of the room, that had tried—and succeeded—to scare her into fleeing the ranch had been the spirit of a lingering serial killer. She shuddered.

Slapping her laptop shut, she propped her elbows on the table on either side of her computer, and shoved her fingers into her hair, cradling her head. What the hell was she supposed to do with this?

Stick to the plan to contact Francis and casually ask him if he knew where Pete was buried? Contact a guy who the ghost of a serial killer seemed to hold a grudge against? Maybe Michael was right; maybe contacting the guy couldn't possibly go well.

But Riley remembered Pete standing at the window of the

ranch, watching her from the top floor. Recalled his laughing, smiling face as his father spun with him.

Pete was fading now. If he could no longer manifest, would he soon be gone forever—lost and forgotten in some in-between plane where even Riley couldn't find him?

She couldn't live with herself if she didn't try everything in her power to set him free.

Even if it meant getting in contact with someone like Francis Hank Carras.

CHAPTER 16

She walked through the forest, music blaring through her head-phones. She hadn't listened to her "Great Composers" cassette in ages, but it always calmed her. Something about the swell of the piano combined with the tranquility of the still woods put her at ease. It'd been a rough week at work and she was happy to get away for a hike. She tried to come out here at least once a month.

Her irritation at her boss came creeping in past the music. He'd chastised her in front of the entire office two days ago—calling her out for something she knew damn well *he'd* been responsible for, but publicly blamed her to save face. But what could she say? She was a lowly secretary who'd only been there for eight months. Even if she'd beaten out dozens for the coveted position, she had absolutely no power there.

The flash of something to her left caught her eye. She glanced that way, thinking she might've startled a deer or rabbit. But she didn't see anything moving amongst the tree trunks or fallen needles and pinecones.

She focused forward again. *Don't think about Daniel. He's not worth it. Enjoy your time out here.*

Willing herself to shift her focus, the tinkling sound of the piano filled her mind again. She adjusted her pack on her back, the space between her bag and her shirt growing damp with sweat. She'd been walking for well over two hours.

Another half hour passed before she realized she'd zoned out and wasn't totally sure where she was. She stopped suddenly and glanced behind her. Had she missed the fork? Crap. If she didn't make it home before it got dark, Nick would make fun of her. He was always telling her that her tendency to get lost in her own head would get her lost in real life one day.

She backtracked, sure the fork was just ahead.

Another blur of color, this time to her right. The hell? She pulled off her headphones, the headband pressing her unbound hair to her neck. The quiet forest seemed even quieter in the absence of her music. The lilting sound of the violin still seeped out, soft and low, from the headphones. "Hello?"

She didn't know why she thought anyone was out here; she rarely ran into anyone on her hikes. From what she heard, there was a ranch somewhere nearby, but she'd never seen it. The forest was open for hiking, seeing as it was a national park and all, but she also knew she ran the risk of crossing onto private property. Though maybe if she'd strayed that far off the path, a kindly ranch hand could set her in the right direction again.

No reply.

She had a hand on either one of her headphones, ready to pull them back up over her ears, when someone appeared from behind a tree off to the right, several yards away. It was a boy a few years younger than her. It looked like he'd been in a fight, though now his cuts and bruises were mostly healed. The area under his right eye was still purpled and there was a cut on his bottom lip that looked like it had split open recently.

Despite being banged up, she was still initially taken aback by how cute he was—like an underwear model who'd been in a bar brawl. He was dressed in jeans and a black shirt, not like someone out for a hike.

"Hello?" she tried again, clicking the stop button on her Walkman after he remained standing by the tree.

"Hi," he said, finally walking toward her. "I'm sorry if I scared you."

She swallowed. "Are you okay?"

When she motioned to her own face, near her eyes and lip, he reached up, mirroring her, fingers pressing gently against the puffy skin. "Oh, this? Yeah, I'm okay. Are you lost?"

Her stomach flopped. "Just a little turned around."

"You're almost to the ranch," he said. "My uncle lives there. If you want, he can drive you back to your car. It's getting late."

She looked up, realizing the sun was much lower in the sky than she first thought. Even if she made it back to the fork and kept going, by the time she hit the spot where the path looped back the way she'd come, it would be well after dark.

Nick would never let her hear the end of this. "How far is it from here?"

"Twenty minutes, tops." He offered her a 1000-watt smile.

Her stomach flipped again. And not in a good way. "I don't mind walking—do you think you could just get me back to the fork? I can walk back the way I came. If I hightail it, I think I can make it before it gets too dark."

The boy's jaw clenched for a moment, but he quickly smiled again. "Of course."

He started walking and gestured for her to follow him. Taking a deep breath, she did, working her hand casually into the side pocket of her bag. She kept a can of pepper spray there to scare off wild animals. Easing it into her hand, she primed it in her palm so she'd be ready in case this went south.

When he looked back, she smiled at him, hoping he couldn't tell how strained it was. His gaze roamed her face and her chest, where the strap of her pack clipped under her breasts, pushing them up more than usual. Ugh. Creep. He slowed a little to allow her to fall into step next to him on the narrow path. They had to walk so close together that their arms lightly brushed every few steps.

She couldn't explain it, but something about this guy made her uncomfortable. Everything in her told her to run in the other direction, handsome face or not. "So you said your uncle lives out here?"

"Yeah," he said after a moment, almost seeming startled—like he'd managed to forget she was beside him. "The place used to be a cattle ranch but my uncle kind of let it go. Now it's like having a *really* large backyard when I come to visit a couple times a year."

"That's cool," she said, hyper alert, actively scanning the area around them, worried whoever did that to his face would show up. "What were you doing way out here? You aren't really dressed for hiking."

He shrugged. "We're not all that far from the ranch. I like coming out here when it's near dusk. I have a couple of rabbit snares out here—I check them around this time."

"Oh."

Where the hell was the fork?

"What's your name?" he asked her.

She hesitated for a moment, then said, "Renee. Yours?"

"Hank."

They walked for another fifteen minutes or so, and she saw a clearing to their left. A large house sat in the distance. Her heart started to hammer in her chest.

"I thought you were taking me back to the fork …"

"It'll be easier just to have my uncle drive you," he said. "It's getting dark."

She stopped walking. "You know … I think I can make it on my own, thanks."

He turned to face her, his brow furrowed. Eyes roaming her body again, he said, "I think my uncle would like you."

"What?"

"Like to help you," he said. "Sometimes we get lost hikers out here. He likes to make sure they get back safe."

She didn't move. Her gut told her she'd be better out in the woods than with this guy.

Quick as a whip, he reached out and snagged her wrist. "What's wrong with you? I'm trying to *help* you."

"Let go," she said, momentarily forgetting the pepper spray she kept fisted in her other hand. She yanked on her arm, but he only held firmer.

"Just … it'll be better for everyone if you come with me."

What the hell was this guy's problem?

Without giving it much thought, she reached up and sprayed him with her mace. To her horror, the nozzle hadn't been facing him directly, and he ducked out of the way of the mist.

"The fuck?" he said, startled enough that he let her go.

They both coughed, the air suddenly heavy with the scent of pepper. She took that as her chance and ran.

She could hear him crashing behind her as she veered off the path and ran full-broke through the leaf litter. She really had no idea where she was going now; all she knew was she had to get away.

If she got out of this alive, she would never hike again.

The pack on her back bounced violently as she ran, and it weighed her down, but she couldn't bear to drop it now. It had snacks and water and a change of clothes—if she lost him and was trapped out here after dark, her supplies might be the only thing to assure she wouldn't meet some other horrible end.

She really wished she'd stuck with the Girl Scout program.

Her headphones still hung around her neck, the padded earpieces tapping against her collarbones as she struggled to maintain her pace.

The guy kept up with her better than she'd hoped, and even had enough wind left to call her a "stupid bitch" every few minutes.

If she hadn't been so damn scared, she was sure she would have been sobbing. She needed to get the pepper spray into his eyes. It'd slow him down for at least half an hour. Enough time to find the fork. Her dad had made her practice with pepper spray so many times, she couldn't believe she'd managed to miss.

Her palm sweated where the can touched her skin. She needed to try again.

He shoved her backpack and she pitched forward and hit the ground, the wind knocked out of her. They wrestled in the fallen pine needles, him grabbing onto her ankles and trying to pull her toward him while she kicked and scrabbled away from him on her elbows. A foot got loose and she kicked with her heel, making contact. He howled and let go. She was up in an instant, moving so fast she almost didn't get her feet back under her as she struggled to remain upright.

She'd only made it a few feet when something slammed into her and she was down again, on her back this time, struggling to get up with the pack still strapped to her. She flailed like an overturned turtle. Kicking and clawing, she tried to get him off her, but he was straddling her now, his bony hips digging into hers as he squeezed with his thighs and reached for her hand holding the pepper spray.

She bucked, hoping to knock him loose.

The smile on his pretty face creeped her out more than anything, like this was the most fun he'd had in ages. When he leaned forward, their chests pressed together, she realized with a whole new horror that he was hard as a rock. Her breath came in shallow, quick gasps. Oh god. No.

One of his hands snaked behind him and he pulled a rock out of his back pocket—one he must have picked up in his pursuit of her through the underbrush.

With renewed desperation, she yanked her arm free, aimed the pepper spray, and pressed the button. The boy screamed, hands flying to his face as he continued to straddle her, sitting squarely on her stomach. The rock dropped with a thud. She bucked even harder now, trying to dislodge him.

A growl that sounded far more animal than human erupted from his throat. His eyes were swollen shut and tears and snot ran from his eyes and nose. Despite all this, he thrashed out with his fists, managing to land a blow to her cheek and light burst behind her eyes. Her head snapped to the side, and she cried out.

Dazed, she clawed at his face, nails slashing across already tender skin.

He howled again, coughing and gagging.

Twisting under him, she caught him off balance and knocked him loose. She struggled to get up, clawing at the clasp of her pack fastened under her breasts. Her head still spun from the blow he'd landed to her face. Her fingers weren't working right.

And now she *was* crying, the world a blur of green and brown and black.

She started to crawl away on hands and knees, body racked with sobs.

He yelled again, coming for her on his feet now. Could he see her? Had it been three minutes yet? Her dad had told her that the first three minutes was the worst of it—that her attacker would be incapacitated.

Something clobbered her from behind and she went down on her stomach, pinned by her bag and his body weight. A sharp thud sounded right by her head. Her hair was a tangled mess, blocking her view of everything. She screamed and thrashed and tried to push off the ground with her hands. But he was too heavy; her arms shook with the effort.

Thud.

She realized then that he had the rock again and was smashing it down blindly in hopes of eventually hitting her. Her thrashing became even more frantic, her sobs so violent, she could hardly breathe.

Crack.

Spots swam in her vision.

Crack.

The pain was so immense, the fight left her abruptly, her limbs going slack. Then her vision blurred at the edges. Blackness seeped in, swallowing up everything. Like the end of a black-and-white cartoon where everything was reduced to a pinprick of white before that disappeared too.

He stilled then, heaving heavily on top of her. After a few moments, wandering fingers slipped under her, crawling and creeping until they found the button on her jeans. The teeth of her zipper gave way, tooth by tooth, as if time had slowed to a snail's pace. The top of her pants slipped down her hips, followed by her underwear. Gruff hands ran over her bare skin.

"Mmm, Renee," he said. "I can't see you too good right now,

but you *feel* good."

A choked sob sounded in her throat and then the tiny sliver of white turned black.

Riley woke with a start, then immediately burst into tears. She couldn't breathe. She gasped and pulled in air as best she could but she felt like she was drowning. Like all the oxygen had been sucked out of the room and she was going to suffocate.

She kicked her blankets off, wanting nothing to touch her. She could feel his phantom hands on her. Creeping, rough hands.

Riley's stomach roiled. Hurrying to her bathroom, she splashed cold water on her face and willed herself not to throw up. When the nausea passed, she slipped to the bathroom floor, the tile cold beneath her legs. She pulled her knees to her chest, hugged them, and cried for what felt like hours. Every time she stopped, something would flash through her head or she'd feel something she knew was both real and not real at the same time and lose it all over again.

She needed someone to talk to. Someone to hold onto her and tell her that these things hadn't happened to her. That she didn't need to hide under her bed and never come out.

But this *had* happened to Renee. And Riley was almost positive that poor girl hadn't lived through it. Riley wanted to contact Hank—Francis, whoever—if only so she could tear his goddamn eyes out.

This assuredly would have come up in her search if Francis had been convicted for it. Or even arrested for it. Had he murdered and assaulted Renee and somehow been living as a free man ever since?

The idea of it made her stomach turn over.

When she found the strength, she got up and found her phone. It was Saturday. Jade would be home. The moment Jade answered the phone, Riley burst into tears again.

"Babe!" Jade said. "God, are you okay?"

"No."

"Call in sick. I'll be there in fifteen minutes."

Riley miraculously found someone to cover her shift in only a matter of minutes—she'd covered for so many of her co-workers, she had good karma built up—and was a comatose mess on her couch by the time Jade let herself into Riley's apartment.

"Jesus," Jade whispered when she saw Riley. "What the hell happened? What did Michael do? I will *destroy* him."

"Nothing. He didn't do anything."

Riley curled up in a ball on the couch, her head on Jade's lap, while she cried for a little while longer. Jade ran a hand slowly over her hair until Riley was calm enough to talk.

It took her a while, but Riley got it all out: Mindy, Francis, the EVPs, Renee.

By the time she was done, she was sitting up, arms wrapped around her knees. Jade's eyes welled up as Riley told her about Renee.

"Damn," Jade breathed. "Oh! That day in the woods at the ranch … you heard music, remember? Was that Renee trying to get your attention?"

Riley's eyes widened. She'd heard the music from Renee's Walkman that day. Did Renee haunt the woods like Pete haunted the house?

"So what's your theory?" Jade asked, clearly trying to pull Riley out of her own head. "That this Francis guy killed Renee and was never caught?"

"Yes," Riley said, never more sure of anything in her life. She wondered if Pete was behind the dream somehow, just as he'd somehow shown her his own death. Had he contacted Renee off in the Great Beyond and told her the best way to get in contact was through a creepy-ass dream? She told Jade as much.

"Weirder shit has happened," Jade said. "Do you think by helping them, you'll find a way to slap this Francis asshole with a murder charge as an added bonus?"

"Maybe?"

"Damn," Jade said again. "What can I do?"

Riley shook her head. "I don't know yet. The guy was clearly a monster …"

"Probably still is."

"Michael says that too." Taking a shuddering post-cry breath, Riley said, "I can't go to the police with nothing but a couple creepy dreams as proof. But unless I talk to Francis directly, I don't know if I'll get any proof at all."

"Just … don't do anything until you've had time to really think about it, okay?" Jade said. "I'll help you. Michael will help you. Police use psychics all the time, right? Maybe you can find someone who will listen to you."

"Yeah, maybe." Riley sighed. "Thanks for coming over."

"Of course," she said, giving one of Riley's hands a squeeze. "You scared the hell out of me. I've never heard you cry like that before."

"Because that was a first. God, when I woke up, I felt like I was dying. I *wanted* to die."

Jade frowned.

"No one was there to help her," Riley said, eyes welling again. "She fought so damn hard and that bastard got her anyway."

"Maybe you can help her now," said Jade. "Her *and* Pete."

Riley nodded. "I need to shower. I'm a disaster."

Jade brushed a lock of hair out of Riley's face. "Yeah, a little bit."

After her shower, the two watched a fluffy romantic comedy before Jade had to leave for yoga with Brie. She tried to convince Riley that she'd just cancel it, but Riley insisted she go.

"I'm okay; I swear," Riley said. "I owe you one for dealing with that."

"Of course," she said, hugging her so tight it hurt. Pulling away and staring at her for a moment, she said, "I think you should let Michael in on this, but if it's too hard to talk to him about it—you call me if it gets bad again, okay? I'll stay here tonight if you're worried about going back to sleep."

Ugh, Riley hadn't even thought about sleeping. "Thank you."

She tried watching TV after Jade left, but she couldn't concentrate for anything. Her itch for information was getting to her. Every time the show broke for commercials, Riley's gaze shifted to her closed laptop. The laptop with the audio files on it. The laptop she hadn't been able to open since she heard Orin's voice.

After pouring herself a glass of wine, downing it, and then pouring a second one, she steeled herself and opened her computer. A third glass followed. She made all her best decisions while wine-drunk, after all.

Francis had still been banged up in the snapshot of the past, so his successful attack on Renee had happened soon after his failed attack on Mindy. Searching for girls named Renee who went missing in 1983, the same year Mindy escaped Orin's ranch, she very quickly spotted a headline of a website that read, "Who killed Renee Palmer?"

The poorly-crafted website sported a gray background, the font a too-bright blue. Below the title in huge font featured a smiling, slightly-grainy picture of Renee.

In her dream, Riley hadn't seen her face. She'd *been* her. Felt what she felt.

Renee had been a Caucasian girl with a bright smile and a head of slightly curled, light brown hair. She looked so normal. Like any other girl Riley might see walking down the street, going about her life.

A brief flashback then of grubby, unwanted hands on her skin assaulted Riley, and she had to close her eyes for a moment and breathe deep. She knocked back the rest of wine glass number three.

The site had been set up like a blog, but only had eleven posts. The first pinned entry had been posted ten years before on September 7th.

Below that, it listed the most recent posts first. The newest one was from last year, also in September. It simply said, "Renee would have been 56 today, had she lived. We love and miss you, Renee!"

The next nine were very similar, each one acknowledging Renee's birthday on the seventh of September. Someone kept up hope—all these years later—that Renee's murder would be solved.

She scrolled back up to the pinned post.

> Renee Beatrice Palmer was the light of my life. She was my only daughter and I treasured her. At only twenty-three years old, she was brutally murdered and assaulted during a hike in the Gila National Park, her body left to the mercy of the elements.
>
> There were no witnesses. She was found by another hiker a day later.

She is survived by her father, Walter Palmer,
mother, Gladys Elise Palmer, and her two
younger brothers, Isaac and Scott.

I have lived without my baby girl for three
decades and my greatest wish before I leave
this earth is to have closure on the darkest
chapter of my life. Any information you can
provide a grieving family would mean the
world to us. We'll ask no questions and offer
no judgement. But maybe with enough
evidence, we can get her case rekindled.

God bless,

Walter

Riley teared up reading the post written by the man who'd done
his best to train Renee to defend herself.

Tracking down newspaper articles for a thirty-year-old crime
proved to be harder than she'd realized. She found short articles
here and there, the most recent one from ten years ago on the anniversary of her death, published in the now defunct *Better News* based
out of Silver City.

Given how tiny both the town and the paper had been, Riley
guessed it hadn't taken much to get the story printed. But she also
suspected no one would know it'd been there had they not been
looking for it.

The article went over many of the same things Walter included
on his website, but also added a little tidbit of information that made

Riley sit up. The park rangers who had come upon the scene after the hiker found Renee's body had then gone to Orin Jacobs' house to ask if he knew anything about the woman found dead roughly half a mile from his property. Little did the rangers know then that the quiet, unassuming man would be arrested later that week for the kidnapping of Mindy Cho, and eventually the murder of five missing girls.

Orin had been ruled out quickly. The MO didn't fit Orin, and Renee had clearly put up a fight. Orin had shown no sign that he'd been in an altercation just days before.

Riley wondered how long the effects of pepper spray would last. After a day, would Francis still have felt the pain of it? Riley hoped so.

She kept searching for some mention of Francis' name—or Hank, for that matter—but found nothing. Wouldn't his DNA have been all over her? He wouldn't have had a record before this, but they would've taken a sample after he was convicted of the statutory rape with the thirteen year old. The link in DNA of the two cases should have put him away.

So why was the asshole still free all these years later, posting smiling pictures online with his friends like he didn't have a care in the world?

DNA, according to her next search, hadn't been actively used in criminal cases in the US until after 1985. Had Renee's ended up a cold case before DNA testing was readily available?

She snapped her laptop shut and rubbed her eyes with the heels of her hands.

How the hell was she supposed to get Francis Hank Carras behind bars?

There were already too many people wrongly convicted of

crimes they didn't commit, years—decades—of their lives lost. DNA was starting to help overturn those convictions. Maybe she could find a way to get the opposite to happen to Hank, someone deserving of incarceration who had somehow slipped through the cracks.

And how the hell was Francis going to lead her to Pete?

She snatched up her phone and texted Mindy. **Do you know who Renee Palmer is?**

The reply came within minutes. No. Should I?

Wanna meet for lunch again?

I have a feeling I'm not going to like what you're going to tell me. But yeah. When and where?

Same place? In an hour?

Lucky for you, I don't have a life. See you then.

It was nearing two in the afternoon.

After getting ready, she shoved her laptop into her bag and headed out for the Redbird Café.

Mindy beat her there this time and managed to snag the same table in the corner. "So what's this about? Who's Renee Palmer?" Mindy asked, arms folded on the table. She wore a flat leather bracelet on her wrist again.

Even though they shared a twenty-year age difference, Riley thought they might be friends one day.

Images from her dream flitted through her head, linking up with the things Mindy had told her when they first met. Mindy's relaxed demeanor likely wouldn't last long. "Remember when you told me Hank said he'd 'done something'?"

Mindy's pale skin paled further.

"I know what it was."

The waiter showed up, and she and Mindy hastily gave him their orders.

When he was gone, Riley launched into the dream. By the end of it, Mindy was in tears. Riley was in tears. Mindy immediately excused herself and hurried to the restroom. Riley felt hollowed out. She hadn't wanted to upset Mindy; she'd even gone a little lax on the details, unlike Jade, who had gotten the full story.

But Francis had tried the same thing with Mindy as he had with Renee. Mindy was likely reliving it now. Pulling up those horrible memories even all these years later. Memories of those rough hands wandering skin uninvited.

Riley's leg bounced under the table as she waited for her to come back. Hoping she hadn't fled. The waiter brought their food and it had been sitting there for a good ten minutes before Mindy returned, her lightly freckled face a bit splotchy now.

"Sorry," she said, sitting down and using both hands to tuck her hair behind her ears.

"Don't be sorry," Riley said. "I'm sorry I—"

"You don't be sorry either," she said, grabbing her napkin out from under her utensils and then softly blowing her nose. "I just got to thinking ..." Her balled fists sat on the edge of the table. Though her gaze was focused on her salad, Riley was sure Mindy wasn't really seeing it. "I was thinking if I had just let Hank—"

"Don't you *dare* finish that sentence," Riley snapped.

Mindy glanced up then, clearly startled.

"You didn't owe that little shit anything then, and you don't now."

Mindy pursed her lips. "He told me he'd done something. I *knew* something was wrong. I could've—"

"No. You couldn't. I think she'd already died by the time ... before he ..."

Mindy pressed the fist still holding the napkin to her mouth, as if that would keep her nausea at bay. "It's my fault."

"No. It's *his* fault. He was the one who couldn't control himself. There's nothing either one of you did or didn't do. Renee fought as hard as she could, right until the end. Even if she hadn't, it wouldn't have changed anything. *He* was the problem, not you. Orin just turned a bad apple even worse."

Mindy's lip quivered. "I know." She took a deep, shuddering breath. "I guess I just need to be reminded sometimes."

Riley reached across the table and squeezed Mindy's hand, who relaxed a fraction.

"So that's her name, huh?" Mindy asked. "Renee Palmer?"

"Yeah. Case went cold after a couple years."

"How do we nail the bastard for it?"

Riley grinned. "I don't know yet."

"I'll help any way I can," she said. "I shouldn't have kept quiet this long."

Riley shot her a pointed look.

"Sorry. Blaming myself for everything is a force of habit."

When the waiter poked his head out the patio door, Mindy said, "We should probably eat before we give the poor guy a complex."

Riley decided she needed to stop having such heavy conversations in public.

Mindy told Riley about the Crooked Horseshoe and their tour across the United States in an old van. Living off fast food, sleeping in motels with neighbors—often ones who paid by the hour—having loud sex, playing shows where one night the place was packed, and the next it only had three people in it, all drunk and who had no idea where they were, much less who was playing. It didn't sound like a life Riley would have enjoyed. But Mindy's face lit up when she talked about it, and Riley found herself smiling too.

After they finished their food and the waiter had cleared away their plates, Riley said, "So, uh … there's one other thing …"

"I'm scared to ask."

"One of the investigators from the ranch sent me a couple of EVPs," Riley said. "I think they're from Orin."

Mindy sat back. "Damn. We *really* need to have our lunches in bars from now on. I'm too sober for this shit."

"Do you want to hear them? I was thinking maybe you could make sense of them."

"No, I don't want to," she said. "But do you think it'll help put Hank away?"

"I don't know. Maybe? Hopefully."

"Okay, I'll listen. I'm very likely going to regret this, but I'll listen anyway."

Riley fished her laptop and earbuds out of her bag, then set it up for Mindy. The other woman's leg bounced so forcibly under the table, the whole thing tottered slightly. Riley couldn't blame her; she'd heard the EVPs only once each and vowed never to listen to them again if she could help it. How closely did the gravelly voice on the recording sound like Orin?

She was just about to hand the plugged-in earbuds to Mindy when she pulled her arm back toward herself. "I'm not traumatizing the shit out of you, am I?"

Mindy gave a full-body shrug. "I was pretty fucking traumatized before I met you."

Riley frowned. "I just don't want to make things worse."

"I wouldn't have come if I didn't want to." Mindy sighed. "Talking to you the other day was more freeing than I thought it'd be. I have a shrink … I talk to her. But … I don't know. It felt different talking to you. You give a shit. You're not just listening to me because my fucked-up life is helping pay your mortgage."

Riley cocked a brow. "Tell me how you really feel."

She grinned. "My shrink thinks I have a rage problem."

With a snort, Riley handed over the earbuds. The laptop was set up on the left side of the round table, so they could both see the screen if they awkwardly craned their necks.

When Mindy gave her the thumbs up, Riley hit play.

Roughly thirty seconds later, Mindy yanked the earbuds out of her ears. They clanked lightly on the iron surface. "*Fuck*," she hissed.

"Yeah," Riley said. "Does it … does it sound like him?"

"It's … uhh … deeper, I guess? But it's him." She stuck the earbuds back in. "Play the other one."

Riley did.

Mindy pulled them out when it ended, breathing deeply. "Hank lying isn't exactly news."

"Do you know what he meant by 'dark room'?"

Mindy chewed on her upper lip for a second. "He called the cellar that sometimes. 'I'm going to the dark room for a while,' he'd say before locking me in my room."

"But he didn't *always* call it that?"

"No. Sometimes the cellar, sometimes the dark room."

Were they the same place?

"Did you stalk Francis online after I told you his full name?" Riley asked.

"Hell no. What if he could trace it somehow?"

"Do you want to see him?"

Mindy fidgeted, chewing on her upper lip. Then she thrust her chin at the computer. "Show me."

Riley clicked out of her email and switched to her browser, pulling up Francis' social media feed.

Mindy was quiet as she scrolled through the pictures. Finally, she said, voice soft and a little faraway, "You can tell his nose never healed right. It's kinda lopsided." She reached up and tentatively touched the screen. "He looks so normal. Still *really* good looking."

"I know." Thinking back to her dream, Riley said, "He's a monster with a pretty face."

While they looked through his page, a red 1 popped up at the top of the screen. A new friend request.

Mindy and Riley looked at each other, then the screen again, having noticed the notification at the same time.

"You don't think …" Mindy started.

"My profile is almost all private." Then a thought hit her. "You can't *actually* trace who looks at your page, can you? I thought you were just being paranoid."

"Gee, thanks. And I don't know. Isn't the government watching us through our TVs now or something?"

Riley laughed, but it was halfhearted. She was going to throw her TV out the window when she got home.

"Do it," Mindy said. "Friend him back. We're gonna have to have contact with him to get his ass caught, aren't we?"

"There's the real Mindy. I knew she was in there somewhere," Riley said, eyeing her. "What do I say, though? *'Sup, Francis. You murder a girl back in 1983?'*"

"No," Mindy said with a laugh. "No one says *'sup*."

Riley chewed on a thumbnail, then clicked the notification. After all, it wasn't necessarily Francis.

But it was.

"Shit," they said in unison.

Before she could convince herself not to, Riley hit accept.

Curiosity sent her on another internet search. They found a way to track the people who interacted with your page the most. Which included views, even if you weren't friends.

"Look up mine," Mindy said.

Riley didn't like the panicky edge to her voice, but she logged out of her page and let Mindy log into her own. Pulling up Mindy's stats, there, at the top of the list, was Francis.

"Goddammit," Mindy muttered. "He can't know it's me, right? I don't even have a picture of myself up there."

"I don't know," Riley said. "Maybe he obsessively checks the pages of all the Mindy Chos in the area."

"Because *that's* a comforting thought," Mindy said. "I've updated my location several times over the years," she said softly, almost like a confession. "What if he's been following me online and now knows I'm back here?"

"You can't know that."

"Should I delete my page?"

"It might look suspicious," Riley said. "Plus, you've been back for two years and he's left you alone. He could just have creepy internet habits."

Riley sure as hell did.

"Crap." Mindy did her two-handed hair tuck again. "I gotta go."

"Are you okay?"

"Yeah," she said, scratching the side of her neck. "I get anxiety attacks sometimes. I just need to walk it off. Sorry."

Mindy grabbed her purse and jacket, gave Riley an awkward side-hug, and fled.

Blowing out a long breath, she turned the laptop to face her head on, then she logged out of Mindy's account and back into her own.

A chat request waited for her now.

She hit accept.

> **HANK CARRAS:** hi

> **RILEY THOMAS:** Hi

> **HANK CARRAS:** thanks for accepting my request

> **RILEY THOMAS:** No prob

> **HANK CARRAS:** Your cute

Riley cringed.

> **RILEY THOMAS:** Thanks … you too

> **HANK CARRAS:** hope its not weird i contacted you i like to know who looks at my page just a curious guy i guess

> **RILEY THOMAS:** No, it's cool. I'm just embarrassed you caught me!

> **HANK CARRAS:** your to cute to be embarrassed

Riley rolled her eyes and sent a blushing emoji.

> **HANK CARRAS:** so whats up?

Riley had no idea what was up other than this dude had a violent past and was paranoid enough to keep tabs on who visited his page. He thought she was cute; she could chat him up for information. But the idea of fake-online-dating him for intel made her want to throw up—plus she'd never do that to Michael.

    HANK CARRAS: common cutie don't be shy

What the hell reason could she possibly have to be creeping around this guy's profile? When she first contacted Mindy, the voicemail message she left had mentioned writing an article. Could Riley say she was a reporter? Her profile didn't reflect that, but she could always say this was her personal page, not her professional one.

    HANK CARRAS: you fall asleep on me?

A story about what, though?

    RILEY THOMAS: Sorry! Got up to grab something to drink

    HANK CARRAS: what you drinking

    RILEY THOMAS: Wine

    HANK CARRAS: mmmm

She hated this guy already. But she kept him talking about nonsense for another fifteen minutes until she came up with a semi-decent lie.

    RILEY THOMAS: So I hope this isn't forward of me
    ...

He sent a winking face. She rolled her eyes again.

> **RILEY THOMAS:** I'm a freelance writer and I'm
> doing a piece about men who have done jail time,
> got out, and turned their lives around. I've been
> very impressed with the work you've been doing
> at your company. I apologize that I'm doing this
> on my personal page, but you caught me while
> I was trying to do some off-the-clock snooping.
> I've always found such strength in people who are
> able to learn from past mistakes. You seem like a
> shining example of that.

She crossed her arms and waited, half expecting him to log off or block her. The other half expected him to gather his wits about him and then curse her out.

Tapping her foot, she saw that he didn't sign out *or* block her. It didn't say he'd gone idle either, so he was trying to figure out what to say. She decided to appeal more to his ego.

> **RILEY THOMAS:** So many young men are convicted
> of crimes and never truly recover—bouncing in and
> out of the system. You found a way to rise above
> that. I think your story could be an inspiration to so
> many others.

No reply. Appeal to vanity.

> **RILEY THOMAS:** Plus, you're gorgeous, so you'd pull
> readers simply from your cover picture

HANK CARRAS: i could be the cover story?

RILEY THOMAS: My editor loves this idea; I think I could convince him to have you be the lead story.

HANK CARRAS: if you can show me some proof of who you are i'd be down to meet with you

Meet with her. In person. Mindy, Michael, *and* Jade would all smack her upside the head for agreeing to that.

RILEY THOMAS: I'll work something up and email it to you. What's your email?

After getting his information, she made up an excuse and logged out. Her heart pounded in her chest.

Oh, this is a bad idea.

Packing up her things, she hustled for the exit. Her waiter seemed relieved that she was finally leaving. It was nearing four, so it was slow—that in-between lunch and dinner time—but she was sure he didn't want to have to keep checking on her to see if she needed anything else when she so clearly didn't and was just soaking up their free Wi-Fi. She had almost made it to the door when she backtracked and tapped the waiter on the shoulder, where he'd been wiping down menus.

His eyes widened.

Fishing a ten-dollar bill out of her purse, she said, "Thanks for letting me hang out back there."

"Oh, you don't have—"

"I'm a server, too. Consider it a professional courtesy."

He grinned, taking the money. "Appreciate it."

As she walked to her car, she pulled out her phone and dialed Michael.

"Hey, Ry," he said after two rings.

"So, I did something stupid."

CHAPTER 17

Once Michael determined Riley wasn't in any immediate danger, he walked around her living room, arms behind his back as if he were a patron in a museum. As if he thought memorizing the exact placement of her furniture would unlock the secrets of her soul.

Riley sat on her couch watching him. She hadn't had anyone over other than her parents or Jade in the six months she'd lived there.

Suddenly he stilled. "Is Pete *here*?" he whispered so fiercely, eyes wide, that Riley laughed.

"He seems to be having problems manifesting lately. He knocks things over or moves them around to let me know he's here, but I haven't seen him in a couple days," she said. "Even though seeing him pop up in my living room scared me, I'm getting a little worried about him."

Michael nodded at this as if it made perfect sense. After a few more minutes of inspecting her apartment, he sat next to her. Pulling her feet up onto the cushions, she wrapped an arm around her knees.

He turned toward her, one leg propped up on the seat. "So what level of stupid are we talking?"

After recounting her stupidity, Michael sat quietly for a spell.

She worried he was going to reconsider this whole thing and see himself out.

"Well. Could be worse," he said. "It shouldn't be too hard to craft some official-looking badge. Choose a paper or magazine and I'll make one—bonus of dating a guy with a design background. If he asks, tell him you're not listed on any websites because you're freelance."

Riley blinked at him. "You're not going to yell at me?"

"I'm building up so much good karma right now by *not* yelling," he said. "In a couple years when I start to have an existential crisis and want to start brewing beer in the bathtub? You won't be able to say a damn thing to stop me because I'll bust out the 'Remember that time I helped you interview a psychopath?' card."

Smiling and shaking her head, she said, "What if he tries to call the whatever magazine I claim to work for?"

"Give him my number and I'll make something up."

"Seriously?"

He shrugged. "I'm guessing you did your obsessive research thing and didn't find anything too alarming, right?"

Riley sucked in a breath, but then closed her mouth, letting her cheeks puff out.

"Aw, shit. You went good news/bad news and didn't tell me."

"Don't forget you said you're not going to yell at me!" Steeling herself, she gave an even more sanitized retelling of her dream than she'd given Mindy. Michael still looked horrified.

"Is that why you stayed home from work?" he asked, voice soft, gaze sweeping over her face.

Riley managed a nod, focus shifting to her hands where she worried at a loose strand on one of her throw pillows. He put a hand over hers.

She couldn't look at him. "It uh … the dream played out as if I was Renee. I could still feel his hands on me even after I woke up. It took a couple hours to stop crying."

"Jesus."

"Yeah."

When he was silent for longer than usual, she glanced up at him. Their hands were clasped in the space between them, his brows were pulled together.

"You don't want me to meet with him, do you?" she asked.

"Can you blame me? If he got away with what he did to Renee, who knows what else he might be guilty of. Maybe nothing. Maybe that was it and he's just paranoid about getting caught. I just …"

"I know."

They fell silent again, him holding fast to her hand.

"What if I go with you?"

Riley raised an eyebrow at that.

"I could be the photographer? I could just as easily make two badges."

"You're really not going to fight me on it?" she asked.

"Do you want me to? Do you want me to try like hell to convince you not to? Because I will."

"I …" She shrugged. "I don't know. Maybe the opposite? Maybe I want to know you're okay with it."

"I'm not. Not even a little bit. But what if I fight you on it and you decide to do this by yourself and something happens to you?" he said. "And, who knows, if I was in your position, maybe I'd be doing the same thing. I can't understand what you've seen or experienced. I know how scared you've been of your ability. I just … I don't want you to feel like you're alone in this. So I'm here to give you whatever you want, even if I think it's batshit crazy."

Her eyes inexplicably welled with tears.

"Hey, what's wrong? What'd I say?"

Shaking her head, she said, "I'm just having a hard time with all this."

"Come here," he said, tugging gently on her hand and lowering his leg so both feet were on the floor.

She truly worried that if he put his hands on her, it would trigger her memory of the dream all over again. But he just pulled her to him and she rested her head on his chest, one arm draped around her. He kissed the top of her head.

"We'll figure it out," he said.

She curled a little closer to his side, letting herself believe it.

By the following weekend, they had a plan. Riley and Michael arranged details via text, as she'd taken on extra shifts to make up for taking the weekend off.

The pair now "worked" at *Albuquerque Life* magazine, which Riley chose because, through another one of her Internet search wormholes, she discovered the magazine had already gotten in trouble a handful of times for their dodgy journalistic tactics. Hiring a couple of freelancers to harass stories out of supposedly rehabilitated criminals wouldn't even be the worst thing they'd been accused of.

Riley and Michael procured a fancy camera from Brie, who was apparently very into nature photography.

They agreed to meet Francis at a coffee shop in Santa Fe on Saturday.

"If anything gets weird, call me," texted Jade. "I'll have the cavalry there in two shakes of a lamb's tail if that psycho touches a hair on your pretty head."

Just after one-thirty, a knock sounded on her door.

"Hey," Michael said when she let him in, hugging her immediately. She hadn't seen him since the weekend before. "You nervous?"

"About meeting a murderer? Nah."

Michael quirked a smile, picking up Brie's camera off the coffee table as if it were made of glass. Its case sat beside it, two additional lenses inside. She hoped they didn't break the thing. It would cost a small fortune to replace.

"I looked up key photography-sounding words," he said, draping the strap around his neck. "Shutter, aperture, image."

Riley snorted. "You had to look up *image*?"

"I'll just talk about the light a lot."

Luckily, he was quite charming and looked professional as hell in his work clothes—which he'd donned for this occasion—so she figured he could fake it.

Riley would be doing most of the talking, anyway. Her stomach had been in knots all morning. She wore the one pencil skirt she owned—black—paired with a dark purple button-down silk shirt she'd gotten for mandatory family photos years ago.

"I can tell you're nervous," he said, "but you look amazing."

She smoothed out the non-existent wrinkles in her skirt by running her sweaty palms down the front of it. Her cheeks heated up, embarrassed for some reason, and kept her gaze focused on the tips of her cream-colored ballet flats.

"You turn a darker shade of brown when you blush," he said. "It's oddly sexy."

When she glanced up to glare at him, he snapped a photo of

her. Hands on hips, she gave him her best "If you don't put that camera down, I'm going to smash it over your head and make you pay Brie back" look. He snapped another one.

Laughing, she held a hand up to block her face. "Stop!"

"There's that smile." He took the camera off and carefully placed it in its case. "You ready? We're meeting him at three, right?"

After tossing everything but her purse in the trunk, she climbed into the passenger seat, greeted by two badges hanging from his rearview mirror. They were on the end of black lanyards, and the cards behind the protective plastic covers had their names, titles, and place of employment, paired with a picture.

"Not bad, Roberts."

"I'm trying to convince myself you're dating me because you like me, and not for my access to Photoshop."

She shrugged.

"Cold."

Leaning over the center console, she kissed him on the cheek.

"Hmm. You're lucky I'm so easy," he said.

Because she'd abused her radio privileges the last time they'd been in the car together for an extended period of time, she'd been banished from even touching the dial. Every time she tried, Michael playfully swatted her hand away. He settled on a classic rock station and stayed there.

When they were ten minutes away from the coffee shop—half an hour early—Riley asked, "Wait. Is it a crime to impersonate a reporter?"

"Kinda late in the game to ask that, no?" he said, laughing. "It's probably not a crime, but I'm sure there's something more than a little sketchy with our plan."

"'Kay. Just checking."

Riley employed her oft-used deep breathing exercises.

He grabbed her hand, keeping the other positioned on top of the wheel. "It'll be fine."

The sun shone in a clear blue sky, birds chirping in the newly flowering bushes surrounding the shop's outdoor seating area. The patio was populated by a handful of bright red umbrellas over black iron tables, and they chose one not far from the group of cheerful sparrows scrabbling in fallen leaves and bouncing around the branches. Thankfully the seating area, enclosed by a low wrought-iron fence, was currently deserted.

She and Michael pressed two tables together so they could set everything up before Francis arrived. Riley hoped that the more professional they looked, the fewer questions Francis would ask—and, hopefully, the more he'd answer.

Riley pulled up her document of questions on her laptop and had a pen and legal pad ready too, the recorder placed beside the pad. She straightened out the lanyard hanging around her neck and made sure her badge faced out.

Michael held the camera from underneath, his hand wrapped around the lens and the base resting on his forearm. She was moments from telling him how believable he looked, when she spotted a middle-aged man walking across the parking lot. Though he was over thirty years older, he was unmistakably the man from her dream. The man who'd chased after Renee, calling her a "stupid bitch."

Michael's face appeared in her line of sight and her attention snapped to his eyes. "Focus."

She blew out a deep breath. Standing up, she took a few steps to the side and raised an arm in the air.

Francis glanced over and stopped dead in his tracks, giving her an elevator scan. Stones dropped in her belly, the weight of each one rounding her shoulders. The fact that he was literally twice her age only made her queasier. A smile slowly inched up his face.

The smile was disarming, even now. Riley saw how women—and likely quite a few men—could be lured in by that smile.

Francis gestured at the entrance to let her know he was going around.

When he was out of sight, Michael said, "If he looks at you like that again, I'm going to strangle him."

"Easy, tiger."

He grunted.

Riley straightened her skirt and turned to face the door, hands folded in front of her. She offered a bright smile when Francis pushed his way outside, turning on her schmoozy waitress charm. "Hello, Francis. I'm Riley," she said, taking a couple steps forward with her hand outstretched.

"Please call me Hank," he said, taking her hand in his. "You're even more beautiful in person than you are in your picture. You actually remind me of someone I knew when I was younger. I'm sure she would've grown up to be as pretty as you."

Would have. Janay?

Riley swallowed, hoping it would soothe her churning stomach somehow. "Well, thank you. And this," she said, turning, "is my partner, Jansen Trombley."

The name sounded even more ridiculous out loud. No more choosing aliases for Michael. Francis knew her name; Michael still had his anonymity.

Francis shot a cursory glance at Michael, but quickly dismissed him.

"Ready to get started, Hank?" she asked.

"Sure."

Gesturing to the chair across from hers, she sat down. Michael hovered nearby, glaring daggers at the side of other man's head.

"Think of this more like a conversation; I want to get to know you—" she tried extremely hard not to let her lip curl when he smirked here, "—as a person more than anything else. This piece is about you and the progress you've made. Jansen is here to take pictures, so just let him do his thing and pretend he's not here."

"Not a problem."

Michael's jaw clenched.

"Perfect," she said. "I also would like to record this. Is that all right?" She picked up the digital recorder.

"Yeah, that's cool."

She hit record and supplied what she hoped sounded like a proper pre-interview statement, rattling off the date, time, and who she was talking to, and asked him to confirm verbally that he gave his consent to be recorded. She placed the recorder beside her legal pad, the microphone facing Francis.

Guys like him, the cocky ones who got through life at least partly relying on their looks, often wouldn't shut the hell up once you got them talking. A compliment here or there and they opened up like a flower in the sunlight. Add in the fact that this guy had gotten away with quite a few crimes with no one the wiser? Riley banked on the fact that once she gave him a little encouragement, he'd start blabbing.

Riley had watched enough shows about guys like him, the ones who slipped through the legal system's fingers, to know that they often found ways to mention the crime in question—wanting to brag without making a confession.

"How long has it been since your statutory rape conviction?"

Francis flinched slightly, as if startled by the question. What did he think they were going to talk about—baking? He recovered quickly, gaze focused on something she couldn't see beyond the barrier of her open laptop. "I … uh … I was eighteen. My girlfriend was thirteen."

Quickly looking up, he pulled his brows together, silently daring her to judge him for having sex with a girl who had barely entered into puberty. Riley kept her face blank.

"I got eighteen months," he said. "So I was almost twenty when I got out. Been thirty years."

"Were you required to register as a sex offender?"

"Nah. That didn't really start until the mid-'90s."

Unfortunate. It also meant she could skip a handful of her pre-pared questions. She scrolled down the list, then looked up at him.

"How did having a conviction on your record affect your ability to find employment?"

"It was absolute shit there for a while. I had to let people know I had a criminal record and no one wanted to hire me—not even as a janitor. Plus, people I thought were my friends started thinking I was a child molester or something. I just had a young girlfriend and her parents were real uptight—religious nuts, you know. Thought it was a sin and all that.

"But we were in love. And we wanted to express our love … physically."

He winked quickly on the last word. Riley threw up in her mouth a little.

"So you felt the verdict was unjust?"

"Of course. It's no one's business who I have sex with other than me and who I'm with." Riley was about to ask something else, but he cut her off. "And none of that 'Oh, she's not old enough to make those kinds of decisions at thirteen' bullshit. That girl was plenty capable."

Out of the corner of her eye, she saw Michael quickly walk away from the table where he'd been hovering, like he'd just narrowly avoided going through with his desire to bludgeon the guy with his camera.

"You were a runaway when you were in your early teens, is that right? Your parents reported you as missing in 1980?"

His head reared back slightly.

"I'm a reporter; I've done my research."

Rolling his shoulders, he nodded. "Yeah, I took off when I was thirteen."

"Why's that?"

"Is this relevant?"

"Children with troubled home lives often wind up in the system one way or another. You're a product of what was done to you."

He sighed, folding his arms on the table, shoulders bunched up by his ears as he smiled at her. The sudden change from guarded to … something else … threw her. She could only see his eyes and half of his partially crooked nose over the laptop. Reaching a hand up—which made Michael close the distance by a few steps—Francis placed a finger on the edge of her laptop, then slowly pushed it closed. She pulled her hands out of the way.

"You said this is a conversation, right?" Francis said, gaze roving her face. "It's easier for me to have a conversation when I can actually see who I'm talking to. Shame to have a pretty little thing like you hiding behind this. Besides, you got the recorder going, don't you?"

Riley swallowed. "Fair enough."

He relaxed a little, keeping his arms crossed on the table. "So, yeah, I left home because my dad lost his job when I was about ten or so. He worked in a factory and messed up his back—was on disability. After rent, we hardly had enough to eat.

"Parents fought all the damn time. Mom developed a drug habit—and they were both alcoholics. She lost her job. Dad beat me pretty good on a regular enough basis that I finally just left."

"Where'd you go? Did you have extended family in the area?"

"Stole some cash and took a bus to see my uncle. He didn't want another kid to feed though. Kicked me out after a week or two."

"Then what?"

"Shelters. Slept on the street. Did odd jobs—mowing lawns, tried a paper route but it was hard to swing without a bike, washed windows and cars."

"That must've been hard."

"I survived."

"Must have been a scary time back then, being on the streets," she said. "That was when that serial killer was snatching up runaways, right? What was his name?"

"Orin Jacobs," Francis said automatically.

"Yeah, him," she said. "Were the shelter kids scared?"

"Not really. I mean, the guys weren't. Only chicks were getting taken." Francis rubbed the back of his neck. "Wanna know something kind of interesting though?"

Riley's heartbeat stumbled. "What's that?"

"Well, funny thing. That girl who escaped? Mindy? I knew her."

"No kidding?"

"Yeah, we were actually staying at the same shelter when she was taken."

"Wow. Must have been scary to know you'd been *that* close to a killer."

"Like I said, I'm not a chick, so it never really got to me. Luck of the chromosome, I guess." He stared at her for a long time.

Riley started to get the impression that he was sizing *her* up now.

"Did you ever see him? Orin, I mean. You know, after the fact, when his face was on the news—did you recognize him?"

"Nah. I'd never seen the guy in my life." He cocked his head. "You seem more interested in that than in me. You into that kinda stuff? Murder mysteries?"

"I'm into finding out the truth."

He smiled. She mirrored it.

Then she folded her arms on the table and slightly leaned forward. "What are *you* into?" Her voice took on a low purr.

Slowly, he licked his lips. "Pretty girls who like searching for the truth."

She laughed. A fake, over-the-top waitress laugh. It brought out the full grin from Francis she'd been expecting. "What's *your* truth, Hank?"

"Ditch the pretty boy and I'll show you."

Riley'd managed to forget Michael was there for a moment. Maybe Jade was right about the incorrigible flirt assessment. "My first priority is always the story. I need to uncover *that* truth before I … explore anything else."

Francis sat back, his arms wide as either hand gripped the edge of the table. "I know a challenge when I see one. I'm game. Keep asking your questions."

Michael stood off to the side, behind Francis, his mouth agape.

"What do *you* think about murder mysteries?" she asked, regaining her focus.

"I think too much time is spent harping on the past when only the present matters."

"You don't think studying past behaviors leads to a better understanding of the present?"

He shrugged. "I think the past should stay there; you can't change it."

"You sound a little bitter. Have you done something you regret?"

"Haven't we all?" he asked. "What's something *you've* done you wish you could take back?"

She considered that for a moment. She regretted a lot about Casey but she wasn't about to get that personal with Francis. "Letting work take over my life when I should be a better friend."

He scoffed. "You can do better than that. Cheating on a boyfriend, shoplifting, hurting someone …"

"I can't think of anything that specific. What about you?"

"Well, if we're going to be vague … I regret the trust I've put in people," he said. "When I was a teenager, I fell in love with a girl who used me. Made me think she cared about me when all she wanted was an out. When I really needed her, she turned on me."

"The thirteen year old?"

"Nah. Before Natalie."

Mindy. Had to be. She said he'd told her he loved her. Then she'd clocked him in the face and left him bleeding—possibly dead—before she made a break for it.

"You've contradicted yourself," Riley said. "You said the past doesn't matter since we can't change it. Why are you still so upset about something that happened decades ago?"

"If we go by your way of looking at things, that betrayal all those years ago made me who I am today," he said. "I learned never to trust anyone."

So he blamed *Mindy* for all this?

"That's mighty bleak," she said. "That why you track who looks at your page?"

He smiled. "Led me to you, didn't it? Paranoia has its rewards."

"Paranoid about what?"

Looking away for a moment, he broke the intense bout of eye contact they'd been maintaining. "What happened to this article being about me turning my life around?" His posture was more guarded now, arms crossed in front of him again.

"I told you this was a conversation. Plus," she said, motioning to her computer, "you closed off my access to the prearranged questions."

"Aw, you don't need those. Something tells me you're good on your ... toes." The disarming smile revealed white teeth arranged in a perfect line.

Maybe she'd let Michael strangle him at the end of this after all. The look on his face said he'd be happy to.

She got in a couple more questions about his parents before a group of six teenagers flooded out onto the patio. They took a spot in the opposite corner, laughing and talking over each other.

Francis immediately lost focus, his gaze continuously flicking over to the boys. Riley couldn't tell if he wanted to join them or hightail it back to his car. Did crowds make him nervous?

"Wanna call it a day for now?" she asked.

"Yeah, that's cool," he said, springing to his feet as if someone had just hit the eject button on his chair. "I got some stuff I gotta do."

Riley stood as well and held out her hand. "I really appreciate you taking the time to talk with me. Maybe we can chat on the phone if I need more material?"

"Yeah, yeah, sure," he said, not even acknowledging Michael as he headed for the exit.

Blowing out an exaggerated sigh, some of the tension left her shoulders as she grabbed the recorder and hit stop. The legal pad didn't have a word on it. As she went to pick it up, she felt someone behind her. Michael, camera halfway back in its case, froze in place, attention focused over Riley's shoulder.

A hand lightly wrapped around her elbow and she stilled, back ramrod straight.

With his chest pressed to the side of her body, mouth right on her ear, he said, "If you want to talk more in-depth, you could always come to my place for a one-on-one session. See me in my element. Uncover the real me." His voice was deep and smooth. "Just make sure you leave *Jansen* behind."

Then he was gone, the patio door swishing shut behind him.

CHAPTER 18

In the middle of packing up her things, Riley looked up. Francis strode across the parking lot as if he hadn't a care in the world. A smartly dressed woman walked past him and he turned to walk backwards for a moment to admire the view from another angle. Then Francis noticed Riley and smirked. He blew her a kiss. Face hot, she diverted her attention back to her belongings. She needed to get the hell out of there.

When she cautiously glanced up again a few moments later, she caught sight of him just as he disappeared around the side of a sporting goods store.

Michael and Riley left the café, loaded up the car, and drove away. It wasn't until they were out of the parking lot, and sure the guy wasn't following them, that she let herself have a full-fledged wiggle-panic-meltdown.

"Oh my *god*! He is the most vile man I've ever met!" Shaking out both hands, goosebumps broke out across her skin at the memory of him standing so close to her. She wanted to take a shower in bleach.

"You ... you two were practically undressing each other with your eyes at one point."

"Michael!"

"What!"

"You can't possibly be jealous of ... of ... *that*."

"Something was happening between you two—that's all I'm saying."

Riley shuddered violently. Then she replayed her encounter with Francis in her head. "Jade says I'm an incorrigible flirt."

He started to say something, then stopped.

"What?"

With a shrug, he shook his head.

"Okay," she said. "You know how some people have that extra … something? Where you're drawn to them because of something beyond physical attraction?"

"Why do you think I'm currently in Santa Fe driving around with a girl who just had a chat with a murderer?"

She laughed, semi-hysterical. "No, I mean, have you ever met someone you were drawn to, but it wasn't sexual? Maybe even another man—like a boss or something where you just want to be around them. To soak up their knowledge or they have a really fun energy that always puts you in a better mood?"

He considered that. "Yeah, I guess so."

"I think flirting is just … I don't know … a result of that. Some instinctual thing that pulls you to another person, regardless of the reason," she said. "There are billions of people on the planet and most of them you don't even look at twice, right? But there are those few who have that something that makes them stand out. Sometimes it's sexual, but for me it usually isn't. It's an … energy thing? Man, I sound so woo-woo, new age-y right now."

"Nah, I think I get it."

"He's got that," she said. "The non-sexual draw. And, I mean, how many times have you flirted with someone based solely on looks and then once they start talking you change your mind and the desire to flirt turns off?"

He nodded.

"Just because you're showing interest on some level doesn't automatically mean physical attraction. When I flirt, the intention isn't to sleep with them, it's just to get to know them. Flirting is fun and makes people open up more. But that's all it is."

"You don't think there's a risk of leading someone on?"

Riley shook her head. "I think that's more about entitlement. You think because someone shows interest in you—and it could be sexual for one person, but not the other, and they're taking things the wrong way—you're owed access to them sexually. But that's bull-shit. You're only allowed access if I say you are, flirtation or not. It's not my fault if you read into my actions what you *want* to be true."

Mouth bunched up on the side, he quietly mulled that over.

"When my ex flirted, he did so quote-unquote *discreetly*. To me, that shows intent to hook up. If you didn't know I was meeting Francis and found me out on that patio with him, me in his lap—" Riley shuddered at this, "—my intent would clearly be different than what just happened. But you were there the whole time and you knew I was only trying to get information out of him, right?"

"Yeah, for sure," he said. "I think I see what you mean. It was still hard to see, but that's also because I had mild Kim flashbacks."

She hadn't considered that and reached over to squeeze his free hand. "I'm sorry it made you uncomfortable."

"So you *don't* want to run off with him and live like Bonnie and Clyde?"

"My god!" She smacked his arm. "I *loathe* him. He fascinates the hell out of me, but more in that 'I want to solve the puzzle' way."

"Well, you *did* warn me that you were really into true crime."

"Maybe I missed my calling as a private investigator."

"Still time."

After a few minutes of driving, the low hum of classic rock the only sound, she said, "Did you really think I *liked* him?"

"The intellectual part of me didn't," he said. "What did he say to you before he left?"

"He wants to meet with just me," she said. "He suggested his place."

"*Hell* no," he said. "You're not allowed alone with that guy—especially not in his house. I don't care if that makes me sound like a possessive asshole, but I'm shutting that shit down right now."

"You're hot when you're feisty."

There was no sign of his usual good humor. "I'm serious, Riley."

"I know. Sorry. I know." After a short bout of silence, she said, "I wonder if *he* knows what the dark room is."

"Come again?"

Then she remembered he didn't know about the EVPs. "You ready to hear something?"

"Probably not."

After prepping the EVPs on her phone, she cranked up the volume. She was half tempted to hit play then shove her fingers in her ears, *la la la*-ing herself out of hearing Orin's voice again, but held firm.

Michael kept quiet through the first one, his hands gripping tight to the steering wheel.

"*Hank ... lied.*"

With a full-body shudder, he said, "Hate to break it to you, Orin, but Hank lies quite often." He sighed. "I just don't want anything to happen to you, Ry. That guy is ... off."

"Totally."

They stopped for an early dinner in Albuquerque, fighting to discuss everything *but* the weirdness of that afternoon. Of the last two weeks.

A thrift shop sat in the same complex as the restaurant, and after dinner they walked hand in hand down the aisles, looking at the random collection of odds and ends. Michael's favorite was a porcelain cookie jar in the shape of a vintage clown, which was already horrifying in its own right—especially since one eye was missing, the paint rubbed clean off—but when you opened it, a voice yelled "Hands off my cookies!" followed by a cackle straight out of nightmares. It startled him so much the first time, he screamed and nearly dropped the lid. Then he would have had to buy the awful thing.

Riley laughed so hard she cried.

Her favorite was a ceramic plate with two humanoid horses on it. They both wore pink, frilly tutus and one had a lock of the other's mane in its hoof/hand. Both creatures looked seductively out at their audience.

"What the hell?" Michael asked as he stared at it over her shoulder.

"I have so many questions," she said, staring at it. The plate itself was white, the edge lined with an uneven circle of gold.

"You want it?"

"Yes! But maybe just so I can smash it in the parking lot."

"Done!" he said, taking it from her and turning it over as they headed for the counter. "It's five dollars. I'm willing to pay any expense for my girl."

She laughed, ignoring the goofy flutter she got from hearing "my girl," and looped her arm through his.

They had just climbed into his car, her hideous plate wrapped in newspaper and stuffed in her purse, when she said, "You want to hang out at my place for a little bit? I don't have to work tomorrow. We can watch a *movie* or something."

He grinned. "Yes. That. Let's do that."

Their last date had been almost a week ago—on Sunday. They'd been on another one of their epic all-day dates, which ended at a drive-in closer to him. Riley wasn't sure she even saw the opening credits, because the moment it got dark enough for them to start the movie, she was on him.

She'd startled him, she knew, but some crazed need to be as close to him as possible sent her over the center console and into his lap, whacking her knee on his seatbelt clip, but she'd been too focused on kissing him to notice until later.

After a few seconds, she'd pulled away, both of them breathing hard. "Sorry."

"Good god, woman, if there was ever a thing *not* to apologize for …"

They'd been slightly less frantic after that. She'd unbuttoned his shirt, wanting her hands on his bare chest, and he'd slipped his hands up her back to unclasp her bra.

When his fingers had trailed down to the button on her jeans, however, she'd stilled.

So had he. "Too fast?"

"Just … it's been a while and maybe it shouldn't happen in a car."

Placing his hands on her hips, he'd said, "Did you want to watch the movie or—"

"Or—that one. Whatever that is."

"My place."

She'd climbed off his lap and he'd given the front of his pants a couple of awkward tugs.

But by the time they'd gotten out of the parking lot—which had taken forever, as the road out was blocked by a string of cars trying to get in—and to his place, she'd lost her nerve.

Hooking up with someone new—which she'd only done two other times—always made her impossibly nervous. Plus, he'd mentioned once that his ex was "toxic." Wasn't that on the same spectrum as "passionate"? The woman likely had been a vixen in the sack. Riley had the sexual prowess of a sloth.

Currently, she was fairly certain she wouldn't chicken out. Sometime during the course of wandering the thrift shop with him, she'd realized how much she liked the idea of being "his girl."

Once they got to her apartment, they spent the next ten minutes finding the perfect display location for the creeptastic ballerina horse plate.

They stood near her bookshelf staring at the tutued horse-people.

"I hate it so much," he said.

"Me too."

"Did you see the little set of numbers near the signature? It says 4 of 15. Does that mean there are fifteen nightmare horse plates?" He took the plate from its new home and flipped it over, squinting at the small writing on the back and scratching off the bright orange price tag. "Oh! It says this is part of the barnyard series."

Eyes wide, she said, "What if there are, like, horse mugs and tiny cake plates?"

"What if," he said, turning the plate back again, revealing the horse-people, "there are *more* plates? Creepy sheep and chickens and cows … if that's the case, we might have to devote our lives to finding the rest of them."

How could she possibly be nervous around this guy? He was just as weird as she was. Safely placing the plate back on its spot on the shelf, she slipped her hand into his and pulled him toward her bedroom.

"You sure?" he asked. "We can take this slow—"

She unzipped the back of her pencil skirt and let it hit the ground, puddling at her feet. Then she closed the distance between them, stood on her tiptoes, and pulled his face down to hers. Groaning softly, he wrapped his arms around the backs of her thighs, hoisting her off her feet. She curled her legs around him as he walked them to the side of the bed, slowly lowering her onto the bed.

Then Michael abruptly let her go and froze, back ramrod straight, eyes wide and scanning.

Riley propped herself up on her elbows. "What's wrong?"

"Is *he* here? Is he watching?"

Gaze shifting to her dresser, she stared at Pete's maroon beanie lying on top. She'd almost forgotten all about him. "No. I mean, he might be nearby, but he's not watching. He hasn't manifested in days."

"Still?"

Riley nodded. "If you're uncomfortable, we don't have—"

Lips pressed to hers cut her off. Then they were both fumbling with their own shirts, shaking fingers struggling to undo tiny buttons. Michael got his off first and then helped her with hers. But they were small, pearl-like buttons that were fastened by loops.

"This is the stupidest shirt I've ever seen," he muttered. "Wouldn't it be super sexy if I ripped it open and the buttons flew off?"

"No!" she said laughing. "This is the most expensive shirt I own!"

When he finally got the last button unfastened, she slipped her arms out of the shirt and tossed it on the floor.

He kissed her. "I'm setting that thing on fire after you fall asleep," he whispered against her mouth.

Unfastening her bra, she tossed that away too. He seemed less concerned about her shirt after that.

He leaned forward, easing her back until she lay on the comforter. Taking her by the hips, he lifted and scooted her further onto the bed in one fluid motion. He did it so quick, she let out a surprised laugh.

Climbing on top of her, he took one of her nipples in his mouth. *Oh hell.* Running her fingers through his hair as she watched his mouth on her, her brain went a little fuzzy.

"Um …" she said.

When he stopped to look up at her, the expression on his face almost sent her over the edge. He looked at her like he thought she was the sexiest thing to ever grace the earth. Sexy sloth women for the win!

"I'm usually all about foreplay, but I need you *now*," she said. "I needed you yesterday."

He didn't need to be told twice. Scrambling off the bed, he divested himself of the rest of his clothes and she wiggled out of her underwear.

"Condom," she said.

"Oh!" He practically dove for his pants on the floor. "Condom, condom …"

When he'd finally slipped inside her, she let out a sound somewhere between a moan and a whimper.

"I'm not going to last very long if you keep making that sound."

Her fingertips dug into his back, her feet wrapped around his calves.

Mouth on her ear, breathing labored, he said, "You feel even better than I thought you would."

After only two more thrusts, his breath hitched and he went still. Like he'd stopped breathing altogether. Lord, had Pete taken this moment to not only manifest, but to do so with enough energy that

Michael could see him too?

"Uhh … Michael."

"Shh. Don't talk," he said. "Don't even breathe."

He sounded pained; she snorted.

Breath hitching again, his back muscles taut, he said, "For the love of god, please don't laugh."

"What's wrong?"

"Just … uhh … give me a second." His head rested on her shoulder, his warm breath on her skin.

After a few long moments, he relaxed slightly. Lifting his head, he kissed her softly on the mouth. She kissed him back, hips rocking into him.

Mirroring her for two more thrusts, he groaned loudly, his body giving a sharp, violent jerk. "*Shit.*"

She bit her bottom lip. "Did you just—"

"It's … uh … been a while for me too," he said, twitching once more. "And you feel really fucking amazing." Twitch. Silence. Twitch. "I would like to state for the record that I'm mortified."

She tried so hard not to burst out laughing that it turned into a silent, internal earthquake. Rising up on one elbow to look at her, he arched a brow, making it even harder to keep it together; his face was bright red, more from embarrassment than exertion. Which made her feel even worse for laughing, but she wasn't sure she could stop. Her nostrils flared spastically with the effort to keep her laughter contained.

The faintest hint of a smile graced his mouth. "This isn't funny, Ms. Thomas. My penis has just failed us both."

Riley lost it, laughing so hard she cried for the second time that day.

He let her cackle like a lunatic, then kissed her nose and climbed off the bed to wash up in the bathroom. She had more or less calmed down by the time he came back. She still lay naked on the bed, arms thrown above her head.

Lying next to her, he propped himself up on his side. "This was supposed to be the most incredible experience of your life."

She snorted, rolling over so she faced him, her head propped up in her hand, too. "I'm just so relieved the pressure is off. Women get performance anxiety too, you know!"

"Performance!" he said. "You literally just laid there and I was done already."

"The first time is supposed to be kind of awkward." Then she leaned forward and kissed him. "Just means we gotta keep practicing."

They talked for a little while and he finally started to relax. At least he was no longer the color of a tomato.

"So, uh … wanna start that practice … now?" he asked.

She nodded emphatically.

Cupping the back of her head in his hand, he kissed her, lowering himself on top of her. He left a trail of kisses down her stomach until he settled between her legs.

It was only a matter of a minute before it was her turn to cry out and twitch beneath him. He kissed the inside of her thigh after she'd settled; her body felt like it'd melted. She was no longer solid.

"I hope that makes up for it?" he asked.

She could only offer a sleepy smile in response.

And, when he slipped inside her again, he made up for it a second time.

CHAPTER 19

Given their vastly different work schedules, Riley had a hard time seeing Michael during the week. He came over to her place after work the following night. They were two insatiable beasts and didn't get to bed until after three.

When he came over the following night, he sat on her couch while she hurried to the bathroom to pee shortly after getting home. She emerged in her skimpiest underwear, only to find him snoring softly, head thrown back on the cushions, mouth open.

Between that, feeling awful for Baxter the cat being left alone night after night, and worrying that Pete would feel abandoned—even if he seemed unable to manifest—she forbade weekday rendez-vous at either residence until she managed to get a better schedule.

Which left her with post-work wind-down time, and her quest to ruin Francis Hank Carras. Every girl needed a hobby, right?

Since going to his place alone to "uncover the real him" was not even in the realm of possibilities, she needed to get to the guy another way.

Ever since she'd read the post by Renee's father, Riley had the niggling idea in the back of her mind that getting the case reopened might be her best bet. Especially since a reformed Francis, eager to confess his past wrongdoings, wasn't in the realm of possibilities either.

And, in order to reopen Renee Palmer's case, she'd need evidence. The police already had a full caseload, with new crimes happening every day, so she'd need something compelling. She knew she was hindered by the fact that she wasn't related to the victim in any way other than psychically from beyond the grave, and oh sweet lord, no one was going to buy that.

Her search for microfilm copies of the newspapers that reported the crime proved fruitless. Both the University of New Mexico and the New Mexico State Library had microfilm available online, but their efforts were focused on preserving the papers with historic headlines—like the Roswell crash of 1947. Neither had papers from the timeframe she wanted, and the library had only started cataloguing ones from the 1990s and later.

By Thursday, she was at a loss. She'd need the officer's name who'd worked on the case, or a case number—something—when she tried to contact authorities about reopening it. But she couldn't find anything.

The "Who Killed Renee Palmer?" tab headline still sat in her browser, wedged between tabs for her email and the 24-hour diner down the street. Clicking on Renee's site, Riley read the post again. It was ten years old—who knew if her father was still alive. It might have been the mother or one of the brothers who kept sending yearly birthday wishes into the ether.

An email address was the only option for contacting the family. Maybe the email was no longer active. Maybe her email would just end up in a spam folder. Maybe she was making up excuses because she didn't want to give this family false hope. Or, even worse, make them think this was all a joke and she was making fun of their thirty-year-old grief.

She copy-and-pasted the address into the "to" line of a blank email.

Subject? "I know who killed Renee"? God, was that too morbid? Too sensationalist?

She settled for "About Renee." Vague had to be better than morbid.

The couple who walked the street where their son and nephew had been hit by the speeding van popped into her mind. The pair had been doubtful at first but warmed to the idea of Riley's gift once she told them details a stranger wouldn't know. Keeping that in mind, she penned her email.

> Dear Palmer family,
>
> My name is Riley Thomas. First off, I want to say I'm sorry for your loss—I'm sure that even though it happened over thirty years ago, the pain is still fresh. I'm writing to you for a slightly unconventional reason, and I hope you finish reading before you discount it as a practical joke.
>
> About two weeks ago, I went to the Jordanville Ranch for one of their paranormal investigation weekends. This, as I'm sure you know, was the house where Orin Jacobs the serial killer had once lived. I know Renee's body was found near the property line.
>
> I'm a medium, though not one who practices it professionally. After I left the ranch, I had a dream about Renee. She showed me

what happened to her. That dream and the information it provided me has now led me to this email address.

I wanted Walter Palmer, her father, to know that she used the skills you taught her to defend herself. She managed to get the guy in the face with her pepper spray—though she missed the first time. She berated herself, thinking she'd done her father shame initially when, even after all her lessons, she didn't get him on the first try. But she eventually did and fought with everything she had to get away. She did all she could.

She had a feeling her boyfriend—I'm assuming—Nick would chastise her once she got home because she'd been so consumed with thoughts about her troubles at work that she'd strayed from her usual path. Nick had told her once that she would get lost in the real world one day as a result of being so lost in her head.

It's my goal to hopefully help get the case reopened. If there's any additional information you can provide me, I would greatly appreciate it.

I just wanted to let you know that Renee

hasn't been forgotten, and that someone who doesn't even know her would like to help bring closure to your family.

I hope this email finds you well despite your tragic loss.

If you are at all uncomfortable that I've contacted you, simply don't reply and I will leave you and your family alone.

Best wishes,

Riley Thomas

She read it about ten times to herself before deeming it worthy. Adding her phone number, she hit send. Holding her breath, she waited for a kickback email informing her that the message was undeliverable. But one didn't come. After ten minutes, she figured it had gone through. Whether anyone would read it was another matter.

On Friday, near the end of her shift, one of the waitresses flagged Riley down on her way to bringing refills to her last table. Usually by nine-thirty, sit-down customers tapered off, and it mostly became takeout orders—they were open until ten. The Laughing

Tiger was the only upscale dim sum place in the immediate area that also catered to the take-out crowd.

"Hey, so there's this guy who just requested to sit in your section," Emily said.

Riley groaned. "Really? I thought I was getting out of here soon."

Emily grinned. "He's handsome!"

Had Michael decided to surprise her? She was supposed to spend the night at his house tonight, since she had Saturday off.

After depositing the refills at the table of a very drunk older couple who were now making out passionately in a back booth, Riley scanned her section looking for Michael.

And found Francis Hank Carras instead. Her stomach bottomed out.

Steeling herself, she took a calming breath, and walked over to him. Aside from the sucking-face couple, she and Francis were alone on this side of the restaurant.

"Hello, Riley." He wore khakis and a white button-down shirt. The picture of normalcy. A black leather jacket was draped on the booth next to him. "Care to have a seat?"

She looked around. Emily and Sasha stood at the maître d' podium, trying to look busy, but watching Riley and Francis out of the corner of their eyes. Their curiosity would hopefully work in her favor and they'd stick around even after he left to get details on this good-looking stranger requesting her by name.

Riley slipped into the hard-backed chair across from him. "What are you doing here? I'm guessing it's not for dim sum."

He shrugged. "I love dim sum—especially pad thai."

"Pad thai is *Thai* food; dim sum is Chinese."

He waved that away with one of his hands as if the distinction couldn't possibly mean any less to him. "I find it very interesting that you work here when you claim to be a reporter."

Keep calm. "A *freelance* reporter. Writing isn't exactly lucrative. This pays my bills."

Pursing his lips at that, he said, "You said your editor loved the story idea."

"He does." How the hell did he find her? Then it hit her a moment later. *I listed my place of employment on my page. Idiot.* "Okay, to be honest? Your story is supposed to be my breakout piece. The pay is shit *now*, but the name recognition will hopefully snag me a gig as a full-time reporter. You're my meal ticket out of here," she said, motioning to the restaurant. She had zero idea where any of this came from, but she ran with it.

"If this story is so important, why haven't you contacted me again?"

"Aw," she said, cocking her head to the side. "Is this little tantrum because I haven't called you?"

She got one of his slow smiles. "You hurt my feelings."

"As you can see, I've got several irons in the fire," she said, motioning to the restaurant at large again. "I'm still working on your story."

"I've been thinking about you," he said, licking his bottom lip.

She suppressed a shudder. "You've crossed my mind once or twice."

He laughed at that. A heartfelt belly laugh. "Such a tease."

When the staring went on a little too long, she said, "So was there a reason for this visit other than to pout?"

"I found out something else very interesting about you."

Good god, what did *that* mean? "Oh?"

"Well," he said, folding his arms on the table and leaning toward her a little, just as he'd done during the interview. She didn't mirror him this time, remaining with her back flat against the chair. "You should really be careful whose friend requests you accept. Opens a person up to seeing all kinds of things."

Hell. Had a picture of Michael and her together been posted somehow? The only pictures she had of them were on her phone; she hadn't posted anything. No. He couldn't know that Jansen Trombley was actually Michael Roberts. Michael didn't have a page.

"You don't seem to post that much. A private girl. Very smart. But that friend of yours—Jade? She posts all manner of things. Checks in at almost every location, posts selfies, often with the location of wherever she is in the background, and has friends who comment with great frequency. She's beautiful, that girl. Missed her obvious calling as a model."

Riley's jaw was clenched, her skin crawling. She didn't trust herself to not say something stupid, so she opted to stay quiet.

"So, after going through all these posts and comments by these insipid girls, I discover that a few weeks ago, you went on a little ghost hunt."

A dramatic pause.

She took the bait. "And?"

"That's where the interesting thing comes in. I hopped over to the forums for the Jordanville Ranch and looked for mention of the weekend you were there. Someone named Angela posted that one of their guests, Riley, had spoken to the ghost of a kid named Pete."

Goddammit, Angela.

"So, what, you a psychic or something?" he asked. "See dead people?"

"Proper term is medium."

"Oho!" he said, throwing his head back as he laughed. "You

admit it."

She shrugged.

Voice a fraction softer, he said, "Some girl named Heather said you had contact with Orin himself."

Goddammit, Heather.

The Skinny Jean Quartet couldn't be trusted with secrets either.

His change in tone gave her pause. He almost sounded reverent. "Why does any of this matter to you?" she asked.

"I got this girl snooping around who's first a reporter and then a waitress and now a medium? Makes a guy wonder if he's got something to be worried about."

Now she mirrored his posture, leaning toward him a fraction of an inch. "There something you need to tell me, Francis?"

His upper lip twitched. "Hank."

"You only need to be worried if there's something you're hiding," she said. "You've told me the truth, haven't you? I trust you as much as you trust me."

A grin crept onto his face at that, gaze zeroed in on her mouth for a moment before his gaze flicked back up to her eyes. "I trust women only about as far as I can throw them. And that's usually backwards onto my bed. Or the couch or ..." He ran a hand, palm down and fingers splayed, on the black surface of the table between them. "Over the side of something hard and flat."

She smiled as she thought about shoving chopsticks into his eyes. "Story first, Hank, story first."

With another award-winning smile, he sat back, nodding. "Fair enough, little medium." Grabbing his jacket off the booth, he started to scoot out.

She was on her feet in an instant, taking several steps back.

Stopping a foot in front of her, his tall frame seemed larger than at the interview. "Have a good evening, Riley Thomas."

"You too, *Francis*."

Expression some combination of smirk and scowl, he sauntered for the door, jacket in hand. "Good night, ladies," he said once he reached door, shooting one of his disarming smiles at Emily and Sasha. They swooned in his general direction.

He didn't look back as he pushed his way out into the cool, springtime night air.

Why the hell had he come all the way over here for *that*? Just to rattle her? She could imagine how Mindy must have felt when he'd done the same to her, but over the course of months. Turning up day after day on her route to and from school.

Emily and Sasha bounded over.

"*Who* was *that*?" Emily asked.

"Does he have a son?" asked Sasha. "Though I wouldn't mind *him*. Older men have more experience."

"Please *swear* to me that you'll never encourage that guy if he comes back."

Sasha's head reared back as if Riley had slapped her.

"He assaulted a friend of mine."

A gasp erupted out of them in unison.

"Yeah, he's bad news. I don't have solid proof of it yet, but he's been sniffing around, trying to see if I've got what I need to go to the police. He's trying to intimidate me."

"Jesus," Emily said, arms crossed over her chest as if she were suddenly cold.

"If you see him again, or if he calls looking for me—"

"No worries, girl, we got you. We'll warn the others, too."

After finally booting the drunken couple—when she went over to tell them the restaurant was closed, the man had his hand up the woman's shirt while she moaned in ecstasy—Riley gathered her things and sent a text to Michael. **Heading your way now. Apologies if you find rice in my bra. I can't be bothered to shower.**

We can take one together, he suggested, followed by half a dozen smirking emojis.

Emily caught her just before she left, Frank in tow. "I told everyone still here about the creep. Frank said he'll make sure all the girls get to their cars safely."

"Thanks, Frank," Riley said, strapping her purse on her shoulder.

"I got daughters your age," he said, as if that explained everything.

It wasn't until she was on the road to Michael's house—too scared to even grab a change of clothes—that she realized *how* rattled she was. Her hands shook on the steering wheel. She might've hit 85 on the highway.

When she finally got to his house and he greeted her on the porch, she was so relieved to see him, she almost cried.

"Whoa, you okay?"

"Better now," she said, wrapping her arms around him. "Hank showed up at the restaurant tonight." Then she winced, waiting for it, temple pressed to his chest.

Michael froze, hands on her waist. "He *what*? Why didn't you say anything when you texted me? I could have come to you instead."

She shook her head. "I needed some distance. Dude scares the shit out of me."

Michael let out a long sigh, then led her inside. For some reason, he decided that what she needed in that moment was hot tea. Once

Baxter was happily curled up in her lap, purring away, Michael bustled into the kitchen. She didn't have the heart to tell him she wasn't a fan of tea.

Her phone dinged. Doing her best to reach for her purse on the coffee table without interrupting the cat, she fished out her phone.

She sucked in a breath.

One of the Palmers had written back.

CHAPTER 20

Riley had expected it would take the Palmers days—maybe weeks—to reply. Not twenty-four hours. She was suddenly terrified to open it. What if they threatened to contact the authorities for harassment if she ever emailed them again? She'd be back to square one.

Dear Ms. Thomas,

I will admit that I was ready to dismiss your letter, sure this was yet another person claiming to have communicated with my daughter—you'd be surprised how many we've gotten over the years.

But by the end, I was crying like a baby. My son came running into the room to ask me what was wrong, sure someone must have died given how I was carrying on.

When I told him to read the email, he had a similar reaction.

It was the details that sealed it for us both. You knew things that no one outside the family would know—not even the police who interviewed us. Especially that last bit about Nick warning her that she'd get lost one day thanks to that over-active mind of hers.

That's what did it.

My hope of finding out the truth has been wavering lately. People tell me it's time to move on. Well, now, thanks to you, I can tell them to go suck an egg!

As for evidence, I'm not sure if I can be any help there. We have since moved out of the house the kids grew up in, " and we're in Rio Rancho now in an "assisted living" facility. More like a "place where people go to slowly die" facility, if you ask me. But they tell me my memory's not what it used to be, so I guess I don't have much choice in the matter.

I read up a little on mediums, and it says some of you folks can pick up information if you handle something of importance to the victim? I've got a box of Renee's things here. All we've got left. You're welcome to give those a try. Have a few newspaper clippings from back then, too.

I read them sometimes. If my memory really is starting to go, I want to make sure Renee isn't something I forget.

Please let me know what you'd like or need to proceed.

And thank you again for reaching out.

God bless,

Walter

Riley read the email twice. She jumped when Michael sat down next to her.

"You were zoned out again," he said.

The heavy scent of cinnamon hit her. She fought the urge to wrinkle her nose. When Michael handed her the steaming mug, she passed him her phone.

Baxter's head jerked up, ears flattened, and then he sprang off Riley's lap, scampering down the hall.

"What did I do?" she asked.

"He hates the smell of cinnamon," Michael said matter-of-factly, gaze focused on her phone screen.

She took a tentative sip of the tea—dismayed that even the cat thought it offensive—and found it not nearly as strong as its aroma implied. It was soothing, actually. She took another sip.

"Damn," Michael said after a minute, handing her phone back. "What are you going to do?"

Glancing at him, she said, "You wanna go for another drive?"

"Just tell me where and when."

"No objections?"

"To an old guy who's grieving over his daughter? Nah."

"I like you a little bit."

Smiling he said, "Only a little?"

She leaned forward to put her mug on the coffee table, then sat in his lap, facing him. With a light kiss, she said, "Slightly more than a little. And we can figure out the other stuff in the morning."

Groaning, he kissed her. Then he grasped her under her thighs, held tight, and stood. She yelped and laughed, legs circling his hips.

"I get you all day tomorrow, right?" he asked, then kissed her neck.

"Mmhmm."

"Good," he said, walking them to his bedroom. "Because you're not allowed to get out of my bed until noon."

On Tuesday, after Walter and Riley had sent several emails back and forth, she and Michael headed to Rio Rancho to meet Mr. Palmer and his youngest son, Scott, at the Ridgeview Estates after Michael got off work. The middle son, Isaac, lived in Houston.

Riley admittedly knew very little about how the whole "medium thing" worked, but between her experience with seeing a snapshot of the past after touching the doorjamb of the Hyssop Room and Pete's beanie, and her borderline-obsessive research on her paranormally inclined peers, she figured trying to get a glimpse into Renee through contact with her belongings couldn't hurt. The worst that could happen was nothing. Which was what she was already working with.

She drove, hoping the act would make her feel less jittery. Give her something to do.

"You all right there, Speed Racer?"

Apparently, that "something" was doing her best impression of a NASCAR driver. She slowed her highway speed from 85 to 70. She still white-knuckled the steering wheel.

"I have a hard time thinking of myself as 'gifted' or whatever," she said.

"I know," he said. "What specifically is freaking you out right now?"

"I guess … I'm scared of both possibilities. What if something *does* happen, but it's Mariah-level batshit and I send the poor old guy into cardiac arrest? But, also, what if *nothing* happens and I crush what little spirit he has left?"

"Don't put so much pressure on yourself," he said. "And, remember, he said himself that just contacting him made him feel better. I think whatever you offer him—even if it's nothing—will be gravy on the cake. Wait, no. I just mixed my metaphors."

She laughed. "And your ingredients."

"I'm a horrible cook."

Some of the tension left her shoulders. Good thing Michael was so level-headed; it kept her from completely losing it.

Ridgeview Estates was a three-storied, L-shaped building with two entrances, one at the top of the L and one in the intersection of the two pieces. The latter was where they needed to go. Residents with memory impairments lived on the first floor. Walter Palmer currently called the third floor home, so they hadn't decided just yet that his memory was gone—just making its slow progression out the door.

As they walked to the entrance, Riley noticed an older woman standing near the doors with her walker, staring out into the parking lot. No one was with her.

"Hi," Riley said as they got closer.

The woman's eyes took a second to focus on her. "I'm not sure where I was going."

Riley frowned. "Maybe you can go back inside and someone can help you."

The woman's nose crinkled. "I hate it in there." Then she started shuffling down the sidewalk, where a bend to the right would take her on what looked like a nature trail around the building.

Michael and Riley shrugged and headed inside.

The lobby, simple and clean, had a receptionist desk on one side and a couple of offices on the other. Both office doors were closed, the lights off. The scent of food hung heavy in the air. Riley guessed it was dinnertime in the cafeteria now.

The receptionist at the desk, a young woman likely no older than twenty, only had eyes for her phone.

"Hello?" Riley said.

Snapping to attention, she put her phone down. "Sorry, I didn't hear you come in. How can I help you?"

"We're here to see Walter Palmer."

"Okay. I'll give him a call and make sure he's up for visitors. Can you both sign in?" she said, pointing to a set of open guest-books at the end of the counter, then picked up the phone.

Michael scribbled in the date, time, and person they were visiting. Riley followed suit. The page was only half full, and even though only a dozen slots were filled in, several had been from the week before. She figured hundreds of residents filled the units here, yet only four had visitors that day. Weekdays were likely hard for that kind of thing, but the weekend visitors had been sparse, too.

"Yep. Two of them. Great, I'll send them on over." The receptionist hung up and offered them a smile. Riley recognized it as a waitress smile—the one you give when you're trying your damnedest to be helpful, but all you want is to go home. "Elevator is right around the corner. He's in room 1345 on the third floor."

The inside of the elevator had small, framed announcements on the walls. The schedule of events for the day included both "Xbox bowling practice" and "interpretive dance with Julia."

"Is it bad that I'm upset we missed most of these things?" Michael asked.

"I need to know what this bowling practice looks like."

As they stood outside Walter's door, Michael placed his hand on the middle of her back. "You've got this."

With a calming breath, she knocked.

Seconds later, a middle-aged, portly man pulled open the door. And mere moments after that, a barking, snarling little puff of white fur came tearing toward them. Riley and Michael jumped back a few steps. Riley couldn't tell if the dog was excited to see new people or if it was ready to go to the mat to protect its owner even though the thing couldn't have weighed more than ten pounds. He wore a collar fashioned to resemble a red bow tie.

"Mr. Marbles!" the man yelped, lunging toward the dog who was now jumping and snarling and circling Riley and Michael like a crazed canine tornado.

The man—Scott, she guessed—scurried out the door, which clanged shut behind him. He alternated between chastising the dog and apologizing for him being a "little hellion," all the while stooped over with his hands out, trying to snatch up the dog. Riley and Michael stood helplessly in the middle of the hallway while they were circled by dog and man.

Mr. Marbles stopped abruptly, lifted his leg, and peed all over Michael's shoes. Michael yelped, not able to get out of the way in time. He shook out his leg; Riley tried not to laugh. Then the dog sat, tongue hanging out, like he'd just had the best time imaginable with his new friends. Riley could have sworn he was smiling.

"Oh my god. I'm so sorry," Scott said, grabbing the dog and tucking him under his arm. "He's the most godawful creature to ever live. I swear. But Pop finds it hilarious that Mr. Marbles hates damn near everyone and particularly hates most of the staff here. He's peed on almost everyone. I think Pop is hoping one day they'll tell him he either needs to get rid of the demon dog, or he has to go."

"He mentioned not being terribly fond of the place," Riley said.

"I hear about it on a daily basis," said Scott, absently running a hand over the dog's head, who still panted, tongue lolling, as if he'd just run a marathon. "Anyway … ready to go in? Pop is excited to meet you."

The dog attack had startled most of her nerves away. "After you," she said, gesturing to the door.

When Scott got it open, he called out, "Pop! Riley's here!"

Michael shut the door behind them and Scott dropped Mr. Marbles to the floor. The dog trotted off and turned toward a bedroom as if nothing happened. Scott handed Michael a handful of paper towels and apologized again.

They had stepped into a kitchen area which was nothing more than a little swatch of linoleum flooring, a fridge, a sink, minimal counter space, and a handful of cabinets. A microwave and a toaster were the only cooking appliances.

Linoleum gave way to thin carpet. The living room was big enough to fit a two-seater, a recliner, a small coffee table, and a TV stand in the corner. A local news station was on, the sound muted.

A slightly hunched-over man with age spots on his bald scalp came shuffling into the room. "Hidee ho! Sorry about the delay. I had to use the little boy's room. Have a seat, have a seat," he said waving his arm in the general direction of the couch. "My wife will be back shortly. She went to the store."

Scott let out a dramatic sigh from the kitchen, like he resented his mother for being out shopping while he was stuck with his father.

Riley and Michael made their way to the sofa.

"Did you offer them refreshments, Scottie? You always forget to offer refreshments." Walter hobbled to his recliner, took his time getting his body angled just right in front of it, then dropped back with a satisfied, "Ahhh."

"I was too busy making sure Mr. Marbles didn't do anything too embarrassing."

Walter chuckled. "I love that stupid dog."

"Did you two want anything to drink?" Scott asked, in the kitchen now with the fridge open and his rather significant butt pointed in their direction as he took inventory of his father's assortment of beverages.

"I think we're okay," said Riley. "Thank you."

They managed some awkward small talk about the short half-hour drive over and the general state of the weather. Scott hovered halfway between the bedroom doorway and the living room. Riley wasn't sure if it was the lack of space on the couch for his large frame, or if he was usually poised to be at his father's beck and call.

"Why don't you go fetch that box of Renee's things for Riley here, Scottie?"

"Sure thing, Pop," he said. "You said it was in the closet in here? You never got it down, did you?"

"It's too high."

Scott gave an exaggerated sigh as if this was the final straw and he could take no more. But he headed for the adjacent bedroom, the same room Mr. Marbles the Terror had wandered off to.

"You're taller than me," Scott said to Michael, as if it was a personal affront. "Maybe you can help me? Pop hasn't sorted through all the crap in this room yet—we might need the Jaws of Life to get us back out."

That didn't sound promising.

When they'd left the room, Riley perched on the edge of the couch with her knees pressed tightly together and her hands placed on either one.

"Been meaning to get that box for you all week, but Scottie usually only comes to see me on Tuesdays. My wife's a spry old gal, but her back isn't too strong, so we've had to wait for Scottie to get here."

"It's no problem," Riley said, managing a small smile, her gaze focused into the bedroom opposite from where she sat. A cane leaned up against the far wall by the bed.

"So when did you know you were a medium?"

When she looked over at him, she found him staring at her, head cocked like the human version of Mr. Marbles.

"The first time I was contacted, I was about ten."

"That young!"

Riley nodded. "I was in denial for a long time."

"I think it's a gift, if you want an old man's opinion," he said. "You came right when I needed you. Like someone sent you to me."

Riley didn't know what to say to that. She wasn't sure what to say, period. Now that she was finally here, she was clamming up.

"Pop!"

"What!"

"The box isn't here!"

"The hell it's not."

A long pause.

"It's not here!"

Walter shot her a long-suffering look so identical to the expression she'd last seen on Scott's face, she laughed. "Dagnabbit," he muttered to himself as he slowly scooted to the edge of the cushion, preparing to stand.

Mr. Marbles came trotting into the room then and gave the tips of Riley's shoes a sniff, tail wagging so hard, his whole back end moved. If he lifted his leg on her, she would dropkick him into the bedroom. Instead, he hopped up on the couch next to her, turned in three circles, and plopped down, head resting on his paws.

Riley glanced over at Walter to gauge his progress. She had visions of him trying to get up and breaking a hip. "Do you need help?"

He waved her off, muttering to himself as he finally got up and started shuffling toward the other room. "Damn kid acts like he forgets I'm seventy-damn-eight years old. Making me walk over to find something when I can barely see my hand in front of my face. What good is it having a son if he can't help you when your body starts to fall apart?"

Riley was left alone in the small living room, listening to the muffled, slightly raised voices of the three men coming from the other room. What was she was doing here? Weren't mediums supposed to be able to "read" the room? Feel the energy? The only thing she could sense was the faint aroma of old food. A plate of congealed mashed potatoes and gravy sat on the counter.

Sighing, Riley held out a hand near Mr. Marbles, wondering if he'd let her pet him. He merely rolled his eyes in the general direction of her hand, not moving an inch.

"Every man in this house is difficult—beast or human."

Startled, Riley looked toward the kitchen to see an older woman standing near the fridge. Riley had been so distracted, she hadn't heard her come in. She walked over.

The "spry old gal" was in her early-to-mid-sixties, much younger than Riley had expected. She wore khaki pants Riley suspected had an elastic waist, a salmon-colored top, a white, unbuttoned cardigan, and a small brown handbag hung from a bent arm.

"I'm Riley," she said, holding out a hand.

The woman slightly wrinkled her nose at it; Riley geared up to be highly offended. "'fraid there's not much use in that gesture for me anymore."

Riley dropped her hand. "Because you're not actually *here*."

"'fraid not," she said. "But I'm Gladys. It's nice to meet you."

Walter's memory definitely had begun to fade if he thought his wife was out shopping, not that she had actually passed. It explained Scott's reaction to Walter mentioning his wife.

Mr. Marbles hopped off the couch, nose to the ground as he loudly sniffed his path to her. Riley recalled Michael asking if he'd be able to see an entity if he stood in the same room with one. Could animals?

The dog stood by Riley's shoe, still actively sniffing the ground. Then his head jerked up. His ears flattened against his head, he let out a low growl, then, with his tail between his legs, scampered off.

Well.

"I never met the dog in life."

Riley was at a loss for what to say again.

"They won't find it where they're looking," the woman said.

"Walter put the box in the closet in his bedroom a couple months ago but doesn't remember doing it. You'll find it in a plastic container with a green lid. It's underneath a pile of old quilts."

Riley pursed her lips. She honestly wasn't sure if the woman spoke to her as any other person would, or if these ideas just popped in her head while she looked at her. Would she ever get used to this?

"The locket he lost when he first moved here is in a bottom cabinet in the bathroom. It's tucked far in the back and the chain's clasp has slipped behind the cabinet's backing. You'll have to do some finagling to get it loose."

Raised voices from the other room caused her to turn toward the sound. Walter came shuffling into the living room, still muttering to himself, though he looked more dejected than miffed now. Michael and Scott followed behind him. When Riley turned back, Gladys, as expected, was gone.

"I think I might know where it is," Riley said.

Walter, who had his head down, looked up, a small smile on his face. "Was Renee here?"

Riley lightly shook her head. "Gladys."

Scott sucked in a breath. "She was *here*?"

"Here in the kitchen, yes."

"Where is she now?" Walter asked, not as interested in this revelation as Scott had been. "She go down to the car to get the groceries? We needed milk."

Scott's sigh was less aggrieved this time. "Pop, you know Mom died. Been five years."

Walter frowned at this. "She's not at the store." A statement, not a question.

"No, Pop, she's not."

He shuffled off to his chair, plopping down again. His shoulders were slumped, his bottom lip sticking out. "I keep waiting for her to come home."

Scott came over to sit on the armrest of the chair, putting an arm around the older man. "I know, Pop."

Riley and Michael stood on opposite sides of the living room. When they made eye contact, he offered her a small shrug.

"Is it okay if I go get the box, Walter?"

"Sure, sure," he said.

She walked into Walter's bedroom and went for the closet, immediately spotting several plastic containers inside when she trundled open one of the sliding doors. When she felt someone come into the room, she knew it was Michael even though he didn't say anything, just watched her.

The only container with a green lid sat underneath two others. She pulled them out, placing them on top of each other behind her, and then put the green-lidded one on the stack.

Michael and Scott both stood in the doorway now.

Her heart hammered in her chest, but she realized it was due to giddy anticipation, not fear. The contents of the container smelled a little musty, like wet towels. She pulled out a pair of thin handmade quilts—old and threadbare.

Walking over with his arms out, Scott said, "I'll take those. My mom made them for Renee when she was first born." He peered into the box when he reached her. "Well, I'll be damned."

An old shoebox sat on the base of the container. Riley grinned. "She found it, Pop!"

"Of course she did!" came the reply from the other room. "Gladys was always better at finding stuff than me."

"Oh, there's one more thing," Riley said, leaving the shoebox where it lay, and headed into the bathroom. A small set of drawers lined the left of the credenza, with a drawer above a cabinet on the right. Riley squatted before the cabinet and pulled it open. Bags of cotton balls and gauze, pill bottles, and boxes of Band-Aids came tumbling out. There were old hairbrushes and half-empty bottles of dog shampoo and an unopened package of adult diapers.

Riley piled it all up in front of her feet.

And then she saw it. The oval pendant. The cabinet was slightly deeper than the length of her arm, so she dropped onto her knees and stuck her head inside. After pushing against the back panel of the cabinet with one hand, and gently pulling on the locket with the other, she wiggled the chain free.

Scooting out, she sat back on her haunches and examined the golden pendant. Clicking the side button, the locket popped open, revealing a picture of a young, dapper Walter on one side, and a smiling, radiant Gladys on the other.

She closed it with a tiny snap, then hurried past Michael and Scott—who still held the old quilts—and stopped in front of Walter, letting the necklace hang from her fingers, the pendant swinging in the space between them.

Walter let out a sputtering sob at the sight of it, putting a shaking hand to his mouth as his eyes filled with tears. He reached out and took the necklace, the locket in his palm. It took him a few seconds to get his fingers to work right and get the pendant open. When he saw his young wife looking back at him, his bottom lip quivered violently.

Wiping his eyes with the sleeve of his sweater, he looked up at Riley who watched him with tears in her own eyes. Lucidity took him over. "I gave this to Gladys on our one-year anniversary. We'd been married fifty-three years by the time she passed." He sniffed, attention focused on the pictures in the locket again as he ran a single finger over her picture. "This is my favorite picture of her. I'd thought I'd lost this thing back at the old house. Thought I'd never see it again."

"Gladys wanted me to find it for you."

Sitting up a little, he grabbed one of her hands, the locket firmly clasped in his other. "I don't know who sent you to me but thank you."

"It was all Gladys. She told me where to look."

He smiled, letting her hand go and sitting back. "Sounds like you're still in denial."

Laughing, she said, "Oh, your memory's not as bad as people say."

"Hear that, Scottie!" he called out. "Still sharp as a tack!"

"I heard it, Pop." He sounded amused this time, rather than upset, at least.

Riley glanced over to find him and Michael watching her from yet another doorway.

When Walter requested a box of tissues and a glass of water, Scott sprang into action. Michael and Riley ducked back into the bedroom.

Wordlessly, they shuffled through the contents of the box. All the worldly possessions of Renee Palmer that remained.

There were a handful of newspaper clippings, some of the words smudged from repeated handling. After taking pictures of the articles, Riley texted herself with all the names of associated police officers and reporters. Some of them might have been deceased or retired by now, but she'd be taken more seriously if it was clear she'd done her homework.

While Michael returned the items to the box, and placed the quilts on top, Riley shoved all the odds and ends from the cabinet back in, hastily shutting the door before it could all come tumbling out.

When they walked back into the living room, Walter was passed out and snoring in his chair, locket still clasped in his hand.

Riley caught Scott's attention and motioned for the door. The three of them slipped out.

"We should probably go now," she said. "Thank you for letting us come by."

"Of course," he said, arms crossed, hands holding his elbows. He stared at her for a few moments. "I'm kind of unnerved by all of this, to be honest."

"I am too if that helps," she said.

He managed a laugh, but it was strained.

"We'll be sure to let you know if we come up with anything," Michael said.

Scott nodded. "You can keep in touch even if you come up empty. Pop would love it."

"You got it," Riley said.

Before she had the chance to react, Scott had enveloped her in a tight hug. It was over just as quick, and then his arms were folded again. "I haven't seen Pop this happy since before Mom died. Even if you can't help get closure on my sister's case, I think you gave him more than he could've asked for. So ... just ... thanks."

"Glad I could help."

It wasn't until they were inside her car, Michael in the driver's seat, that he said something. "You're a freaking medium, dude!"

"Don't call me dude!"

"Dude, it's like my cousin in England who's doing this kind of thing for a *living*. You could do that. You could talk to spirits and help families. This could be your thing. Everyone needs a thing."

"You seem very excited about this."

"I just …" He shrugged. "You're good with people, Ry, even though you think you're not. You said things happen for a reason, right?"

She side-eyed him for using her own words against her.

"You said yourself you don't want to be a waitress forever. Maybe *this* is what you're supposed to do."

"Finding lost heirlooms?"

"Bring something positive to people who are grieving."

She had to admit that even if nothing came from the names she got from the newspaper clippings, seeing that look on Walter's face when he first saw the locket had been worth the trip.

"You're considering it. Good." He started her car.

"Stop reading my face!"

"It's like a freaking neon sign, that face."

Riley did her best to read the photographed articles on her phone while Michael drove, classic rock playing in the background again. A text alert appeared at the top of her screen, breaking her concentration.

It was from Mindy.

I think Hank found me.

CHAPTER 21

Riley called Mindy immediately. She picked up on the first ring. "What do you mean he *found* you?"

"Hello to you, too."

"*Mindy.*"

"Okay, okay. Two days a week, I work at a record store. My friend owns it and knows about my panic attack issues, so she pays me under the table and lets me pick my own hours. The times I go in can vary drastically.

"Anyway, I went in today and one of the guys said someone named Francis has called looking for me the last couple days."

"Shit."

"Luckily the guy knows my history—what I've told him any-way—so he knew better than to tell some random dude when I'd be in. Just said he hadn't seen me in a while. When my co-worker asked Francis yesterday if he could take a message, Francis just said no and hung up." She sighed loudly. "That name wouldn't even *mean* any-thing to me if it wasn't for you. I told them to say I don't work there anymore if someone asks."

"How did he find out you work there?"

"Only thing I can figure is that he's been stalking me through my friends' pages."

"But *yours* is private."

"Even still," Mindy said, "if you visit someone's page, it starts suggesting people you might know. Especially since he sent a friend request; I've been too scared to reject it so it's still pending."

"Cheryl says she's the owner of the store on her page. Maybe he's just shooting in the dark, contacting all kinds of people to see if he hits something."

"Or he's physically following you."

Mindy whimpered. "I feel sick."

Riley hadn't told Mindy about Francis' surprise visit to her work, mainly because she didn't want to scare her. That clearly hadn't been a good call.

"He showed up at my job Friday night."

"*What?*"

"I think he was just fishing for information," Riley said quickly. "He stalked me online too and found out about my ghost-seeing tendencies."

"So, what, he was trying to figure out if you'd seen Renee at the ranch or something?"

"Maybe? I really don't know," she said. "He might have just been trying to get a read on me. See if I'd freak out if he showed up unannounced. I think I played it off okay. He probably assumed I would be terrified about him tracking me down if I knew he'd murdered and assaulted someone."

Mindy sighed heavily. "What do I do?"

"Don't go into work again for a while, that's for sure," Riley said. "Maybe get a restraining order?"

"Not sure what good a piece of paper is going to do if the guy breaks down my door."

"It'd be good to have a record of complaints against him. It'd help build our case later."

"Okay. I can try that tomorrow. Assuming they even issue one … someone asking about me isn't exactly harassment. Can't I just plan to never leave my house again?"

"Don't let him ruin your life."

"Too late," she said. "Talk to you later. I need to go put my head between my knees." She hung up.

When Riley dropped her phone in her purse, she realized they were only a few minutes from her apartment. She turned to Michael, whose mouth was bunched up on one side. "You okay?"

It took him a while to finally respond, and it wasn't until he'd pulled her car into her spot. "Maybe just go to the cops now. Lay it all out. Then back off it and let them do their thing. At least for long enough that you'll drop off Francis' radar."

"I'm not sure one drops off that guy's radar once they're on it."

"You're not making me feel better."

"I'm sorry," she said, reaching up and cupping his face. He leaned into her hand. "Frank and the other guys are still walking the girls out to their cars at night. Everyone's been warned to be on the lookout for him. Unless he's followed me home—and at this point, why would he?—all I can really do is be as alert and as safe as I can."

"I don't like it," he said.

"I was thinking of writing up a sample article and sending it to him. Tell him it's a rough draft, but I wanted him to see the progress I'm making. Maybe it'll make him less paranoid if I keep the reporter angle."

"Maybe."

She unfastened her seat belt and leaned over the console to kiss him.

"Call me the second you think something is fishy, okay? Whether it's here or work, and I'll drive as fast as humanly possible to get to you."

"Okay," she said, kissing him again.

Moments after exiting the car, he had her pushed up against the driver's side door, his mouth on hers. It made her go a little weak in the knees and she needed the resolve to tell him he should go home. They both needed to sleep.

"I can stay with you tonight," he said, lips a mere inch from her ear. Then he kissed her neck and all coherent thought flew out of her head for a moment. "What if we solemnly swear to be asleep by midnight?"

"You're going to be miserable in the morning." She had his shirt bunched in her hands on either side of his waist.

Nipping at her ear, he said, "But it'll be totally worth it."

The next morning, he was twenty minutes late for work. But he was right: it was worth it.

The following evening, she finally replied to Nina. The unanswered email had been in the back of her mind since she received it.

"*Dark room*" and "*Hank ... lied*" replayed in her head at night, Orin's voice sometimes incorporating itself into her dreams. She recalled the tone Francis had taken on during his surprise visit at the Laughing Tiger. Though "dark room" had meant nothing to Nina or herself, and Mindy thought it might just be another term for the cellar, Riley wondered if it'd mean anything to Francis. How on Earth she'd bring *that* up in conversation, she didn't know.

Dear Nina,

Thanks for passing these along. I can't say I
enjoyed them, but they were an interesting
listen. I have no idea what significance "dark
room" has, and "Hank lied" is vague, but it
meant more to me than the first one. Though
the bar was low.

They mean nothing to you? I assume "dark
room" has some connection to the ranch—you
know it better than I do. If only Orin had been
more chatty. Ha ha ha.

Hope all is well,

Riley

That done, she set about looking up all the officers and reporters' names that had appeared in the articles Walter kept.

There were two associated detectives: Perry Mason—which was
a cruel twist of fate, Riley thought—and Reginald Howard. The first
had retired, but Howard was still at it.

Howard had been fresh out of the academy when he'd been
put on the case with Mason. From what she could glean, about four
years after the Renee Palmer case went cold, Howard had taken the
detective's exam, aced it, and transferred to Santa Fe.

Of the two reporters, one woman had written four of the five
articles in Walter's possession. Riley couldn't find a newspaper either
were still associated with. Social media revealed that the reporter

who'd written the one article passed away about ten years before. The other reporter seemed to be taking the grandma thing very seriously in Maine.

If Howard didn't pan out, Riley would put in the work to track down the woman's number.

The following morning, Riley woke early to phone the Santa Fe Police Department. After navigating an automated system and going through a directory, she wound up at Howard's voicemail.

"Hi, Detective Howard. My name is Riley Thomas and I have some questions about opening a cold case you worked on back in 1983. The victim's name was Renee Palmer. If you could please return my call at your earliest convenience, I would greatly appreciate it." She rattled off her phone number and hung up.

Her hands shook. If she hadn't spent the better part of an hour rehearsing that, she was sure the message would have been one long "Uhh ..." followed by expletives and her phone number. Assuming she remembered it.

She told herself to give the guy three days, and if she hadn't heard back, she'd call again. And email him. And call. And call and call and call.

When a blocked number called her cell two days later on Saturday, her heart lurched into her throat. Her first thought was that Francis had somehow found her number. But then she figured it was standard practice for cops to block their numbers. Did cops work on the weekend? She supposed crime didn't care about the day of the week.

"Hello?"

"May I speak to Riley Thomas?" His voice was deep and a little melodic. It reminded her of Morgan Freeman.

"That's me."

"Hi, Riley. This is Detective Howard returning your call," he said. "Do you have a few minutes?"

Still in pajamas, her teeth not yet brushed, and her hair a rat's nest, she was glad he couldn't see her. "Yes. I'm happy you called back so quickly. And on a Saturday, no less."

"No rest for the wicked," he said. "I had to make a couple calls on my end before I called you, otherwise it would've been sooner. The Palmer case was my first."

"I know," she said. "I mean, I saw that when I was doing my research."

"So why don't we start with why you think this case should be reopened."

He wanted to get to it immediately. Wanted to dismiss her as a nutjob right away so he could get back to more pressing cases. But she knew she had his interest piqued, at least. He wouldn't have called back so soon if he wasn't curious.

But if he was skeptical *before* she dropped the psychic/medium/I-see-dead-people bomb, she figured this would be a short conversation.

"You're going to think I'm insane."

"Try me. Not much surprises me anymore."

With a deep breath, she told him about her "ability." "*Pete Vonick, Orin Jacobs' first and only male victim,*" however, was reduced to "*a spirit from the ranch.*" She figured adding in yet another victim to the story would complicate it even further, especially since said victim was semi-haunting her apartment. Somehow, she hoped that solving Renee's murder would lead Riley to Pete's resting place. That one would bring her closer to the other.

"I *have* worked with psychics and mediums in the past," he said. "I won't discount any of what you tell me solely based on your claims of being gifted."

Well, there was that, at least.

The detective remained quiet for the rest of her explanation, though she occasionally heard the clack of keys in the background. Hopefully he was taking notes, not answering work emails while he pretended to listen.

When she got to the part about being in contact with Mindy, he interrupted her. "If Ms. Cho was fearful of this boy, why didn't she come forward sooner, back when she first escaped?"

Riley pursed her lips, glaring ahead as if Howard sat across from her and not in a police station an hour away.

"I'm not passing judgement, Ms. Thomas. I'm merely trying to get the full picture."

"For one, she only knew him as Hank, not his legal name. Two, she'd been kidnapped—lured there *by* Francis—and had been beaten by Orin for months. The other girl who'd been there with her—Janay—died while Mindy was there, so the threat of that was very real. Francis tried to rape her while there. And she was *sixteen* when it happened. She was *scared*. Once they got out, Francis started stalking her. So her nightmare followed her to where she thought she'd be safe."

"Okay, okay," he said, and she could picture him using placating hand gestures. "I'm not accusing or blaming anyone for anything."

Riley's heart pounded.

"Do you happen know where Francis is now?"

"He's in Santa Fe too," she said. "I met with him once—"

"Under what pretense?"

Was this something she should admit to an officer? "Uhh ... I told him I was a reporter doing a piece on him for a magazine about reformed criminals?"

"And you're … not a reporter."

"I'm a waitress."

He sighed very loudly. "I'm going to pretend I didn't hear any of that."

"I guess I was hoping he'd be super repentant and open up about it or something."

She could almost hear his expression. "*Oh, you naïve girl.*" What he actually said was, "If you truly think he's dangerous, it's not a good idea to pursue any of this yourself."

"I know," she said. "He's clearly … *not* repentant."

"If he's truly gotten away with murder, people like him usually aren't. And they grow both more confident and paranoid at the same time."

"So you believe me?"

"Let's talk a little more about Renee."

Which wasn't a yes. Riley heard the shuffle of papers.

"Describe the scene for me as best you can."

So he was testing her. Trying to assess what she knew in comparison to reports and photographs that likely hadn't been made public since it was still technically an ongoing investigation—just a frigid one.

She told him everything she could remember from the dream, closing her eyes to let the images play like a film reel against the backs of her lids. She told him what colors Renee had been wearing, about the pepper spray canister in her hand, the headphones around her neck, the cassette in the player, and how many times Francis had hit her.

"Geez," he muttered when she was done. If she didn't know better, she would think he was actually impressed. "Now, I have to ask—why should I believe you saw all this in a dream and there isn't something else going on here?"

"Like what? I'm twenty-five," she said. "I wasn't even alive when any of this happened."

He remained silent.

"I was drawn into this case for some reason. I don't know why. But I can't figure it all out alone; I need the police's help. DNA is what's going to put him away, not me."

"Oh?"

"In 1985, Francis was convicted of statutory rape of a thirteen-year-old girl when he was eighteen." The clack of his keyboard sounded in the background as she spoke. "He would've given DNA samples when he was convicted, right?"

"Yes. Sexual-related crimes, even then, more than likely would have resulted in a cheek swab at least."

"More than likely? There's a possibility they didn't?"

"The late '80s and early '90s were when DNA profiling started to gain speed, but so many cases from that time have gone unsolved. In 1985, there wasn't even a state DNA database yet."

"No way."

"Yep. In fact, it wasn't until 1997 or so that every state adopted one. The national database launched in 1998."

Riley thought about that. "So, in an ideal world, if his samples from Renee's body had been run and put in some kind of system—"

"The DNA samples collected *after* the statutory rape conviction two years later should've resulted in a match to the DNA sample from the Palmer case." Howard huffed. "New Mexico has the largest backlog of untested rape kits in the country. There are some from as far back as 1980 that haven't been tested yet."

"So it's possible the DNA sample from Renee's case is still sitting in a box somewhere and the statutory rape conviction is the only time his DNA was cataloged? Maybe he didn't get pinned for Renee after the fact because Renee's kit was never processed in the first place?"

Howard huffed again. "It's very possible." After a long pause, he said, "Let me work on this. The evidence should still be in lockup back in Silver City. Requests to open old cases and to run samples can both take a while. I'll see what I can do and will keep you updated. In the meantime, keep your head down, okay? What's the best number to reach you?"

Once they'd hung up, Riley felt a little better. Howard sounded like he was going to try to resolve this and he had more resources than she did. He'd told her just before he disconnected the call this would likely take *weeks*, though.

But, she figured, as long as she kept her head down as instructed—and Mindy did too—Francis' paranoia would mellow. She could still write up that bogus article to keep him under the assumption that she was writing a piece on him. She could drag this out for a couple more weeks.

When Francis was arrested, and Howard realized she was the best damn medium ever, she'd tell him about Pete. Find his body. Put the poor child to rest. Then she could wash herself clean of all things related to that godforsaken ranch.

CHAPTER 22

A full week went by with little fanfare. Riley worked most weekday nights, actually attended a game night at Jade's with the same group who'd gone to the ranch—she and Rochelle started texting obsessively about *Tiana's Circle* a day later when a surprise episode was released—and she had dinner at her parents' Friday night. She spent the weekend with Michael.

Her mild concern about Pete's inability to manifest had morphed into a constant worry that buzzed around in the back of her mind like a trapped fly. Most nights, she'd wander her apartment and ask him to show her a sign of his presence, as if she were conducting a paranormal investigation in her own home. Occasionally she'd see a flicker of something in her peripheral vision. One night she asked for a sign and a broom immediately toppled over in the kitchen. The beanie had yet to move on its own again, but Riley was also too nervous to touch it, so it lay untouched on her dresser.

While Michael was in the shower on Sunday morning—Baxter snoozing in her lap—the game she played on her phone got interrupted by an email alert. She clicked over to her inbox, hoping Detective Howard had sent her an email full o' evidence.

Instead, the message came from a nonsensical address made up of seemingly random numbers and letters. She would've deleted it entirely had it not been for the subject line: "My little medium has been busy."

Heart hammering, she took a screenshot of the address to look up later, then she opened the message, hoping it wasn't loaded with viruses that made her phone explode.

The text in the body of the email said, "What are you up to Riley?" Attached were five pictures, each making her feel more and more nauseous than the last. The back of the Laughing Tiger with Frank walking her to her car; the front of Jade's house; the front of her *parents'* house; the outside of Ridgeview Estates; a cropped picture showing her handwriting in the guestbook the day she visited Walter.

She went through them a second time, searching for any sign of people in the middle three pictures, but there was only her in the first one.

"Shit, shit, shit," she muttered. "Sorry, Baxter." Then she grabbed him, dropped him on the couch, and hurried to the bathroom where the shower had just turned off. She darted in without knocking.

Michael, wearing only a pair of boxer briefs, yelped and froze in the middle of toweling off his hair. She was too scared out of her mind to admire the view.

"I just got this," she said, thrusting the phone in his face.

He cursed under his breath as he clicked through the pictures.

"The middle two are Jade's and my parents' houses," she said. "He's fucking following me."

"You gotta tell that cop you're in contact with. Show him this. That first picture is proof he's watching you."

"Dammit."

Walking out of the bathroom, she called Detective Howard, but ended up at his voicemail again. She hung up without leaving a message, forwarding the email to him instead.

With the slats on Michael's blinds pulled apart, she peered out. Francis wasn't standing there, arms crossed, like the Big Bad in a horror movie. Not that she expected him to be. But, even still, she didn't know what his car looked like. He *could* be out there.

"This seems like a ridiculous question," Michael said as he walked into the living room, startling her. She turned away from the window. "But, uh … you still want to go to breakfast?"

No. She wanted to hide. But she couldn't stay locked up in Michael's house forever. She had friends and a family and a job.

Remembering her own words to Mindy, telling her to not to let Francis ruin her life, she nodded.

Riley scanned the cars lining the quiet street. Once they were in his car, headed for a nearby breakfast diner, she glanced behind them every minute or so, despite not knowing what she was looking for. She resigned herself to the fact that Francis probably knew Michael wasn't actually Jansen Trombley.

Francis was the co-owner of a small, successful tech firm—how did he have time to follow her around town at all hours of the day? Had he figured out who Walter Palmer was? Did he know *she* knew what he'd done to Renee?

Her stomach churned.

The feel of the car stopping snapped her out of her thoughts. They'd arrived at the diner.

"You okay?" Michael asked.

"Not really," she said, glancing over at him and offering the best smile she could muster. "But I'm desperate for French toast."

"Then French toast you shall have."

The compact diner only allowed a narrow walking space between the booths lining the wall of windows to the left, and the long counter to the right. People talked, waitresses called orders to the cooks, silverware clanked on plates, and the faint hum of some top 40 radio station tried to be heard over the din. It smelled like bacon, powdered sugar, and coffee.

She loved it.

The fifteen-minute wait was spent in silence, Riley standing directly in front of Michael—back to his chest—to make room for those also waiting in the cramped space.

Her mind had gone into overdrive trying to figure out the best course. Who knew how often Francis was watching her? Was he in the parking lot now? If she went to the police this minute, he could follow her there too—get spooked and retaliate. He'd stalked and killed before; it was naïve to think he'd grown out of it.

Detective Howard had said it himself: if Francis had gotten away with murder in the past, the longer he went without getting caught made him both more confident *and* paranoid.

If Francis truly thought Riley was a threat to his freedom, what would he be willing to do to quell the threat? God, he knew where her parents and Jade lived.

Pulling out her phone, she looked through the pictures again. Since she was in her uniform in the first one, it was impossible to tell what day it had been. But something occurred to her about the others.

The waitress called their name, momentarily distracting her as they made their way down the narrow walkway just as another couple was heading the opposite way to pay. Riley attempted to make more room for the other pair and accidentally whacked a guy sitting at the counter in the head with her purse. Luckily, he caught his glass of orange juice before he knocked it over.

Michael suppressed a smile when they sat down.

"What?" she said, tossing the offending bag onto the seat beside her.

"You get really clumsy when you're flustered."

She attempted to glare at him.

"What's up? It's not just getting the email …"

Taking out her phone, she pulled up the pictures and then swung it around on the tabletop so it faced him. She navigated the screen upside down. "When I went to Jade and my parents' house this week, it was early evening."

He bent forward, looking at the phone with his hands under the table. His gaze flicked up to hers. "And?"

"And these were clearly taken during the day," she said. "Why show me pictures of places I'd been, but after the fact?"

Michael shrugged. "To show that he could go back any time he wanted?"

"Why am I only in the first one?" she asked. "And …" She opened the last picture. "There's a picture of the old folks' home— also during the day—but he purposefully cropped the guestbook photo. Why?"

Michael stared at it a moment, then shrugged.

"If you zoom in, there's a little bit of handwriting that's below mine. If he took the picture the next day, or even days later, some-one would've signed in under me. The page of the book had only been half filled and there were guests from last week still on that one page. They don't get a ton of traffic."

"So, what, he cropped it so it wasn't obvious that he went there well after you, and not the same day?"

"Maybe?" she said. "Thinking he could be out there right this second is scarier than thinking he might be here sometime in the future even if I'm not."

"So you're thinking he *actually* followed you to the Laughing Tiger since he knew when to find you there, but didn't go to the other places?"

Michael always tried to humor her, but he looked at her now like maybe she'd lost it.

"In the picture of my parents' house, neither car is in the driveway. Which means this was likely taken in the middle of the day when they were at work," she said. "He might not even know who lives there. Just knows I was there and that seeing the house alone would scare me."

She was about to say something else, but the waitress showed up to take their order. Riley clicked out of her email and powered off the screen.

After they ordered, Michael said, "So what's your theory?"

She'd been formulating said theory as she talked it out with him, and now that she had to say it out loud, she felt a little ill. "I think there's a tracker on my car."

Michael stared at her. "Wait, what?"

"I thought it was weird that he made a point to come all the way to the restaurant an hour out from where he lived only to talk to me for like fifteen minutes and then leave. But what if he'd been watching the parking lot for me to show up for my shift, figured out what car was mine by seeing me get out of it, then slapped on a tracker when the lot was deserted? He came to see me in person likely because he knew it'd rattle me and he gets off on stuff like that."

"Then he went back to the places he knew you'd been," Michael said, "and took pictures to let you know he'd been there too."

"Yeah."

"Damn."

"I mean, I could be wrong," she said. "But we should check my car later."

"I hate this guy."

"I'm not crazy about him either," she said. "But if I'm right, at least there's some comfort that he's not lurking around at all hours. He's letting the tracker do that."

The waitress brought them their food and they fell silent for a while as they ate. Though her French toast was even better than she expected, she had to force it down after the first few bites. She kept thinking about a device on her car and Francis getting updates on his phone about her every move. Thankfully, the same fate hadn't befallen Mindy, given her co-worker's unwillingness to tell Francis her schedule. But if Riley found a tracker, she'd warn Mindy anyway.

Her leg jiggled uncontrollably on the ride back. She typed the random-looking email address into a search engine. It was a temporary "guerrilla" address. Emails sent from one were set to erase from the guerilla inbox after an hour so there would be no way to prove who the email had come from. Maybe an FBI tech whiz could figure out the IP address of the sender or some other technological magic she didn't understand, but the FBI would not be helping her with Francis Hank Carras.

What good would that email in Detective Howard's box do if there was no way to prove Francis had sent it? Even if the detective believed her story, he couldn't do anything to Francis based solely on her word.

When they got back to Michael's apartment, they walked to the guest parking area a few slots away. They stood behind her car, arms crossed, like they disapproved of the car's actions. How had she let creepy-ass Francis do this to her? Why hadn't she told Riley what happened?

She patted her car's trunk. "It's not your fault, hon."

Michael ignored that. "Where would it be? What do they look like?"

A quick internet search turned up thin, box-like devices. Most were black. "In TV shows, people just slap them on the underside of cars. A lot of them are magnetized."

Michael dropped to the ground and wiggled as far as he could under the trunk on his back, head first. Riley stood there chewing on a thumbnail, not sure if she wanted to be right or not.

"I think I found it!"

Crap. "Wait … don't touch it. Scoot over." Riley dropped her purse by one of the back tires, then inched her head under the trunk, too, the side of her body flush with Michael's.

And there it was: a thin black box with a very dull green light, and the word "SPYMASTER" printed on the front. The font was also black and slightly raised, but was legible enough.

"Subtle," she said.

"What do we do with it? If we take it off and leave it in the bushes or something, he'll eventually figure out you took it off the car, right? Like if he gets suspicious about why you haven't been home?"

"Yeah, but what'll he do next if he realizes this tactic of keeping tabs on me isn't working anymore?"

"I mean, you're not thinking of leaving it on, are you?"

"Maybe?" When she looked at him, she realized how odd it was to continue the conversation while lying on the pavement partially under her car. After getting back to their feet and brushing each other off, she said, "I could keep going to work like normal, but then maybe take taxis or something for everywhere else? He'll just think I'm at home. Or I can park the car at the *Albuquerque Life* lot sometimes and then take a taxi somewhere for a few hours then go back to get it later."

"Until when?"

"Until I hear from Detective Howard?"

"Why not just tell him about the tracker now?" he asked.

Riley thought of all the times she'd called authorities about things less than dire: non-fatal car accidents, rowdy neighbors, suspicious people wandering the neighborhood. They always said they'd be on their way and never showed, or arrived well after the problem had worked itself out. Unless there was severe property damage or someone was bleeding or dead, no one would show up.

Riley would tell them she was sure it was Hank. Based on what? they'd ask. He was creepy and sent her an email of pictures making it clear he was following her. But there was no way to prove he'd sent it, and the email he'd sent would have disappeared off Guerrilla Mail's servers by now. Maybe there would be prints on the tracker. Maybe he paid for it with a credit card. But maybe he used gloves and paid in cash. Then what?

They'd likely assume Hank was a jilted lover and would tell her to cease all contact with the guy. She had no proof he put the tracker there—though she was certain it couldn't be anyone else. But why would they believe her? She had zero evidence to back up her claim other than gut instinct. And if the tracker *was* somehow linked to him, what would happen then? The police would let him know he had to leave her alone? What if he retaliated?

Riley sighed. "I'll call someone about it tomorrow."

"I don't like any of this," Michael said, glaring at the trunk of her car.

She got up on tiptoes and kissed his cheek. "I know."

Michael stayed with her that night—even though she said it wasn't necessary—but she found it hard to sleep. Hank likely wasn't lurking in the apartment complex. She was on the second floor, so he also probably wasn't peering into her windows at night. But he'd gotten into her head. He was out there.

As she lay awake in bed, listening to the soft breathing of Michael beside her, she thought she could make out the silhouette of a small figure by her window. It shimmered around the edges, both separate from and blurring into the shadows in her room. An overwhelming sense of sadness washed over her as she looked that that flickering image. She couldn't tell if the emotion came from her or Pete. Maybe both.

She'd texted Mindy that afternoon to warn her to be extra cautious and to check her car too, just in case. Riley hadn't heard from her again after she said, I'm freaking out.

Jade and her parents were warned, too. Riley's phone call with her mother had been so long, her throat was sore by the time she finally hung up.

The next day, thanks to a lull in customers, she was able to take a rare, short "cigarette break" around four to make a call about the tracker. Detective Howard was based out of Santa Fe, well over an hour away. Even if he had advice for her, she knew he'd tell her to contact a local police station, as he couldn't do much for her.

Riley went through a series of automated prompts before being put on hold. After half a century, a friendly woman answered. "This is Joanne. How can I help you?"

"Uh … hi," Riley said, shooting a look at nosey-ass Roberto who stood outside with her, smoking an actual cigarette and trying to act like he was engrossed with his phone, not listening to her every word. "So … I think I have a stalker."

"Oh. That's got to be scary," she said, voice flat. "What makes you think you're being followed?"

Riley told her about the guerilla email.

The woman was silent for a moment. "Did you try to do a reverse email search to see where it came from?"

"No," she said. "You can't trace it—that's the whole point."

"And how do you know this man?"

How *did* she know him? "He's … uh … someone who used to be friends with a friend of mine." *Wow, Ry, way to be vague.*

Joanne let out a sound that implied she thought this "friend" was Riley herself. "What else has he done other than send you this email?"

"I think he put a tracker on my car."

Joanne's tone turned a little more serious. "You know for sure it was him who put it there?"

"I can't know for sure, but it couldn't have been anyone else," she said. "He came to my work unannounced too."

"Where do you work?"

"The Laughing Tiger," she said. "It's a dim sum restaurant. He came towards the end of my shift and asked to sit in my section. I think that's the night he put the tracker on my car."

"And how long ago was this?"

"Three weeks."

Joanne fell silent again. "Had the tracker been there for that long before you realized it was there?"

Riley's cheeks flamed. "Yes."

"What has he done in the days since he put the tracker there?"

"Other than send the email—nothing."

Joanne was fond of long-ass pauses. "Without anything more solid than this, I don't think there is much the police can do, to be quite honest. The best thing would be to bring the tracker into your local station—perhaps they can figure out where the device came from and contact the man once they know he's the one who purchased it. The email might be helpful for an officer to see too. You can file a report."

Riley sighed. "Okay, thanks."

"Sure thing, honey," she said. "Stay safe."

Riley hung up and sat back hard in her chair, ignoring Roberto whose gaze bored holes in the side of her head. Joanne had confirmed something for Riley. Francis hadn't made a move since the email, so there was no reason to think he would suddenly come after her violently simply because she knew he was keeping tabs on her now. *Her* knowledge had changed, his hadn't.

But that wasn't terribly comforting.

By the end of her shift, after Frank had walked her to her car, Riley blearily checked her messages, finding the usual assortment of texts from Jade, Michael, and Rochelle. And then she saw an email from Nina.

She'd almost forgotten about her entirely.

Hey Riley,

My resources about the ranch aren't that extensive, honestly. What you can find publicly about the place is the extent of my knowledge, too. The Fredricks (the owners of the ranch house) don't seem to know that much either. I emailed Porter Fredricks' daughter to ask if "dark room" or "Hank" meant anything to her and she said no. She asked her father, too. No dice there either.

But, if you're up for it, a group of us conduct séances once a month. I'm the acting medium, so you wouldn't need to do anything other than offer your energy. If anything comes through, they'll speak through me, not you.

Orin might be the only person who knows what this "dark room" is—he manifested himself to speak to you for a reason. Don't you want to know what that reason is?

Think about it and let me know,

Nina

Xavier had mentioned séances during introductions at the ranch. Nina had made contact with Xavier's mother. Had known things she couldn't have. And Xavier had been so impressed with her that he'd gotten her to join his team. That all had to point to Nina's abilities, didn't it?

But a *séance*? That was basically the same as using a Ouija board—and sometimes mediums used them during séances—except the medium herself sometimes became the board. The crash of

Becca's shelf hitting the floor of its own volition replayed in Riley's head. The word "Mariah" written over and over on the walls. The stories about whatever had come through hitting and scratching and bruising Becca to the point that the Greens moved to escape it.

Maybe that all happened simply because Riley and Becca had been too young to know what they were getting themselves into. Or maybe it had something to do with Riley herself.

On her drive home, her mind filled with questions about séances. She ran through every scene in a movie or TV show she'd seen that featured them. There were sham séances and terrifying ones. Possessions by malevolent spirits and visitations by friendly ghosts.

If Nina did them regularly, it couldn't be *that* dangerous, right?

But then Riley recalled the look on Nina's face when they'd been in that cellar. How the exploding bulbs had sent Pamela out of the room as fast as her feet could carry her, while Nina looked as if she'd just found nirvana. Nina's séances were likely tame. The type of séances where deceased loved ones simply came by to impart messages to those left behind. But was it possible to have a tame séance if the spirit in question was a convicted serial killer?

When had her life turned into this? *That* was what she needed to know.

Still lost in thought, she headed up the stairs to her apartment. She almost tumbled back down when she finally snapped to and spotted a person sitting at the top of the staircase near her door.

It was Michael.

"Jesus!" she whisper-shouted, hand to her chest.

Startled, he looked up from his phone, face awash in the blue glow of the screen. "Hi. I'm staying with you or you're staying with me until this whole tracker thing gets sorted out."

He clearly had that one ready.

Taking a few more steps up, she said, "Michael—"

He stood, sticking his phone in his pocket, the only light now the dim bulb by her door. A small duffel bag sat by his feet. "If you say no, I'll just sleep on your doormat. It's your choice if you want me to be eaten by rats in the night."

"There are no rats!"

"I saw one the size of a small car scurry by here while I was waiting."

She sighed dramatically.

He frowned, hands in his pockets. "I mean … if you really don't want me here I can—"

"No, it's not that. I just don't want you to totally disrupt your life over this."

"Being around you isn't disrupting anything. You're stuck with me until you tell me to go kick rocks."

She joined him on the small landing. "You sure?"

"Yes," he said, stepping out of her way so she could unlock the door.

"Okay then. Because I'm thinking of attending a séance." She walked into the apartment, leaving him standing on her mat with his mouth hung open.

He cursed softly to himself as he grabbed his bag. "You're really lucky I like you so damn much." It was his turn to sigh dramatically. Closing the door behind him, and dropping his bag, he said, "All right. What the hell is a séance, exactly?"

"An invitation sent to the Other Side or the Great Beyond or another dimension or whatever to allow spirits to manifest and speak through a medium."

"Like you."

"Like me," she said. "But Nina will be conducting it."

"Do we trust that Nina knows what the eff she's doing?"

"She was good enough for Xavier."

"True. But how … safe is it?"

"Jury's still out."

"So there's a possibility that it'll be like the Mariah-Ouija board episode all over again?"

"Yep."

"And you're probably going to do it anyway, aren't you?"

"I'm seriously considering it."

"Even though the last time Orin talked to you, he made shit explode."

"Yeah."

He sighed again. "I would like to start drinking now."

Another week passed with no word from the detective, so Riley rang him to check on progress. He assured her that he was looking into it, but the paperwork end of things always slowed things down. Plus, he had current cases to work on. Last week, he'd emailed back to say he'd pass the information about the stalkery email on to a local officer he knew. Riley hadn't heard anything since.

"I promise you I'm working on it," he told her. "It'll just take time. This isn't an episode of *CSI*. The Santa Fe PD doesn't have a homicide division. We have our daily cases and we get to these older ones in the spare moments. Renee is still a priority."

"He's following me."

The detective sighed. "My guy is on it. Have you received anything beyond the email you forwarded?"

She rehashed all of it: the surprise work visit, the tracker on her car, and how she'd called an officer. "The woman said to bring the tracker in and maybe they could figure out where it came from."

A choked sound came out of Detective Howard.

"Are you … laughing?"

"Sorry," he said, coughing now. "Honestly, unless he escalates or there's a record of his behavior or a witness to the harassment, your file will be pushed to the bottom of the pile until someone has a light day and has time to wade through paperwork. We can't come down on a guy just because he's a disgusting human being. Half the population would be locked up in that case."

Riley pursed her lips. Some disgusting human beings did nothing more than leer and make people uncomfortable. Some pushed that boundary and hurt people. How did you know which it would be? And how did you stop it before it happened, rather than just punishing them after the fact?

"I'm not telling you to skip the step of filing a report," he told her. "I probably shouldn't have said any of that. I think the psychic thing makes me a tad nervous. Like you'd know if I was lying."

"Aren't detectives supposed to be stoic and hard to crack?"

"Maybe I'm getting too old."

She managed a laugh. "I'm a medium, not a mind reader."

Clearing his throat, he said, "What are your interactions with him like now?"

"Nothing, really," she said. "We email each other occasionally under the guise of me being a journalist working on a story about him."

"But you haven't seen him? He hasn't made in-person contact other than the night he came to the restaurant? Five weeks now since he put the tracker on your car?"

"Yeah."

"Keep doing what you're doing. If you avoid contact altogether, he might escalate. Avoid meeting him anywhere, especially alone. The second he starts to act shifty, call me. I'll reach out to my guy in your area again."

"Okay," she said, nodding.

"You have pepper spray?"

Riley swallowed, thinking of Renee. "I'll get some."

"Good," he said. "Stay safe."

So she played eager journalist and sent drafts back and forth with Francis. He seemed happy with how the article was shaping up.

The day after she parked her car in *Albuquerque Life*'s lot—and then took a taxi into a nearby shopping area to run errands, before taking a taxi *back* to her car later—Francis was even more chatty in emails than usual.

In fact, the more her behaviors—based solely on the movements of her car—matched up with a good little girl keeping her nose out of things that weren't her business, the more flirtatious Francis got. He'd email her out of nowhere just to ask how her day was, or to tell her he'd been thinking about her all day, or to say he couldn't wait until the story on him was finished so they could "explore what else their relationship had to offer."

Relationship. He was insane.

While she didn't out-and-out flirt back, she didn't discourage him either. She needed him to think their arrangement was as shallow as possible so he didn't ask too many questions.

One of Riley's exhaustive searches led her down a rabbit hole about stalking victims. They had few protections, and once the police really got involved, it was usually because things had turned violent—if not fatal—for the victim, just as Howard said. And with

Francis' past, she was too scared to poke the hornet's nest.

She understood now why so many victims just kept their mouth shut and their head down. Knew why Mindy would much rather lock herself up in her house and not come out unless absolutely necessary. Then she stumbled on a *Dateline* episode about stalking victims—one featuring an actress from a popular primetime show. If celebrities couldn't get help from the police, how could she?

Riley just hoped that this meant Francis was backing off the in-person surveillance and starting to trust her again. That his paranoia was ebbing.

But no matter what she told herself, she was antsy. What if it took months to hear back from the detective about reopening the case? She'd heard countless stories about evidence sitting in storage even with active cases.

She couldn't leave the tracker on her car forever. Couldn't always feel the need to look over her shoulder when she left the house, worried Francis lurked out there, waiting for her to do something he deemed suspicious.

Which was why, almost a week after she first received the email from Nina, she wrote back and said, "I'm in. When and where?"

Then she called Jade.

"Hey, girl," Jade said. "What's up? It's Sunday. Isn't Michael usually cattle-prodding your oyster ditch with his lap rocket by now?"

Riley damn near fell off her couch. "*What?*"

"I heard that the other day! Isn't it great? I've been waiting to use it!"

"Where the *hell* are you hanging out? Seedy taverns by the harbor?"

"Ugh, I wish," she said. "No, really, what's up?"

She'd almost forgotten. "Wanna go to a séance?"

Jade squealed. "This is the happiest day of my life!"

CHAPTER 23

On Friday evening, Riley and Jade sat in Jade's car outside Nina's small corner house on the outskirts of Albuquerque.

The mostly brick house had been painted over white, the door and window trim a faded red, likely similar in color to the bricks beneath the layers of white paint. Four red steps led to the small porch where a pair of black Adirondack chairs sat, a small table with a flowering cactus between them.

"Looks normal enough," Jade commented from the driver's seat.

Then a pair of women in all black—one wearing a short cape—rounded the corner. They had pale skin, wore thick black lipstick, and had dyed jet-black hair. They both wore combat boots with heavy buckles on the sides. Riley watched them walk up the steps to Nina's house and let themselves in.

"Oh hell," said Jade.

"They do monthly séances," Riley said. "They probably aren't going to look like investment bankers."

Jade blew out a long, slow breath. "They just look like they're ready for this shit. I'm not sure I'm ready. Pamela still has nightmares."

"You said you were excited!"

"I am! But I also feel like I might crap my pants," she said. "You're sure contacting Orin is a good idea?"

"Jade!"

"Sorry! She was in a *cape*. Now I'm panicking."

"It's been two and a half weeks since I contacted Detective Howard the first time and he just tells me he's working on it. Creepy-ass Francis has had a tracker on my car for almost six weeks now," Riley said. "In the meantime, I'm going to go broke paying for a ride every time I go somewhere I don't want Francis to know about. I'm sick of waiting for something to happen."

"Good enough for me," Jade said. "Let's go."

Instead of letting themselves in as the Goth Twins had, Riley knocked.

Nina pulled the door open a few seconds later and grinned. "Yay! I'm so glad you could make it. Come on in. Nice to see you again, Jade."

They dropped their purses on the little bench seat by the door. The small, tidy living room had a white-and-blue-striped two-seater couch resting against one wall, framed on either side by low bookshelves. One held books on everything from ghosts to Wicca, the other lined with framed photos. Several featured Nina with a young boy. Her son, she guessed. A couple were of her and a handsome, smiling man. Current husband? Ex?

On the opposite wall sat a TV stand, flat-screen TV, and a set of built-in bookshelves—these crammed with novels. The mantel of the bookcase was covered in owl figurines. Wooden ones, ceramic ones, tall ones, short ones—a few made out of odd materials, like pine cones. Their eyes followed her everywhere she went. It gave her the heebie-jeebies.

To the right of the living room, a small hallway led to the bathroom and at least one bedroom. To the left, Riley could make out the edge of a dining table.

"Come meet the gang," Nina said, and ushered Riley and Jade to the left. A doorway led to the kitchen where the Goth Twins and a middle-aged man stood, each holding a glass of wine.

Riley wanted seven of those.

Nina promised she would be back in a moment, then left the way she'd come.

The five of them made awkward introductions and managed idle chitchat about what part of the city they all lived in. The Goth Twins were Megan and Charlotte; Megan wore the short cape. Theodore—who went by Teddy—poured wine for Riley and Jade.

By the time Nina returned a minute later, Riley had drained her glass.

"Ready?" Nina asked the group, though her focus was on Riley.

Riley managed a curt nod in response as Jade looped her arm through hers. The wooden floorboards creaked slightly beneath their feet, especially Megan's thick black boots. The wine hadn't dulled her nerves as much as she'd hoped.

They turned right down the short hallway on the other side of the house. The sparsely furnished room had a round table that ate up most of the space, covered in a dark purple tablecloth. A single recliner sat in one corner and a small table rested against the wall in another. On top, a small stereo played soft instrumental music— Celtic, maybe—and incense stuck out of a flat, wooden burner that had been lit in front of it, a thin, curling snake of lavender-smelling smoke rising from the tip. Nothing hung on the white walls. A candelabra in the middle of the table holding four flickering candles provided the only light.

"Everyone have a seat and get comfortable," Nina said.

Riley and Jade sat next to each other and Megan sat on Riley's other side. Nina wound up directly across from her.

Charlotte closed the door, causing the shadows thrown around the room by the flickering candle flames to become even more pronounced. The lavender incense left Riley vaguely lightheaded.

Once seated, Nina said, "Everyone hold hands, close your eyes, and breathe. I will say a quick prayer before we get started."

The prayer, whispered more to herself than to the group, featured the word "goddess" a couple times, and Riley wondered if Nina was Wiccan.

"Okay. You can open your eyes now, but keep the link going with everyone's hands," said Nina. "I want you all to think of someone you'd like to hear from today. Don't tell me any details until something comes through."

Their silence stretched on for long minutes, the soft, plaintive cry of wind instruments the only sound. Riley had come in hopes of getting answers from Orin, but the thought of the events in the cellar repeating themselves made her stomach clench painfully.

It felt as if something was *in* her stomach, actually. It knocked around, bumping into the walls. Then stilled.

What the actual hell?

Blowing out a slow breath, she tried to imagine Orin's face. The smiling, younger version of him, rather than the dead-eyed man from his mugshot.

The sensation in her stomach returned. It thumped once, twice, three times. Then stilled for several seconds. Thump, thump, thump. Every time it happened, it came in threes. It felt like being kicked from the inside.

By the sixth time, she felt compelled to say something. It drove her slightly mad. As if it would never stop if she didn't acknowledge it. "Is someone here pregnant?"

Her voice sounded strange to her own ears. She didn't realize what she'd said until the words left her mouth.

Megan, who held one of her hands, tensed at the question, but didn't speak.

Thump, thump, thump.

"Three months pregnant?"

The reply was a shaky, "Me. Three months today."

"*What?*" Charlotte asked. "Why haven't you told me? I'm your *sister.*"

Megan, tears in her eyes, stared at Riley a moment before glancing at Charlotte across the table. "We wanted to be sure before we told anyone. After the miscarriage ... I couldn't ... the thought of telling anyone I was pregnant again and then having to tell them I wasn't ..."

"But this time everything is—"

"I think so," Megan said, nodding emphatically. "The doctor is hopeful. Leo totally fell apart at the appointment this morning when the doctor told us everything was looking really good."

"He's a kicker, that's for sure," Riley said.

"He?" Megan asked.

"Oh, I don't know. I—"

"Trust your instincts," Nina said.

Megan and Charlotte were given a few seconds to pull themselves together. Charlotte had a harder time than her sister.

How had that just happened? Where had the sensation come from?

Jade stared at her in wonder.

"Breathe, Riley," Nina said.

Riley listened to her. She could mull over the details of her "gift" later. She needed information from Orin so she could do something rather than just waiting around for the police. She needed a solution for Pete who was disappearing more and more every day. She wanted to believe that when Pete wasn't haunting her apartment, he was back at the ranch, full energy at his disposal. But Riley knew Pete was fading. That after he'd tagged along with her, after he'd moved over two hundred miles away from his body, he'd gotten stuck in some in-between place. Not able to move on, but not able to manifest either. She was tormented again by the implication of it. What happened when he could no longer make contact with the physical world? Would he just disappear forever?

But there was also Francis to worry about. What happened when he got bored of their current arrangement and decided to push the issue of "exploring their relationship"? She really couldn't think about that right now.

A message via Nina came through for Teddy from his grandmother about checking the pipes below his house because they were sure to burst soon. In the middle of Teddy asking a question, Riley suddenly felt something behind her. Felt *him* behind her.

"He's here," Nina said, voice a breathy whisper, cutting Teddy off. He didn't seem to mind.

Riley's palms sweated. Why did he always have to hover? It was like a black tsunami rising up behind her, leaving her feeling like a tiny fishing boat caught in the shadow of inevitable destruction.

"You can ask questions, Riley," Nina said. "Just start with simple ones that only require yes and no to start."

Something ran across the length of her neck despite her hair being down. She tried to rub the feeling away with her shoulder, both of her hands still clasped by Jade and Megan. It happened again and Riley squirmed uncomfortably.

"*Riley*," a voice whispered right next to her ear, though she felt no accompanying breath.

He was screwing with her. Trying to unsettle her.

"What is the dark room?" she asked, her heart thudding as she tried to control her breathing. Her palms felt slick.

"Simple questions, Riley."

But she'd been plunged back into the cellar. Or her mind was. She couldn't be sure.

Images overlapped. First, the cellar from thirty years ago with massive anatomy tomes open on tables, shelves lined with books and jars and gleaming tools, then the cellar from a month ago with empty, worn wood shelving, a pair of pristine stainless-steel tables pushed end to end, and a string of small, lit bulbs ringing the ceiling.

She stood in front of one of the empty shelves.

"What do you see, Riley?"

Was Nina there with her? No. Riley felt the chair under her, the hands in hers. Could make out the faint, distant scent of lavender.

Something shoved her. Pushed her toward the shelves.

"*Dark room.*"

Whether that had been in her head or not, she didn't know.

When she tried to turn away—look away—from the shelves, she was wrenched back. Shove. "*Dark room.*"

Riley tried to explain what was happening, unsure of what—if anything—the others saw or heard.

"Maybe the dark room is a whole other room," said Jade, sounding as if she were on the other end of long hallway. "Maybe you have to push on the shelf to open a door."

It took her a few seconds, like waking from a deep sleep, but Riley opened her eyes to look at her friend, brow cocked.

"What?" Jade asked. "Haven't you ever seen a spy movie where there's a hidden passage behind a bookshelf?"

Fair enough. With a slow breath, she closed her eyes again.

"What's in the dark room?"

"*You.*"

The hair rose on the back of her neck.

"Is that a threat?"

"*You,*" he said. "*Go.*"

Oh. Well. Returning to the ranch was on the top of her Oh Hell No List, but she kept that to herself and switched the focus of the "conversation." She cleared her throat. "What did Hank lie about?"

No reply.

She simplified it. "Did Hank lie?"

Still no reply.

As she tried to think of an equally simple question, her right arm jerked. Then again. And a third time.

Jade and Riley looked at each other, then down at their hands. Riley's arm slid forward an inch, bunching up the tablecloth.

"What's wrong?" Jade whisper-hissed. "Does it itch or something?"

"I'm not doing it on purpose!" Riley whisper-hissed back.

"Everything okay over there?" Nina asked.

"I … uh … my arm keeps twitching."

"As if someone is pushing it?"

"Yes."

"It might be a call to do some automatic writing."

"Say what now?"

"You essentially grant the spirit access to your body to write messages," Nina said. "It allows for more complicated responses."

"But it … what, possesses you?"

"In a way. Channeling him is a better description." Before Riley could protest, Nina said, "Automatic writing isn't for novices, so I wouldn't recommend you be the one to do it. If he'll cooperate, I can write, and you can continue to ask questions. It's too easy for something like this to go sideways if you undertake it without practice. Plus, Orin's spirit is volatile. I've had a lot of experience with protecting myself."

Riley managed a nod.

Without a word, Teddy let go of Jade and Charlotte's hands and riffled through the drawer beneath the stereo. He placed a pad of paper and pen in front of Nina, then sat again, clasping hands with his partners.

Megan and Charlotte let go of Nina's hands and each clasped one of her forearms. Riley assumed this was to keep their circle of energy in place while Nina wrote. At least it was clear they'd all done this before.

"I'll need to prepare myself mentally, so please give me a few moments. I'll nod when I'm ready for you to begin." With that, Nina picked up the pen, hovered the tip over the paper, and closed her eyes.

Lord, this whole thing was *weird*. Riley's palms were slick, her heart raced, and she combatted her leg's desire to bounce uncontrollably. Jade gave her hand a squeeze and she glanced over.

Offering her a tight-lipped smile and a nod, Jade whispered, "You got this."

Though Riley could still feel Orin's presence, it shifted. He no longer loomed behind her. Scanning the area around Nina, she couldn't see a silhouette—though Riley wasn't sure how much of what she felt had been from a solid, physical entity.

She didn't pretend to understand any of this.

What felt like centuries later, Nina nodded.

Megan squeezed Riley's hand. "I'll read the answers."

"Are you Orin Jacobs?"

It took a few seconds, but then Nina's hand jerked to life. Riley couldn't make out the individual letters from where she sat, but she could tell the handwriting was in all caps.

"Yes," Megan read.

"What did Hank lie about?"

"Name."

"Yes. His first name is Francis and his last is Carras, not Gerber. What else?"

"Mindy."

Riley's brow furrowed as she quickly went through everything Mindy had told her about both men. Francis had lured Mindy to Orin.

"What did he lie about in regards to Mindy?"

"Escape."

After Mindy had clocked Francis over the head and ran, Francis obviously hadn't died there in the forest as Mindy had feared. Had he gone right back to the house? Had he told Orin that Mindy had overpowered him somehow, and not that Francis had purposefully let her out?

Nina's hand moved again. "Hank said I would be safe if I didn't talk. Jail time minimal for only one kidnapping. I would be free if they didn't find others."

Then it clicked. "Francis was the anonymous tip."

"Yes," Megan read. "And it's underlined."

Not only had Francis lied about not knowing Orin, he'd known the inner workings of the ranch enough to alert the cops about the others. Had he hung up after he dropped the anonymous tip on the cops, then just walked away from it all? Riley knew Francis' stunt to get Orin arrested had had little to do with his sudden growth of a conscience, and more to do with his panic about being caught after what he'd done to Renee. And he'd known Orin couldn't rat him out, as Orin hadn't even known Francis' real name.

Only Francis and Mindy knew the secret about Orin's accomplice, and seeing how neither one had ever planned to tell said secret, it would have gone with them to both their graves had Riley not gone to the Jordanville Ranch and met a little ghost boy named Pete. The spirit who'd started this whole thing. Without Pete, Riley never would have met Mindy. Would have never had a run-in with Hank, or learned about Renee, or met Walter, or been in contact with a detective.

She thought about Pete's Batman pajama pants and Scooby Doo shirt with the floppy ear. She thought of his curly brown hair sticking out from beneath his beanie. The way his eyes had lit up when she offered him a bag of tiny marshmallows for his hot cocoa—hot cocoa he desperately wanted but would never be able to drink again. The laughter that had bubbled out of him as his father spun him in a circle, his mother watching with a grin stretched wide across her face.

Laughter that had been snuffed out because of the monster now lurking in the shadows.

"Where is Pete Vonick buried?" Riley asked, something like anger roiling in her stomach now.

"Not buried."

"Where is he?"

A small, slow smile inched up Nina's face. Her eyes remained closed. It was not Nina's smile.

"That's enough, creepy bastard," Charlotte said, taking hold of the pad of paper and yanking it out from underneath Nina's hand.

That act seemed to sever whatever connection Nina had with Orin, because the smile vanished in an instant. Nina's brow wrinkled, and she put a hand to her temple, eyes still closed. Another prayer was muttered, and Riley heard both the words "goddess" and "goodbye."

The crucial step Riley and Becca had missed with the Ouija board.

Riley couldn't feel Orin in the room anymore.

Even still, Riley held her breath and fast to Jade's hand; Megan had already let go. Riley waited for Nina to open her eyes and prove she was still Nina and that she hadn't been body-snatched by a long-dead serial killer, because Riley's nerves wouldn't survive that.

Nina's eyes fluttered open.

"You okay?" Riley asked.

"Yep."

Letting out a dramatic sigh, Riley let Jade go and slumped back against her chair. "Oh, thank god. I was worried we'd need to call in a priest for an exorcism."

Charlotte and Teddy laughed.

"We've only had one time we genuinely thought a spirit had taken her over," said Megan. "We didn't break the contact soon enough. Now we know to cut it off as soon as things get dicey."

Nina looked over the words and phrases she wrote, then up at Riley. "Get the answers you need?"

"Enough for now."

"Any time you want to come back, girl, you're more than welcome," Nina said. "Let me show you the ropes and you can even start conducting your own."

Michael's words came back to her. "*This could be your calling.*"

She glanced over at Megan, her hand resting almost protectively on her stomach. Megan smiled at her. Initially, Riley had hated the idea of turning her gift into a profession.

But she wasn't so sure anymore.

1983

O rin shouldn't have been surprised that he had rivals and betrayers. John Hunter had them, too. Men of renown were always plagued by those jealous of their skills and innovation. Why would he be any different?

Orin's Edward Jenner had morphed into an odious, mean-spirited Jesse Foot. John Hunter and Orin both had attempted to teach their rivals, tried to bring them into their fold, and yet when both men realized their abilities were vastly outdone by their superiors, they turned petty. Vindictive.

Jesse Foot had spread lies and slander about the incomparable John Hunter wherever he could. Hank Gerber now undermined Orin's entire life plan.

He knew the moment he returned from one of his carnal outings with Roxanne—the prostitute who dressed like a Catholic school girl for him—that something had gone horribly wrong. Hank had been frantic when Orin pulled up to the house, his eyes swollen, his broken nose spewing blood down his face.

Despite coming twice with Roxanne—she'd let him choke her that evening, which he always had to pay extra for; just the feel of her struggling for breath beneath his hands had given him his first release—Orin felt a twitch in his pants at the sight of Hank's mangled face. He wondered what his nose breaking had sounded like. The twitch was even sharper then. He had to think about something else.

"What the hell are you doing out of your room?" Orin asked, trying to be stern without focusing too hard on the blood.

"Mindy escaped."

All other thoughts flew out of his head. "What did you *do*?"

Hank darted out of the way as Orin went tearing into the house. He wove around boxes and cages and pounded up the steps, calling Mindy's name, voice echoing in the open air of the bonus room to his left. The windows opposite him showed not a trace of light beyond.

Mindy couldn't be out there. Not alone in the dark. She was such a delicate thing; she'd never survive on her own.

Hank's door had been kicked down, the wood around the lock smashed and splintered. Mindy's door stood open. Her bed was empty.

Orin wanted to go after her. Would she think he didn't care about her if he didn't find her? She'd run from Hank, not him. She was his girl. They all were.

A deep, guttural sound came from a place Orin didn't know he had. He'd break the rest of the bones in Hank's scrawny little body. His manhood gave another twitch.

Hank was still outside when Orin came charging after him. Despite Hank frantically pleading his case, Orin grabbed him by the back of the shirt and hoisted him up, heels dragging and scrabbling against the wood as Orin pulled him inside.

"Mindy tricked me!" and "You were right: Mindy doesn't love me!" and "Mindy needs to be caught before she ruins everything for us!"

Us.

Ha! As if Orin considered him part of his operation anymore. He wondered how long it would take to dig another grave. What could he learn from burying someone alive? But he needed to hit him first. The ache between his legs grew almost unbearable. How many times would he have to pummel Hank before he got his release?

As Orin dragged him through the house, Hank grabbed hold of a box to slow their progress; the whole tower of boxes toppled, sending magazines spilling out onto the floor, their slippery covers sending them sliding every which way. Orin might just strangle the boy right there in the middle of the living room. The feel of his fragile neck beneath his hands would be even more satisfying than Roxanne's.

He grunted, making a fist and digging his fingernails into his own hand to keep himself from finishing right there in the middle of the room. The mere thought of listening to Hank's dying gurgles for breath nearly put him over the edge.

If only he had Roxanne to bury himself in.

"What if she runs into someone out there?" Hank asked, voice full of desperation. It sounded ridiculous to Orin, though, given the nasally tone. His nose had definitely broken. Massive bruises had welled up on either side of it, his eyes puffy and swollen.

"Not likely, boy."

"But she might! If she finds a park ranger or something …"

Orin halted a few feet from the door to the cellar. He still had Hank by the back of the shirt, holding him up, the tips of his shoes barely touching the ground. It reminded Orin of Hank just a few days ago, walking in with a pair of rabbits, holding them up by their ears.

"We gotta go find her," Hank said. "If she talks, we're screwed."

Yes, getting her back was the priority. He needed his girl back. He'd deal with Hank later.

Orin growled again, then dropped Hank, who fell awkwardly to his feet, his knees almost giving out. "Which way did she go?"

They ran out the front door and into the dark. Orin wasn't sure how the boy had grown to know the dark woods so well, but he hardly stumbled even with only faint assistance from the moon.

After reaching the road, they ran alongside it, Hank heading up toward the highway, Orin heading down toward the neighboring dude ranch. Orin kept his ears peeled for the sound of something crashing through the underbrush, the sound of a crying girl. But the night was eerily silent save for the occasional hoot from an owl or the screech of some other night bird.

Running downhill, some of his wind returned, but his lungs still burned.

Almost to the turn-off for the neighboring ranch, a sweep of headlights through the trees startled him. Crouching low, he watched as a car pulled onto the road, a couple in the front seat, and—his heartbeat stumbled—Mindy in the back.

He stood as they rushed past, his body hidden behind the trunk of a ponderosa pine. Mindy looked out the window at him. *Through* him. She hadn't seen him. She was *leaving* him.

His Mindy.

Hank waited on the porch for Orin. The boy looked a frightful mess. Red stained his shirt and a smear of dried, cracked blood ran from one nostril, his nose crooked. His normally pretty face was a rainbow of blue and pink and purple. Orin was sure the boy had been crying just before he walked up.

Not the slightest hint of pity twinged in his chest at the sight of him. This almost-brother. This almost-son.

Orin had taken his time to return—crushed more by Mindy's desire to leave than the fear of what she might tell someone. He'd given her a house to sleep in, food to eat, books to read. He'd given her a home when she had none, and this was what she did? She left?

"What have you done, Hank?" Orin asked, his rage more like a gentle simmer than a pot boiling over now.

"She knew how I felt about her," Hank said, sniffling. "She called to me after you left. Said she needed me. Said she realized she wanted me now—that she loved me too."

Orin's lip curled. "And you believed her?"

Giving a helpless shrug, he said, "Have you discovered the mysteries of the human heart during your experiments? Because I can't explain what power she has over me."

Orin never thought the boy terribly bright, but wondered now if Hank was pulling a fast one on him. The pathetic nasal whine didn't help.

"I kicked my door open, desperate to get to her. I've never loved anyone this much, Orin, you have to believe me." Hank's lip quivered, but his eyes remained dry. "When I picked the lock, she was waiting there with a weapon of some kind—I don't even know what it was. She hit me with it. Broke my nose, clawed at my face, kicked me when I was down. And then … then she ran. She left us, Orin."

The reality that Mindy was gone and not coming back hit him. Orin swayed on his feet.

"The police will come looking for you," Hank said. "But if you're cooperative and tell them you only took Mindy, there's no way they'll find out about the others. You can tell them you took her because you always wanted a daughter.

"Throw a deer carcass on the table in the cellar and tell them you use the place for curing meats—they'll never know.

"I'll disappear until this blows over. I won't say a word to anyone and when they slap you on the wrist for child endangerment, I'll be back to help you again." Hank managed a small smile. Orin assumed it hurt. "We'll be better than ever. Two girls a year instead of one."

Orin still very much wanted to bury him alive. But the idea of more patients intrigued him.

"You're all I've got, Orin," Hank said, his puffy eyes downcast.

There was a twinge at that. Somewhere deep in his chest. Orin knew the boy meant it.

"You're like a father to me. I'm sorry I screwed up. But we can fix it," he said. "Lie low, confess to nothing, and we'll be back in business in a couple months. I swear it. No one will care that much about a missing homeless kid."

"*You* did."

Hank swallowed hard. "It'll never happen again."

When the police showed up with cadaver dogs a week later, Orin knew how foolish he'd been. How the mysteries of the human heart truly *were* unexplainable.

Orin vowed never to care for a homeless kid ever again either.

CHAPTER 24

Jade remained uncharacteristically quiet for the drive back. When they pulled into Riley's apartment complex, she spotted the yellow glow of her living room's lights behind the closed blinds. Riley had left Michael a key under the mat just before Jade picked her up.

"I feel like I'm supposed to say something insightful," Jade said.

"About?"

"About the fact that you can do what you just did. I mean … how did you know Megan was pregnant? You just met her."

Riley explained the thumping in her stomach. How she had just known how to interpret the message. How had she known it was three months and not three weeks? She couldn't answer that. Or why she was sure it was a boy and that he'd be perfectly healthy.

"I'm … it's … how can you be like a sister to me and I didn't know this about you?"

"I'm still figuring it out myself."

Jade nodded. "Just … you can tell me anything, okay? I hate the idea that you had this, I don't know, talent and you felt like you couldn't talk to me about it."

Riley couldn't remember the last time her friend had looked so … dejected. Jade idly rubbed a thumb back and forth along the bottom of her steering wheel.

"The cops say they need evidence if I want to get Francis caught for the stalking," Riley said. "Vaguely creepy behavior isn't enough."

Jade perked up, turning in her seat. "And?"

"He's crazy flirty," she said. "What if I actually flirt back for once and make him think he's got a chance, but try to get him to confess to the tracker first? I could, I don't know, pretend his persistence is hot or something twisted."

"Maybe," she said. "But you won't, like, *meet* with him, right?"

"God no." Riley shivered. "I can tell him I want to see him sometime soon, but I have a super jealous boyfriend and I have to wait until he's out of town before we can go there?"

"Then when he admits he's been stalking you, you can show your cop friend the proof," Jade said, nodding.

"It's the best I got."

"Go for it," Jade said. "Once you have that, can't they follow him and pull him over for some minor traffic violation to get him in custody?"

"Something like that," Riley said. "Thanks for coming tonight."

"Duh," Jade said, then pulled her into an awkward hug across the center console. "Keep me in the loop! And stay safe."

As Riley hurried to her apartment, she felt buoyant. She had something to *do*. And Jade thought she was only half off her rocker.

She was so preoccupied as she jogged up the steps that she almost tripped when she saw the small bouquet of flowers sitting by her door. Half a dozen red roses in a small, cream-colored vase.

Smiling, she picked it up and plucked out the card. Then her stomach dropped.

I was thinking about you today. It's been so long since I've seen you. Since I've heard

your voice. Write faster, my little medium.
I'm going crazy waiting...

Francis had been watching her enough to figure out which apartment was hers. He'd found a way through the gate, and then watched her come and go from her apartment. More than being fully creeped out that he'd been here lurking around, she hated that he'd been watching her without her realizing it.

How many times?

What if he'd seen her put the key underneath the mat and had grabbed it before Michael had gotten here?

Hands shaking, she opened her door and was greeted by the smell of garlic and pasta sauce. She placed the vase on the coffee table but kept the card.

"Hey," she said, a slight wobble to her voice as she tossed her purse onto the couch and heading for the kitchen.

"Hello!"

She stilled in the doorway. How the hell one person could have made *that* much of a mess was beyond her. A pot of bubbling spaghetti sauce sat on one of the burners, a red ring of splatter decorating the white surface of the stove top. Sauce had splattered on the backsplash and the handle of the oven. Noodles lay in a strainer positioned above a pot, a lone one lying on the stained stovetop as if crawling to safety. Crumbs, mashed garlic, and an unsettling amount of grated cheese lay scattered across her cutting board. A quick glance toward the trashcan he'd pulled out from underneath the sink told her he'd already burned the first attempt at cheesy garlic bread. A line of pasta sauce had smeared across his cheek.

This she could deal with. Her goofy, sweet boyfriend doing his damnedest to be there for her.

"You made dinner," she said, trying to sound lighthearted. "I thought you said you were a terrible cook."

"Oh, I am. I burned the noodles the first time."

"*How?*"

He shrugged. "Also, you didn't have everything you needed for sauce, so I just added a lot of spices and garlic to ketchup."

She snorted. Then she crossed her arms to hide her shaking hands. "You're joking."

"What! They're both made from tomatoes! I followed the recipe I found …" As if determined to prove her wrong, he took a spoon and dipped it into his concoction, then defiantly swallowed the heaping spoonful. Then gagged. "Holy shit." He coughed. "That's … that's not good."

She waded through the mess, wiped a thumb across his cheek, and kissed it. "Thank you for trying. But I'm not eating that. I'm ordering a pizza." That damn waver to her voice returned.

"Hey, what's wrong?" he said.

Dragging him into the living room, she gently pushed him onto the couch. Normally he would have arched an eyebrow or said something racy, but he had just spotted the vase on the table.

Sitting next to him, she silently handed him the card.

Her hands shook again.

"Fuck." He looked up at her. "I got here about two hours ago—he left this while I was *here*."

The shaking wasn't just fear. She was pissed. Even though she'd only been living her life on pins and needles for over two weeks with the knowledge of the tracker, he'd been watching her for well over twice as long. Francis was in this for the long haul and Riley was fucking sick of it.

"He was *here*," he said. "What if he'd decided to force his way in and you'd been alone?"

She grabbed his free hand. "But that didn't happen."

"It could have." He tossed the card onto the coffee table. "I want to beat this guy's fucking face in."

Without preamble, she told him her plan.

"You still want to interact with this asshole after *this*?" he said, gesturing at the card and flowers.

"The police side of things could take months, if not longer. Both the non-emergency operator and Detective Howard said there isn't much they can do without proof. I think Howard believes me, but they can't just go arrest the guy for being unsettling, can they? He hasn't acted in a way to threaten my safety yet. An email, a surprise visit, and flowers. Plus, there's no way to even prove Francis is the one who left these here. He didn't sign his name or use mine.

"Let's say we convince a cop to go talk to him. What if it spooks him or pisses him off? What would Francis do then? And I hate to play the damsel-in-distress card, but unless a cop agrees to watch me and my house twenty-four-seven, I don't want to risk pissing this dude off. All he'd need is a window when I'm alone and I could be in deep shit."

Michael sighed. "I can't just beat his face in?"

Riley ran her thumb across his palm. "If he can be a creepy, sneaky piece of shit, then so can I." After patting his leg, she fetched her laptop.

"You're going to do this *now*?"

"You bet your ass." Plopping down next to him, she powered on her computer.

When she signed into her page, he was logged in too. She often set her profile to the ghost setting so no one knew she was on—he almost always logged in at night, the circle by his name orange now. Idle. Riley was keenly aware of Michael next to her, watching her every move.

Pulling up a chat window, she told herself to keep her bubbling rage in check. She needed him to admit to the tracker *and* the flowers now. She wasted no time.

> **RILEY THOMAS:** Got your flowers.

Orange flicked to green within seconds.

> **HANK CARRAS:** like them?

> **RILEY THOMAS:** Yes, but are you stalking me, Francis?

> **HANK CARRAS:** you drive me crazy. not my fault i cant get you out of my head. i want to see you

> **RILEY THOMAS:** They're very pretty.

> **HANK CARRAS:** just like you. i got you a dozen but you have to come get the other six in person

Michael grunted.

> **RILEY THOMAS:** So you've been thinking about me too? Why can't you get me out of your head?

> **HANK CARRAS:** you look in a mirror lately?

RILEY THOMAS: That it? You think I'm hot?

HANK CARRAS: you dont back down. i like a woman
thats honest about what she wants

Riley wasn't sure how to respond to that, fingers hovering over
the keys.

HANK CARRAS: you should come get the rest of
these flowers

Riley swung the conversation back to asinine chitchat for a few
minutes, partly because flirting with Francis had lost its minor appeal. She felt like she "got" him now and didn't at all like what she'd
found. The urge to curse him to hell and back for putting her—putting Mindy ... putting *Renee*—through all this made her so angry she
swore red seeped into her vision.

HANK CARRAS: you got plans this weekend?

RILEY THOMAS: My usual

Silence.
Riley found it hard to believe this guy was so delusional. He saw
the anonymous flower drop as, what—romantic? Thoughtful? She
felt nothing short of unnerved. Violated.
But this was the same guy who'd lured Mindy to Orin knowing
she'd die, then somehow convinced himself he loved her.

HANK CARRAS: so when we going to do this?

Riley's heartbeat stumbled. *Get him to confess without pissing him off, without him catching on that you don't mean a word of any of this.*

RILEY THOMAS: Do what?

HANK CARRAS: dont be coy. you say you want to finish your story but you wouldnt keep talking to me if you wanted to keep it professional. wouldnt chat me up in emails all the time

HANK CARRAS: you wouldnt thank me for the flowers. youd tell me to leave you alone

RILEY THOMAS: Happen to you often?

HANK CARRAS: never. i know women and i know how to tell what they want

RILEY THOMAS: And what do you think I want?

He only allowed a few seconds to pass before he replied.

HANK CARRAS: i think you want me to fuck you

Michael clenched his fists and folded his arms, like it was all he could do to keep himself from putting said fists through her computer screen.

Francis then proceeded to tell her in rather graphic detail what he wanted to do to her. Riley took screenshot after screenshot. She assumed he kept going because she didn't tell him to stop. Even if she did, she wasn't sure he'd comply.

Maybe he thought she was so hot and bothered by what he said that she was getting herself off to his words. *Have to get him to confess and then I can shut this down.*

Finally there was a lull in his barrage of X-rated suggestions.

"This guy is fucking disgusting," Michael said.

HANK CARRAS: well?

HANK CARRAS: how does that sound?

RILEY THOMAS: Like I know what I'm going to be doing in the shower later

HANK CARRAS: you're driving me fucking crazy, baby

RILEY THOMAS: Same

RILEY THOMAS: I gotta ask you something though. Been bothering me for a while

HANK CARRAS: whats that?

RILEY THOMAS: I found a tracker on my car. You leave that for me like you left the flowers?

Silence. A *long* silence. Long enough that his green dot turned idle-orange.

Shit. She hoped he'd been so riled up that he wouldn't rabbit on her now. That he wasn't on his way here now in a rage. *Appeal to his ego, appeal to his ego …*

RILEY THOMAS: If you did, I'm not mad

Nothing.

RILEY THOMAS: I know you must have been so worried about trusting me. I was worried about trusting you, too. But I feel like we've really gotten to know each other these past weeks. Honestly, I could have been done with the article weeks ago, but I've been stalling so we can keep talking

RILEY THOMAS: I can't even tell half the time if my boyfriend still wants me. It's nice to feel wanted

Orange flipped to green.

HANK CARRAS: hes a moron if he doesnt know what hes got

HANK CARRAS: i'll turn you out in 30 seconds

RILEY THOMAS: I can't wait for the day he leaves town in two weeks

HANK CARRAS: you wont be able to walk when i'm done with you

RILEY THOMAS: so … ?

HANK CARRAS: yeah, the tracker was mine. i'm sorry i had to do that … but you can't blame a guy for being suspicious

RILEY THOMAS: I knew it! I'm glad you told me.

HANK CARRAS: i'll make it up to you

RILEY THOMAS: You better

HANK CARRAS: two weeks is going to kill me

RILEY THOMAS: Haha. I gotta go. I'm crawling out of my skin

HANK CARRAS: haha. id say im sorry but im not

He typed out his phone number.

She logged out, slammed her computer shut, tossed it onto the couch, and all but bolted for the kitchen. A colorful string of curses poured out of her when she realized she'd finished the last of her wine. She'd never been a huge fan of hard liquor, but she had vodka in the freezer for emergencies.

If this wasn't a goddamn emergency, she didn't know what was.

She considered pouring herself a shot like a civilized person, but then thought "fuck it" and swigged directly from the bottle. The grunt she let out was one of disgust, but she wasn't sure how much of it was due to Francis and how much was due to the vodka. It burned her throat on the way down. It burned her eyes and her nose. She ran a hand across her mouth; her nose was running. Was she crying? Dammit, she was crying.

Michael stood in the doorway, watching her lose her shit. He'd become good at letting her fall the fuck apart both without abandoning her *or* crowding her before she was ready.

The reality that Francis had been keeping tabs on her with the tracker was one thing—still spying, but detached. She'd convinced herself she could get around that. That she was still safe.

The fact that he'd been on her doorstep—with Michael inside her apartment—was what got to her. Michael worried about what could have happened if Francis forced his way in. But, dear god, Michael could have been just as easily surprised if Francis came in armed. Francis was imposing, overconfident, and paranoid. Pair that with the fact that he'd both sexually assaulted and murdered some-one before …

Sniffling hard, Riley put down the bottle of vodka—she wasn't sure how much of it she'd actually drunk—and wrapped her arms around Michael's middle, her temple against his chest. He returned the hug.

When she'd finally calmed down, she loosened her hold on him and took a step back, glancing up at him, not sure what expression she'd find. It was some combination of hopeless and devastated. She supposed she was getting good at reading his face, too.

"If you give me some macho bullshit about it being your job to keep me safe, I swear I'm going to slap you," she said.

He tried not to smile. "I can't help it. I don't want anything to happen to you. And I know it's stupid, but I feel guilty that he was creeping around outside and I didn't even know."

"I know the feeling."

He huffed out a breath. "So what's next?"

"I send that conversation to Detective Howard and hope it's enough. Then we eat pizza and watch a movie and pretend every-thing is normal."

"Can I pick the movie this time?"

"Absolutely not. You're still on probation after *Monster Babes on Mars.*"

CHAPTER 25

The following day, Riley took the tracker off her car and smashed it with a hammer in the parking lot. It was a weekday around noon—so she hoped not too many people saw the ridiculous girl in the lot breaking a small black box into a million pieces. She sent pictures of the destruction to Jade and Michael.

Then Riley waited several more days to see what reaction she'd get from Francis. But he remained his usual flirtatious, disgusting self in IMs and emails. She didn't call or text him; she didn't want him to have her number.

When nothing happened, and she didn't see any mysterious cars following her home or loitering in random places, Riley finally followed up on the information she'd gotten from the séance. This dark room, whatever it was, was back at the ranch. Though it likely wasn't the wisest decision to heed suggestions from dead serial killers, she couldn't ignore the feeling that she needed to get back to Jordanville.

How much time did Pete have before he disappeared? His beanie tied him to her apartment. She'd need to take it back to have any hope of restoring him back to what he was, even if she couldn't find the dark room or his body. She'd rather have him trapped at the ranch again than being gone entirely.

So Riley called the ranch bright and early on Monday.

"Thank you for calling the Jordanville Ranch. This is Angela speaking; how may I help you?"

"Hey, Angela. This is Riley Thomas. I—"

"Riley! It's so good to hear from you!" Then, in a stage whisper, she added, "You're practically a legend around here now. Nina mentions you every time she starts her session in the cellar."

Riley sighed, but feigned excitement. "Oh, that's so cool!"

"Nina also told me about that séance you had," Angela said. "She said Orin *himself* contacted you!"

If this isn't the gossipiest pair of women … "It's true. And, well, I don't know if this is even in the realm of possibility, but I've gotten a message from the other side that there's something at the ranch I'm supposed to find. I don't suppose I could come by some day and take a look around?"

"I can check with the Fredricks, the owners, you know? But I don't see why it would be a problem. There's been a spike in reservations since we posted your story on the forum. The Fredricks know *all* about you."

I'm sure they do. "I'm hoping to bring a friend of mine—a police officer—just in case we find anything."

"Oh, goodness! This *is* exciting," she said. "I'll talk to the Fredricks and then give you a call. But let's plan on two days from now, on Wednesday? We won't have guests until next weekend, but there's a wedding on Saturday so we're prepping for that. Any time after three on Wednesday would work for me!"

"Perfect." Riley rattled off her phone number and hung up.

After getting the all-clear from Angela later that evening, Riley called Detective Howard in the morning. "Hi, it's me again."

The detective sighed. "Hello, Ms. Thomas. We're putting together a case for you about Francis … Hank. My contact called you, didn't he?"

"Yes," Riley said. "He's very nice." But they were still moving at a snail's pace and Riley had a creepy motherfucker stalking her and a fading ghost child and she really needed to take control of this situation before she lost her damn mind. "Do you stand by what you said when we first talked ... that you wouldn't discount anything I presented simply because I'm a medium?"

After a beat of silence, he said, "Yes?"

"There's something else about the ranch I haven't told you."

He stayed silent this time.

"I had a dream similar to the one I had about Renee. Except in this one, it was a young boy named Peter Vonick. I believe Orin also killed this boy and his body is still on the property."

Riley heard the rapid clack of a keyboard.

"Pete went missing in 1973," she said, hopefully confirming what he saw on his screen. "I think he was Orin's first victim. He was a reckless grab, so he won't fit the MO of the others." Riley waited a few moments, knowing the detective was searching for Pete—or at least taking notes. "He won't be buried with the others either."

"I'll look into this."

She tried not to grunt in frustration. "I ... uhh ... have a favor to ask. I know one of the employees at the ranch and she's granting me access to the house tomorrow so I can look around."

"Riley ..."

"Would you like to come with? You know, just in case?"

He didn't reply.

"It's either you or I invite someone from *Albuquerque Life.*"

"You can't be serious."

"Quite."

He sighed.

"I've learned not to ignore these signs," she said. "For some reason, I'm being told that now is the time to find Pete. Maybe it's tied to Renee and Francis. But I'll be making the trek tomorrow either way. I'd much rather have you there than a reporter."

"An *inept* reporter," Detective Howard said. The pause stretched out for so long, she wondered if he'd forgotten he was still on the phone. "I'll be in touch soon."

Well, it wasn't a no.

The following morning, Riley was abuzz with anticipation. She had no idea what she'd find at the ranch, but she was glad both Michael and Mindy were going to make the drive with her. Jade couldn't get the time off work.

Riley had been surprised Mindy volunteered to come with her, but the woman had jumped on the "things happens for a reason" bandwagon.

"I was fully prepared to only use my therapy sessions to deal with what happened to me until you came along. Renee and Pete deserve better. *I* deserve better. If I can help them, maybe it'll help my healing process or whatever the fuck," Mindy said. "Besides, I've been in that cellar a bunch of times. Maybe being in there will help jog my memory and I can help you find the dark room."

"I'm still worried about traumatizing the shit out of you," Riley said.

"I'm already pretty fucking traumatized," Mindy reminded her.

Since they planned to get to the ranch around four, Michael—

who had taken the day off work—and Riley swung by Mindy's place just before noon. And then off they went, Pete's beanie stuffed into her purse. When she'd taken it off the dresser, she'd gotten no flash of memory.

She feared Pete was already gone.

When they reached Santa Fe, she called Detective Howard and met him at the station. He was a black man in his fifties, rocking salt-and-pepper hair, a step above a dad bod, and an agreeable, clean-shaven face.

After exchanging a few pleasantries in the parking lot, Riley, Michael, and Mindy piled back into Riley's car, and the detective got into his dark sedan, Riley leading the way.

The first three and a half hours of the drive were relaxed, though Riley often found herself drumming her hands on the steering wheel. Michael and Mindy had similar tastes in music and spent a large chunk of time talking about bands Riley had never heard of.

What if she was leading the detective on a wild goose chase and this dark room didn't exist? What if this was all part of Orin's plan from beyond the grave to lure more girls into the belly of his house?

Michael placed a warm hand on her leg and kept it there.

About half an hour away from the ranch, Riley rounded a tight turn, and when she straightened out again, the sedan was no longer behind her.

"Where'd he go?" Riley asked.

"Chill, girl," Mindy said.

But Mindy and Michael both threw occasional looks over their shoulders out the back windshield.

Riley glanced up for the hundredth time and let out a shriek, the car swerving. The tires thud thud thudded along the rubble strip lining the right side of the road. If they went over the side, it would send the car into a ravine or headlong into a tree.

Michael grabbed hold of the wheel, straightening her back out.

At the same time that he yelped, "What? What happened?" Mindy shrieked, "What the *hell*?"

Riley's eyes flicked back to the image of Pete, still wavering slightly, in the back seat beside Mindy. He sat with a sheepish smile on his face, wayward curls peeking out from underneath his maroon beanie. "It's good to see you, kid."

"*Oh*," said Mindy, side-eyeing the empty seat next to her. "Awesome. I'm sitting next to a ghost."

Michael turned in his seat, scanning the area behind him. After several long seconds, he waved and said, "Hi, Pete," despite being unable to see him. He sounded vaguely disappointed.

When they pulled up to the open gate, Riley heaved a sigh of relief. Angela had said she would be on the property that day, but over on the dude ranch side where the wedding reception would be. She'd said the house would be unlocked and to just let herself in. Riley wouldn't have been surprised to find out later that she'd been hiding out, hoping to catch a glimpse of something exciting to add to the website.

The little gravel lot to the left of the house was empty.

Once they all piled out of the car, Pete disappeared again. She hoped he was inside somewhere, restored. Pulling the beanie out of her purse, she shoved it into her back pocket.

Riley turned to Mindy. "You sure you want to come in?"

"I never thought I'd see this godawful place ever again." Mindy stared at the house, her chest heaving slightly. "But I'm sure."

Riley gently took hold of Mindy's elbow. "If you start to panic, I'm right here, okay?"

"What, you mean don't run off?"

"I just want you to be safe," Riley said.

Mindy shook out her arms, rolled her shoulders. "I'll be all right."

"Detective Howard should be here any minute." Riley couldn't call him to see how far out he was, given the lack of reception.

They loitered for about ten minutes, but still no sign of him. The air had a bite to it and Mindy's teeth started to clack.

"Should we just go in?" Michael said. "At least we know anyone we could run into in there is already dead."

Riley and Mindy looked at him, heads cocked.

"I realize that could have been worded better."

With a laugh, Riley headed for the front door.

Once over the threshold, Riley stopped dead in the middle of the rug just inside the door. She had talked to Mindy about panic, but she hadn't accounted for how hard being here would hit *her*. She'd been nervous about failing Renee and Pete. Of wasting Detective Howard's time.

But the panic at experiencing what she had in the cellar, of encountering the dark, looming presence of Orin again, hadn't fully registered as a possibility until that moment. Her gaze shifted from the chairs she'd sat in with Michael, to the spot where Pete's spirit had stood in the middle of the lobby, to the closed door of the cellar beyond the barrier of the reception desk.

"I'm right here, okay?" Michael asked, his voice pulling her back to the surface, his warm hand on her lower back.

"Me too," said Mindy from her other side.

"Orin is helping you for some reason," Michael said. "He told you where to find this other room. Chances are it'll be more of a Casper the Friendly Ghost situation rather than a vomiting pea-soup possession type deal."

"Thanks ... I think."

Riley squeezed her fists into tight balls, then marched forward. She would not freak out, she would not freak out.

The house being dark and deserted without the faintest trace of life didn't calm her nerves. It felt as if the building waited, holding its breath. Hints of wedding preparations were scattered here and there. Large boxes sat stacked randomly throughout the room. A set of giant white wreaths lay on the dining table. The corner of a creamy white cloth poked out of an open box on a chair.

The candles were unlit in their sconces along the stairs.

She would not freak out, she would not freak out.

Pulling open the door to the narrow, claustrophobic hallway that eventually led to the cellar, all Riley saw was white walls eaten up by shadows and she couldn't do it. She pressed her back against the wall near the now-open door and shut her eyes. Her breath came shallow and quick.

She was freaking out.

"Hey. Hey, look at me, Ry." Michael had a hand on either side of her face, gently tipping her head back so they'd make eye contact once she got up the nerve to open them. She did. "I'm with you, okay? This is for Renee and Pete."

"What if there's something really awful in there?"

"There probably is. We'll likely both have nightmares." He shrugged. "I know a really great therapist."

She laughed, despite everything.

"We'll deal with it—whatever it is."

Giving herself a short mental pep talk, she nodded. Then, with another deep breath, she pushed away from the wall.

Mindy stood a few feet away, wide eyes focused on the door, a finger running back and forth under one of the leather bands on her wrist.

"You good?" Riley asked.

Mindy's attention snapped to her and she dropped her hands to her sides. "Yeah. I can do this. I didn't do anything for Renee back then. Maybe I can now."

Michael went in first, flipping on a switch that illuminated the single bare bulb in the middle of the ceiling. Reaching a hand out behind him, Riley laced her fingers through his. Though she appreciated not walking into the cellar first, not even Mindy's presence behind her, the woman's hand on her shoulder, could stop the hair on her neck from standing on end.

Riley could almost feel the looming presence of Orin behind her, herding her down below the house as he had with so many others before her. As he had with Mindy before. Her free hand out to her side, Riley let her fingertips graze the smooth drywall, finding comfort in the solid feel of it.

Michael turned left, led them down a short hallway, and then stopped at the cellar door. He turned the knob and pressed the door open. As he flipped on another switch, light cascaded over the deep steps. They let go of each other's hands so they could brace themselves against the walls as they made their way to the cellar floor.

Quietly uttered words poured out of Mindy behind her.

"You've got this, Mindy," Riley said. "You'll—"

The feeling hit her. That otherness of Orin. Not nearly as overwhelming as before. He merely watched now.

When they made it to the base of the stairs, they just stood there, shoulder to shoulder.

"Dear god. I can't believe I'm in this fucking hellhole again," Mindy said, breath coming in quick, shaky bursts. Eyes wide and roaming, as if she saw all those dead girls crawling out of the walls and creeping toward her, Mindy's hands opened and closed into fists. She stepped back.

Riley took Mindy's face in her hands, just as Michael had done to her. Mindy's wild eyes locked on Riley's. "Breathe. Slow and steady."

Mindy took a deep pull in through her nose and slowly let it out her mouth.

"Again."

Mindy obeyed.

"Orin is dead," Riley said. "He can't hurt you anymore."

Though Riley didn't know how true that was, given his presence in the room. When Mindy had calmed, Riley let her go and surveyed the cellar.

The only light in the room came from the dim glow of the bulb above the stairs. All three of them pulled out their useless cell phones and turned on their flashlights. Well, partly useless.

On the long sides of the room stood two tall shelves—almost to the ceiling—flanked by a short one on either side. The individual shelves were about four-feet long and three-feet high. They looked sturdy as hell, as they'd been used to hold massive anatomy tomes, thick glass jars, and metal tools. According to Riley's ghostly intel, the bookshelf in question was one of the tall ones to the left.

They swept their lights across the room, casting eerie shadows. Orin's presence was still here, observing rather than circling and assessing.

The string of shattered bulbs ringing the ceiling had been taken down but not replaced, the glass gone.

Michael stood before the left wall of shelves, the pair of stainless steel tables to his back. "You sure it's these ones?" he asked, fingers running tentatively over empty shelves and bookcase backs.

Riley closed her eyes and tried to remember what Orin had

shown her during the séance. But all she could recall was seeing *these* bookshelves and experiencing the sensation of being pushed.

Michael started pushing on the bookshelf's frame. But that immediately felt wrong. If it was that easy to find the dark room, the police would've done so already. Or some guest who came down here for one of the investigations would've leaned against the wall and accidentally triggered something. There had to be a reason why no one found it.

"Shit," Mindy said.

Michael and Riley turned to her.

Swallowing hard, Mindy pointed at the shelves in question. "There was a day Hank and I were in here—cleaning up, you know? And Hank was goofing around by the bookshelf, jumping around like he was trying to reach the top shelf, and saying that if he found the right book, he could show me something cool. I didn't know what the hell he was on about, and Orin came in while he was hopping around and screamed at him to get back to work before thwacking him upside the head so hard, he hit the ground."

Something Jade had said replayed in Riley's head then, and Riley tried to think of all the secret doors she'd seen in movies and TV shows. If it wasn't some elaborate hidden passage opened by stepping on certain floor tiles in an old cave, it was a door opened by pulling on a book on a shelf.

Only problem was, these shelves were empty.

Michael still probed every available surface, undeterred. Even at 5'10," the topmost shelves stretched taller than him. On tiptoe, he barely reached the top shelf, let alone the shelf's back.

She tried to picture Orin loping around here. All six-feet-plus of him. Mindy's memory of Hank jumping to find the correct book.

"Can you give me a boost?" Riley asked, immediately abandoning the idea of scaling the shelves like a ladder, sure she'd fall and crack her skull open.

Michael looked at her, the shelves, and back again before shrugging. Lacing his fingers together, he formed a basket for her foot and stooped.

Bracing her hands on one of the shelves and the other on his shoulder, she stuck a foot in his hand and pushed off the ground. He hoisted her up. With her arms folded on the topmost shelf, she sneezed violently at the cloud of dust she kicked up.

"Hang tight," Michael said, and next thing she knew, he'd gotten underneath her, positioning her to sit on his shoulders as he wrapped his arms around her shins.

Now on his shoulders, she had a better view. Her cell phone light bounced erratically as Michael adjusted his hold on her. With one hand holding her phone, the other poked and prodded at the shelf and bookcase backing. Nothing seemed out of the ordinary.

"I think it was the other one," Mindy said, watching them as she chewed nervously on a thumbnail.

Michael shuffled sideways.

Riley poked and prodded this shelf's backing, too. Moments away from giving up, her fingertips grazed a small, splintered hole. A piece of what might have been a nail or a wire had been poking out, but when her finger touched it, it fell away. A muted scrape and clang reverberated from the other side.

Riley looked down; Michael looked up. They wore identical wide-eyed expressions.

"Oh hell," said Mindy.

"I need something to smash through this," Riley said, shoving at the bookcase backing with the heel of her palm. It gave a little, but not much.

Getting Riley back on her feet wasn't remotely graceful, but the second she was on solid ground again, they split off to find any blunt object they could. All three settled on the thick metal candleholders decorating the various surfaces, tossing the candles aside.

Resting their phones on the shelves, giving them enough clearance so the light wasn't blocked, they started hacking away. The first hit against the wood with the metal candleholder reverberated painfully in Riley's elbow. The back of the bookshelf shifted a little.

They took turns trying to smash through the same area. Riley, Mindy, Michael. Riley, Mindy, Michael.

After several more hits, the wood started to splinter. Riley turned and gave it a couple of sidekicks, using the force of her heel. One kick, two—and her shoe went through. Those aerobic kickboxing classes she used to take had just paid for themselves.

They smashed through the broken wood even further with their candleholders until there was a hole big enough for one of them to crawl through. The space was about four feet off the ground, in one of the middle shelves.

Though it would be a tight squeeze, either Mindy or Riley would fit through.

"Sorry, but that's a solid fuck no from me," Mindy said, thumbnail wedged between her teeth again.

"Dammit," Riley muttered.

"I'll be right here," Michael said. "There's gotta be a latch or something on the other side."

Grabbing her phone, Riley bent down and shone the light inside the opening. If this were a scary movie, that would be the exact moment a disease-ridden zombie appeared in the hole to scare the shit out of her. But she couldn't see much of anything and heard even less.

"Dammit," she said again, shoving her phone into her pocket.

Gingerly climbing onto the third shelf, sure the wood wouldn't be able to hold her weight, she held her breath. So far, so good. Holding onto the lip of the shelf above her, she inched toward the hole so her feet faced it and her back faced Michael and Mindy.

In as fluid a motion as she could manage, she went feet-first through the hole, her shirt snagging on a jagged piece of wood as she went. Her boots hit solid, slightly uneven ground, and aside from the weak light of the two cells in the next room, it was pitch black. And smelled musty—like wet sawdust.

Aside from a small tear in her top, and possibly scraping a little skin from her back, she was unscathed. And there still weren't any zombies, so she figured luck was on her side. She *assumed* there were no zombies, anyway. She couldn't see a damn thing.

Fishing her phone out of her pocket, she turned on her flashlight again and turned to face the bookshelf. A quick scan revealed a latch, like one you'd find on a gate, in the upper left corner, a pull wire hanging uselessly from it. The wire she'd inadvertently knocked loose with her finger.

Luckily the latch was lower here than on the other side. The base of the bookcase rested on a pair of wheels, one askew. A handle sat about chest height.

Since releasing the latch meant pulling the wire *up*, she jumped to knock the top of the latch loose with the tips of her fingers. She miraculously got it after a handful of jumps, sweat beading on her forehead. She gave the handle a pull, but the wonky wheel kept it from moving. Poking her head through the gaping hole, Riley said, "It swings toward me, but one of the wheels is busted. Push as hard as you guys can when I tell you."

"Got it!" said Michael.

Riley returned to the wonky wheel, and with a combination of pulling up on the case's frame and kicking the wheel back into alignment, was able to get it semi-straight. "Push!"

The case jerked toward her and she barely got her fingers out of the way in time. Hurrying to her feet, she grabbed hold of the handle and pulled the door toward her while Michael and Mindy heaved from the other side. A horrible scraping sounded followed by a thud—Riley was ninety-eight-percent sure the wheel had fallen off—but they'd opened it enough that they could squeeze through.

Riley swept her light over their handiwork and found the bookshelf-door resting at an awkward angle, the wheel lying a few inches away.

"Think we're gonna have to pay for that?" Michael asked.

With a snort, Riley swung her light the other direction. They stood in a crude hallway, the walls made of what looked like nothing more than packed earth, the air damp and musty. A faint sound of dripping water would have really tied the whole creepy vibe together, but it was silent.

Riley looped her arm through Mindy's. "You're doing great."

"I feel like I'm going to throw up."

They walked for about a minute, flashlights up, then the path veered left, where they quickly came across a white, rusting metal door. It had a spinning handle in the middle like a submarine door or an old-time bank vault.

"No way there's anything good in here, right?" Michael asked.

"Probably not."

Plus, Orin had followed them, waiting to see where he'd led them.

The moment Riley reached out to touch the handle, she was assaulted by images. Orin lumbering down the hallway with a black trash bag hung over his shoulder, a smile on his face like a perverse Santa Claus. Another of him with a young Francis by his side, the pair pushing a stretcher with a body bag on it.

Riley reeled back, removing her hand.

"Hey," Michael said. "What happened?"

Shaking her head, heart racing, she said, "Can you open it?"

Mindy shifted from foot to foot in Riley's peripheral vision. Like a little kid who needed to pee. Like a nervous animal getting ready to bolt to safety.

Michael took hold of the handle with his hands at two and eight and turned. The lock disengaged with a long, grinding metal shriek that made the hair on Riley's arms stand up. Shoving the door open, they were hit with another wave of musty, stale air and something else. Something faint, but sickly.

It was dark in here too—the room aptly named—and they crept over the slightly raised threshold. Riley was scared to lift her flashlight beam and see what was in here. But she didn't need to, because seconds later, the room flooded with light.

Michael had found a switch, power still running to the hidden room.

Riley and Mindy both let out muffled screams; Mindy clamped a hand over her mouth. Michael unleashed a string of colorful curses.

The cellar-sized room's back wall—the one across from them—had a freestanding set of shelves, and next to it sat what looked like a giant refrigerator with drawers. Either of the side walls had long, thin tables pushed against them.

Riley couldn't keep her gaze from the shelves for long. The top two rows were stuffed with books and papers. And below that sat row after row of jars filled with floating body parts and organs. A small one with a pair of eyes, medium-sized ones with severed feet and hands, and even two larger ones with heads. One was missing its eyes and stared at Riley from across the room with empty sockets. There were jars of brains, hearts, and the snake-like coil of intestines. Dried bones, and what Riley could only guess were muscles and dried tissues, sat in neat little rows before carefully written tags.

Riley swayed on her feet.

Mindy stumbled back and grabbed hold of the wall, head leaned out of the dark room. She emptied the contents of her stomach onto the floor. Then she turned and slid to the ground, back to the wall, knees to her chest, head in her hands. Riley thought she could hear her muttering to herself again, the other woman's eyes screwed tightly shut.

There was no drain in the floor here beneath the steel tables. And that was because, Riley figured, once the girls had been moved in here, they'd long since been killed and drained of any fluids. This was a room Mindy had been lucky enough to escape.

She was an asshole for agreeing to let Mindy come with her. This surely would traumatize her further. How had she let her see this? She needed to grab Mindy and Michael and get the hell out of here now. But she couldn't look away from Orin's "work."

On one of the thin tables lay yet more books held in place by bookends, loose papers sticking out at odd angles. More tomes littered the space, including biographies of John Hunter. An open sketchbook with a partially drawn bone sat beside the bone in question.

Riley inched towards the table, eyeing the spines of the leather-bound journals. Names were written vertically in black marker. Names she didn't recognize from reports. Kristy, Maddie, Paula.

And one for Hank. Riley grabbed it and flipped it open. Orin's handwriting was small, neat, and in all caps. The first page listed Hank's incorrect name, the day he'd been taken, and a description of him both physically and emotionally. Realizing her fingerprints were now all over it, Riley wiped the cover with the long sleeves of her shirt—Crap, had she just wiped off other fingerprints as well?—and returned the journal.

On the other table were more dried bones and tissues.

And, on the middle tables, rested two fully intact skeletons. One skeleton had brown bones, as if they'd been painted with furniture varnish. The other had clean white bones.

Riley eyed the steel locker in the corner, reminded of the metal drawers in morgues she'd seen on TV. But she knew those drawers had never held flesh-covered specimens.

She crept past the laid-out skeletons and the table covered in bones and dried tissues. Something told her she knew what was in the drawers, but she needed to see it anyway.

Mindy was still on the floor, head in her hands as she employed deep breathing exercises. Michael stood just inside the doorway, silent and watching—like Orin.

There were four drawers, the fourth one at eye-height. A jar with a severed hand floating in a murky brown liquid sat atop the bank of drawers, forever waving at her. Her stomach churned.

Taking a deep breath, she pulled her sleeve over her hand and then took hold of the handle. Pulling the handle down, she released the latch, then pulled it toward her, sliding the drawer out. She took several steps back as the preserved skeleton came into view. A choked sob vibrated out of her throat when, by the skull, she saw the neatly folded brown shirt, Scooby Doo's floppy ear standing at attention as if in greeting.

"Hey, Pete," Riley whispered.

She stared at him—what was left of him—for a few moments before trundling the drawer closed and pulling out the next. A skeleton with a string bracelet lying beside the skull, the name Maddie spelled out in individual painted beads. Drawer three had a Mickey Mouse watch by where a skull should have been, the hands—Mickey's arms—stuck at 1:33.

Rattling the drawer closed, she opened the last, finding it empty.

Tears in her eyes, she turned to the skeletons on the tables. She hadn't noticed it before, but items lay by both of their heads, too. The one closest to her had a small ring with a red gem in the middle. The other had a silver ring circled in little squares of turquoise, strung on a silver chain.

Riley just stood there in a daze, not really looking at anything, fighting the urge to collapse. She'd hoped she'd find Pete. She had no idea she'd find four others.

Orin hadn't killed five girls. He'd killed nine and one boy. Ten victims.

The police only knew about half. Five families with no closure.

Her chest ached.

Mindy silently cried now, shoulders shaking, arms wrapped around her middle as if trying to hold herself together. Riley wanted to go to her, to comfort her, but she felt numb. Helpless.

Michael moved toward her. When she looked at him, his skin had paled. "Five in all?"

Riley nodded. The back of her throat hurt from how hard she tried not to cry.

"And Pete?"

Riley nodded again.

"I don't know what to say."

But before Riley could come up with the suggestion, a loud

scrape made all three of them jump. It startled Mindy out of her tears.

Jesus! She'd half forgotten what she'd been doing before she found this room of horrors. Why she'd been here in the first place.

It had to be Detective Howard. How long had they been down here?

The time on her phone said it was nearing five. Had it really been forty-five minutes since they'd arrived?

"I know you're down here, Riley!"

Michael and Riley's attention snapped to one another.

Mindy sucked in a breath. "Holy. Shit. That's not the cop." Then her breath started coming in short, quick pants. Her hands shook. Her eyes darted this way and that.

Full-blown panic attack.

Riley darted over grabbed hold of her hands. "Mindy." No response. "*Mindy!*" she hissed.

The other woman's gaze focused on her.

"I need you to breathe, okay?" Riley said.

"How the *hell* is he here? How did he know we'd be here?" Mindy asked, her voice nearing shrill. "Where the hell is Detective Howard?"

"*Shit,*" whispered Michael.

Francis' voice had sounded far away, carried to them by the echo off the hallway's walls.

Riley turned to Michael. "Hide."

"Excuse me?"

"There's no way to know who he thinks is here with me, if anyone," she said. "He might think we got separated or something. But you've got a better chance of ambushing him than either of us do. What if he's armed? Hopefully Howard got delayed somehow and he's still on the way."

"Riley," Michael said. "I'm never going to fucking forgive myself if something happens to you."

"Same," she said. "Now hide."

"What about me?" Mindy hinged forward, hands on her hips and head bent toward her knees. "I can't do this."

"What do you think you're doing down there, Riley?" His voice was closer now—too close.

"*Hide*," she snapped at Michael.

Michael cursed again, then scrambled for a place. He ran around like a chicken with his head cut off for a moment, then scurried behind the still-open door. Getting the tips of his shoes onto the ledge of the door so his feet wouldn't show, he held onto the crank handle in the middle. Riley ran over and pushed it until Michael's back was against the wall. If he stayed wedged into the corner made by the door and the wall, he'd be out of sight if no one looked too closely.

Riley grabbed hold of Mindy's hand and then scurried to the other side of the room and hid behind one of the steel tables. She yanked Mindy down next to her. All Francis would have to do was look under it, but it gave her a mild sense of safety.

Heart hammering so hard she could hear it, she held fast to a table leg on one side of her, and Mindy's sweaty hand with the other. What the hell were they going to do? What had happened to Howard? She felt the gaze of the floating heads behind her, of the detached eyes trapped in formalin.

She stared through the open door and down the short hallway. His footsteps echoed closer. It was only a matter of seconds before Francis appeared.

One, two, three, fo—and there he was. All swagger and confidence. He didn't appear to be covered in blood, but his white shirt and one cheek were smeared with dirt, his hair mussed. God, Riley hoped Detective Howard was all right.

Francis only slowed his swaggering pace once he reached the door of the dark room. For a moment, Riley feared he'd somehow seen Michael. For ten solid seconds, nothing happened. Riley squeezed Mindy's palm so hard, she was surprised she didn't break her hand.

Maybe he would turn away. Maybe he'd think he was too late. But the pile of Mindy's sick was puddled just outside the door.

Hank squatted abruptly and spotted them. "Peek-a-boo."

Mindy screamed, quickly muffling the sound with her hand. Hair rose on Riley's arms.

His composure slipped for a moment. "*Mindy?*"

"Jesus Christ, how is this happening?" Mindy muttered under her breath.

Riley popped up to her full height, amazed her knees hadn't given out. She yanked Mindy up beside her.

Francis stood, too. "Fancy seeing you here, huh, Mindy?"

Mindy held fast to Riley's hand with both of hers, her chest pressed against Riley's arm. She felt Mindy's heart hammering.

"I smashed the tracker," Riley said.

"I like watching you," Francis said, shrugging. "Started to miss knowing where you were after you destroyed it. I follow you sometimes. Waiting."

His tone was almost sultry, as if picking up from where they'd left off in their instant message conversation. As if they were still waiting for her boyfriend to go on that business trip so he could seduce her. As if Mindy wasn't standing there beside her. As if they weren't standing in a nightmare.

"How many of these girls were you here for?" Riley asked, motioning to the set of morgue-like drawers behind her. "How many of them did you help cut up?" Her voice had grown shrill.

"What does it matter?"

"Because I want to know! How many?"

"Three live ones before Mindy," he said. "I helped him unearth two of the ones who died before I got here. Once they were dead, he buried them six feet under and gave them several years until their bones were clean."

He said it so causally. All this time later, even after being reminded of it in this room of the dead, he still showed no remorse. He had claimed to love Mindy, to be hurt by her betrayal, and yet he'd brought her here to end up just as the others had.

Placing his hands on the steel table, he said, "If you wanted to know about this place, why wouldn't you just talk to me? I'm back to thinking you can't be trusted."

Riley almost laughed.

He moved to the right, around the table. She mirrored him, moving left, dragging Mindy with her.

"The police are on their way," Riley said.

"*Were* on their way." Francis reached behind him and pulled out a gun tucked into the back of his pants. Though he kept it by his side, Riley heard him flick off the safety.

Mindy kept up a steady stream of whispered curses that only grew more frantic at the sight of the firearm.

The door where Michael was hidden gave the faintest movement out of the corner of her eye. Riley struggled not to react.

"What do you mean?" she asked.

Francis offered a dramatic eye roll. "Meaning I ran into your cop friend and he's not coming to help you any time soon. Terrible luck busting a tire out in the middle of nowhere. Poor bastard didn't see me coming."

Shit. Shit shit shit.

"My friends know I was coming here today," she said. "They'll come looking for me."

He shrugged again. "I'll be long gone by then."

The door shifted and Riley caught sight of Michael's profile. Jesus, he was going to do something incredibly stupid and she knew there was nothing she could do to stop him, especially without giving him away. She would not recover if Michael got shot.

So she decided to buy him some time. But Mindy beat her to it.

"You said you loved me."

Francis stared at her. "I did. Until you tricked me."

"I didn't trick you."

"You did!" He slammed his free hand on the table and they both jumped. "You said you'd help me with that girl. It was your fault anyway. We could have been together. Could have left this place, but you wouldn't let me. And then I was … I was so out of my mind because my goddamn heart was broken and that girl was just in the wrong place at the wrong time."

"Her name was Renee," Riley said.

"The fuck does it matter what her name was?" Francis asked. "It was a long time ago. Water under the bridge."

In a flash, Michael was on the move. Francis turned his head at the sound of Michael grabbing a femur off the nearby table before Michael whacked him square in the temple. The gun clattered to the floor and went off. Riley's heart stopped for a moment, but neither Mindy nor Michael had been hit. The gun slid under one of the thin tables.

Francis grunted and collapsed past Riley's line of sight, past tables between them and Francis.

Michael rose the femur over his head and came down on Francis with a *thwack*. Michael had hit a back or a side. Riley wished he'd just smash the guy's skull in. But Michael had paled. "Run!"

Riley snapped to, pulled out of her shock. She bolted past the tables, Mindy fast on her heels, and toward Michael who stood in the doorway, his free hand out for them. The energy in the room— the watching, lifeless eyes; Francis's presence; the sheer fear coming off all three of them—was almost enough to drag Riley to her knees.

Riley launched over Francis' prone form, making it to Michael, but whirled at Mindy's yelp. The woman's elbows broke her fall as she slammed into the cement. Her phone bounced out of her pocket and skidded across the ground, a hand around her ankle. Riley flashed back to her memory of Renee. Of the girl kicking and crawling to get away from this very same man. Mindy screamed and thrashed.

Francis yanked her toward him, her shirt riding up as her belly dragged across the dirty floor. Michael, still armed with the bone, darted forward. But Riley snatched him back when she saw the glint of a knife in Francis's hand, the blade's tip now pressed into Mindy's side.

A trickle of blood ran down Francis' temple. "Yeah, back the fuck off, *Jansen*."

Michael put his hands up, one still clutching the femur.

"*Up*," Francis hissed in Mindy's ear.

Riley itched to reach out for her friend. The tension in the room was building. Riley was near dizzy with it.

Francis sneered at Riley over Mindy's shoulder. "Probably regretting you brought this one along now, huh? Girl cracks under pressure at the drop of a hat. Besides, you can't believe half of what she says. She's looney-bin crazy. I mean, it was lucky she was cute, 'cause that helped balance out how fucked up in the head she was. *Is*. All she needed was some pretty words from me and she willingly followed me into Orin's trap. Desperate for attention because she had *daddy issues*. Boo-fucking-hoo."

He buried his face in Mindy's neck for a moment, breathing deep. The low moan that rumbled out of his throat turned Riley's stomach. She wished she had a clear path to the gun. She wasn't a violent person, but she wanted to put a bullet through the bastard's skull right then.

"Fuck you," Mindy growled.

"Not really my type anymore," he said.

The lights above flickered. Riley's cell phone gave a chirping cry before it beeped twice and went dead. Michael's, Mindy's, and Francis' did the same.

Orin's presence suddenly grew overwhelming, just as it had been in the cellar. *That* was what she'd been feeling both then and now. Orin gaining strength. The looming black tsunami of a pissed-off spirit's energy. Riley felt him shifting back to his predatory state. The circling. The calculating way he sized up his prey.

Perhaps Orin had *lured* Riley here. Maybe he'd known somehow that Mindy would come with her. Maybe he wanted to reclaim her, the ungrateful girl who'd run away. Passing the torch onto his protégé now. Giving him permission to take out yet another girl trying to disrupt the life they'd created here. His life's work.

The string of tiny lights running along the inside of a plastic tube circling the ceiling flickered again.

With the force of a moving vehicle, something slammed into Riley. It shoved Francis and Mindy back, pushing the tables with the scrape of metal legs on cement. Michael stumbled, pushed by a hand unseen.

"The hell?" Francis snapped. "You a witch, too?"

Riley gasped for a breath; the shock of the sudden shove loosened Francis' hold on Mindy's neck for a moment. But Riley couldn't do anything to help her. The elephant-sized weight pressed on her chest, threatening to crush her ribs and lungs to a pulp.

Another shove, harder this time. Riley cried out and Francis cursed, dropping the knife as he instinctively reached back with one hand to steady himself on the table behind him while still gripping Mindy with the other.

Lights flickered and winked out for a moment. Michael rushed forward. They flicked on. With a millisecond of a facial cue from him, Mindy ducked and Michael landed another direct hit with the femur to Francis' temple. He howled and Michael yanked Mindy out of his grasp. The lights winked out again.

When they blazed bright a moment later, Francis rested on one knee, blood trickling from an even bigger gash on his forehead. A hand went up to grab hold of the thin table covered in bones and dried tissues, but he was disoriented. Eyes closed, his balance was unsteady even while grasping something solid. He shook his head like a dog, trying to de-scramble his brain.

"Let's go," Michael hissed in Riley's ear, hand wrapped tight around her wrist.

Riley wanted to shut the door, lock him in there somehow, but the door swung in—she'd have to lurch forward to grab it and then back up to pull it closed. Francis might be woozy, but he'd have the wherewithal to lunge for her if he thought she'd trap him inside. He could still dart for the gun.

The lights flickered, muted pops sounding in a corner of the room, a whole section of the tiny bulbs going dark. And then Riley felt him behind her, the lingering person-shaped tsunami. Given the yelps from Michael and Mindy, Riley knew they felt it too. And just like in the cellar, Riley was locked in place. Just like in her dream of Pete, she couldn't move, feet welded to the floor.

It felt like a tide violently pulling back from shore. The pullback that let you know what came next would be destructive and all-consuming and would drown you if you didn't get the hell out of the way.

Michael had hold of her, tugging her arms, begging her to move. But her limbs were fused in place, her thoughts lost in a panicked fog. In this overwhelming surge of wrongness.

And then it shoved her. Shoved *through* her. Sent her hurtling forward so she stumbled and hit the ground on all fours and scraped the skin from her palms and felt like she had just run a marathon—energy expended.

In that same second, Francis was heaved through the air like he weighed nothing more than a sack of feathers. He slammed with a sickening crunch into the shelves of jars. Wood splintered, dried specimens knocked loose, and jars wobbled on their shelves. Francis lay in a heap.

The tidal wave of wrongness vanished, a gentle lapping in its place. Hardly a ripple on the surface of a lake. There, but fading fast.

Had Orin just saved them?

No. Immediately she knew Orin had acted on revenge, not altruism discovered on the Other Side. Francis had betrayed him; this was Orin's payback.

A thirty-year-old grudge.

Pounding footsteps stole Riley's attention and she saw a figure running toward them.

"Are y'all okay?" Detective Howard. Riley almost fainted at the sight of him. His arm hung limp at his side; blood soaked through his white shirt. Despite his dark skin, he looked ashen, his lips almost gray. But he was alive. When he was met with nods, he asked, "Where is he? Bastard shot me."

"In front of the bookcase," Riley managed.

Michael squatted in front of Riley now, hands cupping her face, the femur-turned-weapon abandoned on the ground. "Jesus, Ry. Are you okay?"

"Are *you*, Babe Ruth?"

"I think I soiled my pants."

Riley managed a laugh, then they helped each other to their feet. Riley listed to one side, still inexplicably exhausted, but Mindy caught her under the arms before she toppled over. Had Orin used her like a battery? Drained her of her energy to help himself manifest?

Detective Howard had his gun drawn, wincing in obvious pain, and he gave Francis' side a tentative kick. "If you're conscious and playing possum, I will shoot you if you try anything funny."

Francis groaned.

Riley watched as Detective Howard placed a knee on the small of Francis' back, then yanked one of his arms behind him, cuffing him. Then the other. Eyeing Michael, he said, "You okay to help me get him up? Arm hurts like a sonofabitch."

Michael hurried over and the two managed to get the unconscious man sitting, Michael with a hand on his shoulder. Detective Howard kept hold of one of Francis's wrists, then backhanded him.

The man fully awoke then.

"Oops," Howard said, deadpan. "My hand slipped. On your feet, asshole."

He and Michael yanked him up.

"His gun is under the table," Riley said.

"I've got backup coming. They'll take care of it." With a hand wrapped around Francis' arm, and his gun pointed at the back of Francis' head, Howard said, "You are under arrest for assault of an officer." Then he read him his Miranda Rights. "We'll figure out the rest later."

Detective Howard proceeded to march Francis out of the dark room and toward the cellar. But Mindy stopped in front of them before they reached the threshold. Despite the dirty face and red eyes, some of her confidence had returned. "Who's the fucked-up mess now, *Francis*?"

Francis snarled at her. She grinned as she stepped out of the way and let them pass.

"If this goes to trial, you bet your ass I'm going to be there every damn day until he's convicted."

"Let's get the hell out of here," Michael said.

Riley glanced behind her, catching sight of the drawers again. Of the place where Pete lay. Trundling the door open again, she took the neatly folded shirt and held it to her chest. She took the beanie out of her back pocket and laid it where the shirt had once been, leaving the other trophies beside their owners. Some part of her couldn't stomach the idea of Scooby Doo being catalogued and put into evidence. Pete had chosen her to help him. He'd been the first. Patient one.

Shutting the drawer, she headed for the door, only to come up short when she saw Pete standing by the threshold. He wore the same outfit from the dream now, his blue-and-black checkered jacket done up to his neck, presumably covering up the shirt she now held in her hands. His skin was sickly white again, the bags under his eyes purple. But he smiled at her.

She managed to smile back.

He flickered as the lights had earlier. Still not quite there. Not quite solid.

Then the others shimmered into view, too. The faces of the girls she hadn't known about. All sickly pale. All gaunt and tired-looking. Names popped into her head. Maddie, Kristy, Laura, Paula. The forgotten children.

And, just like that, they were gone.

Tears in her eyes, she whispered a goodbye to them all by name.

Michael and Mindy watched her. They clearly hadn't seen what she'd seen but waited patiently for her.

Slipping her hand into Michael's, Riley held fast to Pete's shirt with the other, and they headed for the surface.

CHAPTER 26

Backup came in the form of two squad cars as Riley, Michael, and Mindy walked out the front door, squinting. The house had been so dark. Riley watched as Detective Howard shoved Francis into the backseat of one of the cars before slamming the door in the bastard's face.

After talking to the huddled-together officers, Detective Howard headed toward Riley. Pete's shirt was hidden under her own now. His lips were still gray.

"You should probably get to a hospital … like yesterday. You look awful. Need us to drive you?" Riley asked.

She could imagine the detective having one of those face-altering smiles. But he was scowling now and ignored her question. "Are sure you're all okay?" he asked.

Riley nodded. "Mostly. What happened to you?"

Aside from the gunshot wound, he looked like he'd taken a tumble down a large hill. Bits of plant debris were caught in his short hair. "Blew a tire while on my way here and that asshole stops to help me," the detective said. "He's making small talk as we get the jack and spare out of the back, asking what I'm doing way out here. Blah blah. I tell him I'm heading to the ranch. Things are going fine until he sees my badge clipped to my belt. He asks me if I'm a cop, and next thing I know, he's whaling on me.

"We get into a scuffle and he pulls his gun. Luckily he's a shit shot and only hit my arm; I end up falling down the ravine—swore I was going to break my neck, but managed to only get banged up. He hops in his car and takes off. Took a damn lifetime to get back up the ravine and then get the spare on. I thought about hoofing it, but …" He patted his stomach. "I think I need to work on my cardio. Plus, you know, the bleeding."

Riley tried to smile. "I'm sorry. If I hadn't asked you out here then—"

"It would have been worse if you came out here alone." He took a step toward her and lowered his voice, Michael and Mindy instinctively inching closer too. "To see that asshole thrown in prison? Worth it. I'm going to feel like I was hit by a bus tomorrow, and my wife is going to have a conniption when she finds out I've been shot, but it was worth it. Renee Palmer's case has haunted me for decades."

"We gotta get you to the hospital, Howard!" one of the other officers called out.

Howard waved in acknowledgement with his good arm.

Remembering Francis's journal, Riley told the detective about the books. "All the victims had one. Looks like Orin saw Hank as part of his experiment—so he took notes on him, too." Riley hadn't read much beyond that first page, but just holding it had creeped her out. "At the very least, it's proof he was living here when Renee took that hike."

He nodded. "I might have to seriously reconsider how often I use psychics."

"Medium," Riley said, correcting him again.

He took several steps back, smiling. She had been right about it being face-altering. "I'll be calling you all in for questioning soon—

assuming I don't pass out from blood loss. Get on home, okay?"

"C'mon, you stubborn old man!" the cop called out again. "You were *shot*."

Detective Howard offered them a sheepish smile and shrug, then walked away, clutching his arm close to his side.

After another brief deliberation, two of the cops—Detective Howard included—piled into a car with Francis in the back. The other cops ushered Riley, Mindy, and Michael to their own car and told them, again, to go home.

Michael drove.

Staring out the back window as they left the Jordanville Ranch property, Riley's gaze focused on the top window. Pete wasn't there this time. The inside of the house was dark, but it didn't feel wrong anymore. It just felt like a house.

Hopefully she hadn't just ruined business for Angela and the Southwest Ghost Investigators.

Riley hoped that even though his body—and the bodies of the others—were still physically there, that they'd find rest now. Whatever that meant. She didn't want Pete to ever be stuck again.

Turning in her seat to face Mindy, Riley asked, "You okay?"

"Yeah," she said, swiping a strand of hair out of her face. "Somehow."

"I'm proud of you, Min."

"Girl, we ain't close enough for nicknames." But she smiled as she said it.

Riley reached into the back to squeeze her hand. "We got him."

Mindy grinned.

Once she had reception, she sent a text to Jade. **Francis is in police custody and we found Pete's body!**

This is the best, creepiest text I've ever received

and I've never been so upset to miss something in my life. Never leave me behind on your crime-solving adventures ever again!

Over the next several days, Howard called them in for questioning. Thankfully, they only had to go as far as the Santa Fe police station. Detective Howard insisted he'd meet them closer, but they all opted to make the hour-long drive to help make up for the wear and tear to his body. His arm was in a sling.

Next of kin were eventually informed of their loved one's discovery after the crime lab ran dental records. One of the decapitated heads floating in a jar belonged to a girl named Alice Kellen, finally identified. But, three weeks later, due to Riley's obsessive searching online and her periodic phone calls to Detective Howard, she knew no one had come to claim little Alice.

Riley still had Pete's Scooby Doo shirt tucked away. She couldn't explain or ignore the compulsion to return it to his mother. But the woman lived in Arizona and Riley worried Detective Howard would find a creative way to have her arrested if he caught wind of the delivery, since she'd technically stolen evidence.

Riley and Michael had returned to staying most nights in their own places of residence now that the threat of Francis Hank Carras was gone—and because Michael had gotten sucked into another involved work project. Riley missed having Michael around all the time, even if it meant destroying her kitchen with ketchup-based spaghetti sauce or leaving his dirty socks all over the house or opening every drawer and cabinet looking for something and then forgetting to close them again.

Weeks later, Detective Howard called to tell Riley that Francis had officially been charged with the murder of Renee Palmer. Riley cried for twenty solid minutes. She called Walter—who got the news an hour before she did—and they cried together. She promised to come see him soon.

"I'll take you and Scottie and your boyfriend to a fancy restaurant. We'll get shitfaced!" he'd told her. Then hung up after he fell to pieces again.

Exactly four weeks after Francis was carted off in handcuffs, Michael called Riley just before her shift started. She stayed in her car so nosey-ass Roberto couldn't listen. Rumors had spread through the restaurant staff about her ever since a piece appeared on the news a couple nights before where Francis' mugshot was featured along with a brief summary of his conviction. It should have been an open and shut case, but it potentially could go to trial, as Francis was expected to plead not guilty.

Detective Howard and his team were working to find a way to charge him with being Orin's accomplice. Riley guessed it would happen eventually, if Orin had kept as detailed a series of "case notes" on Francis as he had with the other kids.

"What's up, Mikey?" she asked now, amazed she no longer needed to worry about being watched or photographed in the parking lot of the restaurant.

"Ugh."

Riley laughed.

"So, I have amazing news."

She straightened, her heart thudding. "Oh?"

"I found pigs."

"Uhhh … what?"

"The ballerina-animal plates from our nightmares. The back of the plate says it's part of the barnyard series, remember? Yours features horses. I found pigs."

"No way!"

"Yep. Ballerina pigs. One is lounging on a blue fainting couch while the other files its hooves. They're giving each other sex eyes."

"It sounds horrific."

"Oh, it is," he said. "The owner is getting rid of a bunch of stuff—she's an eighty-year-old, self-proclaimed hoarder—and is moving in with her kids soon. They told her to purge as much as she can."

"Wow."

"Only catch? It's in Arizona," he said. "So. What if we go pick up the nightmare plate and you finally take Pete's shirt to his mother? If this isn't a sign from the universe, I don't know what is."

That panic about meeting Pete's mother hit her again. What if this didn't bring her closure, but somehow more pain? "I … what? We can't just go to Arizona."

"Why not? I have a week of vacation time saved up, and all this stuff with Orin and Francis is going to hit the fan soon, right? Might as well get a trip in before everything blows up," he said. "It'll be a nice break before we set up your psychic slash medium website so you can become super famous and have your own TV show and I can be your house-husband."

She flushed at the word husband. This was also the first Riley had heard of said psychic slash medium website, but she laughed. "Just want to ride my coattails, huh?"

"I have zero shame."

Chewing the inside of her cheek, she didn't say anything.

"You've wanted to help Pete since that first moment he made contact with you," Michael said, his voice more serious now. "I know some part of you misses him. Misses the possibility of him popping up in your apartment to knock shit over. *And* I know how much you want to bring closure to his mother. She already got the news. She's already grieving. It could help her deal with it a little better to get a piece of him back."

He wasn't wrong; Riley did miss Pete. "I *would* really like to see the godawful pig ballerinas."

"Yes. Yes, you would."

The giddy sense of anticipation almost made her laugh. "When do we leave?"

About the Author

Melissa has had a love of stories for as long as she can remember, but only started penning her own during her freshman year of college. She majored in Wildlife, Fish, and Conservation Biology at UCDavis. Yet, while she was neck-deep in organic chemistry and physics, she kept finding herself writing stories in the back of the classroom about fairies and trolls and magic. She finished her degree, but it never captured her heart the way writing did.

Now she owns her own dog walking business (that's sort of wildlife related, right?) by day … and afternoon and night … and writes whenever she gets a spare moment. The Microsoft Word app is a gift from the gods!

She alternates mostly between fantasy and mystery (often with a paranormal twist). All her books have some element of "other" to them … witches, ghosts, UFOs. There's no better way to escape the real world than getting lost in a fictional one.

She lives in Northern California with her very patient boyfriend and way too many pets.

The Forgotten Child is her debut, the first in a paranormal mystery series.

If you enjoyed *The Forgotten Child*, a review would be greatly appreciated.

Acknowledgments

While the day-to-day act of writing might be a lonely experience, I'm lucky enough to have a wonderful group of supportive readers and critique partners. When I told a select number of friends that I was thinking of publishing this book, I was terrified. But I was met with such enthusiasm, it helped drown out (some of) my self-doubt. Thank you to Jennifer Laam, Garrett Lemons, and Lindsey Duga for being there for me every time I have a writing meltdown (which, let's face it, is often). You guys always know how to pull me back to the surface.

Beta readers are my favorite people. This book wouldn't be what it is today without feedback from others. Every little suggestion helps. I appreciate all of you who took time to get to know Riley and offer me your time.

Thank you to my first wave of beta readers who gave me the courage to try this in the first place: Krista Hall (Sorry for the nightmares!), Brittany Gray, Noel Russell, Christiane Loeffler, and Susanna Woods.

Thank you to my new critique partners, who are all on some part of the publishing journey: Sylvia Shipp, Rose Erickson, and Sheralan Marrott.

Thank you to Dawn Klemish, Kayla Henley, Cathie Bucci, Caren White, Tessa Osbourne, Heather Nelson, Saundra Norton, Molly Sardella, Nikkie Witbrod, and Cathy McMahen for all your amazing feedback.

Thank you to Margarita Martinez for not only being a great copyeditor, but for being one of the most fangirly cheerleaders I've ever met. Benedict and David don't know what they're missing!

Thank you to Maggie Hall for the gorgeous cover (And the swag! And the map!) and Michelle Raymond for the beautiful interior design.

Thank you, Mom, for being one of my first readers, and for the great drawing of Orin's house. I still find it terribly rude I didn't inherent any of your skills.

Brittany … I know you low-key panicked when I offered you the job of reading the audiobook, but I'm so glad you said yes. I'm sorry for all the mens, though. I really am. But I downloaded Snapchat for you, so I think we're even.

And, finally, thank you to Sam for simply being you. You're more supportive than you know, you're my favorite person on the planet, and I heart your face.